To Have and To Hold

Also by Jane Green
in Large Print:

Babyville

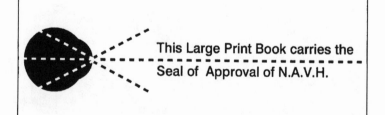

To Have and To Hold

Jane Green

Thorndike Press • Waterville, Maine

This Large Print edition is published by Thorndike Press®, Waterville, Maine USA and by BBC Audiobooks, Ltd, Bath, England.

Published in 2004 in the U.S. by arrangement with Broadway, a division of The Doubleday Broadway Publishing Group, a division of Random House, Inc.

Published in 2004 in the U.K. by arrangement with The Penguin Group.

U.S. Hardcover 0-7862-6589-2 (Basic)

U.K. Hardcover 1-4056-1037-9 (Windsor Large Print)

U.K. Softcover 1-4056-2029-3 (Paragon Large Print)

Copyright © 2004 by Jane Green.

To Have and To Hold was originally published as Spellbound in the United Kingdom by the Penguin Group.

The publishers gratefully acknowledge permission to reprint extracts from the following: 'Let's Get It On' Words and Music by Ed Townsend and Marvin Gaye © 1969, Jobete Music Co. Inc./Stone Diamond Music Corp./Cherritown Music Pub. Co. Inc., USA. Reproduced by permission of Jobete Music Co. Inc./ EMI Music Publishing Ltd, London WC2H 0QY; 'This Be the Verse', from *Collected Poems 1909–1962* by Philip Larkin. Reproduced by permission of Faber and Faber Ltd.

The text of this Large Print edition is unabridged.

Other aspects of the book may vary from the original edition.

Set in 16 pt. Plantin by Liana M. Walker.

Printed in the United States on permanent paper.

British Library Cataloguing-in-Publication Data available

Library of Congress Cataloging-in-Publication Data
Green, Jane, 1968–
    To have and to hold : a novel / Jane Green.
        p. cm.
    ISBN 0-7862-6589-2 (lg. print : hc : alk. paper)
    1. British — United States — Fiction. 2. New York (N.Y.)
— Fiction. 3. Married women — Fiction. 4. Adultery —
Fiction. 5. Large type books. I. Title.
PR6057.R3443T6 2004
    813′.54—dc22   2004047915

*For Harrison, Tabitha,
Nathaniel and Jasper*

PROLOGUE

This is a story about Alice Chambers, who moved into a house that once belonged to the writer Rachel Danbury and who, in doing so, discovered something about herself, her marriage, and her capacity for love. Who changed her life.

Rachel Danbury was a writer who moved to the town of Highfield in the late 1930s. Long after Scott and Zelda Fitzgerald spent a summer in the neighboring town of Westport, Rachel was part of a thriving artistic community of ex-Manhattanites who had escaped to the suburbs and beyond, looking for a more relaxed, peaceful way of living.

She wrote two novels that disappeared without trace, but her third, *The Winding Road*, caused a huge scandal, a scandal that ultimately forced her to move away from the town she loved, to a place where nobody would know who she was.

For Rachel Danbury wrote about her life. She wrote about her marriage, about her womanizing husband, Jefferson, and about her love for a man named Edward Rutherford.

She wrote about a small town in Connecticut called Highfield, about the people who lived there, the people who considered themselves friends. She exposed the town and its inhabitants with warmth and humor, but with dangerously sharp accuracy, and they never forgave her for the betrayal.

Rachel Danbury tried to ignore her husband's infidelities. She told herself he was simply possessed of extraordinary charm, but when he had an affair with a woman called Candice Carter, a former starlet for Paramount and owner of the town theater, she could no longer pretend she didn't know what was going on.

Rachel sought solace, and revenge, in the arms of Edward Rutherford, a neighbor who had always been pleasant, had always been willing to stop for a chat, and until Rachel set out to — successfully — seduce him, nothing more.

But Rachel and Edward fell in love, and

eventually Rachel had to make a choice between a love that was more meaningful than anything she had ever known and her husband.

She chose her husband.

And for the rest of her life Rachel learned to turn a blind eye. She learned to switch off the light in her bedroom, trying not to think of the fact that her husband was not lying beside her, trying not to think about where he was or whom he might be with.

The story of Rachel and Jefferson became famous in America in the 1940s. Everyone in Highfield knew the people involved, and for years the house in which Rachel and Jefferson lived — even after Rachel sold it — was thought to have a curse. Does history repeat itself? The cottage changed hands several times, and then Alice Chambers and her philandering husband, Joe, moved in.

And this is where Alice's story starts.

1

December 24, 1996

Alice takes a deep breath as she opens the closet door and pulls out her dress. She lays it carefully on the bed, gathering her shoes, her veil, her stockings and garter, draping them gently next to the dress, amazed that in just a few hours' time she will be wearing all of this. In just a few hours' time she will be Joe's bride.

"Here comes the bride," she sings to herself, taking small, gliding steps down her hallway into the kitchen, smiling despite the butterflies, putting on the kettle to make herself another cup of coffee. She thinks she needs the coffee to stay awake, so badly did she sleep last night, but the adrenaline is already pumping, and she's waiting for Emily — her maid of honor — to arrive, someone with whom she can share the excitement.

Walking back into the bedroom, she stands for a while gazing at the dress. While not exactly what she would have chosen, she can't deny its beauty, how elegant it is, how impossibly stylish.

Alice had always thought she would have a country wedding. She dreamed, even as a little girl, of a small stone church; of walking through a white wooden gate in a soft, feminine puff of a dress, fresh flowers in her hair and a bouquet of hand-picked wild daisies in her hand. The groom had been unimportant: her fantasy had ended at the church door, but she knows the groom — even in her fantasies — would never have been as handsome, or as successful, as Joe.

At university, when she and Emily sat up late into the night discussing their knights in shining armor, Alice said she thought her ideal man would probably be an artist, or a craftsman, or a gardener. She had laughed as she said it, laughed at the unlikeliness of any lasting relationship, let alone marriage, given that her longest relationship at that time had been three weeks.

And before meeting Joe, her longest relationship had been three months. Not a good record, she had groaned to Emily when they were both planning on growing old together. "Means nothing," Emily had reassured. "Once you find him you'll be married for life. Me? I'll probably get divorced after six months." Alice had laughed, but even as she laughed she was thinking she wished she could be more like Emily, Emily who didn't want to settle down, who was quite happy flirting and flitting from one boy to the next, who claimed to have been born with a fatal allergy to commitment.

So a country wedding with a group of smiling toddlers (she had hoped that by the time she got married, *if* she ever got married, someone somewhere would have been able to provide the smiling toddlers) throwing down a blanket of rose petals and giggling as they walked up the aisle behind her.

She had envisaged a sea of straw hats and floral dresses, the sun beating down on her bare arms as she emerged from the church hand in hand with her other half.

When Joe proposed, she had told him about her dream wedding, and he had smiled at her indulgently and said it was a lovely fantasy, but they couldn't possibly get married in the country when both of them lived in London, and anyway, didn't she agree that winter weddings were so much *smarter?* She didn't agree, but felt she had to, because after all, Joe was paying for it. Alice's parents didn't have a penny, and Joe was determined to have a wedding that he judged fitting for the head of the healthcare business in Mergers & Acquisitions at Godfrey Hamilton Saltz.

They would have a lovely old Bentley to drive them to the church (bye-bye, shire horses and lovely old carriage), she would wear a simple but elegant gown (so long, cream puff of a dress), and a friend of his who was a jeweler would almost definitely lend her a stunning diamond tiara for her hair (see you later, fresh flowers).

So Alice went through the motions of planning her wedding. Every evening she would tell Joe of her decisions, and every morning she would have to phone florists, dressmakers, photographers to inform them that actually, she'd discussed it with her fiancé and the plans would be changing. Would they mind terribly, she would say, if instead of pretty mauve hydrangeas and tulips, they had dark red roses and berries, and not the dress she had designed with a tulle skirt to rival anyone in *Swan Lake*, but a sleek, simple sheath of a dress with long bell sleeves and a matching coat (Joe had flicked through some bridal magazines and showed Alice what would suit her), and so sorry, but actually they didn't want informal fun pictures as they had discussed, but formal family groupings that would take place during the reception.

Alice drains her coffee and steals a quick glance in the hall mirror to confirm what she already knows: deep bags under her eyes proving that last-minute nerves are not just an old wives' tale. Alice has spent the night tossing and turning, fear rising up in a wave of nausea, common sense trying to push it back down again. After all, isn't she the luckiest girl in the world? What woman would not want to marry Joe? Joe with his winning smile and easy charm. His broad shoulders and playful humor. Joe who could quite feasibly have married anyone he wanted, and he chose Alice. *Alice!*

Men like Joe did not usually look at women like Alice, or if they did, it was one quick, curious glance followed by instant dismissal, for the Alices of this world held nothing for men like Joe. The only child of adoring parents, he had been brought up to believe he was God (his mother's fault), to believe that every woman would fall in love with him (his mother's fault), and to believe that a woman's role in life was to do whatever Joe wanted (naturally, his mother again).

Even now, on her wedding day, Alice feels like she has to keep pinching herself. Thirty years old and used to unrequited crushes on men who never seemed to notice her, Alice didn't seriously think she'd ever find her other half. She might have had her dream wedding in mind, but in truth she was secretly convinced she would grow old with her cats, a kimono-clad spinster who would surround herself with eccentric people and end up living vicariously through her younger, prettier friends.

Alice has always thought of herself as rather plain. Everyone who knows Alice has always thought of her as rather plain. She was the shy, mousy girl in the playground who was always last to be picked for teams, and even then she knew she was only ever picked because it was a choice between her or Tracy Balcombe, and Tracy Balcombe had flat feet and B.O.

Alice was left until last because no one ever seemed to notice her. At age fourteen she had become known as Wallpaper, a name that would be said with a snigger, although frankly it never bothered her. She quite liked the fact that she faded into the background, that she could watch her classmates and think her thoughts without anyone ever bothering her.

It only started to bother her when she discovered boys. Up until then Alice had been quite happy with her horses. Her sketchpads were covered with badly drawn pictures of horse heads, mostly of her favorite, Betsy, complete with hearts saying "Alice loves Betsy," and "Betsy 4 Alice," and her daydreams consisted largely of Betsy and Alice steaming ahead to victory in local gymkhanas.

But one morning the girls of Lower IV awoke to discover hormones raging through their developing bodies, and Alice found herself dreaming of Betsy less and less, and more of faded jeans and a cute smile that belonged to a boy named Joe at the boys' school round the corner.

They were on the same bus route, and Alice would stand in the newsagent's for what felt like hours, pretending to flick through magazines, waiting for Joe to arrive. She would stand behind him, staring at the back of his head, willing him to notice her, and although, once or twice, he clearly felt her gaze and turned to meet her eyes, there was not a flicker of interest and he turned away to laugh with a friend.

It was to become a familiar pattern. Throughout her twenties Alice fell head over heels for men who didn't notice her. Strong, handsome, confident men. Men who walked through life with an assurance that Alice coveted, that Alice hoped would somehow rub off on her if she got close enough, which she never managed to do.

Until she met Joe again.

She had known Joe for years. He had been a friend of Ty's — her older brother — at school, one of the boys on whom she had had a huge, and painful, crush. She remembered watching him chat up the prettiest girl in her school at a local disco, watched him laugh and smile with her, his face moving closer and closer as he leaned in for a kiss, before taking her hand and leading her out the door.

Rumor had it that he had gone back to her house, kissed her good night, then an hour later shinned up the drainpipe and stolen her virginity. It was the stuff of which legends were made, and Joe was, even then, a legend. At fourteen years old he was going out with a twenty-year-old Danish au pair girl who lived round the corner. According to the boys in the class she was a cross between Farrah Fawcett and Jerry Hall.

Joe was responsible for a thousand broken teenage hearts, and Alice and Emily would sit for hours and talk about how much they hated him, each of them secretly longing for him to notice them.

And then one day the doorbell rang, and Alice ran to answer it, nearly fainting when she discovered Joe standing on the doorstep. Her fifteen-year-old heart threatened to give way as a hot flush crept up her cheeks, staining them scarlet.

Joe had raised an eyebrow, amused. Not his type at all, but he liked to see the effect he had on women. It reassured him, made him feel secure, and what harm would it do to encourage her a little, it was only a bit of fun.

"Hello, Ty's sister," he smiled, his voice low and flirtatious. "You look lovely. Are you going somewhere nice?" It amused him to see her blush further, and still more to see she had quite literally lost the power of speech. Alice managed to mumble something and stumbled away when Ty appeared.

"Hey, Joe," he said, grabbing his coat. "Hope you're not chatting up my sister," and they both laughed at how ridiculous that would be, as they disappeared up the path.

But Alice had been spun into a fervor. She had called Emily immediately, and Emily had come round to analyze, inspect, and dissect every word. They had locked themselves in Alice's bedroom, each slumped on a beanbag, squealing with excitement as they went over and over the one sentence he had uttered, trying to understand what it meant.

"Say it again," Emily pleaded. "Tell me again what he sounded like when he said, 'You look lovely.'"

They formulated a plan of action. Worked out exactly what Alice would say to Joe when she next saw him, what tone of voice she would use, what she would wear when he took her out, because clearly, he was interested, and whether she would let him go to base one or base two on the first date.

Joe never noticed Alice again.

Fourteen years later Alice had a thriving catering business. She had finally managed to get over Joe and pass six O and two A levels, had gone to catering college, and from there to a yearlong cooking course.

At twenty-nine years old she had an occasional staff of three who helped her prepare and serve gourmet dinners for women too busy, or too lazy, to cook.

Alice tended to stay in the background at these dinner parties. She loved cooking the meals beforehand, but stayed in the kitchen making sure nothing got burned while the other girls served canapés and cocktails. Occasionally, should the host or hostess demand, she would come in to receive praise, reluctantly but graciously, smoothing back the loose curls that had escaped her ponytail as she handed out business cards.

She had a small flat with a large kitchen in Kensal Rise, her two cats, Molly and Paolo, and a tiny social life thanks in part to the success of her business and in part to her natural shyness.

Her last relationship — the three-monther — had been with an actor called Steve, but three months of massaging the chip on his shoulder had taken its toll, and she was grateful when one of his auditions actually came to fruition and he took off to Manchester to do rep for three months. They promised to stay in touch, she would come up to visit, but she knew it was just a formality.

So there she was, in the kitchen of her dreams, in the basement of a large house in Primrose Hill. The kitchen was almost back to its pristine state, the plates stacked neatly in the dishwasher, the crystal goblets already draining next to the sink, and her casserole dishes cleaned and waiting in the boot of the car.

The guests were drinking espresso, with homemade petits fours, and Alice said good-bye to the two girls helping her out, knowing that the only thing left to do would be to wash up the coffee cups, and she could manage that perfectly well by herself.

"Oh, you must meet Alice." She heard the hostess banging down the stairs in her high heels. "She's an absolute angel, and the food's fantastic. Also" — her voice dropped an octave or two — "not at all expensive compared to some of the others."

Bugger, thought Alice. Time to put my prices up. She grabbed a cloth to appear busy and practiced smiling, a bright sparkly smile that would invite more business, quickly polishing the granite worktops as she heard the footsteps come into the room.

"Hello, Alice," said a voice that she would have known anywhere.

"Hello, Joe," she said, the smile replaced with a deep scarlet flush.

Joe walks up to greet his ushers, who all crowd round him in a conspiratorial huddle.

"Well?"

"Did you do it?"

"Was she worth it?"

"Could you resist?"

"Bloody better have been worth it, the amount we paid."

"Didn't know whether you'd have the energy."

"So come on then, Joe, what was she like? Did you succumb?"

Joe smiles beatifically and raises a hand to quiet the masses. "Boys," he says, as they wait with bated breath. "It's my wedding day. Show some respect."

"Seriously." Adrian, his best man, puts an arm around Joe's shoulders and leads him away from the boys. "She cost a fortune, and I just want to know if you got your money's worth."

"You mean *your* money's worth?" Joe grins.

"Well, yes. So did you?"

"Don't you mean, did I actually fuck her?"

"No," Adrian shakes his head. "I've known you since you were eleven years old. Of course you fucked her. So did you get our money's worth?"

Joe had sworn his womanizing days were behind him, had vowed he would be faithful, causing much mirth among his friends. The evening before, on his stag night, they had organized a high-class call girl to be waiting in a limo. It was a test, they had said, a test to see whether he really would be faithful.

"I *will* pass," he had said assuredly when they told him of their plan, and several saketinis later made his way out to the limo, fully intending to tell the call girl thanks, but no thanks. He was greeted by a mane of the exact shade of honey-blond hair that he loved, legs that went on forever, and a Wonderbra that was truly wonderful to behold.

"Oh, shit," he groaned, climbing into the car. "I suppose a final fling wouldn't hurt."

It was a marathon, extraordinary, incredible night. He had woken up this morning at the Sanderson Hotel feeling guilty as hell and then felt a hand start to slowly stroke his thigh, and, oh, what difference would a morning screw make? After all, she'd clearly been paid for the night. And it's only sex.

And Alice will never know.

"So did you get our money's worth?" Adrian persists.

"She was a six-foot Russian blonde with a figure that would make Lara Croft jealous and a mouth that never slept. What do *you* think?"

Adrian doubles over and groans in envy. "Fuck," he spits through his teeth. "I knew it. So was it the best night of your life?"

"Adrian! Please!" Joe looks shocked. "Tonight will be the best night of my life."

"But it was a close second?" Adrian grins.

"Very, very close. And as a final fling Svetlana couldn't have been more perfect."

"Svetlana?" Adrian snorts with laughter. "Was that her real name?"

"Do you know," Joe says nonchalantly, turning to head back to the church, "I don't actually care."

Joe had never thought he was going to get married. Had been quite happy living the quintessential bachelor lifestyle, but by his early thirties he'd started to think it might be quite nice to have some permanence, someone to come home to, to look after him.

25

The problem was that the girls he went out with were about as far away from wife material as you could possibly get. Yes, they looked great. Tall stunning blondes, the occasional brunette or redhead, they were all polished to perfection, but were so cold, so brittle, Joe sometimes thought that if he bent them the wrong way they might snap.

They were women who were waiting for a rich husband to provide them with a life-style their beauty had led them to believe they could expect. They had no careers, avoided the news as if they could catch something nasty from it, couldn't cook, didn't clean, had never ironed a thing in their lives ("Darling, if God had meant us to iron he wouldn't have invented dry cleaners"), and had a deep-rooted fear of marrying a man who couldn't afford a "woman that does."

They expected certain things of Joe — dinners at the Ivy and Hakkasan, nights out at Atticus and Home House, the odd treat from Harvey Nicks — and in return they gave him unlimited performance sex, little pressure (these girls knew that the best way to hook their fish was to let the line run as long as possible), and the guaranteed envy of every man he knew. It was

only once they started expecting commitment that Joe would turn around and tell
them in the nicest way possible that they'd
had a wonderful time together, but that he
knew it wasn't meant to be, and on he
would go to his next conquest.

He knew he didn't want to marry a
woman who wanted him only for his bonus
(although his looks and personality weren't
exactly negligible), and he knew he wasn't
going to find the woman he would marry
in the trendy bars, restaurants, and clubs
he frequented, but there was something
about glossy, streaky blond hair, a leg clad
in Wolford stockings, breasts pushed up in
La Perla that he just couldn't resist.

And then he met Alice. Alice who turned
scarlet when he said her name, who remembered him from school, even when he
had no recollection of ever meeting her.
Alice who had loose mousy curls and
didn't wear a scrap of makeup. Who wore
cheap black leggings and baggy shapeless
sweaters to disguise her curves. He
wouldn't normally have looked twice at a
girl like Alice, but he was amused by the
way she blushed every time he looked at
her, and there was something very sweet
about her, and sweetness was not a character trait he was used to in women.

She was sweet, and she was grateful, which in turn made Joe feel generous and kind, rather like a benefactor. She didn't expect anything of him other than his company, and when he gave her what she wanted she seemed in a state of permanent disbelief that he would be with a girl like her.

Plus, he realized very quickly that Alice had a huge amount of potential. She was a lovely girl, she could cook fantastically, she'd definitely look after him, and it wouldn't take much to make her look a whole hell of a lot better. With a diet, a decent hairdresser, and a new wardrobe, she'd be a whole new woman by the time he'd finished with her.

2

December 24, 2001

"Need help with your bags, love?" The cab driver makes a halfhearted attempt to open the door, but the woman stops him.

"Don't worry." She smiles with uncharacteristic warmth (because God knows, he knows the type, and he's usually lucky if he gets a thank you, let alone a smile). "I'll manage. Merry Christmas!" And she collects her bags and walks up to her door.

The cab driver sits and watches her for a minute. Great legs. Great smile. Great hair. If only he were a few years younger. But see that huge rock on her left hand? The alligator handbag that screams money and class? Look at the address, must be where she lives. Belgravia indeed. He shakes his head as he drives off to the Lanesborough to try to pick up some rich American tourists (the tips make the wait

29

worthwhile). Girls like that were always out of his league.

After clattering up the front steps and opening the door, Alice dumps her bags just inside and kicks off her heels. "Bloody Jimmy Choos," she mutters, leaning down to massage her instep, grateful for the cool limestone floor against her aching feet. "Bloody Beauchamp Place. Bloody shopping."

She pulls some beautifully gift-wrapped boxes out of the bags at her feet and leans down to arrange them underneath the huge Christmas tree, sweeping aside the iced white crystal balls that hang from the branches and catch in her straightened, streaked hair.

During their first Christmas together, Alice had planned to decorate the tree with Joe. She'd spent hours searching for Christmas decorations: brightly colored wooden soldiers, colorful beads, multicolored fairy lights, and strings of glittering tinsel. Joe had phoned to say he was stuck in a meeting, so Alice had decided to surprise him by decorating the tree herself.

She loved every minute of it. When she'd finished, she sat on the floor gazing up at the tree while eating popcorn out of a huge bucket, remembering all her childhood Christmases, dying for Joe to come home and see the tree, how lovely, and festive, and homely it looked.

When Joe walked in and saw the tree, he froze.

"What. Is. That?"

"That's our tree," Alice laughed, putting down the popcorn and running up to kiss him.

"But what is all that stuff on it?"

"Those are our decorations." Alice spoke slowly, as if to a child.

"No." Joe shook his head as Alice tried to understand. "No."

Now Alice understands.

Joe had taken everything off the tree and come home the next day with new decorations. Everything, he said, had to be white, or he refused to have a tree. White crystal balls, the best money could buy, tiny white fairy lights, and white velvet bows as a concession to tradition. Even the fairy had to go, and now their tree is topped by a brushed silver pyramid.

Alice has never managed to feel the same way about Christmas again, although now, gazing up at her twelve-foot Norwegian spruce, glittering icily in the subdued lighting of the lobby, she has to admit it may not be festive, or even particularly pretty, but it's certainly impressive.

Their whole house is impressive, for that matter, although Alice has become immune to it now. They had employed an architect known for his modern, minimalist style to gut what had once been an old garage that specialized in redoing vintage cars and turn it into a designer haven.

Limestone floors and glass ceilings. Stainless steel fixtures and hard square modern furniture, shades of coffee and cream, not a color to be seen. And then that huge, impressive foyer, two storys high, large enough to house a Christmas tree bigger than Alice had ever seen before outside of Trafalgar Square.

Alice walks upstairs to the open-plan kitchen and switches on the kettle (Alessi) for a quick cup of tea. Tonight is their five-year anniversary, and they're off to Nobu — Joe's favorite — for dinner. She checks the clock on the microwave — 6:14. The table's booked for eight-thirty, but she has learned to be twenty minutes late for everything, and even then she usually arrives before Joe.

Alice has become used to walking into restaurants, parties, events, alone. She has perfected the art of small talk, of wearing a serene smile on her face at all times to hide her discomfort and awkwardness.

Joe is invariably late, or away. Alice used to try to cancel if Joe suddenly announced he was going to be away, but she has obligations now, commitments, and it is not always easy to come up with a new excuse. If Joe is in London, merely working, she knows he will eventually turn up, his tie askew, his mind clearly elsewhere, and Alice, who would once have been appalled by his rudeness and disrespect, has learned to accommodate even this, but she is not happy about it.

This is not the life Alice imagined herself leading. This is not the marriage Alice imagined herself to have. And Joe is not the knight in shining armor she had once thought.

She hates sitting in restaurants by herself, feeling the other diners glance at her with curiosity (I haven't been stood up, she feels like announcing, my husband will be here in a minute), yet she puts up with it because there is a small part of her that still enjoys seeing Joe walk in, stepping outside her role as his wife, pretending she is just another diner, feeling again the thrill of her attraction to this man.

So tonight, their anniversary, Joe will be late. He may or may not phone first and apologize in advance, but she is quite sure he will make it up to her with wonderful flowers and a wonderful present, probably jewelry, at which she will gasp with delight, although she now has a safe full of wonderful jewelry, which she neither needed nor particularly wanted.

Alice would happily exchange her jewelry for more time with her husband. She married him dreaming of their shared lives together, but finds that she is far lonelier now than she ever was before. At least in her single days she had her career, and Emily, but the only cooking she does these days is when entertaining Joe's business clients and occasionally friends, and Emily is so busy living her single life, Alice just doesn't seem to see her much anymore.

Alice takes her tea upstairs and starts to run a bath, sitting on the edge of the tub as she examines herself in the mirror opposite, feeling as she so often does these days that she is looking at a stranger, barely able to recognize the person she has become.

There have been occasions, over the last few years, when she has run into former clients at parties. They are always charm personified, and not one of them has ever recognized her.

There have even been times when she has mentioned that she once had a catering company, and they have said, "Really? What was it called?" because these are people who use catering companies on a regular basis, and when she has told them the name they have said, "Oh, yes. I think I might have used them once a long time ago." They have no idea that Alice has studied their kitchens, knows their cupboards, their fridges, what brand of kitchen towel they use.

But why should they recognize her? Alice thinks, sipping her tea, remembering the girl she used to be. Gone now is the mousy, curly hair. Gone the pale, wan skin free of makeup. She crosses her legs and looks down at her tight Gucci trousers that show off her long, lean legs, splays her fingers to look at the short, square nails, French-polished to perfection, stands up and leans on the counter, moving her face toward the mirror to better examine what she sees.

Her hair now falls in a streaky sheet, all hint of mouse hidden by honeys and caramels; her skin is lightly tanned, her makeup subtle and her clothes sophisticated. She now wears only the best of the best, even though she has a pathological hatred of high heels and feels like a trussed turkey in the little fitted jackets Joe likes.

Her favored, favorite old Levi's are still in her closet, but she couldn't wear them now. Sometimes she tries them on as a reminder of who she is, who she once was, but the jeans are now so big she can pull them on and off without even undoing them.

The jeans she wears these days, on the rare occasions she wears jeans, are Earl, or Diesel. They are dark denim, low-slung on the hips, flaring ever so slightly and sexily over her pointed boots. She wears them with delicate chiffon Alberta Ferretti tops, under a long shearling coat with a huge fox collar. These are her outfits for pretending she and Joe are trendy, hip Londoners, for pretending they are ten years younger than their age, for those nights they go to Hush, or Home House, or the K Club.

Alice can pull off this look, despite her age, because she doesn't really care. Clothes have never interested her, do not interest her now, but she knows she has to play the part, and she has always been good at fitting into different roles. Not to mention different clothes.

There used to be mornings, before her transformation was complete, when Alice would come down for breakfast in one of her old, baggy sweaters, but Joe has taught her always to look her best, even if only nipping out for milk, because, after all, she never knows whom she might bump in to. Alice doesn't much care whom she bumps in to, or what she looks like, but she wants to make Joe happy, and if looking perfect keeps Joe happy, then she will do her best to look perfect, twenty-four hours a day.

At night she wears delicate silk negligées, with matching robes and Loro Piana cashmere slippers. She still has a pair of men's flannel pajamas from days of old, and when Joe is away she clambers into the pajamas and snuggles up in bed, television remote control in one hand, thickly buttered toast and honey in the other. (Joe does not allow breakfast in bed: the crumbs might — God forbid — get into the sheets.)

The phone rings sharply, bringing her running from the bathroom, and her heart sinks as she sees Joe's mobile number flash up on caller display.

"You're going to be late, aren't you?" Her voice is flat.

"Oh, darling, I'm so sorry. I'm stuck in

this bloody meeting, and" — he drops his voice — "I did tell them it was my anniversary tonight, but work is work, and it shouldn't go on too late. I just want you to make the reservation nine. I'll definitely be there for nine."

"Joe, it's our anniversary. Why tonight of all nights? Why are you always working?" Alice cannot help the anger in her voice. Their arguments are always the same: his work, his traveling, his absence. "What do you want me to do?" he usually hisses. "Leave my job? We'd have to sell the house, change our lifestyle. You'd like that, would you? You want to have no money? Fine. Just say the word and I'll leave."

Or her personal favorite: "I'm doing this for you, you know."

"You think I like the traveling?" he'll try from time to time. "You think I like getting up at four in the morning to go to the airport, flying to meeting after meeting, missing you and just wanting to be home? You think it's any fun for me staying in hotel rooms all the time, with no friends, no family, going to one boring business dinner after another?"

I am not stupid, Alice thinks. I know all about your business trips. I know about the big, black plush Mercedes that drives you to Heathrow. I know about your first-class travel and your gold executive card for British Airways. I know about your hotels — the Four Seasons and nothing less. I know about your six-course gourmet client dinners, with rare, fine wines, Cuban cigars, and vintage ports. Oh, the sheer hell of it!

Alice does turn around from time to time and say, "Yes. That's exactly what I want. I'd love to sell this bloody museum of a house, and I'd love to change our lifestyle. You think I care about all this stuff? I don't care, I'd love a little house outside London. Go on. Leave. Leave your bloody job."

"Fine!" he would say defiantly. "I'll leave tomorrow." And usually that's the last she'll hear of it until the next row.

Now, on the telephone, Joe takes a sharp intake of breath and drops his voice low. "Alice, I do not need to have an argument now. I am in a meeting, and it will run slightly later than I had planned. I am not prepared to get into this on our anniversary." His voice is stern, and Alice doesn't have the energy to fight.

"Please don't be later than nine," she says eventually.

"I'm sorry, darling." The relief in his

voice is audible, relief at Alice's acceptance, her lack of anger. "I promise I'll be there for nine and I'll make it up to you."

Alice sighs. What else can she do? "I'll see you at nine. I lo—" She stops. The phone has already been cut off.

She leans back on the pillows and looks at the photographs on the wall at the end of the bed. Three photographs, black and white, blown up, of Joe and Alice looking like the happiest people on earth. It could almost be an ad for Calvin Klein, so perfect do they look. But Alice remembers that day well. The photographer grew more and more impatient waiting for Joe to arrive, and Alice remembered trying to placate him, to make him laugh. When Joe finally did arrive they had five minutes before the photographer had to go to another job (he couldn't let them down — *Vogue*). Both Alice and Joe were amazed that in such a short space of time he managed to produce pictures this beautiful.

Alice gazing directly into the camera, the sadness in her eyes already apparent, looking pensive, and wistful, and very beautiful. Joe kissing Alice's forehead, an apology for the delay, his profile in shadow, her profile a sharp chiaroscuro of light. Joe cuddling Alice, his strong arms wrapped tightly around her, chin nestled in her shoulder, a cheeky smile on his face, her eyes lit up with laughter and love.

They had been taken three years ago, but it felt like a lifetime. What had happened to them in the last three years? Where had the laughter and intimacy gone?

At three minutes past nine (of course Nobu accommodated the last-minute change — Joe Chambers is, after all, one of their best customers), Joe takes the steps, three at a time. He charges through the restaurant to the table at which he knows Alice is waiting and scoops her hair gently away from her neck, leaning down to kiss her cheek.

"Three minutes," she warns, grateful that he did not make her wait tonight.

"I told you I wouldn't be late," he grins. "You look beautiful. I'm sorry. Happy anniversary." And he places a small turquoise-blue box on the table in front of her.

"Yet another guilt present?" Alice jokes, as Joe stiffens.

"What do you mean?"

"I mean every time you're late you bring me a present."

"Not every time, darling." He relaxes. "And this is our five-year anniversary."

"Five years. Can you believe it?" Alice is playing with the white ribbon on the box, wondering whether tonight would be the night for another talk, whether tonight he might listen when she says she needs Joe to spend more time with her. But she knows it will probably descend into another argument, and tonight is their anniversary. Perhaps she will try to save it until tomorrow.

"The happiest years of my life," Joe says, as he says every year on their anniversary, and Alice still doesn't know whether he means it.

"Are they really?" she says tonight, putting the box down and staring at him. "Are these really the happiest years of your life?"

"Alice," he warns with a sigh. "I'm not prepared to have that discussion tonight. I'm not going to sit here and talk about how unhappy you are with my hours because I can't change that right now, and I'm not going to have an argument on our anniversary. Open the gift. Let's just have some champagne and have a lovely evening."

Alice unwraps the Tiffany box and opens it to reveal a small diamond heart on a long platinum chain.

"It's beautiful," she says.

"Here. Put it on."

Alice leans her head forward obligingly and Joe slips it on, sitting back to admire his good taste and his beautiful wife. He is aware that he is not the only one, that these days Alice always garners admiring glances. He chose well. She is a good wife, and she makes him happy. She's not as passive or as forgiving as he had once thought, and he could live without the rows that seem to be more and more frequent, but he doesn't think many women would put up with him, and on the whole Alice is probably far less demanding than any of the others.

And look how beautiful she has become, how the Plain Jane has blossomed into this stylish, sophisticated creature. She is everything he has ever looked for, and he leans forward, taking her face gently in his hands as he says, "I love you."

"I know," she smiles.

"No. I really love you."

"I really love you too."

"I love you the most," he smiles, for this is their game.

"No. I love you the most."

"Okay," he shrugs with a playful smile,

and they both laugh and kiss, all animosity now forgotten.

They have a wonderful evening. The chef's specials were, as always, delicious, the champagne warmed their hearts, and they have been both tender and playful. Alice is almost high with joy, for this is the Joe she fell in love with, this is the Joe she doesn't often see anymore.

He has been charming and funny and flirtatious. Perhaps he has flirted with their waitress a little more than Alice is comfortable with, but she is used to his ways now, and pretends not to notice.

"Doesn't it bother you," Emily once said, "how he flirts with anything in a skirt?"

"Absolutely not," Alice had lied. "He's all mouth and no trousers. He'll look but he won't touch." And although she knows this to be true, knows that he would never be unfaithful, that he is basically just an insecure little boy at heart who needs to be constantly reassured that women still find him attractive, she still finds it exasperating that he continues to flirt in her presence.

"What?" he says, shrugging. "Why are you giving me that look?"

"You know why."

"I'm not flirting. God, Alice, you always think I flirt with everyone."

"That's because you do."

"I'm just being charming."

"Smarmy, more like."

"Anyway. You're the one I chose. You're the one I'm married to."

"Hmmm." Alice raises an eyebrow. "I'm not sure if that's a good thing or a bad thing."

The bill has been paid and Alice and Joe are just finishing their coffee. Joe's hand is already stroking Alice's thigh under the table, and they are smiling at each other, knowing what that means, knowing that to-night will not be an early night after all.

"Alice! Joe!" A piercing French accent rings out, and Joe's hand leaps off Alice's thigh as they both turn round to see Valerie and Martyn.

Alice doesn't like Valerie. She has known her for some months now, has bumped into her at several charity events, and on each occasion Valerie has said they must have lunch, but of course neither one has phoned the other.

Truth be told, Alice is more than a little scared of Valerie. While Alice is aware she now looks the part, she also knows that, much like a little girl playing make-believe, she is pretending. Valerie, on the other hand, is the real McCoy. Originally from Geneva, Valerie was brought up in New York, and now flies between London, New York, and Paris. So polished she's almost gleaming, and so hard you'd hurt yourself if you bumped into her, she is witty, caustic, and the current darling of the society pages.

She also flirts mercilessly with Joe every time she sees him, and the only small mercy is that — extraordinarily — Joe doesn't flirt back. "She's a ball-breaker," he said, when Alice first mentioned her. "A scary woman. Not sure I like her." Alice breathed a deep sigh of relief.

"Valerie." Joe stands up, plants a kiss on each cheek, and shakes hands with Martyn, her current, and rather insignificant save for his small fortune, boyfriend.

"Alice!" Valerie bends down to kiss Alice, enveloping her in a cloud of Calèche. "You look so in love, the two of you, sitting here gazing into each other's eyes. So romantic!"

"Do we?" Alice says brightly, thinking, Yes, see how happy we are? *That* will teach you not to flirt with my husband. "It's our anniversary."

"Oh, chérie, congratulations. How

wonderful. How long?"

"Five years." Alice continues to stake her claim.

"Mon Dieu! That's practically a lifetime! My first marriage lasted nine months and that was long enough, thank you. Aren't you getting bored?" Valerie turns to Joe and raises an eyebrow.

Joe looks nervous. "Bored? With my beautiful wife? Absolutely not."

"But they say that variety is the spice of life," she says lightly. "After five years" — she turns to look at Alice — "I'd be looking for a little variety."

"We don't need variety," Alice smiles through gritted teeth. "We have each other. Come on Joe, love. Let's go home." A dramatic pause. "To bed."

Valerie raises an eyebrow and smiles. "Enjoy yourselves, my darlings. And don't do anything I wouldn't do."

3

They fuck you up, your Mum and Dad
They may not mean to but they do
They fill you with the faults they had
And add some extra, just for you . . .
                              —*Philip Larkin*

Joe finishes buttoning his shirt and reaches
for his tie, draped neatly over the back of a
buttery toile armchair in the corner of the
bedroom. He puts his tie around his neck
and stands in the soft glow of the bedside
lamp for a few seconds, gazing down at the
figure in the bed, her back toward him, her
head resting on her arm, looking exactly like
a model for an Impressionist painting. How
lovely she is, the light glancing off the curve
of her hip, her hair fanned out on the Frette
pillowcases.

He leans down with a regretful smile and

plants a gentle kiss on her shoulder, at which she turns over and stretches, giving him a lazy smile.

"You have to leave already?"

"I do."

She reaches a hand up and strokes his cheek. "When will I see you again?"

"Soon. I'll call you." He sighs, knowing that this has to end, that her appearance at the restaurant last night crossed the line of acceptable behavior, that although it might just be a game to her, it could cost him his marriage.

"And what if I call you first?" Valerie smiles, then slowly pushes herself up on to her knees, stretching her arms up around his neck, waiting to see his reaction.

"Valerie," he warns, nervous now. "You know the score. Alice is my wife and I love her, I don't want to hurt her and I'm not going to leave her."

"I know, darling," she purrs, because this is a game she has played many times before, and as much as she likes to tease her married lovers, she has no intention whatsoever of breaking up their marriages. She just likes to have fun, to push the limits, to see how far she can go. "This has nothing to do with your marriage, I know, I know."

"No, Valerie," he says gently, disentangling himself from her arms. He has to end this, nearly had heart failure last night when she turned up at Nobu, only three hours after he had left her bed, when he had told her where he was taking Alice for their anniversary.

In the beginning he would have found it flattering. Would have found the element of danger exhilarating and sexy as hell. But he's been seeing Valerie for a while now, and although the sex is fantastic, the thrill of the chase has now well and truly gone, and the prospect of getting caught — particularly after last night — is far more worrying than exciting.

There are, after all, certain rules about playing away, certain expectations that each of you must have, and an implicit agreement that you will abide by these rules.

First, and most important, a mistress must conspire to protect your marriage, must understand that your marriage comes first, and that however much you profess to love your mistress, you will never leave your wife.

She must never acknowledge you publicly in anything other than a platonic way, must understand that arrangements are made to be broken and that your family will always come first.

She must wait for your phone call or phone you on your mobile phone, which will be switched off when you are with your family. If you are with your family when the phone rings, you will have a code, and she will understand and immediately say good-bye. She will never phone you at home, not even when the urge to hear your voice becomes unbearable, and she will make herself available whenever you wish to see her.

Joe knows the rules by heart, knew the rules long before he planned to play the game. He has been observing the rules since he was a tiny boy, too young even to understand the meaning of the word, but old enough to know that what his father was doing was somehow wrong, would hurt his mother, that he would have to shoulder the burden of secrecy to please his father and protect his mother.

We are all the product of our parenting, and Joe, although a kind man, a loving man, could not have turned out any other way.

Eric Chambers was twenty-seven when Joe was born in 1964. He had been married for a year to Ava, whose dark good looks always reminded people of Ava

Gardner, after whom she was named. Eric had fallen in love with Ava after she repeatedly turned him down, rejected his advances, told him she was not interested.

She knew of his reputation, had seen him around town in his E-type Jag, always with a glamorous blonde in a headscarf and large black sunglasses at his side. Ava had known he would be a heartbreaker, that he had indeed broken the hearts of many of the girls she knew.

But Eric persisted. He was not used to being turned down, and her indifference only fanned the flames of his desire. For a while, just like his son, he thought he could be the perfect husband, thought that one woman would be enough.

For a while he thought he could look and not touch, appreciate the myriad of beautiful women around him, admire the miniskirts brushing their thighs, the sleek bobs brushing against sharp cheekbones, but once Ava's pregnancy started to show, Eric found himself longing for the unfamiliar touch, the thrill of a new body, a new taste, a new smell.

He fought it as long as he could, but one brief dalliance before Joe was born became several during Joe's first year, eventually becoming one permanent mistress, who was subject to change, plus a couple of one-night stands, should he be lucky enough to find them, the free love of the 1970s taking rather longer to hit Guildford.

It didn't, however, take Eric long to realize that Joe was the perfect foil. "I'm just taking him out for a walk," he would tell Ava, who would gratefully retire to her room for a break from the exhausting demands of motherhood. After bundling Joe up, Eric would put him in the carriage and walk him down the road to Betty's house, where Joe would gurgle happily on the floor of the living room while Eric helped "Auntie Betty" in the other room.

After Auntie Betty there was Auntie Sandra. Then Auntie Sally, followed by Auntie Terry, Auntie Pat, and Auntie Barbara. Auntie Pat was Joe's favorite. She'd scoop him up into a big hug, saying, "Whaddyaknowjoe?" had a color television set, and let him eat sherbet fizzes and drink pop while he watched *Captain Scarlet.*

All the aunties made a fuss of Joe, but by the time Auntie Barbara came along, Joe was refusing to cooperate. He didn't need any more aunties, he had decided, and there was no point being nice to them because they never seemed to stick around for long anyway.

"I don't want to go and see Auntie Barbara," he'd said. "Why can't we go and see Auntie Pat?" But of course he'd never say this in front of his mum, because Eric had already told him that he worked for the aunties on the quiet and that Mum wouldn't be very happy about it, and he was only doing it to make a bit of extra money to buy nice things for Mum, so Joe mustn't say anything.

Joe knew, even at five years old, that there was more to it than that. He knew that his father was somehow guilty, and hated the fact that he would buy him a treat on the way home to buy his silence. He hated that moment when they would both walk in the door, and his mother would give him a big kiss and ask whether he'd had a lovely time at the park, or the museum. He'd shrug and stay silent, and would go up to his room as quickly as possible to avoid any more questions.

"Good boy, Joe," Eric would whisper as he ruffled his hair. "Who's Daddy's best boy?"

"I am," Joe would mumble, unable to look his father in the eye.

The best times were when his father was

away. Then it would just be Joe and his mum, and he could look after her and make her laugh, and make sure that she didn't have to worry about anything. And best of all, he didn't have to lie, although his father said it wasn't lying, it just wasn't telling the whole truth, and that was something entirely different.

His parents were married for thirty-one years, until the unthinkable happened. Ava left Eric for Brian, a man they had played bridge with, a man they had known for years, whose own wife had died of cancer a long time ago.

It came completely out of the blue. Joe was at the office when the phone rang and he heard a series of short, sharp sobs. For a man who had never seen his father cry, it was possibly the most shocking thing Joe had ever heard. "She's gone," his father kept repeating. "She's gone. What am I going to do?"

"Of course I knew," his mother said when Joe got hold of her later that day. "I've known for years about your father but I didn't want to know, I pretended not to notice. I kept thinking that if I kept quiet he'd eventually give the women up, and I kept hoping that maybe it wasn't true, but I've heard all the rumors, I know there's no smoke without fire."

"But he loves you," Joe pleaded, devastated that his mother had actually left, that the only security he had ever known could be shattered so quickly. "He's devastated. He doesn't know what to do with himself."

"He'll get over it," she said sadly. "I love him but I can't live with the lies anymore. I can't live with the phone calls saying he's just going to the pub, when I know he's with another woman. I don't want to live with him going into the other room and whispering when his stupid mobile phone rings. He's nearly sixty, for heaven's sake, and he's still at it, and I've had enough."

Ava had married Brian — a very nice, but very dull accountant — and Eric had finally got used to being on his own.

"You'll be fine," Joe had said to him in the beginning. "Think of what a wonderful time you'll have now you're a free man, think of all those women who are dying to meet a handsome man like you."

But Eric hadn't ever really been fine since Ava left. It had shocked him to the core, and it was only once she had gone that he realized not only how much he loved her, but how much he *needed* her.

Eventually he met Carol, a divorced woman in her mid-fifties, and they settled down together. Joe doesn't spend enough time with either of them to know whether the aunties are still around, but he rather suspects they are. What leopard, after all, ever manages to change its spots?

Joe had sworn he wouldn't do the same thing as his father. Even as a young boy he had vowed he wouldn't have a series of aunties, wouldn't hurt his wife like his father had hurt his mother, wouldn't spend his entire married life lying to his partner.

But really. Did he ever have a choice?

Joe does love Alice. Truly and absolutely. He loves her as much as a man like Joe can ever possibly love a woman. He loves her and wouldn't ever want to hurt her. But he also loves women, and he has come to justify his love of women by thinking, as his father did before him, that it is merely satisfying a physical urge, that as long as he does not hurt his wife, as long as his wife never finds out, what harm can it possibly do?

There was only ever one woman who didn't understand the rules. Sasha was Joe's first transgression after his marriage, and had she not made it so obvious she was interested, had she not blatantly pursued him, perhaps he would have managed to stay off the slippery slope. Not forever, you understand, just for a while longer.

Sasha was supposed to be a one-night stand. He had two hours of frantic, animal sex, then slunk home feeling sick and guilty, creeping into bed next to Alice, resolving not to let it happen again.

He left early the next morning, unable to look Alice in the eye, and returned home that night with a large bunch of white lilies to hide his relief at not being found out. He'd gotten away with it, and although he hadn't planned to see Sasha again, if he had gotten away with it once, surely he could get away with it again, and Alice would never need to know.

But after four months of secret trysts with Joe, Sasha was fed up. She had been single long enough, had wasted too much time looking for a man like Joe, without the attachments. It had taken thirty-three years, and finally she had figured out that men like Joe — attractive, intelligent, good sense of humor, bucketloads of money — were never unattached. She would simply have to steal her man away from somebody else. What else could she do?

She took Jerry Hall's words to heart, becoming a cook in the kitchen, a maid in the living room, and a whore in the bedroom. Joe had never had sex like it: She would do anything, anywhere, at any time. At first it was as addictive as a drug — the sex, then the food, and all completely under his control, she was entirely at his beck and call.

And when Sasha knew he was hooked, she started exerting pressure, not much, just enough to show Joe she meant business. A few dangerous text messages. The odd phone call at home to hear his voice, blocking her number first for the couple of occasions when Alice would pick up and Sasha would have to put the phone down. Love notes hidden in his coat pockets in the hope that Alice would find them.

Alice didn't find them. Joe did. He was furious. This wasn't part of the deal, he told her in a rage, trying hard to disguise it for fear of causing further damage. She knew he wasn't going to leave his wife, how could they possibly continue when Sasha had breached his trust like this?

Sasha realized immediately that she had overstepped the mark by leaving the love notes in his pocket, and she tried to apologize, to persuade him to carry on, promised she wouldn't do it again, but Joe couldn't take the chance.

Some men might have been put off by such a close shave, and Joe was, temporarily, shocked into being the faithful husband. For a while. He was home every night by eight o'clock, and when he phoned to say he would be late because he was in a meeting, he was in a meeting.

He went away on business and stayed in the best hotels, and met clients in the bar for a drink, wined and dined them, then went back to his room, on his own, and phoned Alice just before climbing into bed to tell her how much he loved her.

Then during a trip to Denmark he met Inge, a waitress at the coffee shop next to the hotel. He met her on the first day and was in bed with her by the third. A business trip doesn't count, he told himself, pushing away the guilt, as long as I don't do anything in London, on my home turf.

That lasted precisely four more months.

And now his latest is Valerie. Valerie who is sophisticated enough not to be taken in by his charm, who is dangerous enough to have her own agenda, to want to play games just to see what kind of reaction she can incur.

He knows that on one level Valerie is a safe choice. Far too experienced a woman, a lover, a mistress, to believe that sex is anything other than sex, she would not actually do anything to seriously jeopardize his marriage, he knows, but Alice is not stupid, and until last night, when Valerie turned up at the restaurant to play a little mind fuck, Joe had not realized quite how close to the wind she was prepared to sail.

Joe is much more careful now about the women he chooses, but clearly not quite careful enough. And then, at times like this, when he is nearly caught, when he is shocked into realizing quite how much he stands to lose should Alice ever discover his affairs, he vows to stop, to settle down and become a proper husband again.

"Valerie." He gazes down at her, knowing that this is the last time he will sleep with her. "I can't do this anymore."

"I thought you might say that." Valerie reaches over and grabs her robe, for as hard and ruthless as she may be, the prospect of being dumped while naked makes her instantly vulnerable, and she needs to cover herself for protection. "And was it because I turned up last night? Or were you growing bored with me?" She isn't upset, merely curious, and they both know full well that there will be another Joe in a matter of days, that there may in fact be a number of Joes already waiting in the wings.

"Ah, well. *Tant pis.* I had a lovely time."

She cups his cheek in her hand and kisses him on the lips, stroking his cheek tenderly. "You are going to try to be a faithful husband now?"

Joe nods.

Valerie smiles. "Until the next Valerie comes along." She turns and climbs back into bed. "Take care, my dear."

"And you too." Joe is relieved, grateful that she has taken this so calmly, like such a professional, and now wondering whether he is doing the right thing.

Valerie sees the light go on in his eyes and shakes her head. "No, Joe. No last good-bye fuck. I prefer my endings clear and clean cut." She blows him a kiss. "Go home to your wife and treat her well. Tell Alice I said hello."

Joe sighs with relief as he walks down the stairs from Valerie's apartment. No second thoughts now. With that last statement from Valerie, Joe knows beyond a shadow of a doubt that he's doing the right thing.

"I hate these bloody things." Alice is on her hands and knees, phone cradled snugly between her chin and shoulder as she brushes paint stripper thickly onto the legs of a cherry demilune table she's picked up in a junk shop.

"I know, darling," Joe says beseechingly on the other end of the phone, "but it's only an art gallery opening, and I promise we won't have to stay long."

Once upon a time Alice would have loved going to the opening of an art gallery. She would have felt blessed to have been able to go to such a glamorous occasion, would have been awestruck at being allowed to see paintings before anyone else, would have stood in front of each painting for minutes at a time, drinking them in, forming an opinion.

But she has learned not to do that anymore. She has learned that an art gallery opening is just another place to see and be seen. That you take a glass of champagne from a waiter bearing a silver tray when you arrive, then walk around the room airkissing all the familiar faces, commenting on how marvelous the art is when in fact you can't possibly see anything due to the hundreds of people crammed into one small gallery.

"You promise we can come straight home afterward? No other parties?" She drops the paintbrush into a can and picks up a small wad of steel wool.

"I promise. What are you doing now, Alice? What was that noise?"

"Stripping a table I found."

Joe laughs. "I don't know why you always insist on doing it yourself. You can buy these pieces of furniture anywhere you want."

"Because I enjoy it," Alice says. For the hundredth time. "You know I get pleasure from it."

"That's because you're strange. You're the only woman I know who actually enjoys getting filth under your nails and getting covered in paint."

That's because, Alice thinks, I'm the only woman you know who thinks there's more to life than manicures and appearing in *Tatler*.

"I promise I'll clean up by tonight."

"I promise I'll have you dirty again by the time we get to bed."

"Will you ever lose that schoolboy sense of humor?"

"Would you want me to?"

Alice smiles, feeling loved and wanted, loving this feeling of closeness to her husband. It happens so rarely these days, but there are times when the pressure lifts and the cloud that seems constantly to overshadow her seems to disappear for a while, when Joe is not distracted and distant, when he reverts to the Joe she fell in love with.

Times like now, when work doesn't seem to be as demanding and he is not required to be in the office all hours, when the business trips are few and far between.

And when the pressure of work has been relaxed, Joe is more relaxed. He is back to being the loving, playful husband he was when they met, and she has learned to enjoy those times, for she knows they will not last.

She has heard the occasional rumors about her husband, but she chooses to ignore them. Infidelity is something she is simply not prepared even to think about.

4

The cab driver pulls up with a screech outside the gallery in Cork Street. Even from this distant vantage point Alice can see Joe is already inside, standing head and shoulders above everyone else, chatting animatedly to a couple they see from time to time at gallery openings such as these and the odd dinner party.

Not friends, exactly. Acquaintances. Alice and Joe don't have many of what Alice calls friends, not friends in the sense that Emily is a friend, not friends in the true sense of the word.

Of course there are people who consider Alice to be their friend, particularly those who feel it may benefit them in some way to be seen with Alice Chambers, but Alice is fully aware they mix in superficial circles, and she has learned to judge each overture of friendship with just the right amount of friendliness and suspicion.

Yet people want to be friends with Alice. They want to know more about her, want some of her luck and success to rub off on them. Women are drawn in by Alice's natural warmth and intrigued by her air of mystery.

They don't know where she came from, just that Joe, hugely eligible and unlikely ever to settle down, suddenly announced he was getting married, and to a woman none of them had ever heard of.

And they have tried to get close to her, but with a charming smile she always manages to turn the conversation back to what they are doing, what they are thinking and feeling, and these women so love talking about themselves that after a while, flattered and charmed, they find that they haven't found out anything more at all.

Of course people have talked about her. The cattier women in the circle claim she was a waitress, claim to have seen her serving sushi at parties many years ago. Others say it was her own business, that she was a hugely successful businesswoman in her own right, that the current hot caterers — Rhubarb and Mustard to name but two — modeled themselves on her unique and innovative style.

Neither is true, but they love to talk. Particularly when they have so little to go on.

Alice is frequently at their lunches, always impeccable in the latest designer outfits, always gracious as the others gossip away, but she doesn't ever let anyone get too close, and the longer she has been married, the more rumors have started swirling.

She refuses to have sex with Joe, they say, which of course is why he's off sleeping with anything in a skirt. She's into swinging, they say, and in fact the two of them have been known to share Joe's racier girlfriends. She's clearly a dominatrix, they say, and a friend of the architect said the cellar had been converted into a dungeon complete with torture rack and chains.

The fact remains that the ladies who lunch are fascinated by Alice Chambers because they simply don't know who she is. They long to be a fly on the wall in her bedroom, love seeing her walk into a restaurant, or a premiere, or an opening, to see what she's wearing, whether she might do anything that would give them more fodder for gossip.

Alice pushes open the door of the gallery and gives Joe a half-wave and a smile.

She has to squeeze through hordes of tightly packed people to reach him, and already she has seen more than half a dozen familiar faces, and she knows by the time she air-kisses and does the "Hellohowareyous?" it will be several minutes before she reaches him.

No one is looking at the paintings. The loud buzz of conversation fills the air as people talk, and laugh, and constantly turn to see who else has walked in the door.

Clearly the gallery is the place to see and be seen tonight. Look over there, at the platinum blonde in the one-shouldered top, isn't she the famous It girl? And the tousle-haired brunette with the miraculously growing pout, isn't she you-know-who? And the fresh-faced pop star in the corner.

They're all here tonight, the paparazzi scattered around going into a frenzy, not sure whom to photograph first.

The celebrities turn and flash large sparkling white smiles for the cameras, careful to show off only their best sides, gracefully extending a leg in the most flattering of poses. They chat up the photographers, knowing it will work to their advantage, knowing that they will stay in the papers only for as long as they continue to court the press.

The women who are not famous glare furiously at the paparazzi, wishing that they were, hoping that their expressions of disgust may convince the photographers they might be famous too, may convince them to take their photographs as well.

The photographers turn to look at Alice with interest, a couple of them recognizing her from the diary pages, and as soon as one raises his camera to flash a quick snap, the others run over just in case they've missed anything, and soon, much to Alice's horror, the entire room has turned to stare at her.

No posing for Alice. No white-toothed smiles and smooth brown thigh peeping out from a long, slashed dress. Alice drops her eyes to the floor, lowers her head, and pushes past them, trying to reach Joe quickly, wishing that these people would just leave her alone.

"Alice?" She looks up as Emily puts her arms around her tightly and squeezes her. "What a fucking nightmare."

"Oh, Em!" she whispers. "I hate these bloody people."

"Great." Emily releases her with a smile. "So why did you invite me?"

"Because I didn't think you'd come. You

never come to anything, Emily. How come you're even here?"

"You're right, I never come because I hate these people too, but you're my best friend, and I love you, and I haven't seen you for ages so I decided to brave it."

"You haven't seen me for ages because you're always so busy."

"Bollocks, Alice. You're the one going off to this charity do, and that film premiere, and dinner at the Ivy all the time."

"Okay, we're both busy. That's the best you'll get from me."

Emily laughs. "Okay. That I'll accept."

"Come and see Joe." Alice can see Joe has stopped talking, is waiting for Alice to reach him. "He'd love to see you."

Emily can never quite decide what to make of Joe. She's never been comfortable with his flirtatiousness (and no, of course he hasn't flirted with Emily — he wouldn't dare), and although Alice has said she trusts him, Emily does not, but there is something so irresistible about Joe, something so inherently likable, that as much as she wants to hate him for his smooth charm, she can't.

Of course Emily hasn't heard the rumors. Emily mixes in a different social circle entirely, and although she does, from time to time, enter Alice's world, she's not comfortable with these people, and they are not comfortable with her.

When Alice went off to catering college, Emily went off traveling for a year. By herself. She filled a tiny rucksack with one sweater, two sarongs, three pairs of shorts, four T-shirts, five pairs of panties, and eleven bottles of hair conditioner — her only luxury, although she would claim it as a necessity for her corkscrew curls — and hopped on the hovercraft to France.

Everyone told her she was mad. Travel? Yes. By herself? Absolutely nuts. Only Alice was completely supportive, and devastated that she couldn't go too.

So Emily went to France, fell in love with Laurent, the son of a wealthy hotelier from St-Paul-de-Vence (whom she met in a bar in Paris one busy, drunken night), traveled down to the Côte d'Azur to stay with Laurent's family in their fabulously luxurious home, from where they both crossed the border at San Remo into Italy, and traveled to Naples, before driving down the Amalfi coast to Sorrento and Positano.

It was the most romantic and exciting time of Emily's life. Laurent had to leave after Positano, had promised to start working in his father's business, and there were rivers of tears when they said good-bye. Emily was tempted to follow him back to the south of France, but she had been planning this trip for months, years, and although she loved Laurent, she knew that if she didn't do everything she had planned she would regret it for the rest of her life.

So from Italy she went to Greece, and in Greece she hooked up with a bunch of rowdy Australians, and, thankful that she had saved enough money to be able to do this, she booked a cheap flight to Sydney and spent the next eight months working as a waitress in Australia, taking off the last six weeks to travel around and see the country.

She'd write Alice long letters about the adventures she was having, the people she was meeting, and Alice wrote back, trying to make her course at catering college sound as exciting as Emily's life, but failing miserably. How could she possibly compete?

By the time Emily returned to London she had had two flings and three relationships with large, tanned Australians, and Laurent had been well and truly forgotten.

Alice and Emily's friendship continued as if Emily had never been away. "That's the mark of true friends," Emily always used to say. "That we might not see each other for a year but when we do it's as if we were never apart."

That was until that fateful night when Alice ran into Joe. Alice had phoned Emily the next day, so excited she could barely breathe, let alone talk.

"You won't believe it," she said. "You won't believe who I saw last night, who" — Alice paused in disbelief — "took my number!"

"It better be good or I'm putting this phone down," Emily groaned, never her best first thing in the morning, particularly at 8:15 a.m. when she hasn't got to bed until two. "It's the middle of the bloody night."

"It's not. It's 8:15. I thought it would be okay to call now."

"Of course it's not bloody okay. You know I try to lie in on the weekends."

"Oh God. I'm really sorry."

"Don't be sorry, just tell me and then I can go back to sleep."

"Joe Chambers."

"Joe Chambers. Gorgeous Joe Chambers?"

"Yes!"

"Noooo!"

"Yes!"

"And is he still gorgeous?"

"Yes!"

"Noooo!"

"Yes!" Alice giggled in delight.

"And he asked for your number? Are you serious?"

"Yes!"

"Noooo!"

"Oh, fuck off!" And they both started laughing.

"Did he really ask for your number?" Emily thought back to the years of Alice waiting for Joe at the bus stop after school.

"He really did. And, Em, he's so lovely. Really. And I can't believe he asked for my number."

"Did he remember you then?"

"I don't think so, but he said he did, and he remembered my brother. Actually I hope he doesn't remember me. God, I was a horror at school."

"Everyone was a horror at school. Remember how they called me Afro Girl?"

"I wasn't much better. I was Big Bird."

Emily started laughing.

"Fuck off, Em. It's not funny."

"Sorry. But we were all ugly."

"Except Joe Chambers."

"Except Gorgeous Joe Chambers. Jesus. I can't believe he asked you out."

"He didn't ask me out. He just asked for my number. Do you think he's going to ask me out?"

"How old are you? Twelve?"

"What? I'm just asking."

"Of course he's going to ask you out. Why else would he ask for your number?"

"Duh! To cater a dinner party."

"Oh." Emily had forgotten about that.

"Bugger. He probably just wants me to do a dinner party for him. Oh, damn," Alice moaned. "I wish I hadn't blushed so much. He probably thinks I'm a complete idiot."

"Probably," Emily concurred.

"Oh no. Do you really think so?"

"How the hell do I know? Now you'll just have to experience what the rest of the single sisterhood goes through every time we give out our number. We sit glued to our phones for days on end, hating mankind, and thinking that if only we were thinner, or fatter, or blonder, or darker, or louder, or more quiet, he'd phone."

"Sounds horrific. Is it really that bad?" Alice of course has been so busy with work, she's managed to rather successfully avoid the trials and tribulations of the dating scene, although, as she has said on numerous occasions, Emily has more than made up for it for the both of them.

"It's worse. But thankfully you'll now be able to discover that for yourself."

Two weeks later, two weeks during which time Alice had begun to seriously hate her telephone, and hate Emily even more for being on the end of the line when it did ring, Joe finally called.

Unfortunately he was ringing her for the exact reason she feared — he wanted her to cater a dinner party for him.

What she didn't know was that he was using this as an excuse to see her again, and after the dinner party he asked her out on a proper date.

And Alice, at least as far as Emily is concerned, has never been the same since.

Where did shy, mousy, curvy Alice go? What happened to the girl who loved animals, and children, and dreamed of a cottage in the country with roses climbing over the porch?

Emily blames Joe for Alice's transformation. The Alice of old would never have been caught dead in heels higher than an inch, let alone — Emily looks down at Alice's feet — these pointed, four-inch, doubtless horrifyingly expensive shoes. The Alice of old would never have dreamed of dyeing her hair (apart from a disastrous experiment with Jolene bleach and green Crazy Colour when they were sixteen), let alone visiting Jo Hansford every six weeks and — presumably — spending hundreds of pounds on her honey highlights. The Alice of old would have been happy snuggling up on a sofa in her Garfield slippers, tucking into a pizza (albeit one she had made herself with fresh buffalo mozzarella and shredded basil leaves plucked from the terra cotta pot on her patio), watching crap TV for the evening, would have hated the idea of dressing up and going to a snazzy, sophisticated soirée such as this.

The Alice of old used to laugh at the women for whom she used to cater, the same women who are milling around this art gallery, but now Alice has become one of them.

Emily remembers that a few months after Alice started dating Joe, she and Alice had met at Prêt à Manger for a quick lunch.

"I'm on a diet," Alice had said, picking out a small salad and a Diet Coke as Emily was carrying a huge club sandwich, chocolate fudge slice, and banana smoothie to the cash register.

"Diet? But you don't need to *diet*." Emily

had looked at her in horror. This was Alice. Alice who cooked for a living. Alice who adored food.

"I know" — Alice had said — "but Joe keeps looking at pictures of models in magazines and commenting how amazing their figures are, so I thought I might try and lose a few pounds."

Oh, he's good, Emily thought. Subtle. "That's ridiculous," she said. "You have a great figure, and he loves you for you." At least, she thought, he *should*.

"I just want to lose a few pounds," Alice shrugged. "Not much."

And then a couple of months later a new, skinnier Alice turned up to lunch with straight hair.

"Where have your curls gone?" Emily had ventured.

"I just wanted to see what I'd look like with straight hair."

"And Joe didn't just happen to suggest that he loves women with straight hair?"

"Well . . ." Alice had shifted uncomfortably in her chair.

"I suppose he'll be telling you to go blond next. Men like Joe always prefer blondes, they see them as some kind of status symbol."

"Actually . . ."

"Oh no! Alice! For Christ's sake, that's ridiculous. You're not seriously thinking of going blond? For Joe?"

"Not for Joe, no. I'm going to the hairdresser on Thursday and I thought I might have a few highlights. It was my idea," she huffed, seeing the expression on Emily's face.

"And what does the beloved think?"

"The beloved thinks it would really suit me."

"I just bet he does."

"Joe!" Emily forces a large, fake smile as she reaches up to kiss him hello.

"Emily!" Joe beams from ear to ear, giving the distinct impression that he could not be more delighted to see her. "How lovely that you're here, as cute as ever, I see."

Emily raises her eyebrows and shakes her head. "That charm just never stops a-flowin', I see."

"I say it as I see it," he grins. He likes Emily. Doesn't fancy her — far too strong and opinionated for him (not to mention far too close to Alice), but he actually respects her, and that's something he honestly can't say for a lot of people.

"Emily's cool," he used to say to Alice. "She gets it."

"So what are *you* doing here?" he says. "Either my lovely wife — hello, my darling" — he turns to Alice and kisses her — "my lovely wife invited you, or you're here to gather some dirt about the hoi polloi."

"How many times do I have to explain that I write serious features, and that just because I'm a journalist doesn't mean I'm interested in who Tamara Beckwith happens to be snogging right now?"

"So who *is* she snogging right now?"

"I don't know," Emily smiles. "But I passed her on the way in so perhaps you could ask her."

"Aha! Caught you. I thought you said you weren't interested in celebrity gossip, and yet you just happened to notice Tamara Beckwith on your way in. You are here dirt-mongering. I knew it!"

"Just because I have a personal interest in the goings-on of my favorite *OK!* and *Hello!* heroines doesn't mean I have a professional interest."

"A hack is a hack is a hack."

"Not when the hack in question is a freelance feature writer who tends to write stuff mostly for the broadsheets, I'm afraid."

"Children, children," Alice chides, stepping between them as if to prevent a fight.

"Will you just behave yourselves." But she is pleased to see the gentle teasing, relieved that Emily is not being — as she can be with Joe — confrontational and aggressive.

"It's not me, it's her," Joe whines before breaking into laughter as Emily elbows him sharply in the side.

For once, Alice has fun. It is lovely to see Emily, even in these unfamiliar surroundings, and she is relaxed and happy that she is with her two favorite people in the world. Joe is affectionate, attentive, and only has eyes for her, and she finds herself basking in the attention.

Tonight she is able to truly relax, amazed that every time she looks at Joe he is not gazing at a thrusting cleavage across the room or at a pair of endless legs a few feet away. He is gazing at her.

This is why I married him, she thinks, leaning into him as he puts an arm around her waist and squeezes her tight while laughing at something Emily has said. Now I remember.

5

"So come on, fill me in on all the gossip." Alice leans forward on her chair, nursing her cappuccino as Emily tries to unravel Humphrey's leash from the chairs and coffee tables.

"Hang on," Emily says. "Humphrey!" She drags the little terrier reluctantly back to the table, knowing that, this being a warm sunny spring Tuesday in Primrose Hill, it is only a matter of minutes before yet another dog strides past their outside table at Cacao, and Humphrey — a newly acquired rescue dog from the local animal shelter with a distinct lack of training — makes a mad dash to say hello.

"For God's sake, Humphrey!" Emily picks him up and puts him on her lap. "Anyone would think you'd never seen another dog before."

"How's the training going?"

Emily and Humphrey have enrolled in Doggie Dos and Don'ts, a local obedience class that meets on Hampstead Heath for an hour every Sunday morning, armed with a clicker and a pocketful of treats.

"Great. As long as we're in the living room in the flat, he's the best-trained dog I've ever had."

"You've never had a dog before."

"Exactly. Although he does sit when I tell him to when we're at home, and we've nearly mastered *down* as well. Watch." Emily puts Humphrey back on the pavement and says sternly, "Sit. Humphrey, sit." Humphrey looks at her, then turns around and starts sniffing the table leg. "Oh, fuck it," Emily sighs. "Humphrey, you're hopeless. If it wasn't for Harry, I wouldn't bother going to the class at all."

"Ah yes. Harry. So how is the sexy dog trainer?"

"Sexy. And distracting. Which is probably why Humphrey's so crappy at following orders. I spend most of the class focusing on Harry's lips."

"Just his lips?"

"Well, no, but" — she lowers her voice and gives Humphrey a sidelong glance —

"I wouldn't want to corrupt Humphrey too much."

"So has anything happened yet?" Alice had heard all about the first lesson, how Harry had repeatedly singled Emily and Humphrey out for demonstrations to the rest of the class, how Emily had flirted outrageously and been rewarded with several glances that lasted just a few seconds too long and a long conversation at the end of the class that had rapidly left the subject of dogs and moved swiftly into the personal.

And then, the following week, Harry had asked if anyone was interested in going for a coffee after the class, and given that most of the class had already left by the time he asked, and that the only people still around were Emily and an elderly man called Lionel, it was pretty clear that he was interested in getting to know Emily better.

("I always knew I should have got a dog years ago," Emily had said, after their third date. "Just think, if Humphrey and I had met ten years ago I'd probably be married by now with a swarm of screaming children around my feet.")

"Has anything happened? What on earth can you mean?" Emily asks.

"What on earth do you think I mean? Have you slept with him?"

"Of course I haven't slept with him!" Emily shrieks in mock horror, immediately lowering her voice as the Primrose Hill wannabes break off from their conversations on their mobile phones to look at her with interest. "He's lovely. I'm not going to screw it up by jumping into bed with him this early."

"So what have you done?"

"Lots of snogging and a bit of feeling up."

"Feeling up top or feeling up bottom?" Alice grins, knowing that the only person in the world she could possibly ask a question like this, be as childishly silly with as this, is Emily.

"Feeling up top, of *course*," Emily says. "There won't be any feeling up bottom until I've had my legs waxed."

"You *still* haven't had them waxed? That's disgusting!" (Alice, who goes to the waxing salon every six weeks without fail, has never understood how Emily can go for months without touching her legs. "Why bother," Emily has always said, "unless I'm having sex? Of course *you* have to do it because you have a husband who expects smooth thighs, but the only person I sleep with on a regular basis is Humphrey, and frankly, as far as Humphrey's concerned, the more hair the better, the more he relates to me.")

"But I think I may have to make an appointment this week."

"So D-Day is approaching?"

"I think the time is nearly here for me to relinquish my born-again virginity."

Alice bursts into laughter.

"It's all right for you," Emily says crossly. "You think it's funny because you can have sex whenever you want. All you have to do is roll over and prod Joe in the stomach."

"Yes, because there's nothing guaranteed to warm up my husband more than a good sharp prod in the stomach."

"From what I've heard, Joe has a permanent erection anyway." Emily was making a joke, but it falls flat, floats uncomfortably for a while in the silence as the smile is wiped off Alice's face and the color in her cheeks quickly fades.

"What do you mean?" Alice says icily, as Emily wishes she could take the words back, wishes she'd never said anything, not that she knew where it came from anyway. But she knows there are certain subjects about which she has to be sensitive, and Joe's priapism is clearly one of them.

"I was joking," Emily says softly. "I just meant you always used to say that Joe's always up for it, that was all I meant."

They both know that's not true, not now, not anymore. Once upon a time, when they were first married, Alice did say exactly that. How can a man want this much sex? she'd ask Emily in amazement, after the nights when Joe had rolled over in bed and made love to her twice, three, often four times.

"I don't know, but if I were you I wouldn't question it." Emily had groaned in jealousy. "Just be bloody happy you found him."

Now, five years on, months go by when Joe barely touches Alice. Alice has tried everything. She has spent fortunes on sexy, lacy underwear from La Perla, then tried the other extreme and — she shudders with embarrassment when she remembers how desperate she was — attempted cheap nylon crotchless panties and even a maid outfit from Ann Summers.

She has tried talking dirty to Joe, stroking his thigh softly as she whispers in his ear what she would like to do to him, blushing furiously as she speaks, then having to deal with the humiliation when he doesn't move, continues to pretend to sleep.

She even phoned Ty and told him she

was planning a hen night for a friend, and they thought it would be a laugh to get some porn films, did he know where she could get them, or would he get them for her? She had ended up watching them on her own, masturbating miserably and wishing she'd invested in a vibrator that time she'd been to Ann Summers for the underwear.

Joe claims it's the pressure of work, sheer exhaustion that's killed his sex drive, and the alternative is too terrible for Alice to consider. She knows that at some point it will come to an end, that one night he will come home with flowers, or jewelry, and he will kiss her and put his arms around her and say a major deal has come to an end, and that night they will go to bed and have sex all night, and Alice will pray that she has her husband back for good.

Alice looks at Emily, sees how innocent her remark was, and forgives her. Emily would rather die than do anything to upset Alice, and Alice knows that.

"It's okay," she says finally, after an awkward silence, the color slowly returning to her cheeks. "Don't worry about it. As it happens, the last few weeks he has pretty much had a permanent erection. It's lovely.

For once I'm thrilled to have these bags under my eyes."

Emily laughs with relief as Humphrey starts to bark at a Rhodesian ridgeback walking past. "Poor Humphrey. He needs to have a run around. Shall we take him for a walk?"

At the mention of the word "walk," Humphrey starts to leap up and down in a frenzy, and the two girls laugh as they unravel him yet again and set off.

Alice strides ahead, loving that she's not dressed up, that when she's with Emily she doesn't have to put on an act, she can wear her oldest, most casual, comfortable clothes, and really be herself. Her jeans may be Earl, but today she's wearing her gym sneakers, a Gap sweatshirt, and a baseball cap pulled down tight over hair scraped back into a ponytail. She can really *walk* in these clothes, can sit with her legs apart, resting her elbows on her knees, can run and play games with Humphrey, scooping him up for a cuddle without worrying that he might be getting mud on — heaven forbid — a Chanel jacket or a shearling coat.

They walk up the hill, stopping every few minutes to watch Humphrey excitedly greet other dogs. Emily chats away to the owners, sharing Humphrey's story, explaining how she went to the shelter with the intention of getting a cat but fell in love with Humphrey and ended up with him instead, while Alice watches the dogs with a smile, offering Humphrey treats when he comes running back to her.

"God, I envy you," Alice says, as they pause on the top of the hill to watch the people flying their kites. "This is so wonderful, to be able to come here every weekend and do this."

"You envy me?" Emily starts to laugh. "Look at you, Alice. You live in a fantastic fuck-off house in Belgravia while I'm in a tiny one-bedroom flat in Camden. You have a husband while I'm still miserably single and my only permanent Mr. Right is Humphrey. Not to mention the fact that you lead the most glamorous lifestyle of anyone I've ever met, whereas my idea of a glam night out is Marine bloody Ices on Chalk Farm Road. Plus you've actually been in *Tatler*, and the only time I'm in the paper is on the rare occasions when they bother to print my by-line. How can you envy me?"

"Because you have so much freedom. You can do the things you love, whenever you feel like it. You can come to Primrose

Hill every day of the week if you feel like it, and walk Humphrey, and talk to people, and go wherever you want to."

"And you can't?"

"No. I can't." Alice shakes her head. "I can't have a Humphrey because our lifestyle isn't conducive to a dog, it wouldn't be fair. We haven't got a garden, we live in town, and we're always out. Joe hates animals."

"I remember. He hated Molly and Paolo, didn't he?"

"God, did he hate them. My poor babies. He pretended to tolerate them until he proposed, and then it was the cats or him." Alice sighs. "At least I found them a good home. I suppose I have to be grateful for small mercies."

"Didn't we always say never trust a man who doesn't like animals?"

"Don't remind me," Alice sniffs. "But animals aside, Joe would never do something like this. He can't see the point in walking for the sake of walking. Actually" — she laughs — "I think he's completely allergic to nature."

"God. And you were the girl who thought she'd end up living in a thatched cottage in the Cotswolds. Weren't you supposed to have horses and chickens?"

"Yup. And weren't you supposed to have married a millionaire?"

"Yup. Shit. How did you end up living my life and I end up living yours?"

"Good point. Wanna swap?" Alice smiles.

"Only if I can keep Harry."

"Nope. If we swap you have to have Joe and I get to have Harry."

"You've never met Harry, how do you know you'd even like him?"

"A man who trains dogs for a living? I'm in love with him already. How bad can he be?"

"So can I ask a question?" Emily pauses and stops to look at Alice. "Just why exactly *did* you marry Joe?"

It's a question Alice has asked herself many times over the years. When he's loving and kind, she thinks she knows why she married him, but when he's distant and distracted, she has absolutely no idea.

Even when he's being the perfect husband, Alice is forever questioning her life, because she knows that Emily is absolutely right, she has not ended up with the life she daydreamed about.

On a good day she is quite happy. Can find her lifestyle fun, amusing despite its superficiality (of which she is well aware). Can appreciate the trendy restaurants, the beautiful people, the endless round of cocktails and canapés. Looks at her husband and thinks he is the most wonderful man in the world, is happy just to be by his side.

On a good day she thinks that daydreams are just that: daydreams. That if they were ever to come true they wouldn't be nearly as wonderful as the fantasy.

On a bad day she wants to run away. Wonders whether she could make it on her own, thanks God there are no children as yet (again, that is Joe's doing, Joe wanting to have at least five years together to enjoy themselves as a couple, to be able to take off to Italy, or Spain, or France whenever they feel like it, without having to worry about the responsibility of children).

The five years is now up, and Alice is waiting for the right time to broach the subject of children, because thirty-five is already far older than she wanted to be as a first-time mother, and she knows that time is not on her side.

On a bad day Alice thinks about just upping and leaving, taking one suitcase with her, the barest essentials, and going to live in the country somewhere, getting as far away from this world as she possibly can.

She lies in bed those nights when Joe is absent, emotionally or physically, and dreams of divorce. She doesn't cry, not anymore, just lies there thinking about another Alice, an Alice who isn't a trophy wife.

When Joe first took her out, when he took her to the best restaurants, lavished her with presents, cuddled her in the mornings and told her she was cute, she felt as if she had stepped out of her rather dull life and into a movie.

Everything suddenly became so exciting that she left the old Alice behind without a second glance, didn't think she needed the old Alice anymore, didn't think she *was* the old Alice anymore.

"Joe loves me." Alice turns to Emily, trying to justify her marriage. "And I love him."

"Is that enough?"

"I don't know. But I think right now it has to be."

Sometimes Emily knows she just has to back off, and this, quite clearly, is one of those times. She swiftly changes the subject. "So I can't believe you're going to meet Harry! I'm so nervous! Where do you think we should go for dinner?"

"Would you come into town even though it's on a Saturday night? Should we go somewhere special?"

"Of course we'd come into town, just as long as it's not too expensive. Dog trainers aren't investment bankers, you know."

"I know, I know. Of course it won't be expensive. Let me have a think and I'll let you know."

"Hi, darling." Joe phones while Alice is crawling along Baker Street, sitting in the car at a standstill while throngs of shoppers rush from Selfridges to Marks & Spencer, intent on a bargain. "Where are you?"

"Nearly home. I've been with Emily and Humphrey."

"That's nice. I'm just phoning to say that tonight's canceled. Eddie's got flu. Do you want to go anyway? Just the two of us?"

"You know what I'd really like? I'd really like it if we stayed home tonight. I'll make something lovely for dinner and we can have an early night."

"Sounds perfect," Joe smiles. "There's nothing I like more than an early night with my wife. I'll be home by eight. I love you."

"I love you the *most.*"

"I love *you* the most." Alice smiles.

"Okay."

Joe laughs, and puts the phone down, turning to watch a pair of long legs cross the office floor. A tall woman, perhaps in her early thirties, glides in front of his desk, golden hair in a tight chignon, voluptuous curves squeezed into a fitted chocolate-brown suit. She has a mixture of sensuality and confidence, and absolute knowledge that every man on the floor is watching her, given away only by the fact that she refuses to take her eyes off the middle distance as she disappears out of the double doors to the lifts.

"Je-sus." Joe swivels round in his chair and lets out a long, low whistle. "Now who was that?"

Dave looks up from the phone just in time to see the back of the blonde before the double doors swing shut. "That is the new office ball-breaker. Josie Mitchell. Used to run Risk Arb at Goldmans, is here to be COO of Equity Capital Markets."

"*That's* Josie Mitchell? Christ, I always pictured her as a frump. She's not the new office ball-breaker, my friend. Did you see those legs? She's the new office babe."

Dave raises his eyes to the ceiling. "You mean Joe Chambers's new office babe. Careful, Joe. She's not some bimbo. You want to be careful with this one. You know what the Goldmans bonuses were last year, so you know we must have paid a fortune to tempt her over here."

"Maybe she heard there was a better class of man at Godfrey Hamilton Saltz."

Dave snorts with laughter. "She's not some bimbo you can screw and forget. That's all I'm saying. Be careful."

"Careful? It's my middle name. Anyway, I have no intention of screwing her. I'm a reformed man, not to mention a married one. Which reminds me" — Joe checks his watch and picks up the phone again — "I have to call the travel agent before I leave." He punches the number in and sits back on his chair.

"Jackie? Hello, darling, it's Joe. Did you manage to get a room at the Lygon Arms? You did? Oh, that's great, you're an incredible woman, did anyone ever tell you that before?"

"What's this?" Alice looks down at the white envelope Joe has just slid on to her pillow. They have feasted on minted lamb salad and tabbouleh, on succulent fresh raspberries and homemade vanilla ice cream. They have drunk a 1990 Bordeaux and two espressos each. They have undressed in the privacy of their dressing rooms and have met again in bed, where Joe has smiled his come-to-bed smile and reached out for her to come into his arms.

And now Joe is lying on his side of the bed reading the *Financial Times*, and Alice is lying on hers, reading the latest novel that everyone is talking about.

"Open it." Joe puts the paper down and watches her with a smile.

Alice tears the envelope and pulls out a brochure for the Lygon Arms and a faxed piece of paper confirming a reservation for two in the Charles I suite for Friday, April 15, and Saturday, April 16. The coming weekend.

"What's this for?" She's smiling.

"For us to have a romantic weekend away. I thought you could do with a rest from our hectic London life, and I know how much you love the country so I thought I'd surprise you."

"Oh, it is lovely." Alice grins and rolls over to kiss him. "What a lovely, lovely surprise. I can't wait. Oh no." She groans, remembering that Saturday night is dinner with Emily and Harry. "What shall I do about Saturday? Emily and Harry."

"Cancel them," Joe says. "They won't mind."

"But I'm always canceling Emily," Alice says, "and she's so excited, and anyway, I want to meet Harry. Can we change our booking? Could we go the weekend after?"

"Absolutely not. I've already arranged everything and I'm not changing it." Joe crosses his arms. "I'm telling you, Emily will understand."

"No. She always understands and I promised her I wouldn't do it again. We won't be able to go."

"Alice, you're being completely irrational. If we canceled now we'd still have to pay for it, which is crazy. I'm not going to cancel it."

"Okay. Then let's bring them with."

"And who's going to pay for it?"

"You are. This will be my birthday present."

"Your birthday isn't until May."

"I know. Consider it an early gift."

"Alice, the point of this weekend is to have time together."

"But you love Emily, and anyway, don't we always have much more fun when we're with friends?" This last isn't strictly true in

Alice's case, but she knows that Joe is almost always happier in a crowd, and sure enough, Joe shrugs in agreement.

"Go on then," he says, seeing how happy it makes her. "You can phone her tomorrow."

"I hope they come," Alice says happily. "They haven't even had sex yet. It might be a bit awkward."

"They haven't had sex yet? Well, this will be a golden opportunity for them. She ought to be paying me, not the other way around." Joe folds up the paper and stretches over to turn off his bedside light.

6

Joe pushes through the City boys crowding round the bar and manages to catch the attention of the bartender.

"Two Cosmopolitans, two single malts, no ice, and a pint of bitter," he shouts slowly, enunciating carefully so as to be heard over the Friday night din.

As usual for six p.m. on a Friday, Corney & Barrow is packed. Jackets are slung over the backs of stools, ties are being loosened, and the men and women who keep the money pumping through the financial heart of the country are finally able to have a few drinks and relax.

They deserve it. Most are at their desks by six a.m. Monday to Friday, and many are lucky if they make it home before ten. Long hours are made bearable by the promise — not always fulfilled — of absurdly large January bonuses and the knowledge that working hard guarantees early retirement and the ability to play even harder.

Joe takes the drinks over to a noisy table in the corner. Dave drains his old pint glass to make way for the new, and the others follow suit, all except Josie, who didn't want another Cosmopolitan, doesn't really want to be here at all, but has to get to know her colleagues, can't be seen as standoffish or distant, and knows the Friday night drink after work is the best possible place to prove she is one of the boys.

That Josie Mitchell is one of the boys is the very last thing on Joe's mind. He's been watching her for the last couple of days, looking up from his phone calls with interest as she passes his desk, more interested because she has not noticed him, has not even looked his way.

He had finally found himself in a meeting with her this afternoon, mustering all his charm to introduce himself, and had been surprised by her coolness and lack of interest, so that he was even more surprised when she agreed to join him and a few of the others for a drink.

Naturally Joe is inspired by her apparent

lack of interest. He likes cool women, sees them as a challenge, and has maneuvered the seating so he is sitting next to her. Right now he is ignoring her, chatting with other colleagues, biding his time, for he is quite sure that his time will come later that evening, that he will manage to melt her icy exterior, discover whether she is as intriguing as she looks.

"Right, I'm off." Dave drains his third pint and stands up, reaching for his jacket. "Need to get home to the wife," he says. "You coming?" He looks at Joe, a hint of a smile, for he knows what Joe is up to.

Joe gestures to his full glass of single-malt whisky. "Not yet," he says. "I still need a drink or two to relax."

"I'd better get going too." Sarah stands up, and within a few minutes the only people left at the table are Joe and Josie.

"I should leave," Josie says, standing up and offering a smile to Joe for the first time that week.

"At least finish your drink." Joe nods to her untouched Cosmopolitan. "Can't let a decent Cosmopolitan go to waste."

Josie checks her watch and sighs. She has nothing to rush home for, after all, just a stark empty flat in Chelsea, a chilled bottle of Chardonnay, and *Patrick Kielty Almost*

Live. And it is quite nice sitting in this cozy corner in this busy bar on a Friday night, and it is only one Cosmopolitan, and she's curious to see if Joe Chambers really does live up to his reputation.

Hell. It's only a drink. What harm can it do?

Emily has refused point blank to let Joe pay for her and Harry to go to the Lygon Arms, particularly as she has a perfectly good cottage in the country that the four of them can go to. As she said to Alice, it's not very grand and the food probably won't be Lygon Arms quality — unless of course Alice decides to take over on that front — but it's certainly cheaper and they'll have just as much fun.

And so here they are, Emily and Harry, on a Friday afternoon, standing just inside the foyer of Alice's house, on their way to driving down to the country, and Harry's jaw is almost on the floor as he looks around, taking in the vast ceiling, the walls of glass, the sheer size of the place.

"Bloody hell!" he says.

Alice starts to laugh. "I know. Welcome to my museum."

"It's amazing," Harry says, when he finally recovers the power of speech. "I've never seen anything like this."

"You get used to it after a while," Emily says. "So now say hello to my best friend, Alice."

"God, I'm sorry." Harry grins as he extends a hand. "That was incredibly rude. It just took my breath away for a minute. I'm Harry. Hello, Alice."

"Hello, Harry." Alice likes him immediately. He has kind eyes, she thinks. Good teeth. A strong handshake. Yes. He's good enough for Emily. "Would you like a coffee or something before we go?"

"Do you want to see the house?" Emily nudges Harry, who is again gazing around. "Alice will give you the guided tour if you want. The dogs will be okay outside for a few minutes."

"We only charge five quid for the tour, or six if you include the coffee."

Harry laughs. "I'll do a deal with you. If you give the house tour I'll do the driving."

"You mean I should waive the five-pound fee?"

Harry looks indignant. "My chauffeur fees are usually twice that."

"Okay. Done!" Alice smiles, walking up the stairs and beckoning for them both to follow.

"See?" Emily scoots up behind Alice and

whispers in her ear. "I told you you'd like him."

Alice is not what he expected. Emily has spoken of her glamorous best friend and shown him pictures of the two of them together. He has seen a pictorial history of Emily and Alice throughout their lives — the two of them as beaming little girls holding on to each end of a skipping rope, Emily and Alice sitting on a beach, clutching their knees and grinning, their eyes hidden behind huge sunglasses.

And then more recently Emily with the same wild hair, the same wide smile, but Alice looking completely different. "This is the same girl?" he'd asked in amazement, looking at pictures taken at Emily's birthday dinner last year, staring at the glossy beautiful woman, immaculately made up, her smile for the camera doing a bad job of hiding the sadness in her eyes.

He had known he would like the woman in the earlier pictures, had been able to imagine exactly what she was like. "You'll love Alice," Emily had said excitedly, but then, when he'd seen what she'd become, he'd had an abrupt change of mind.

He knew high-maintenance women like Alice. They were the ones who bought designer dogs from breeders, then farmed them out to dog trainers, refusing to have them in the house until someone else had trained them. They treated them as accessories, buying them the very latest in designer dog gear, but didn't spend any time getting to know them, or understanding the unique relationship between a dog and its master. Or mistress.

If Alice had a dog, he had already decided, it would be a bichon frise. Or a Maltese. Not a dog like Humphrey, whom he already adored. Nor a dog like his own collie cross, Dharma, also from a shelter.

He thought he knew what to expect, and was beginning to dread this weekend. Joe sounded like a first-class wanker, and Alice looked like a snotty cow, even though Emily had sworn blind she wasn't, had said he mustn't judge a book by its cover.

On the whole Harry tried not to get involved with his students. Most of the time he managed to be friendly while maintaining his reserve, but there had been the odd slip, and there was something about Emily he just found incredibly appealing.

He'd never admit it, but he was immediately more inclined to like those students of his who had rescued, rather than paid for, their dogs, and Emily seemed like such fun, had laughed uproariously as Humphrey created chaos in the class, and he was delighted when they ended up having coffee together.

She made him laugh, and he found he couldn't wait for the next lesson, to see her again. He had finally kissed her last week, catching her unawares as she was making coffee in her tiny galley kitchen, a mug of Nescafé Gold Blend in each of her hands as he reached down, seizing the moment, knowing that he couldn't wait any longer.

She had stepped back afterward, smiled up at him while still holding the coffee. "I was wondering when you were going to get around to that," she said, and they spent the next couple of hours kissing on the sofa.

"Not yet," she whispered when he had tried to take it further. "I'm not ready yet."

He had seen her all day Thursday, and on Saturday night they went to a movie and grabbed a pizza, then a coffee back at his place. Most of Sunday they spent walking the dogs on the heath, and Monday, when Harry was planning on taking a break, he found himself phoning Emily to see what she was doing for lunch. The deadline could wait, she said with a laugh, rushing out the door to meet him at

Nando's for grilled chicken and more frozen yogurt than she'd ever eaten in her life.

Monday night they had agreed to have an early night. Respectively. So instead of meeting for supper, they sat on the phone for two and a half hours, reluctantly yawning good night at a quarter to midnight. Which was when Emily — nervously — invited him to Brianden for the weekend.

Harry had immediately said yes, laughed long and hard at how the name Brianden came to be conceived (the poor man's Cliveden, Emily had said), and had already organized other trainers to take over his weekend classes.

While Harry didn't want to jump in too fast too soon, he was having too good a time to play games or pretend to be less interested than he was. He hadn't had a serious relationship for a while, but he hadn't met a woman like Emily for a while either. He couldn't wait for this weekend, for their relationship to be consummated, and couldn't wait to open his eyes in the morning and see Emily lying beside him.

"Are you sure you don't mind?" Harry is nervously eyeing the floor of the trunk, which is already being covered in large muddy footprints. "Your car's getting filthy. I'll clean it up when we get there."

"Don't be silly." Alice climbs into the driver's seat. "It's a Range Rover. It's supposed to be dirty." Emily and Harry start to laugh, the Range Rover being immaculate, not a speck of dirt anywhere other than the floor of the trunk, thanks to Humphrey and Dharma discovering a large puddle outside Alice's house.

"I'll sit in the back," Emily offers. "Harry's got longer legs and needs the room. But" — she holds up a warning finger — "I must have equal say in terms of what radio station we listen to, and if you ignore me I will refuse to give you directions."

"Kiss FM?" Harry offers.

"No!" Alice and Emily shout in unison.

"I thought you said I'd like him?" Alice turns around to Emily. "You didn't say anything about him liking Kiss FM."

"I don't," Harry grumbles. "I was just trying to be trendy. Magic?"

"Yes!" the girls shout, as Harry groans.

Five minutes later Humphrey and Dharma are lying panting on the floor of the trunk, Harry is leaning his head against the window groaning, and Alice and Emily are singing *"I've been through the desert on a horse with no name . . ."* at the top of their voices.

Fifteen minutes later, as they get on to the A40, Alice, Emily, and Harry are all screaming along with Marvin Gaye: *"Let's get it on . . . mmm I love ya . . ."*

"If the spirit moves you, let me groove you," Harry croons, closing his eyes and really getting into it. He opens them again to find the girls laughing at him.

"Oh, he's good," Alice laughs. "Have you ever considered a career alternative?"

"You know," Harry sings in a loud falsetto, *"what I'm talking about!"*

"You have a reputation for being exceptionally bright" — Joe pauses — "and a ball-breaker." He wasn't sure whether to say beautiful or not. She is beautiful, of course, but something tells him she is used to hearing she is beautiful, and that he will score more points if he focuses on her other qualities.

"A ball-breaker?" Josie smiles as she raises an eyebrow. "That's the first time anyone's had the temerity to say that to my face."

"I didn't say *I* had said that," Joe says smoothly. "But that is your reputation.

112

Does it bother you, or do you, as I suspect, quite enjoy it?"

"Let's just say I'd rather walk over than *be* walked over."

"That doesn't surprise me."

"And what about you?" She turns to face Joe, three Cosmopolitans emboldening her. "You have a reputation for being a serial adulterer. Does that bother you, or do you quite enjoy it?"

"Christ." Joe is genuinely taken aback, liking to think of himself as a ladies' man, heartbreaker perhaps, but serial adulterer? That sounds far too sleazy, plus it implicates his marriage, and as far as he can he likes to keep Alice out of his extracurricular activities. "You're not serious, are you? Serial adulterer? That's terrible."

"I agree. It is terrible. Is it true?"

Joe sighs, not quite sure which tack to pull. Does he go for the charm offensive and tell her he's faithful but he's never met anyone quite like her before? No. He suspects she'd be out the door before he even started.

Does he go for honesty and say that he loves his wife, but sex was sex, and the two were distinctly unrelated?

Or does he tell her he's unhappily married, he and his wife don't sleep together anymore, and he's only with her because he can't face hurting her, but that it's just a matter of time?

He can see she's interested. Look how the Cosmopolitans have loosened her up. Watch her body language, see how she's twisted her body to face him now, notice how she's circling the top of her cocktail glass with her index finger, giving him a come-on smile.

Christ. He could fuck her right now.

He can see she's interested but he has to play his cards right, has to make the right choice or he'll blow it forever.

"I've been married for five years," Joe says slowly, careful not to look at Josie, trying to sound as sincere as possible, "three of which were fantastic. My wife is an amazing woman, but the last two years we've both been incredibly unhappy. It's not that I don't love her, I do . . ."

Josie barks with laughter, stopping Joe in his tracks. "Let me guess, you're just not *in* love with her, and you want a divorce but you don't want to hurt her."

"Yes, how did you know?"

"I've met you before." Josie shakes her head in amused disbelief. "I've slept with you before. Jesus, I've fallen in love with you before. I can't believe you're coming out with that line and you expect women to believe it. That's the saddest thing I've ever heard in my life."

"But it's true!" Joe blusters, embarrassed at his transparency, furious that he made the wrong choice.

"Yes. And I'm a virgin," Josie laughs.

Back on familiar flirtatious territory, Joe relaxes. "Now that," he says, charm oozing from every pore, "is definitely not true. After all, you just said you'd slept with me before. Although there you must of course be lying, because I know I'd never forget a woman like you."

"I love motorway service stations!" Alice announces just past Oxford.

"Er, why?" Harry looks dubious.

"I love motorway food. Egg and chips, sausage and chips, bacon and chips. Mmmm." She licks her lips.

"I told you deep down she was one of us." Emily grins.

"You mean you're not a salad, no-dressing kind of girl?"

"Of course I am," Alice says in mock in-dignation. "But the salad no-dressing girl is only a superficial exterior to hide the greedy pig beneath."

"Do you want to stop and get some egg

and chips then?" Harry is amused, even though he doesn't quite believe her.

"Okay. Next service station."

"I can do better than that," Emily announces triumphantly. "If you can wait ten minutes there's a Little Chef!"

"Perfect!" Harry laughs. "Alice eating egg and chips doused in ketchup. This I've got to see."

Alice frowns. "Who said anything about ketchup?"

"If you're going to do it" — Harry shrugs — "you may as well do it properly."

Alice leans back in her chair and undoes the top button of her jeans. "That," she announces, "was disgusting. It was so greasy my insides feel like an oil slick. Delicious."

"I cannot believe how much you just ate." Emily is still at the relationship stage of pretending that she doesn't eat and has played prettily with her own egg and chips while pretending not to be hungry, although, given that tonight is *the* night, her appetite does seem to have left her this afternoon.

"I can't believe how much you just ate." Harry shakes his head. "You're tiny. Where do you put it, for God's sake?"

"Here," Alice laughs, lifting up a size

116

seven-and-a-half boot. "It all goes into my big toe."

Emily looks at her watch. "So what train is Joe getting? Do you know what time he'll be in?"

Alice shrugs. Full and happy, for once she does not mind that Joe is not here, can relax and enjoy herself without worrying if Joe is happy, comfortable, getting on with Emily's new boyfriend.

"Who cares?" Alice laughs, knowing that Joe will be, as always, stuck in a late meeting somewhere, and even if he thinks he will be arriving at 8:10 p.m., it is likely to be at least an hour and a half later. "He'll be here. Eventually." And with that they leave.

"I'll drive if you like," Harry says, when they reach the car.

"Okay." Alice hands him the keys, not caring if he's insured or not. Joe would never let a stranger drive the car, not even Emily's new boyfriend. *Especially* not Emily's new boyfriend.

Alice climbs into the backseat and stretches out. "Wake me up when we get there," she says with a yawn before closing her eyes and dozing happily off.

7

"I'd like to tell you it's beautiful" — Harry squints through the windshield as he pulls up in front of the house — "but I can't see a bloody thing."

"That's because it's the country," Emily says. "Wake up, Alice, we're here."

Emily fumbles in the dark for the key, eventually managing to open the door. She walks quickly around the house turning on the lamps, filling the rooms with a warm apricot glow as Alice and Harry stand in the front garden shivering, waiting for the dogs to empty their bladders after the long journey.

By the time Humphrey and Dharma are done, there is a roaring fire and the kettle is already whistling away on the stove.

Alice hasn't been to Brianden for a long,

long time, and she stands in the doorway for a few moments, amazed at what Emily has done, how she has transformed a rather ugly, characterless 1980s house into such a welcoming home.

The salmon-pink carpet has gone, replaced by a thick woven wool in a rich honey. A squashy biscuit-colored sofa faces the fireplace, a red-check armchair tucked into the corner. A brown leather ottoman is piled high with books and knickknacks, and underneath the window is a large oak table that Emily found in Stow.

Tall silver candlesticks stand on the table, which Emily now lights, not caring that it might be over the top.

The kitchen used to be high white gloss, with sleek silver doorknobs and granite-look Formica tops. Emily found a local carpenter to make Shaker cupboard doors, which she painted a soft sunny yellow, and the counters are now thick industrial butcher's block.

At one end is a long scrubbed pine table, with a mishmash of chairs that Emily has picked up at various places, none of which match but all of which work. The walls are covered in framed photographs of friends and family and small paintings she has picked up at local art galleries. It is warm, and welcoming, and quite clearly, as every kitchen should be, the heart of the house.

Harry brings the shopping bags in — they stopped at a supermarket *en route* — and puts them on the kitchen table. Alice expertly unpacks the bags and puts things away, and Emily places three oversize mugs of tea on a tray and grabs a packet of Bourbons, opening it with her teeth, then shaking the biscuits onto a plate.

"Come on, you can finish that later." She carries the tray into the living room and sets it down gently on the coffee table before collapsing on the sofa with her tea.

Alice takes a mug and sits next to her, kicking off her boots and curling her legs beneath her as Harry sits in the armchair.

"This is so lovely!" She looks around the room happily. "I can't believe what you've done since I was last here. It looks amazing."

"I haven't been here before, obviously," Harry says with a nod, "but I have to agree this is lovely. I thought you said it was a modern council house."

"It is." Emily laughs. "Wait until the morning and then you'll see what the outside looks like. Still, it's lovely inside, and we've got the most amazing views over the valley. Every time I come down I wonder why I don't spend more time here."

"I don't know how you manage to go back to London after you've been here," Alice sighs. "If this were mine I'd never leave."

"But you have your museum to take care of," Harry smiles.

"God. Don't remind me."

"I know you won't believe me but this is actually much more Alice's style," Emily says to Harry with a laugh, as somewhere in one of the bags a phone starts to ring. "God, is that mine?" Emily jumps up and starts to rummage in her bag as Alice wearily stands up and crosses the room to hers.

"Nope. It's probably mine. Doubtless that husband of mine is ringing to tell me he's missed the train or he won't be able to make it. Here we go again." She pulls the phone out and flicks it open.

"Darling, it's me."

"Yes, Joe. I know."

"Look, the meeting's over but the client wants to have dinner, so I think tonight's going to be impossible. I think the sensible thing for me to do is go home and get the first train out tomorrow morning."

"Fine." Alice's voice is cold.

"Alice, don't be like that. I can't help it,

it's work. There's nothing I can do."

"Okay, okay. I'll see you tomorrow. Have a nice evening."

"You too."

"Bye." Alice doesn't wait for an "I love you," just sighs and puts down the phone.

Joe flips his phone closed, smiles to himself, and heads back into the bar. He's sure his luck is in tonight, sure that he'll manage to conquer the ice queen, although surprised that it's happened this quickly.

They've spent the last two hours talking. Joe has learned his lesson and has said as little as possible about himself and his marriage, instead drawing her out, asking her questions about her career, her opinions, her ambitions. Josie may not be stupid, but she's flattered by the close attention Joe is paying and softened by the amount of alcohol she's had to drink.

As the evening wears on, Joe moves his chair a little closer, leans forward a little more to hear her better, and Josie is surprised to find herself responding. It's been such a long time since she allowed herself to be attracted to anyone, and even though this is clearly not going to result in anything — he's married and they work together, a recipe for disaster — it's more fun being here with an attractive man than it is being at home on her own.

What harm can it do?

Josie Mitchell didn't get to run Risk Arb at Goldmans by partying and having a social life. She joined Goldmans' analyst trainee program straight from university and quickly learned that she was going to be able to rise to the top only if she forgot about friends, boyfriends, and socializing, and focused entirely on her career.

She has had the odd relationship — she's only human — but her boyfriends have never been able to understand her commitment to work, her drive to succeed, and there was only so long they would put up with being second best.

The only person who understood was James. A managing director at Schroder Salomon Smith Barney, he worked as hard as she did, but knew the importance of keeping a balance, and for a while he made her forget that work was the only thing that mattered in her life. For a while James was the only thing that mattered.

Josie fell in love with James, and when James left her saying he loved her but wasn't ready for commitment — "It's not you, it's me" — she vowed not to make the same mistake again, vowed that no one would hurt her like that again.

She stopped caring what people thought of her, toughened up her act, and refused ever to put men before her career again. Of course there was the odd brief relationship, but Josie made sure she was always in charge, made sure no one could even come close to bruising, let alone breaking, her heart.

"Sorry about that." Joe sits down, pulling his chair closer, brushing her knee with his own. "Just had to make a quick phone call."

"To tell your wife you're stuck in a meeting?" Josie is amused.

"No, actually. I told her I was with a particularly brilliant and beautiful colleague, and I'm having much too good a time to leave, so I'd probably be late home tonight."

Josie shakes her head. She knows he's probably tried this on with a million other women before her. She wants to tell him that he's being an arse, that he's completely transparent, that she's not some bimbo who's going to fall for the whole married man line, but she doesn't.

She doesn't because up until this evening she has genuinely forgotten what it is like to feel turned on, to feel that thrill of attraction, of anticipation. She can feel Joe's knee gently pressing her own, and she's astonished to feel a surge of heat in the pit of her stomach.

She knows this is ridiculous. Dangerous. She's only just started at Godfrey Hamilton Saltz, the last thing she needs is to get involved with someone at work. She ought to just leave now, go before she gets herself into a situation she might not be able to get out of. The attraction is strong, but her survival instinct is stronger.

"I have to go." Josie shakes her head and reaches for her jacket, ignoring the disappointment on Joe's face.

"Where do you live?"

"Chelsea."

Joe's face lights up. This is going to be easier than he thought. "I'm in Belgravia. We can share a cab."

Alice cooked: smoked haddock kedgeree, a large mixed salad, and hot crusty bread warmed in the oven. Harry washed up, Emily dried, and by the time everything had been put away they had drunk just over two bottles of wine.

The dogs are stretched out in front of

the fire when Harry volunteers to walk them before bed. He puts his jacket on, pulls a woolen hat over his curls ("Don't say I didn't come prepared"), and clips their leashes on to take them out.

Alice and Emily wave good-bye, smiling, and as the door firmly shuts behind him Emily exhales loudly.

"Go on then, what do you think?"

"The house is fantastic. I told you."

Emily hits Alice hard.

"Ow!"

"Sorry, but you know I didn't mean the house. What do you think of Harry?"

"Harry's fantastic too."

"He is, isn't he?" Emily sighs happily.

"Yes." Alice nods. "He really is."

There's a silence for a few seconds then Emily nudges Alice. "Go on then, tell me what's fantastic about him."

"You know what's fantastic about him."

"But I want to hear what you think is fantastic about him."

Alice laughs. "Okay. He's funny."

"He *is*, isn't he?" Emily hugs her knees.

"Yes. And he's got a great smile."

"*Hasn't* he though? I told you he had a great smile."

"I know, and he does." More silence.

"What else?"

"He's really interested in people, and interesting."

"I *know!* I love that about him."

"He knew how to make kedgeree."

"I *know!* He can cook!"

"He loves animals." Alice is running out of fantastic things to say about him.

"How perfect is that?"

"That about sums it up," Alice laughs. "He seems to be pretty perfect."

"He *is,* isn't he?"

"There must be something wrong with him," Alice muses. "No one's that perfect. Maybe he's got really stinky cheesy feet."

"Yeuch! That's disgusting!" Emily makes a face as she starts laughing.

"I bet that's it," Alice continues. "Cheesy disgusting feet with long yellow toenails."

"Oh God, you're horrible," Emily groans through her laughter. "That's the most disgusting thing I've ever heard. I don't think I want to have sex with him anymore!"

The front door opens and Dharma bounds into the room, followed closely by Humphrey, with Harry taking up the rear. Emily pales.

"Shit," she whispers to Alice when Alice stops laughing and Harry goes upstairs to the loo. "Do you think he heard me?"

"No, definitely not," Alice giggles. "Although even if he did, he's not exactly an innocent, he must know it's on the menu tonight."

"Shhh." Emily nudges her as Harry clumps back down the narrow staircase and tries to make her voice as natural as possible. "So he said yes, did he?"

Alice looks at her strangely. "Yes. He said yes."

"Oh, good." Emily's voice is unnaturally bright and breezy. "Anyone fancy a game of Scrabble?"

In the end they can't find the Scrabble, decide that Trivial Pursuit is too boring unless you have teams, and they can't be bothered to play Monopoly, so Boggle it is.

Forty-five minutes later Harry offers to make tea and disappears into the kitchen.

Emily leans over to Alice.

"Alice," she whispers, "I think it's nearly time for bed."

"Is it?" Alice looks at her watch. "It's only ten and I'm not tired at all."

"Al-ice," Emily sings slowly. "I think it's nearly time for *you* to go to bed." She raises an eyebrow as Alice gasps.

"Shit, I'm being so obtuse. I'm having such a lovely time I completely forgot I was being a total gooseberry. Oh God, you're supposed to be having sex in front of the fire and I'm sitting here like a total idiot. I'm so sorry, I'll go now."

She jumps up and walks quickly toward the stairs until Emily runs after her and grabs her, leading her back to the sofa.

"You're not being a gooseberry," she whispers. "We're all having a lovely time, and it will be a bit bloody obvious if Harry comes back with a cup of tea for you and finds you gone. Just drink your tea quickly and then go to bed."

"Okay. What underwear are you wearing?"

Emily listens to check Harry is still in the kitchen, then quickly lifts her sweater to flash a cream lacy bra.

"Oooh, nice." Alice whistles her approval.

"I thought so. Black's always a bit obvious, don't you think? Is it sexy though?"

"Oh yes. If I was a man I'd definitely fancy you."

"That's why I love you." Emily puts her arms around Alice and gives her a brief hug. "You always know exactly the right thing to say."

"Tea for three." Harry comes back into the living room holding the tray, Dharma running around his heels, joined swiftly by

Humphrey, the pair of them clearly sensing the rest of the Bourbon biscuits on the tray. "Dharma, down!" he says, as Dharma collapses to the floor. "Good girl!" He turns to Humphrey, who is currently weaving between his legs. "Humphrey, down!" Humphrey jumps up, placing his paws on Harry's thigh. "Emily," he says sternly, "I thought you said you'd been practicing."

"Ah yes." Emily is embarrassed. "It looks like I still have some work to do."

Alice snuggles under the duvet, book in hand, and smiles to herself. She is having the nicest time she has had in ages, with nothing and no one else to worry about.

Part of her is dreading Joe coming up tomorrow. Brianden is tiny, but the three of them — Emily, Harry, and Alice — fit perfectly. The house feels just the right size, and Alice is nervous that Joe's arrival will cause the house to shrink, will give her the sense of claustrophobia that she feels so often these days.

And she knows Joe won't be comfortable. He'll moan about the lack of a shower, the shared bathroom, the bed, the *everything*. She knows he'll want to move, will try to convince her to come up with some excuse and go to a fancy hotel on Saturday night, but, she determines now as she lies here, she will not be swayed. For once she will do what *she* wants to do.

Downstairs, Emily and Harry are lying on the sofa, smiling at one another as they gently kiss.

"So what do you think of Alice?" Emily strokes his cheek as she marvels at finding such a lovely man in such an unlikely place.

Harry smiles. "She's not what I expected," he says. "She's really down to earth and sweet."

"She is, isn't she?"

"What's her husband like?"

Emily frowns. "I like him but I think he's probably a bit of a bastard. You kind of have to like him, he's incredibly charming, but also very controlling with Alice, and I'm sure he's unfaithful."

"Why would anyone want to be unfaithful if they were married to someone like Alice?" Harry is confused.

"I know. Alice swears he's just an old flirt and would never do anything, but I'm not so sure. But the Alice you met today is the real Alice, just incredibly loving and natural and playful, and you'll see how she changes when Joe's around."

"In what way?"

"She's much quieter, she allows Joe to be the center of attention, and she's much more careful."

"Do you think they're happily married?"

"Oh God. I don't know. I know that I would never have expected her to marry someone like Joe, or live the life she's living with Joe, but who really knows what goes on behind closed doors?"

Harry leans forward and kisses Emily again. "That's enough about Alice. I'm far more interested in you right now."

"Oh, good." Emily shivers as Harry lifts her hair and softly kisses her neck. "I was hoping you would say that."

The cab takes a hard right around a corner, causing Josie to slide sharply into Joe.

There's an intimate silence in the cab. Josie is wondering whether she should have stopped drinking Cosmopolitans a few hours ago, while Joe is wondering whether they should go to her place or his. Have to be hers, he decides. However much of a bastard he is, he's too careful to bring anyone back to the house. You never know what they might accidentally on purpose leave behind.

"Just here on the left." Josie leans forward, gathering her coat and bag as Joe starts to rise. Josie turns to him, knowing what she has to do. The air is filled with promise, she is so attracted to him and he to her, and it would be so easy for her to go to bed with him tonight, but it would be a mistake.

She knows absolutely it would be a mistake.

"Don't get up," she says brusquely. "I'll be fine."

"Ah. That means I'm not getting invited in for coffee, doesn't it?" Joe sits back, disappointed but not deterred. If not tonight, another night. He knows he'll get there in the end.

"You're not getting invited in for coffee," Josie smiles, and Joe leans forward just at that moment, and in the darkness of the cab he kisses her. Once, twice. Three soft kisses on her lips. No tongues, nothing overtly sexual, but a guarantee that he will not settle for friendship, that it may not happen tonight, but it *will* happen. Of that he is absolutely sure.

8

Alice yawns as she tiptoes down the stairs trying not to wake anyone, rubbing her neck and shoulder as she groans.

The bed was not as bad as she remembered, it was worse. She had slept fantastically for three hours, then spent the rest of the night tossing and turning, eventually waking with a stiff neck at six o'clock.

She has lain in bed reading for an hour, then come downstairs to be met by an excited Humphrey and Dharma, who jump all over her then run to the front door whining, their tails wagging furiously.

Pulling her coat over her pajamas, she looks for her boots by the front door, realizing she has left them upstairs. She can't be bothered to run back up, so she slips her feet into Harry's huge Timberlands, grabs one of Emily's hats, pulls it down firmly over her ears, and clips the leashes on the dogs as she tries to shush them before quietly going outside.

It's a beautiful morning. The air is cold and crisp, the frost glitters on the grass, and the sky is a bright clear blue. Crunching over the lawn, Alice pushes open the gate and leads the dogs into the field. She bends down and unclips their leashes, smiling as the pair of them eagerly take off, racing round in circles, tongues hanging out of their mouths with joy.

She had forgotten just how wonderful the view is, how much she loves being in open spaces, breathing fresh air. She crosses her arms to keep out the cold, and follows the dogs, sliding her feet across the lawn to stop the huge boots falling off.

Twenty minutes later she's about to die of cold. Calling the dogs as quietly as she can, she clips the leashes back on and leads them across the country lane back into the house to make some coffee and warm up.

"Morning!" Harry's sitting at the kitchen table with a mug of steaming coffee. He's wearing jeans and a large sweatshirt, and Alice is relieved to see that his bare feet seem to be completely normal.

"You look disgustingly happy for first thing in the morning," Alice laughs, knowing that a night of sex will do that for you. As it happens, Alice is a morning person herself, has always had the ability to bound out of bed wide awake, without the need for caffeine to give her that first boost of the day.

"I'm always good first thing," Harry smiles. "I saw you outside walking the dogs. I hate to be the one to tell you this, but I think your boots are a little too big for you."

"Ah, yes. They're yours, actually. I couldn't find mine so I borrowed them. Do you mind?"

"Not at all. Glad to have been of service. And the hat suits you too. Can I get you some coffee?"

"Mmm, that sounds lovely."

"So how did you become a dog trainer?" Alice is clearing up the cereal bowls while Harry stands by the stove cracking eggs into a frying pan.

"I was supposed to be a vet" — Harry laughs — "but I didn't have the discipline."

"You mean you went to veterinary college?"

"Yup. I dropped out halfway through my second year."

"But that's terrible."

"Is it? Why?"

"You were so close. Don't you have any regrets?"

Harry hands Alice the package of bacon to open, then slaps six rashers into the pan. "Sometimes. But I don't think I'm the sort of person who would be happy working in a nine-to-five job."

"Do you think being a vet constitutes a nine to five?"

"Actually it's longer, you'd have to be on call all the time even when you weren't at your practice, but it's more about routine. I didn't have the discipline to do the same thing every day, and although I do sometimes think I should have finished, just to have got the qualifications, on the whole I'm very happy with my life."

"And is dog training everything you thought it would be?"

Harry laughs, walking over to the table and sliding the eggs and bacon onto plates as Alice puts a pile of toast on the table and sits down. "Dog training is fantastic, but best of all is the time it gives me to do other things."

"Such as?"

"Such as gardening. And pottering round the house. And I'm a bit of a dab hand at woodwork."

"What kind of woodwork?"

"Bookshelves. Benches. That kind of stuff."

"For yourself or for other people? God, this is delicious! I don't even remember the last time I had fried eggs and bacon for breakfast. This feels so decadent!"

"What do you normally have for breakfast?"

"Fruit."

"And?"

Alice shrugs. "Just fruit."

"That's not breakfast!" Harry is horrified. "You need something much heartier for breakfast. I'll have to have a word with Emily about you."

"What do you have for breakfast then? Surely not this every day. You'll be having a heart attack any moment now."

"Nope, these breakfasts are only for the weekend. My usual breakfast is a bowl of porridge, toast, and fruit. Oh, and sometimes pancakes."

"Pancakes? How are you not the size of a house?"

"Gardening's bloody good exercise. It's hard physical labor."

Alice laughs. "You could start a new fitness craze: Harry's hard-core gardening workout."

"I'm serious."

"I know. I'm sorry. So go on, which is it? Do you do the gardening and carpentry for yourself or for other people?"

"Both. I took them up years ago just because I wanted to learn new skills, but now I do quite a lot for other people, usually friends, or friends of friends. I try to work only with people I like. Life's too short to be doing something you don't want to do. So what about you, Alice? What do you do?"

There is a silence while Alice thinks about how to answer. How can she possibly tell him she has lunch? Or she is on various charity committees? How can she say she goes shopping? And has manicures?

"I don't do very much really," she says eventually, preferring nothing to the truth.

"Okay. Next question. What would you want to do?"

"You mean if I wasn't living this life?"

"Yup, if you could do anything at all."

Alice sits and thinks for a while. "Probably a bit of gardening and carpentry," she says, and they both laugh.

"Morning!" Emily, in a dressing gown, stretches in the doorway and grins, first at Harry, then at Alice. She walks over to Harry and puts her arms around his neck, leaning down as he looks up at her with a smile, and kissing him on the lips.

Alice watches them with envy. How exciting a relationship is when it's this new, when you're still discovering one another, when you still have the capacity to fall head over heels in love.

"Did you sleep well?" Alice manages an innocent expression, laughing as Emily blushes.

"I slept terribly, thank you for asking," Alice continues. "That bed is a bloody nightmare. I can't believe you haven't changed it yet."

"Why would I change it? I don't have to sleep on it."

"Oh, thanks a lot." Alice harrumphs as Emily sits on Harry's lap. "Can you two just try and keep your hands off each other first thing in the morning?"

"It's not first thing in the morning," Emily laughs, twining her arms around Harry's neck. "It's nearly ten."

"Oh God. I'd better switch my mobile on. Joe's probably standing at the station in a fury, waiting for me." Alice runs out to her bag as Emily shakes her head sadly at Harry.

"See what I mean?" she whispers. "Joe says jump, Alice asks how high." Her voice resumes its natural pitch. "Is there a message?" She looks up as Alice walks back into the room listening to her mobile.

Alice nods. "Yup. He'll be at Stow at 10:55. I'd better get ready. Do you guys want to come?"

Emily looks at Harry. Harry grins at Emily and Alice groans in disgust. "Young love. Doesn't it make you sick? I'll see you later." And she goes upstairs to get dressed.

Joe is an expert traveler. He likes planes, trains, and long car journeys. In first-class on a plane, he immediately pulls on the complementary socks, puts on the eye mask, and instructs the stewardess to wake him for the final meal before arriving. In the car he makes sure he has his favorite CDs and a good supply of snacks, and on trains he ensures he arrives early enough to buy a baguette sandwich and every newspaper he can lay his hands on.

Today he doesn't bother with the newspapers. Today he spends the entire journey with his eyes closed, a faint smile on his face, lost in a fantasy world of what it must be like sleeping with Josie.

By the time the train pulls into Stow, Joe is in an excellent mood. It's a clear, sunny day, there is his beautiful wife waving at him, and he's about to embark on a sexual adventure — life surely does not get much better than this.

"This is *it?*" Alice pulls the Range Rover up on the verge opposite Brianden, and switches off the engine as Joe sneers at what he thinks is one of the ugliest houses he's ever seen.

"Yes, this is it. Come on, Joe, don't be nasty. It's only one night."

Joe shakes his head. "I can't believe you dragged me to the Cotswolds to stay here. This is going to be awful."

"It's not awful, it's lovely inside, and for God's sake it's one night."

Joe sighs deeply and shakes his head as he reaches into the backseat for his Tumi overnight bag. "And to think we could have been at the Lygon Arms right now. Talk about the sublime to the ridiculous."

Alice feels a flash of fury. She's about to say something, but the front door opens and Emily waves excitedly to Joe, who composes his face and gives her his most charming smile.

"Emily!" he says smoothly, getting out the car. "How lovely to see you and how lovely to be here." He leans down and kisses her on each cheek. "And you must be Harry," he says, extending a hand. "I'm Joe. It's very, very nice to meet you."

The four of them set off over the field with the dogs. Emily, Harry, and Alice all wrapped up in scarves, hats, and gloves, sensible boots on their feet. Joe is in a Barbour, a cashmere sweater, and John Lobb custom-made shoes on his feet. His entire outfit is probably worth about as much as Emily's house.

"Isn't this wonderful?" Joe takes a deep breath. "Just breathe that fresh air. I love the country. Darling, why don't we come to the country more often?"

"Because we're always so busy on the weekends?" Alice ventures. "And because I thought you hated the country?"

"Hate the country? Who hates the country? This is marvelous."

The dogs run ahead as the four of them cut across a field, ending up on a puddle-ridden path. Within minutes their boots are sinking into the mud, and Joe's country-loving smile is replaced with a deep frown. "Shit," he mutters, gingerly trying to avoid the puddles, his Lobbs now hidden under a thick layer of mud.

"Is anyone hungry?" Joe asks five minutes later. "Are we nearly there?"

"Hungry? We haven't been out long enough to build up an appetite," Emily scolds. "Anyway, the pub's another two miles."

Joe stops in his tracks, sinking an inch or two into the mud. "Two miles? You're joking, aren't you?"

"No."

"Joe." Alice can't help herself, she starts to laugh. "What did you think we meant when we said we were going for a walk?"

"I thought you said walk. Not John o'Groats to Land's End."

"Oh, don't be such a baby," Emily chides. "It's good for you."

A few minutes later Joe has a horrifying thought.

"How exactly are we supposed to get back from the pub?" The three of them start laughing as Joe shakes his head. "Nope. Count me out. I'll be getting a taxi."

"He *is* charming," Harry whispers to Emily as they stand at the bar, waiting to order, "but he's a bit of a wuss, isn't he?"

"He's just not a country boy." Emily leans into Harry as he puts an arm around her shoulders. "Shame. We almost would have had more fun if he hadn't come."

"Oh, I don't know. That look on his face when he realized he'd be walking back was a classic — gave me the best laugh I've had in weeks."

Two plowman's lunches, two scampi and chips, three sticky toffee puddings, and one apple pie later, Alice, Emily, and Harry stand up and stretch, holding their stomachs and groaning, preparing to walk off some of the calories on their way home.

"Come on, Joe," Alice says, standing over her husband, who is still sitting at the table, perfectly happy with a coffee and to-day's copy of *The Times*, which someone has left on the neighboring table. "Are you coming?"

"Nope. I'll get a cab back. See you at home. Cheers!" And he raises his coffee cup and smiles as the three others shake their heads and troop out of the door.

"I cannot believe what a total wimp my husband is."

"I hope he's prepared to stay there all afternoon." Emily laughs.

"Really? Why?"

"Where does he think he is, Oxford Street? Does he think cabs grow on trees? My guess would be by the time he finds a cab to bring him home it'll be dinnertime."

"Good. Serves him right. Oh God. Dinnertime." Alice moans. "Can we just not mention food ever again?"

"You mean you don't want to go for a proper English cream tea this afternoon?" Harry smiles as the girls groan.

"Tomorrow," Emily says. "Right now I just want to go home and sleep."

"Are you sure that's all you want to do?" Harry takes her hand and winks at her as Alice makes vomiting noises behind them.

"Can you just save it for the bedroom, please? Some of us are about to throw up."

By the time Joe arrives a log fire is roaring, the dogs are stretched out asleep, and Harry and Emily have retired for an "afternoon nap."

Alice is curled up in the armchair, reading, and she looks up with a smile as Joe walks in. He comes over to her and kisses her, as she makes a face.

"I can smell whisky," she says. "Have you been drinking all afternoon?"

"I started talking to the farmer up the road" — Joe's hands start to wander up her thigh — "and he bought me a drink and gave me a lift home."

"Not just one drink, I take it. Look at

146

you, you always get randy when you're drunk."

"Not drunk, just pleasantly mellow, and very turned on by my lovely wife. Where are the others?"

"Doing what you presumably wish you were doing."

"Come on, darling, let's go upstairs." Joe kisses Alice, and leads her, smiling, up the stairs to the lumpy, bumpy bed.

"Good sleep?" Harry looks up from the kitchen table, from a huge doorstop cheese and pickle sandwich he's nearly demolished.

"I can't believe you're eating!" Alice shakes her head. "After that lunch you had? And yes, it was a good sleep." She tries not to blush, knowing she cried out as she came, hoping that she couldn't be heard. "And you? Did you sleep well?"

"Nothing like an afternoon nap to work up an appetite." Harry grins. "Do you want some?" He proffers the remaining half of his sandwich, and Alice finds she's suddenly ravenous.

"I'm going to be huge after this weekend." She takes a big bite. "I'll have to do the cabbage soup diet next week."

"That sounds disgusting," Harry says in

horror. "What the hell is the cabbage soup diet?"

"It *is* disgusting. You make a cauldron of vegetable soup and eat it for five days. It's completely disgusting but you lose pounds."

"And presumably fart for your country at the same time."

"Please!" Alice looks shocked. "Ladies don't fart."

"Oh, so sorry. What do ladies do then?"

Alice stops to think. "We do windy pops," she says eventually as Harry bursts into laughter.

"What are you two laughing at?" Emily walks into the kitchen. "Alice! I can't believe you're eating after that huge lunch. I'm never going to be able to eat again. What are you eating anyway?"

Alice shrugs. "I don't know but it's delicious. Harry made it."

"Cheese, ham, pickle, mayonnaise, tomato, cucumber, and the secret ingredient, onion," Harry says proudly.

"It's really good," Alice says with her mouth full, offering Emily a bite.

Emily bends down and takes a small bite. "Mmm," she says. "That *is* good. Harry, will you make me one too?"

"Of course," he says. "Just as long as you

promise me not to do the windy pop diet next week."

"The what?"

"Promise me first, then ask Alice what it is."

"Okay, whatever it is, I promise not to do" — Emily starts to laugh — "the windy pop diet next week."

"Okay. One Harry ham and cheese special coming up."

"Emily, don't take this personally but that bed is horrific." Joe walks into the kitchen rubbing the small of his back.

"I know, sorry. At least it's only one night," apologizes Emily.

"What's that?" Joe looks over with interest as Harry places another doorstop sandwich in front of Emily, who eagerly tucks in.

"A Harry special," Alice laughs. "Do you want one?"

"God, no." Joe leans back in his chair and rests a hand on his stomach as he shakes his head. "After that lunch? I'm completely stuffed."

"That's because you didn't walk back," Emily says through a mouthful of sandwich. "The country air has got all our juices going."

"Oh, my juices are going" — Joe winks — "don't you worry about that."

They wander around the garden center at Burford on Sunday, Emily buying a few herbs to plant in her back garden, then on to Broadway to wander the cobbled streets looking at antiques.

"Isn't this exactly what we've been looking for?" Joe stops in front of a window to gaze at a large ornate limed French armoire. "Wouldn't that be perfect for the guest bedroom?"

"It is lovely," Alice agrees, moving her face closer to the glass to block out the reflection and see it properly. "I didn't think you liked that style."

Joe doesn't usually. The monolithic modernity of their house is entirely Joe's taste, but Joe likes collecting, and Joe likes expensive pieces. Just last week he was reading an article in *Architectural Digest* about eighteenth-century armoires almost exactly like this one.

"Let's go in," Joe says. "See how much it is."

Forty minutes later the four of them walk out of the shop, a large smile on Joe's face. There's nothing he likes more than a bargain, and, because he bought a Louis XIV chair as well, he managed to get the two pieces for just under ten thousand pounds.

"Did you *see* how much that thing was?" Harry is still in shock as the two couples split up for a while, Joe and Alice to do some serious shopping, Emily and Harry to window-shop. "Did you see how much he just spent?"

"I know," Emily says. "That's almost my annual salary."

"Tell me about it." Harry shakes his head in amazement.

"Joe's hobby is spending money." She shrugs. "I've accepted it now. I've decided that in this world there are the haves and the have-nots, and I'm definitely a have-not."

"You have me." Harry squeezes her hand as Emily's face lights up.

"You're right. Forget what I just said. I now definitely qualify as a have."

"Do you know, I'm really having a nice time," Joe says, four shops, one rolltop desk, and one Eames chair later.

"Good," Alice says as he takes her hand. "I'm glad." She doesn't say that's because you're shopping, even though she knows that to be the case.

Alice is aware that Joe's success has always been defined by material possessions. The more things he has, the more he can show off to the world, the better he feels about himself.

Everything in Joe's life has to be the best. He can't just wear socks, they have to be cashmere. He won't stay in a hotel unless it's a Relais & Châteaux or Four Seasons. His car has to be an Aston Martin DB7 Vantage, his wife beautiful and blonde. Even his mistresses are the crème de la crème.

Alice doesn't care about any of those things. Alice just wants to be happy, and today, seeing Joe is in a good mood, having him take her hand and kiss her fingers affectionately, Alice forgets about his moodiness, his regular withdrawals. She feels grateful to have such a wonderful, caring husband.

"So you do carpentry?" They are sitting in a tea shop smothering homemade scones with thick clotted cream and jam, and Joe appears to be genuinely interested. "That's an amazing coincidence. Our carpenter's just let us down badly, and we've been looking for someone to build some shelves in my study." Joe is eager. "Are you any good?"

Alice wants to kick him, but doesn't.

"Yes, but I try not to work for friends," Harry lies with a smile. "I find it usually leads to trouble."

"Oh yes. I completely understand. Well, if you know anyone else, do let me know." Joe drops the subject, for which Alice is grateful. It's only later she groans when she remembers that Harry said he did most of his work for friends. He must think Joe is awful, she realizes.

"Not awful," Harry says to Emily later that night when they are back in London and lying in bed. "Just patronizing, and from a different world. Not someone I could see myself socializing with on a regular basis."

"But you liked Alice?" Emily snuggles closer into Harry's side.

"Oh yes. Alice is great. I just can't quite understand why she's married to him."

"I know," Emily sighs. "But as long as she's with him I'll support her. I have to. I'm her best friend."

9

There are days when the very last thing Josie Mitchell wants to do at five-thirty in the morning is go to the gym. At five o'clock, on the dot, Capital Radio screams from her bedside table, forcing her eyes open as she groans and throws the covers off, trying to muster the energy to move.

Throwing on a T-shirt, running pants, and sneakers, she scribbles a note for the cleaning woman before picking up her gym bag (carefully packed the night before), her work clothes carefully draped in a hanging bag, and heads out the door to the Harbour Club.

Her daily routine rarely changes. A brief smile and nod to the receptionists (and who could really expect more at that time in the morning?), then Josie strides to her locker, hangs her clothes, and is in the gym doing her stretches by 5:40.

There are already numerous people in the Harbour Club. Mostly bankers, fellow workers in the City, and occasionally someone she knows, although she rebuffs anyone who wants to chat. She takes her exercise seriously and is in no mood for small talk when in the gym.

Twice a week she does weights, twice a week cardio, and once a week, on a Sunday morning, she does a spinning class.

She has breakfast on the way into work. Always the same thing, every day: a skim latte and a dry bagel. She doesn't have time to sit and enjoy it, although food is not something she ever enjoys.

As a child she was overweight, never feeling as if she belonged, never feeling as good as her peers, turning to food for comfort, to stop her from feeling anything at all. At university she went to the other extreme and discovered that not eating empowered her unlike anything else had before, and the less food she ate, the stronger she felt, even as her body shrank to almost nothing.

She would refuse to eat anything that wasn't "natural," as she termed it, subsisting on lettuce, tomato and cucumber, apples and oranges, with the odd bit of whole-meal bread as a rare treat.

When she became ill, weighing less than ninety-eight pounds, she was sent to the university counselor who diagnosed anorexia, and although she now thinks she has a healthy attitude toward food and is a "normal" weight, she still feels uncomfortable eating in front of people, still worries that, despite being a small size ten, people who watch her eat will think her greedy, or worse, fat.

Her addiction to food has been replaced by an addiction to the gym. She fights to keep her gym visits down to five times a week — she could easily go every day, and occasionally, when she's home early enough with nothing to do, it's a battle not to go a second time in the evening.

And of course there is work. The more she can lose herself in work, the better she feels about herself, the less she has to think about a life outside the office.

For Josie really doesn't have much of a life apart from work. Too tough and intimidating ever to be a woman's woman, she has never really had girlfriends, has never known the joys of a close group of women, and has never shared the intimate details of her life with anyone.

On rare occasions when female bonding

has been required — if she has been trying to woo a female client and knows that a spot of moaning about men will create a false intimacy — it has never felt natural to her.

And yet she takes enormous pride in her appearance, is careful to ensure she looks perfect at all times: her hair is streaked at Daniel Hersheson, her suits are Gucci, her nails immaculately manicured. If you didn't know her reputation as ball-breaker extraordinaire, you might mistake her for a wealthy wife, or a glamorous girlfriend.

You might expect to see her lunching at E&O or shopping on Bond Street. You might indeed expect her to share these lunches with someone just like Alice. Certainly what you would least expect is for Josie to stop at Marks & Spencer on her way home and pick up a bag of salad or a ready-cooked meal to throw into her microwave prior to reading or watching television on a hard, uncomfortable mushroom-colored sofa before going to bed.

Al Bruckmeister jokes that her flat is the quintessential bachelor pad. And Al should know. Her only true friend, or at least the only person she sees on a regular basis, he was her second boss at Goldmans, her mentor, and finally her friend.

Al was the only person who knew when Godfrey Hamilton Saltz approached her to come and work for them, and although he was sorry to see her leave, he knew it was much too good an offer to turn down, and told her so.

Al, a native New Yorker, has been living in London for eight years, in a large loft apartment on the river, where he reads the *FT* and the *Wall Street Journal Europe* every day, the *New York Times* on Sunday, and still bemoans the fact that nowhere in this city can you get a decent bagel.

Forty-three, attractive in a Jerry Springer-ish kind of way, and hugely wealthy, there is no shortage of gorgeous young girls for Al to play with, but none of them thus far has interfered with his friendship with Josie.

He adores Josie. Knows that if he were ever going to settle down again (which is something he won't even consider, given the variety of younger and younger women out there), Josie would be exactly the sort of woman he'd choose.

He loves the fact that she's opinionated. She's strong and tough, and he has the best and most provocative arguments with her. She's the perfect companion for the various functions a man like him has to attend and the perfect date for dinner with friends.

Very early on, many years ago, he made a pass at her. They were at a black-tie dinner, and he invited her back to his loft apartment for a nightcap. He had known she would be impressed by the place, and imagined she would, like most of the other young girls he brought back, immediately fantasize about living there, jumping swiftly into bed with him in a bid to become the next Mrs. Al Bruckmeister.

He had poured her a vintage port, dimmed the lights, put Barry White on the stereo, then sat back on his sofa and looked deep into Josie's eyes as he asked her why such a beautiful woman didn't have a man.

And Josie had laughed.

She had laughed and laughed until tears were pouring down her cheeks.

"That is pathetic," she had finally spluttered, wiping the tears and mascara away as Al sat there wondering what the hell was so funny. "Is that how you lure innocent young girls into your bed?"

"Well, yeah," he'd said after a while. "And I have to tell you it usually works."

"You don't expect me to fall for that shit?"

"I was kind of hoping you would," he said hopefully. "Do you think you might? I mean, is it worth me carrying on?"

"With what?" Josie was giggling, enjoying herself immensely. "More smarmy flattery? Al Bruckmeister, you are hopeless. I'm telling you now that even if I were interested in getting involved with someone at work, which I'm not, you would be at the very bottom of my list."

"Oh, thanks." His ego was instantly bruised.

"Oh, please. Don't pull that hurt-little-boy act. Al, you're a wonderful man, but cheesy beyond belief, and you and I would never work. Plus those lines are terrible. If you want I'll help you come up with some better ones for your next victim."

"I've always thought my lines were pretty good. They've never failed me before."

Josie shook her head. "I'm sorry, but you have to do better than that. Pour me another drink and I'll tell you what women really want to hear."

"How would you know?" Al stood up and grinned. "You're just a man in woman's clothing."

"Touchy, touchy," she soothed. "Just because I won't sleep with you. But the good news is I'll be your friend, and, trust me, you'll have a much better time with me as your lifelong friend than as a quick fuck, which would be over in a few weeks."

Al raised an eyebrow. "A few weeks? It would last that long?"

"Only if you were very lucky."

As it turned out, she had been right. They had been friends now for over six years, and he was the one person she could always rely on, the one person she was never too tired to see.

Once or twice a week they'd get together, go for a local meal, or to the movies. On the weekends, if Al didn't have a date, Josie would accompany him to a cocktail or dinner party on a Saturday night, or they'd spend a Sunday together walking in Hyde Park, followed by brunch at the Bluebird with a group of Al's friends. If Al was dating someone, they'd see each other slightly less (the girls in his life invariably felt threatened by Josie), and on the rare occasions Josie was involved with someone, Al would moan for a while before finding another playmate, knowing that Josie's involvements never lasted long, and he'd soon have his friend back.

The last time Josie had sex was eighteen months ago, a fact that never fails to astonish Al, who regularly offers to change that but is always met with rolling eyes and laughter.

Josie tells herself she is too busy to think about men, work is too important to her and a relationship would be too distracting. But something strange has happened in the last few weeks. Something called Joe Chambers.

Josie knows she should find his advances smarmy. She knows of his reputation and knows he should be avoided. But her head and her loins don't seem to be in agreement, and she's shocked to discover that Joe Chambers seems to have awoken feelings in her she thought she'd forgotten about.

It had started that night in the cab, when he'd kissed her. She'd wordlessly stepped out of the taxi and let herself into her flat, leaning against the wall for a few seconds trying to steady her breathing.

You are being ridiculous, she had told herself. He's a colleague, he's known for being a slut, and worst of all, he's married.

But that night she had lain in bed unable to stop herself imagining what might have happened if she'd invited him in. Her breathing had quickened, her hand had lowered as she'd imagined him smiling at her as he unbuttoned her shirt, bending his head to kiss her as he slid her skirt up her thigh.

On the Monday she'd been unable to look at him in the office, had prayed he wouldn't talk to her in case he'd somehow been able to tell.

She had managed to avoid him for the whole week, despite feeling his eyes burning into her. Then on the Friday she had been working late, finishing a presentation, when she sensed someone behind her.

"Well, well." Joe pushed his sleeve up and looked at his watch. "Eight o'clock on a Friday night and you're still working? That's extremely conscientious of you."

Josie shrugged and turned back to her keyboard. "Just finishing a presentation. Can I do something for you?" The coldness in her voice masked her nervousness.

"I don't know. Can you?"

Josie didn't say anything, just carried on typing.

"Okay," Joe sighed, walking around to the other side of the desk so he faced her. "I'm sorry that I kissed you. I'm sorry that

163

I can't help but find you completely gorgeous, but I promise I won't do it again. Are you happy now?"

No! Josie thought. Of course not! But she sighed and nodded. "Thank you."

"I know you'll take this the wrong way, but it is eight o'clock and I'm starving. I was going to go out to grab a quick pizza. Do you want to come?"

It's pizza, Josie thought. He's not inviting you out for a romantic candlelit meal where he's going to make a pass at you (more's the pity). It's pizza, for God's sake. What could possibly happen with pizza?

"I'm still stuck in the office with Dave." Joe went into one of the private offices off the trading floor to call Alice so Josie wouldn't hear. "We're going out to grab a quick pizza, then we'll probably have to come back. Don't wait up, darling, it might be a late night." Please God, he thought, crossing his fingers. Please God, let it be a late night.

Alice sighed and sadly put down the phone. Please don't let it be starting again, she prayed. You've been so lovely for so long. Please don't do this to me again.

Pizza Express was hardly romantic.

Hard-tiled floors, a monochromatic color scheme, and bright white light weren't supposed to fill diners with thoughts of love, and indeed love was the very last thing on Joe and Josie's mind as they sat at a corner table and ordered their meal.

Pizza Napolitana for Joe, a mixed salad for Josie, with a bottle of Montepulciano and a bottle of San Pellegrino to wash it down.

I don't remember, Josie thought, watching Joe loosen his tie and run his fingers through his hair, the last time I found someone this attractive. What is it about him, why am I ready to have an orgasm just sitting here looking at him?

Home run, Joe thought, being his most boyishly charming, asking all the right questions and smiling in all the right places, but careful not to be too flirtatious, careful not to come across as too charming, too well versed in this.

Nearly there. He felt a familiar flutter of excitement, the thrill of the new. Tonight, my son, could very well be the night.

The pizza had been eaten, the salad had been moved around the plate and left, half the water and all the wine had been drunk. The conversation was largely irrelevant, for both of them knew where this was leading. Josie tried to pretend this was innocent, but Joe had left the table to go to the bathroom, and watching him walk back into the room Josie knew that, dangerous as it undoubtedly was, dangerous as *he* undoubtedly was, she would be sleeping with him.

Soon.

There was a lull in the conversation just as they finished the second bottle of wine. Joe leaned his chin in his hand, gazing at Josie. His eyes clouded over with lust as her stomach did somersaults.

"I probably shouldn't say this," he said, his voice low and slow, the smile leaving his face for the first time that evening, "and I know you probably won't believe me, but the only thing I've been thinking of all evening is taking you to bed and fucking you."

"I know." The words were out before Josie even had a chance to think about them. "Are you coming back to my place?"

Wordlessly they paid the bill and left, and as soon as they were out on the deserted city street they stood and looked at each other and within seconds were kissing furiously, Joe's hands everywhere, Josie biting at his lips, wanting him inside her now.

Josie lay in Joe's arms in the back of the cab, eyes closed, savoring every sensation as he traced his fingers along her thigh, gasping softly as they slid beneath her skirt, over the lace of her stocking, and finally, finally, on to bare flesh. (Thank God, she thought, I put stockings on this morning and not tights. Thank God I'm wearing new underwear. Thank God my legs were waxed only last week.)

Higher, she held her breath in anticipation, lust screaming through her body as she waited for him to hit the spot. Higher. Higher. And his fingers gently brushing the outside of her panties, so softly she might almost have imagined it, then harder, then disappearing back down her thigh, teasing down to her knee. Josie sighed as she turned her head to meet Joe's tongue.

No going back now.

Up the stairs and into her flat, the door barely closed before they kiss again, laughing softly at the intensity, then serious as Joe grinds his painfully stiff cock against her.

Walking clumsily, still kissing, into the bedroom, falling onto the bed, tongues and fingers and mouths everywhere, feeling, tasting, sucking, lapping. Whispering, sighing, increased urgency, bodies sliding over bodies, over and over.

And finally relief as Joe lies back, hands on Josie's naked hips, lips on hard nipples, her breasts as full and firm as he had imagined, sliding into her, a gasp from both at the forgotten and forbidden pleasure.

Joe watching Josie as she rides him, eyes closed, biting her lip and gasping as he thrusts deeper, quicker. Reaching fingers down to stroke her as he thrusts, enjoying her smile of surprise, her pleasure, her body stiffening, contracting as she comes, giving up to his own orgasm immediately after.

Lying in bed smiling at one another. Joe tracing her lips with his fingers, watching her taste herself as she takes his fingers into her mouth. Kissing gently, stroking hair, whispering.

"That was amazing." Joe smiles, tracing her hair behind her ear.

"I bet you say that to all the girls."

"I do, but I rarely mean it. This was incredible." He kisses her. He means it. "*You* are incredible."

"It was, wasn't it?" Josie smiles like the cat that got the cream, feels like the cat that got the cream, had forgotten how satisfying it is to *be* the cat that gets the cream.

Joe stretches and rolls over to look at the clock. "Fuck," he hisses.

"Your wife?"

He rolls back and kisses Josie again. "I wish I could stay."

"It's past midnight," she says. "You should go."

"This won't be the end of it." He leans over to kiss her again. "God, you're incredible. Tomorrow?"

Josie laughs softly. "Tomorrow's Saturday."

"And? Tomorrow afternoon? What are you doing?"

Josie wants to say she's busy. She wants to say she won't be available, this was just a one-off and she's not the sort of girl who gets involved with married men, but she doesn't.

"Tomorrow afternoon?" She lies back as Joe starts to stroke an already stiffening nipple again. "I'll be lying here waiting for you to fuck me."

"Oh God," Joe groans, climbing back onto the bed. "I can't leave you alone."

10

"I can't stand it anymore." Alice's throat almost closes, choked up with the tears that so far she's managed to contain. "I don't know why I ever bloody got married, I never see him, and I didn't think I'd ever say this, but I swear to God I can't see the point in carrying on."

Emily sits next to her on the sofa and puts her arm around Alice's shoulders, squeezing gently, not knowing what to say, waiting for Alice to cry and wanting to let her know that she will be there for her.

Alice looks up at Emily. "Imagine if you never saw Harry. You wouldn't put up with it, would you?"

Emily shrugs.

"You wouldn't. I know you wouldn't. I don't know anyone who would. Except stupid old Alice."

"You're not stupid old Alice. You're lovely Alice and it's just a phase. You've been through it before, you'll come through it, you always do."

"Oh God, Emily. I just can't stand it. I think he's having an affair."

Time stands still.

Minutes go by as the color drains out of both their faces.

"Do you really think he's having an affair?" Emily speaks slowly, cautiously, unable to believe that Alice has finally, after all these years, said what she and everyone else have always suspected.

"Yes. No." Alice sighs. "Oh God, I don't know. I mean, on one hand, I don't think he'd do that to me, he knows I'd just leave, but on the other . . ." She sinks her head into her hands then looks up at Emily again. "If someone were telling me about my life, I'd think he was having an affair. For the last three months he's hardly ever been at home before ten p.m. He says he's always in meetings and never answers his mobile when I call. He goes off on business trips without telling me where he's staying, I just have to wait for him to call, and we haven't had sex for three months."

"Are you serious?" Emily cannot hide her shock. "Three months? What's his excuse?"

"He says he's just exhausted, and when he's working this hard the last thing on his mind is sex."

"Is that true?"

"Well, when we've gone through this before and he's been working this hard he's gone off sex, but now I'm wondering whether every time he says he's been working hard he's actually been having an affair. Oh God." Alice stands up clutching her chest, a hot flush suddenly enveloping her, a sweat breaking out on her forehead. "I think I'm going to be sick."

Five minutes later Alice returns from the bathroom, pale and subdued, the sweat washed from her face.

Emily is in the kitchen making tea. She brings it in and watches as Alice gratefully sips the hot, sweet liquid.

"Ali, have you talked to him about it?" she says gently.

"Of course. He just says I'm being ridiculous. I'm so lonely, Emily." Alice finally lets go as the tears start to roll down her face. "I just don't know what on earth I'm supposed to do."

Alice had tried to talk to Joe about it just three days ago. Three months is a long time to go without sex, to go without any warmth or intimacy of any kind when you love your husband and want to be with him, and Alice had thought that perhaps she wasn't making enough of an effort. Perhaps if she looked fantastically sexy and seduced him, she would be able to win him back from whatever had removed him from their marriage.

Alice has tried this before, when Joe has been distant in the past. Has bought the underwear, tried to ply him with wine, and even though it has never worked, she has renewed vigor this time.

And so she waits up for Joe in a lacy negligée. And waits. And waits. At six minutes past midnight, when she hears the front door open, Alice is so tired all she wants to do is sleep, but she has come this far, she will see it through.

She expects Joe to come straight to bed. After all, it is late, and he has been working, but when he hasn't appeared twenty minutes later, she pads downstairs to see what he is doing.

No sign of him in the living room, or the kitchen. She hears the murmur of low voices coming from his study, and immediately her heart starts beating faster, the nausea starts to rise in her chest.

She wants to stand outside the door and listen, have the proof she finally needs, but she can't. She doesn't want to catch him having a seedy affair, doesn't want to hear incontrovertible evidence, wants instead for Joe to reassure her, to tell her that everything's fine.

She hears low laughter, and pushes open the door, loudly, so he knows she's there. She's heard enough to be suspicious, but couldn't bear hearing enough to condemn him.

Joe turns around instantly, fear in his eyes.

"What are you doing up?" he says, trying to sound as normal as possible, still holding the phone.

"What are *you* doing?" Alice hisses, pointing at the phone. "Who are you talking to? Are you having an affair?"

"I'll have to phone you tomorrow," Joe says into the phone, his voice now loud, professional, businesslike. "Don't do anything with the fairness opinion until then."

"Will do," Josie laughs huskily. "Naughty boy, nearly being caught. See you tomorrow." And she blows a kiss down the phone as she puts it down.

"Yup," Joe says into the receiver, now talking to the dial tone, stalling for time.

"Yup, we'll talk about the valuation to-morrow. I'm sorry, but I really have to go." He turns around to Alice, who falters nervously, now starting to doubt herself. Did she really hear soft laughter as she stood outside the door? Did she really hear the soft murmur of conversation, the tone of voice that sounded like he was talking to a woman, a lover?

"What the *fuck* are you doing?" The fear has been replaced with anger. Joe has pulled it off, knows he has pulled it off, and is now furious and defensive, with the righteousness of the guilty who knows he is walking free. "How dare you," he continues, "how dare you walk into my office when I am on the phone to a client in Japan, and accuse me, within earshot, of having an affair."

Alice hates raised voices. Hates arguments. Her first inclination is always to back down and run, and sure enough, she starts to apologize.

"I'm sorry," she says. "I thought you were . . . you sounded like you were . . ."

"*What?*" he spits. "I sounded like I was *what?* You mean you were standing outside listening to my conversation?" For a second the fear is back, but no, she couldn't possibly have heard or she would have known, she wouldn't be backing down so quickly.

Josie is turning out to be somehow different from the others. They have been sleeping together for three months, three months during which Joe has found that unlike all of the other women with whom he has had affairs, he is not the one in control.

Frightening and unbelievably exhilarating, Josie has become like a class A drug for him. The more he sees her the more he wants to see her, and the more he wants to see her the more control she seems to have over him.

For a while he was worried he might have fallen in love with her. Worried because the very last thing he wants to do is hurt Alice, and worried because he knows he couldn't handle a woman like Josie full time. Now he thinks it's not love, merely an obsession that will, eventually, work its way out of his system.

Joe has had these obsessions before, but usually, as soon as the woman starts making demands, starts falling for Joe emotionally, he switches off and moves on to the next challenge.

But Josie is still a challenge. She finds

him amusing. The lines that have worked so well on the others only arouse laughter, and scorn, in Josie.

He finds her toughness, her unwillingness to do whatever he wants, intoxicating, and has, like tonight, started to take more risks.

He left her only forty minutes ago, but he thought of her all the way home, and had to have one last phone call with her before going to bed. Alice, who would, if she possibly could, be in bed by eight-thirty every night, was not supposed to be up.

Oh God, he came close. He looks at Alice, standing there in a negligée he hasn't seen before, and thanks God he got away with it again. This was close. Too close. However addictive he finds Josie, he does not want his marriage to end, and he knows that had Alice heard what he had been saying to Josie, heard him tell Josie that he wanted to take her to the country, to a hotel with a four-poster bed, to tie her up, legs spread wide as he does whatever he wants, his marriage would be over.

"Well?" he repeats, anger and just a hint of fear flashing in his eyes. "What did you hear? What did you think you heard?"

"I . . . nothing. It was just the tone of

your voice, it didn't sound like a business call."

"I don't know what you're talking about." Joe stands up, pushing past Alice. "I've had a long day, I'm exhausted, and I come home to find my wife standing here making ridiculous accusations. Do you have any idea how hard I'm actually working right now? Do you have any idea how busy I am, how exhausted I am by the time I come home?"

"I'm sorry," Alice says meekly.

"Well, it's a bit late for sorry." Joe is on a roll now. "The last thing I need is for my wife to make ridiculous accusations about affairs when I get home at" — he looks at his watch — "gone midnight."

"But, Joe." Alice tries to find the words to express herself, not wanting to give up this easily, wanting to have a conversation about her fears, wanting to be reassured. "We haven't made love for three months. You go away all the time and don't leave me a contact number, and you're never at home. You have to admit it's suspicious."

"So you really think I'm having an affair?"

"No . . . I don't know." Alice sighs. "I suppose I don't really think it, I don't really think you'd do that to me, but when you don't seem to want me anymore I don't know what to think."

"Oh, darling." Joe's won. He can placate her now. He walks up to her and puts his arms around her, hugging her tight. "Of course I'm not having an affair. I love you. You're my little chicken, no one else."

Alice smiles with relief, sinks into his arms. "I love you too." She sighs, nuzzling his neck.

Joe smiles into her hair. "I love you more."

"I love *you* more."

"I know." Alice's nuzzling becomes more insistent, she moves around and kisses his mouth. Joe kisses her in return, but as her lips start to open, he pulls back and squeezes her tightly before turning away. "It's very late," he says, taking her hand and pulling her out of the study. "Bed-time."

Alice slides over to Joe's side of the bed and snuggles into his back. Joe keeps his breathing as still as possible. He loves her, but he doesn't want to make love to her. Doesn't want to make love to anyone right now other than Josie, and even that isn't really making love but fucking.

" 'Night," he mumbles, as if already

asleep. Alice strokes his back for a few moments in a halfhearted attempt to arouse him, but eventually she gives up and moves back to her side of the bed.

"So if you didn't think he was having an affair the other night," Emily ventures once Alice has told her the story, "what makes you think he's having an affair now?"

"I know it sounds crazy, but when he's there, reassuring me, I know with absolute certainty that I'm being ridiculous. But when he's gone, or phoning me yet again to tell me he'll be home late, my mind starts working overtime and I convince myself he's got someone else. And you know the worst thing of all? The worst thing of all is that I'm thirty-five years old and I want to start having children, and how the hell am I supposed to get pregnant when my husband doesn't sleep with me?"

"You mean Joe's finally agreed to children?"

Alice snorts. "Don't be ridiculous. My husband's never at home anymore to even discuss it. But time's running out, Em. I'm ready, God, I've been ready for years, and who even knows if I can get pregnant? It might take ages, and if we don't start soon it will be too late."

"And how can you get pregnant when your husband's not sleeping with you?"

"Exactly. I tell you, I've even fantasized about going to a sperm clinic."

"You haven't!"

"Yes, but I wouldn't. I want to have a child with my husband, not a test tube. I can't believe I even entertained the fantasy."

"I'll tell you what's really sad. My fantasy involves handcuffs, silk scarves, and three big burly men who each have a master's degree in sex. Yours involves a test tube of sperm."

Alice chokes on her tea. "Three? Three men? Are you serious?"

Emily blushes and shrugs. "Was that oversharing?"

"Just a touch. So go on, tell me more. Where do you meet these three men?"

"Uh-uh. I'm not giving you any more information until you tell me your fantasy."

"Okay. My fantasy is a thatched cottage . . ."

"Oh, shut up!" Emily hits Alice, who dissolves into giggles. "Your sexual fantasy. Come on. I've told you mine, now you tell me yours."

"Not until I've had further information

about the three big burly men. Is one of them Harry?"

Emily shakes her head firmly. "Absolutely not. Fantasies should never involve the men you love, not when they're this decadent."

"Oooh, this is getting better and better. Go on then, tell me more."

Half an hour of giggling later, Emily leans over and strokes Humphrey's head. Humphrey closes his eyes in bliss and immediately rolls over, offering Emily his rather fat stomach, which she rubs while laughing. "You're such a big baby, Humphrey. You know what, Ali, if you're not going to have a baby just yet, you need someone else."

"What?" Alice looks up in shock. "I don't want anyone else. What are you talking about?"

"I'm talking about someone like a Humphrey."

"A what?"

"A dog. If you're that lonely, why don't you get a dog?"

"Because Joe hates animals. I'd love a dog."

"Well, that's tough on Joe. Tell him that either he has to spend more time at home, or you're getting a dog to keep you company."

"I don't think he'll buy it. Look what happened to Molly and Paolo."

"But it's worth a try. All men hate cats, but dogs are different, and what harm can it do to try? One of the girls in the training class has a gorgeous Westie that's just had puppies, and she's looking for homes."

"Oh, cute! I love Westies."

"Well, the puppies aren't purebred. Actually the dog was pregnant when she rescued her, so God knows what the puppies will be, but they're incredibly cute."

"My luck the puppies will be half Westie, half Rottweiler."

Emily laughs. "At least it will be a good guard dog. And it would be amazing, you could join the training class. Oh go on, get a dog. Please!"

Alice has brightened up considerably at the prospect. "Well," she says finally, "you've definitely got a point, and it's definitely worth a try. If my husband ever comes home at a reasonable hour again, I promise to broach the subject."

A week later Snoop came home. Of course Joe protested, but Alice had been practicing her argument, and really he didn't have a leg to stand on.

Alice was deliriously happy to finally have someone on whom to lavish love and attention, someone who would love her unconditionally, would want to be with her all the time.

She had already started the dog-training class, and, thanks to Harry's relationship with Emily, was already getting special treatment. If she had any questions or wanted help with anything, Harry had said she could call him any time.

Owning Snoop was opening up a whole new world for Alice. She could turn down invitations with the excuse that she had a new puppy and couldn't leave him alone, or if restaurants wouldn't take Snoop she was sorry but she'd have to decline kind invitations to lunch.

She walked Snoop at least five times a day around their neighborhood, suddenly noticing how many other people had dogs, and stopping to talk to all the other dog owners.

The neighborhood consensus on the other half of Snoop was beagle or basset. An odd combination, certainly, but one that might explain the large brown splotches all over what otherwise looked very like a West Highland terrier.

It was a world that Alice discovered she loved, and even though Joe wasn't around any more than he had been in the past few months, was still distant and detached, Alice found she didn't care nearly as much. Now she had something other than Joe to think about, and it suited her perfectly.

Even Joe started to think Snoop was rather a good idea. He was turning out to be the perfect excuse for a late-night walk and a late-night phone call to Josie. And, given that Joe had no Joe Junior, the perfect alibi for a weekend rendezvous.

"You have a lie in," he'd say to Alice, kissing her as he stood at the foot of the bed in jeans and a baseball cap. "I'm just going to take Snoop to Hyde Park for a long walk." Alice would snuggle back under the duvet with a smile. Who would have thought that Joe would be this smitten with a dog? And if he was this good with Snoop, just imagine what he'd be like with children. Surely they'd be able to start trying for a baby soon.

And Snoop was quite happy. There wasn't an awful lot for him to do in Josie's living room, so he'd pee merrily in the corner while he waited for Joe to emerge from behind the closed bedroom door.

⭐ ⭐ ⭐

"No, Joe, don't be ridiculous." Josie shivers as Joe runs an experienced hand up her inner thigh. "Not in the office."

"And why not?" Joe murmurs. "Eight o'clock on a Friday night, just who exactly do you think is around?"

Josie is silent. He has a point. The trading floor is always deserted by, at the very latest, six on a Friday. She stops to listen, then gets up and looks outside the door. He's right. It's deserted.

"Leave the door open," Joe grins, enjoying the thrill, as he leans back against the conference table in the meeting room at the end of the corridor. "And come here."

Josie leans against the doorjamb in the doorway. "Don't tell me what to do." She raises an eyebrow as she surveys the rise in his trousers. "And if you're serious, unzip your trousers now."

Joe unzips them and raises an eyebrow as Josie walks over to him with a smile, bending down to kiss him as she slips a hand through the zip and Joe moans.

11

"This is Steven from Human Resources. We'd like to have a meeting with you. Could you make it up here for six this evening?"

Shit. No. Six this evening Joe is planning on going straight back to Josie's flat for a couple of hours before the opening of a new restaurant he'll be going to later that evening with Alice.

"Actually six isn't a good time, and Steven, can I ask what this is about?"

"We want to discuss some career options with you. How does five sound?"

Joe sighs. Career options. What the hell does that mean? Whatever it's about it sounds like it's going to be a long one. Still, he should be out of here by six. That would be fine.

"Okay. Five sounds fine."

"Great. We'll see you up here on our floor at five."

Joe intranets a message over to Josie's computer, careful not to use any provocative language, to keep things as professional as possible just in case it's overseen. "Meeting with HR at five. Should be over by next meeting at six. Wait here if it overruns." He picks up the phone to call Alice, tells her he'll see her at the restaurant at seven-thirty.

Steven Webster is sitting with his back to the window, Jacqueline Astley, the head of European Human Resources, on his left. At the head of the table is Richard Nilsson, global head of Investment Banking, and Joe's boss.

Joe was prepared for Steven Webster, a man he knows and likes. The man, in fact, who originally recruited him for the job. He's not prepared for Jacqueline Astley, and nor is he prepared for his boss. This doesn't look good, and as he sits down he remembers the door clicking quietly shut when he and Josie were fucking on the desk in the conference room late last Friday night.

They had stopped abruptly, fear instantly replacing the passion, but by the time he had pulled his trousers up and run to the door, checking the dealing room outside and the corridor, there was no one there.

"Fuck," he hissed. "Do you think someone saw us?"

Josie was white. This was the last thing she needed. Shit. Why did she ever take this risk?

"There's no one there," Joe said. "Maybe it was the wind."

"Maybe," Josie said hopefully. "Or maybe we just imagined it."

But now, seeing the serious expressions on everyone's faces, Joe starts to feel rather sick. Maybe they hadn't imagined it after all.

"Thanks for coming, Joe," Steven says. "Take a seat. You know everyone here?" Joe nods as Steven gestures to the empty chair and offers him coffee, which Joe declines.

"Do you know why we asked you up here?" Jacqueline leans forward and looks Joe square in the eyes.

He shrugs. "Steven said career options."

"Joe, this isn't easy for us," she says after a pause. "In fact this is probably the hardest part of my job, but it's come to our attention that you are involved with a work colleague, and I'm afraid you know the rules about that."

Joe blusters, becomes defensive in humiliation. "Frankly, Jacqueline, I don't think that's any of your business."

"I'm afraid it is our business, Joe," she says gently. "When you become involved with a work colleague it involves everyone you work with, including the people who may or may not walk in on you in a meeting room." She looks at him pointedly and Joe looks away. There's nothing he can say.

"We've discussed the various options, and the one thing we all agree on is that you are too valuable to us to let you go. Doubtless you also know, possibly better than most, why we brought Josie Mitchell to the team, and we would also be extremely reluctant to lose her."

"So where is this going?"

"Do you know Simon Barnes?"

"Vaguely. He's in the States, isn't he?"

"Not for much longer. He's coming back to London to head up the Investor Client Group. I can't express enough how under normal circumstances this would result in instant dismissal. However, because of the revenue you have brought in and your importance to the firm, we would like to send you out to the States on a three-year contract as his replacement."

Richard chooses this moment to interject. "Joe, all things considered, I think it's an extremely generous offer, not to mention an interesting move for you, and one that may in fact work out very well for you. We feel you've accomplished great things in Europe, and I, for one, will be sorry to see you leave the team, but we'd like you to change your focus away from banking and toward capital markets. We want you to head up the Americas Issuer Client Group, to look at bringing in some serious new issue and derivatives business in the Americas, including South America."

"No." Joe shakes his head. "I'm sorry, but my life is here. I'm extremely unhappy about this, not to mention humiliated at the way you've chosen to deal with it. I accept what you say about relationships at work, and I would be more than happy to terminate my friendship with Josie Mitchell, but a move to America is not acceptable to me. I've brought in nineteen million dollars already this year, and I'm extremely happy in my position. I feel there's still far more revenue I can bring in, and I'd like to be given a second chance."

Joe speaks with a confidence and an assurance he doesn't feel, but it's the only way he can mask his deep humiliation and shock. It's one thing to have an affair, but quite another to be caught.

Of course relocation isn't a possibility. His home is here, his wife, his life. He has no intention of moving anywhere, and his only regret is that he may have to give up Josie. Either that or be far more careful in the future. It's his own bloody fault, he berates himself. Josie was right, what was he thinking of, having sex in the office? They were bound to get caught, and he can't believe, sitting here, that he could ever have found that prospect the slightest bit exciting.

And more to the point, what can he possibly tell Alice?

"We are fully aware of the amount of revenue you've brought in," Richard says firmly. "Which is why we believe you're the right person to take over from Simon Barnes. We need someone dynamic and motivated to take the team forward."

"I appreciate what you're saying, Richard, and I'm flattered that you think that. However, I have to reiterate that I would be extremely unwilling to relocate. Quite apart from anything else, you're aware that I'm working with two continental drug companies at the moment, and it looks like the combined deals will bring in an additional twenty million."

"We know, and we're very pleased with the relationships you've built up on the continent, and not to repeat myself that's exactly why we want to send you to America."

Jacqueline speaks quietly and authoritatively. "Joe," she says. "I'm afraid you have no choice."

"Ah." Joe leans back in his chair and exhales. Shit. What is he going to say to Alice?

"And may I ask the time frame of this decision that it appears I have no control over?"

"We'd like you to take the remainder of this week to organize everything. We are aware that you will have things to take care of, but we would like you to start in the Manhattan offices on the ninth of July."

"But that's in a week and a half! You have to be joking!" Joe gasps.

"I'm afraid not."

"How am I supposed to organize everything in less than two weeks?"

"HR will do everything we can to assist

you. We know you're . . ." Jacqueline tries to suppress her distaste at this situation with a cough ". . . married. The firm will provide roughly two months' accommodation in a hotel — you already know the Godfrey-approved hotels — and we'll arrange for someone to help your wife organize everything at this end, including the packing, naturally. We would suggest you arrange for your wife to join you as soon as possible to start looking for a home. Gayle Messler is our preferred relocation agent, and she's expecting your call. You will naturally get the full expat allowance for three years." Jacqueline pauses and checks her watch. "I'm afraid I'm expected at another meeting. Steven will be able to answer any questions that you have. Thank you for your time, Joe, and good luck." She shakes Joe's hand, while he remains speechless in shock.

Richard stands up as well. "I'll call you at home later," he says. "We'll talk about it then." And he too disappears out of the door.

Joe takes the lift back down to his floor, still in shock, but armed with a sheaf of papers Steven has given him. There is his formal job description, details of his new, increased salary, his monthly housing allowance, healthcare insurance, various other minor benefits, and the contact numbers for the relocation agent.

He sees Josie sitting at her desk, and as soon as he sits down a message appears on his screen. "Ready?"

"Something's come up. Will have to go home. Meet me at the café in five."

"I don't fucking believe it!" Josie's in a fury. "What business is it of theirs what we do? How dare they relocate you, and how dare they not involve me in this?"

Joe sighs and puts a hand on her arm to placate her. "Josie, it's so much better this way. I agree, it stinks, but it's much better you don't get involved. I have to go, I don't have much choice."

Josie sits and thinks for a while. "You do have a choice, you know. You could always get another job."

"I know. I've thought about that. But I don't want to have to start proving myself all over again. I've established a good reputation here, and my bonus is virtually guaranteed. Even though the last thing I want to do is leave the country, and leave you, I have to."

Josie doesn't say anything for a while. She tries to digest what Joe is telling her, tries not to let her true feelings show on her face. She thought she could handle this, thought that Joe would be just an affair that wouldn't mean anything, but now, sitting in front of him, hearing that he's leaving, she knows she's been fooling herself all along.

She had never planned on falling for him. God, she of all people was cynical enough to know what happens when you get involved with married men, but the longer she continues seeing him, the more involved she feels.

The only person who knew, up until — she thinks with horror — last Friday, was Al. And Al had been warning her for months, had told her that not only was it unbelievably dangerous to get involved with a colleague, but this was a colleague who was married.

"This is going to end in tears," he said repeatedly, when she first entrusted him with the information. "I don't like the sound of this at all."

After a few weeks she had stopped mentioning Joe, and Al stopped asking. The friendship they had didn't really allow for relationships, and certainly not ones of which one of them disapproved.

Plus Josie was becoming aware that she didn't want this to end. That the more she saw Joe, the more she wanted to see him. That she had started thinking about him when she wasn't with him, that every time he swung his legs out of bed to go back to his wife she started to feel slightly sick inside.

Most of all, Josie had started to think about Alice. She knew Joe wasn't happy, and half entertained the fantasy that he would eventually leave Alice, would move into Josie's apartment, and live happily ever after.

She had started to hate Alice. Alice who seemed so irrelevant in the beginning, who had nothing to do with Josie, with the relationship she had with Joe. And yet over the last few months Alice had grown into this mythical, hateful figure, this Medusa who had cast a spell over Joe, a spell that always brought him running back home.

She was careful never to say anything to Joe, and hated herself for even entertaining the thought that he and Alice might break up, for being that much of a cliché. The more she got to know Joe, the more she could see that the minute she stopped being a challenge, the minute she became the slightest bit needy, or demanding, he would be bored and would move on.

And so, even as she was falling for him, she made herself as unobtainable and interesting as possible. Of course it was hard, particularly when she wanted to see him all the time, and it wasn't so much that she was physically unobtainable — when Joe wanted to see her she almost always said yes — but that she was emotionally unobtainable, impenetrable. She kept Joe guessing, knowing that was the only way to hold his interest.

It had worked, thus far. And now here he is, sitting opposite her at Ponti's near Liverpool Street Station, telling her he's moving to another country and she may never see him again.

Immediately a vision of her life as it was before she met Joe flashes into her mind. The ready-cooked microwaveable meals, the bottles of wine she drank on her own, the mindless television she'd watch in bed before falling asleep knowing that the next day, and the day after, and all the days stretching ahead of that would be exactly the same.

Nothing to look forward to, nothing to dream about, nothing to grow excited about or plan for, only the monotony of work, eating, and sleeping. A monotony broken only by the occasional nights out with Al, which, while pleasant, were hardly anything to look forward to.

Joe has given her something to look forward to. She would never be as dramatic as to say that Joe had given her a reason for living, but he had certainly made her life more interesting, had provided her with hours of colorful fantasy, not to mention hours of colorful reality.

Al would say there would be other Joes, preferably available ones, ones who might actually have long-term prospects, but Josie knows this wasn't necessarily the case. She knows because it had been eighteen months before Joe, and she knows because there was nobody else in whom she had the slightest interest.

The other thing she knows is that however hard it is to hear that Joe is going away, however much she dreads him leaving, however hard she may have fallen for him, she is not going to let him know.

"So when are you going?" she says finally, a false brightness in her voice.

"A week and a half. They've given me next week off to sort things out." Joe sighs again and runs his fingers through his hair, reaching across the table to take Josie's hand. He looks down at her fingers as he entwines them through his own, rubbing her hand gently with his thumb. "I'm going to miss you, Jose," he whispers, not raising his eyes from their hands.

Josie's heart skips. She remains silent.

"What am I going to do without you?" he says.

"You'll find another Josie," she says, with a smile masking her true feelings.

"Josie! How can you even say that?" He withdraws his hand in genuine hurt, but Josie merely shrugs.

"Joe, you and I both knew this wasn't going to last. You're married, for God's sake. It's a miracle we've even managed to survive this long. You love your wife, you're not going to leave her, and you need to be with her." Even as she says this she's praying Joe will refute it, will tell her that she's wrong, that he's realized he is now in love with her and is planning on leaving his wife.

But there is silence as Joe listens to what Josie is saying. "I'll still miss you," he says. "The past few months have been, well, wonderful. Really. *You're* wonderful. And you deserve someone incredibly special, someone who will be able to take care of you properly."

"Someone who isn't married," Josie says, unable to keep the bitterness out of her voice, for what he has just said is tantamount to him saying, "It's over. I don't want you anymore."

"Yes," Joe says gently, surprised that she seems genuinely hurt. "Someone who isn't married. At risk of saying something incredibly clichéd, you really do deserve someone better than me. I wish I'd met you years ago. I wish you and I could be together, but now it's too late. Maybe this is the best thing that can happen. Maybe this is God's way of saying I need to commit to my marriage, need to stop looking outside it for things to make me happy."

"So is this it?"

"What do you mean?"

"Will I see you again before you go?"

Joe looks shocked. "God, of course! I mean, I have to go home now, I have to tell Alice. Shit, what the hell am I going to tell Alice? Oh God. Anyway, I'm at home the rest of the week, maybe we can have lunch or something?"

Lunch. He really didn't have to say anything more.

"Joe." She takes a deep breath and smiles sadly. "I think maybe it's better if

201

we say good-bye now. You're going to have so much to do, and I'll be at work, and it's easier if we stop pretending that we're going to have a final fling before you leave. This is the right time to say good-bye."

They gather their things and walk outside, standing on the pavement for a few minutes as each of them tries to think of the right way to say it.

Eventually they look up and catch each other's eye, and within a split second they are hugging tightly.

"Thank you," Joe whispers into Josie's ear as she blinks her eyes furiously over his shoulder, trying to get rid of the tears. "You're an amazing woman. I'll miss you."

"Go on." She disengages herself, looking at the pavement so he doesn't see her eyes brimming. "Take care." And she turns on her heel and walks off down the street, a tear slowly making its way down her left cheek.

Joe stands and watches until she disappears around the corner. This doesn't feel real. Nothing about this afternoon feels real. How is it possible that he is standing here, in the City, in London, about to go home to his house in Belgravia, and next week his entire world will have changed?

He pulls his mobile phone out of his

pocket and clips the earpiece on to the lapel of his jacket as he sets off to the tube station. The machine picks up, and Joe takes a deep breath. "Hi, darling. Good news, the meeting has been canceled so I'm on my way home. And, Ali, there's something we need to talk about when I get home. Make sure you're there."

"What? I don't understand. Tell me again?"

Joe starts at the beginning again. Simon Barnes is transferring to London and they need a replacement, and Joe has been asked to move over to America to fill the position.

"But that's ridiculous," Alice keeps saying. "They can't expect us to pack up and leave in less than two weeks. And why is this happening so quickly? Don't you have a choice? Couldn't you say no?"

Joe is silent, guilty and uncomfortable. He can barely look her in the eye.

"Joe? I can't just walk away from my life here. We have nowhere to live there, and how am I supposed to get everything done by myself? It's just ridiculous. Plus I don't want to live in New York. God, London's bad enough, but at least I have a few friends here. I want you to say no,

Joe. I don't want to go."

"I can't say no. I've already said yes. And *I* have to go in less than two weeks. You're not expected to join me until you're packed up here, and they're organizing for someone to help you move. You don't have to come until you're ready."

"Oh, great. Well, that makes it so much better. And what do you mean, you *have* to go? Do you mean you've said yes without speaking to me? Thanks, Joe, thanks a lot." Alice starts shouting before taking a deep breath. "Tell them you've changed your mind."

Joe shakes his head. He doesn't know how to explain there is no going back, he can't get out of this. New York. Something shifts in his head. A way forward. A way to make Alice happy.

"We don't necessarily have to live in Manhattan," he says.

"What do you mean?"

"They're offering me a huge monthly housing allowance. We could get an apartment in Manhattan and a place in the country." He sees the spark of interest in Alice's eye. "Maybe Vermont, or Connecticut somewhere. Go out there every weekend. Maybe somewhere on a lake or by the beach."

Alice doesn't say anything for a while. Connecticut. The country. What she's always wanted. "You're not just saying that to make me say yes?"

"Of course not. Alice, darling." He puts his arms around her and hugs her. "Think about it. This could be the fresh start we need. I know you don't want to live in Manhattan, but you've always wanted to live in the country and we really could afford it. I think we'll be happy there. I think *you'll* be happy there."

"I don't know," she mumbles, pictures of a Vermont farmhouse flashing through her mind. "Maybe I'd be willing to try it for a while. A fresh start. Maybe you're right."

"Of course I'm right," Joe says, thinking suddenly that perhaps he is. Perhaps this *is* what they need, a fresh start in a new country. No more affairs, no more messing around. Time to fall in love with one another all over again. He pushes the memory of Josie out of his head, and determines to make a go of it this time.

"I love you," Alice says, eyes filled with a mixture of apprehension, hope, and happiness.

"I know, darling. I love you too." He puts his arms around her and hugs her close. It's been a while since they hugged like this. The feel of her, the smell of her is so familiar. He breathes in deeply and kisses her neck, moves around to find her mouth waiting for his.

They kiss softly and then he smiles, rubbing a hand down her back. "Let's go to bed."

12

"Can't we just live *here?*" Alice stretches out her arms as she lies diagonally on the huge bed and smiles lazily at Joe, a thick terry-cloth towel wrapped tightly around his waist as he wanders in from the bathroom.

"At the Mark? Now that really would be pushing it." Joe laughs, sitting on the edge of the bed and leaning over to give her a kiss. "Our housing allowance, my darling, is big, but it's not that big."

"But wouldn't this be perfect?" Alice gestures around the one-bedroom suite. "It has everything we need."

"Everything except a large country kitchen for you."

"That's okay. I can make do with that little kitchenette. I'll have my large country kitchen when we find our house in the country."

"Speaking of finding houses, or flats for that matter, we're meeting the relocation agent in about an hour, and then we've got lunch with Gina and George. Come on, lazybones, or we'll be late."

Alice hooks her arms around Joe's neck and pulls him closer, smiling lasciviously. "I don't mind being a tiny bit late."

"A tiny bit?" Joe kisses her softly as he unwraps his towel. "Or a big bit?"

Alice giggles as he rolls on top of her. "Rather a big bit is what I'd prefer."

Half an hour later Alice jumps into the shower, grinning all the while. It appears that Joe has been right about this being a fresh start for both of them. She has flown out every weekend for the past month, joining him at the Mark hotel, flying back to London during the week to sort out their house and the move, and every weekend she spends with Joe she feels more and more like a newlywed.

He hasn't been this attentive or affectionate in years. She takes the one o'clock British Airways flight on a Friday, arrives at JFK at around four in the afternoon, and is at the hotel by six. Joe will either be waiting for her in his suite or will arrive about twenty minutes later, and will throw his arms around her in a huge hug, clearly delighted to see her.

They are, much to her delight, making love again with an enthusiasm she hasn't felt for a very long time, and she knows that despite her initial reservations, New York really does seem to be the answer to her prayers.

The city is vibrant and buzzing, and far more friendly than she remembers. She strides along Madison Avenue feeling happy and energized, but just can't get excited about the prospect of living there.

"A great place to visit," she confides to Emily, "but I'd be exhausted if I had to live here all the time."

"So how's the hunt for the country house coming along?" Emily asks.

"Nothing yet. Joe wants to find somewhere in town first. As soon as we've found something here, we'll know how much money we'll have left over for a place in the country."

"Just remember, Harry and I have to be your first guests."

"Of course. So how is heavenly Harry?"

Emily laughs. "Heavenly."

"You sound so happy."

"I am. And so do you."

"I know. I am. Who would have thought it?"

"I miss you, Ali."

"But you saw me last Thursday."

"I know, but you're there now. For good. It's horrible that I can't just jump in the car and come over to see you."

"But you can pick up the phone whenever you want."

"I know," Emily grumbles. "But it's not the same."

"Couldn't you come over and live here too? You could come and live with me in the country."

"Because Joe would love that."

"Ah yes. Actually, he's being so lovely at the moment he'd probably agree to anything I asked."

"Quick, ask him if he'll give me a thousand quid for my birthday."

Alice laughs. "Come and see me soon, won't you, Em? Even if I don't find my country house, will you come and stay?"

"Of course. As soon as you're settled I'll be on the first plane."

Alice still can't believe that she is here. To stay. For good. It seems only yesterday that the removal firm came and spent three days packing the contents of their home, all except Joe's office, for he insisted on doing that himself.

Was it really a month ago that Foxtons had been to their house in London? Two rental agents had gone into paroxysms of delight over the "exquisite" Belgravia home and assured her it would be rented in no time.

Final bills had to be paid, the Royal Mail forwarding service organized, and hasty farewells had to be made. Nobody could believe they were going, and everybody wanted to say good-bye.

Those last few days were a whirlwind, and although people offered to throw a going-away party, the last thing Alice needed was to worry about saying good-bye to people she was secretly thrilled to be leaving behind.

They had to make do with phone calls, with everyone saying they couldn't believe they were just going, and they'd come and stay in the summer. "You must come," Alice would say brightly, hoping that she'd be able to make an excuse, that their promises to come were as empty as her promises to host.

Her only real sadness was in leaving Emily. Emily, who had come over every day and helped her pack, who had taken

Snoop out for walks while Alice had been on the phone, who had spent hours poring over the information the relocation agent in New York had supplied, oohing and aahing over the excitement of living in Manhattan.

The night before they flew, Emily insisted on having Alice over for dinner. At the end of a subdued evening, the sadness hung heavily in the air, and Alice and Emily hugged long and hard, both of them choking back tears. "You'd better e-mail every day," Emily squeezed. "Or I'll get on a plane and come over there and kill you." Alice laughed to hide her sadness and reached up to give Harry a hug.

"Make sure you find a good class for Snoop," he said. "I've already told him to look after you and make sure you're happy."

"We will be," she smiled. "And you make sure you look after Emily."

"Oh, I will." He put a protective arm around Emily's shoulders. "Don't you worry about that."

Alice and Joe step out of the elevator to see a smartly dressed middle-aged woman sitting on the bench in front of the reception desk.

"Is that her?" Alice whispers.

"Yup. Gayle, this is my wife, Alice. Alice, this is Gayle, our relocation agent."

"Oh, it's so good to meet you." The woman smiles brightly as she shakes Alice's hand. "Joe's told me so much about you."

"I'm very excited about seeing some apartments," Alice smiles back.

"That's great! I have a couple that your husband's already seen that he likes and wants you to see, and then there are three more that I'd like to show both of you."

"We've narrowed it down to the Upper East Side," Joe explains to Alice. "Sixtieth to Eightieth."

Gayle nods. "We started on the West Side as well, but we decided it was too young and busy, and downtown is out for obvious reasons. We toyed with Midtown, but as I've got to know Joe a little bit I can see that he'd definitely be happier on the East Side, and I'm sure you'd love it too."

"That's here, isn't it? Where the hotel is?"

"Yup. Prime Upper East Side neighborhood."

"Good. I love it around here. So where are these apartments?"

Gayle hands her a bundle of papers as

they turn the corner, past the Issey Miyake shop, onto Madison Avenue. "The first is a couple of blocks from here, Seventy-fifth and Park. It's a great apartment, lots of light, twentieth floor — so a great view too. Naturally it's a doorman building."

"They're all doorman buildings, aren't they?" Joe interrupts.

"Yes." She turns again to Alice, assuming, as with most of the couples she meets, that it is Alice she has to woo, Alice who will be making the final decision. "They're all desirable doorman buildings, which all of our other investment banker clients demand."

"Well, if it's good enough for the Joneses," Alice laughs.

"Excuse me?" Gayle doesn't get it.

"Nothing. Don't worry about it. What a beautiful day." Alice links her arm through Joe's and smiles at nothing in particular.

"Well, it's a bit of a change." Alice doesn't quite know what to say. She's come from a huge house in Belgravia, and a smallish apartment, even in a doorman building, isn't quite what she's used to.

Ugly modern windows look out onto what is, admittedly, a decent view, and the ceilings are high enough to give the illusion of space, but there are no features, no moldings, no character in the apartment at all.

Boxy rooms, a tiny kitchenette, and a second bedroom that's little more than a closet.

"It's a great address," Gayle says. "It's a lot smaller than some of the other apartments, but you're paying for this building, which is one of the best in the city."

"I'm not sure this is quite my thing," Alice says. "I think we'd probably kill one another in something this small."

Gayle laughs. "That's fine. The more we look the better idea I'll have of what you're looking for. Right. Let's head over to Second Avenue. I think you'll like that one much better."

Three apartments later, Alice is beginning to lose patience.

"Doesn't anyone have kitchens here?"

"The larger kitchens are mostly in the prewar buildings, and the only ones we have right now aren't doorman buildings. They do have an elevator man, but it's not nearly as prestigious, and I did show your husband but he said no."

"But they're all so, well . . . so ugly."

"Darling!" Joe is embarrassed, but of

course Gayle, used to forthright New Yorkers, doesn't bat an eyelid.

"You have to remember that New York is not London. You have to have different requirements here, unless you're prepared to compromise. Most of my clients would take anything in that first building we went to, no matter how small. It's address that counts here."

"I just don't understand it," Alice shrugs. "They're all so small."

"You'll get used to it," Gayle says. "I've relocated hundreds of people from Europe, and all of them end up loving it." She looks at her watch. "Let's go on to the next. I think you'll like it more. It's Seventy-third, between Lex and Park, and a really great apartment. It might be perfect for you."

"I like it." Joe walks around again, for the third time in the fifteen minutes they've spent in the apartment.

"Well, it's definitely the best we've seen," Alice agrees, walking over to the window and looking down onto Park.

"It's a great price, and a fabulous apartment. Actually, this is probably my favorite of all the ones on our books right now."

"So how long has it been on the market?" Joe calls from the master bedroom.

"Only around two weeks. I know another couple came to see it the other day who put in an initial offer which the owner turned down, and I believe they're about to put in another higher offer."

"Presumably their initial offer was below asking price?"

"I believe so. Not much, but I'm sure if you were to offer asking price they'd say yes. An apartment like this isn't going to stay around for too long. Why don't I wait in the other room and you can have a talk about it?"

"Thanks, Gayle," Joe smiles. "That would be great."

Joe perches next to Alice on the windowsill. "What do you think?"

"I don't know," Alice shrugs unhappily. "I can't say I love it, but I don't know anything about the real estate market here. I do know that I wouldn't even consider any of these flats if they were in London, but . . ."

". . . we're not in London."

"Exactly. But you like it, don't you?"

"I do. I think that second bedroom would make a perfect study for me, and I like the fact that there's a large entrance hall and a dining room as well. It has a good feel to it, and it's a great size. You have to admit even the kitchen's the biggest we've seen."

"I know. You're right. It's just so strange to go from a big house to a flat that's probably only a bit bigger than our very first flat. Remember our flat in Kensington?"

Joe smiles. "Yes, and remember how lovely and cozy it was?"

"That's true."

"And this is a good price." Joe looks at the details again. "It leaves us with enough to buy a really nice place in the country."

"Okay, done!" Alice laughs, as Joe puts his arm around her and squeezes.

"I told you I know the way to a woman's heart."

"Hopefully just this woman."

"Of course just this woman, my lovely wife."

Gayle walks back in. "Whoops." She laughs. "I hope I haven't caught you at an inopportune moment."

Joe stands up and laughs. "Not at all. We want to make an offer. This would suit us perfectly."

"Your husband tells me you're thinking of a place in the country as well?" Gayle has walked them back to the hotel and is telling them she'll phone the owner as soon as she's back in the office and put a formal offer in writing on the fax to him later that afternoon.

Alice nods.

"It's a wonderful idea. So many of my clients do that. Often the men stay over in the city during the week then join the wives out in the country on the weekends. It's wonderful to have that choice."

"I like being with Joe, though," Alice smiles. "I'd come into the city as well, I think."

"Of course! You'd have the best of both worlds. Where in the country are you thinking of?"

"Probably Connecticut. I haven't really investigated anything yet, but we'd like it to be somewhere near enough to enable Joe to commute if he needs to."

"Fairfield or Litchfield County would probably suit you perfectly. We have a few offices there. Why don't you visit our website and have a look at the towns? I can put you in touch with someone who could show you around."

For the first time that day Gayle sees Alice's face truly light up. "Really? Would you? That would be fantastic!"

"I wouldn't have thought you'd be a country girl," Gayle says in surprise, having assumed that Alice is exactly like all the other high-maintenance banking wives she is used to dealing with.

Joe shakes his head. "Underneath that sophisticated exterior my wife's really a secret chicken farmer."

"You know, alpaca farming's all the rage these days," Gayle says with a smile.

"Oh God. Don't even start." Joe shakes his head as Alice gives him a pleading look.

"Alpacas? Oh, go on, Joe, let me have alpacas."

"First you have to find a house, then maybe, just maybe, you can have a goldfish."

"Great. My husband the animal lover."

Gayle laughs.

"Anyway," Joe says, "Snoop would hate alpacas."

"Snoop?"

"Our dog," Alice explains. "He's staying with friends until we're settled, then we'll fly him over here."

"Alice's dog," Joe says firmly.

"But you love him too. Admit it. You do."

"I don't love him, but he is rather sweet."

"What about all those Saturday morning walks you used to take him on? Honestly!"

She turns to Gayle. "He'd go out for hours with Snoop every Saturday. And now he tries to pretend he doesn't like being with him."

Ah, yes. Those Saturday morning walks. Josie has thrown herself into work, anesthetized the pain with meetings and phone calls and clients, allowing herself to think about Joe, to dwell on her loneliness, only late at night while she's lying in bed, praying for sleep to come and take her away.

She had hoped to hear from Joe. Had thought perhaps he'd phone her, or send an e-mail, or something, but she hasn't heard a thing.

And Joe? Joe is trying his hardest to be the faithful husband. He is trying to be true to his word, to see America as a fresh start, to be the loving faithful husband he once promised to be.

During this last month when he's been largely by himself, he's allowed himself to look but not touch. And how could he not look when he's never seen such beautiful women in all his life? Everywhere he looks temptation is looking back at him, but he is determined to make it up to Alice, to stop the indiscretions for good.

"So I'll be in touch with you later this afternoon. I have your cell phone number, and hopefully I'll have some good news by the end of the day."

They say good-bye to Gayle and walk down to Annie's restaurant to meet Gina and George for lunch.

"You'll love them," Joe had said. He'd got to know George on a business trip a few months earlier, and had got in touch with him as soon as he was transferred to New York. They lived in a large old brownstone on Seventy-first and had invited Joe over for drinks as soon as he arrived. He hadn't met Gina before that evening, and had been impressed with her warmth and loveliness, knowing that Alice would feel the same way, that she and Gina would become friends.

"There they are," Joe pushes through the line of people waiting for tables as a couple stand up in a corner booth at the back and wave.

Joe shakes hands with George and kisses Gina, who turns to Alice and kisses her in turn. "We've been so looking forward to meeting you, Alice. Welcome to America. I'm so excited that you're here."

Joe is right. Alice takes to her immediately, and within minutes Joe and George are talking about business, and Alice is describing the apartment to Gina.

"It sounds great!" Gina is enthusiastic. "And you'd be so close to us! I have a great decorator if you need someone. Actually I have loads of great people, we'll have to get together, just us girls, with our address books. I have plumbers, painters, dog walkers."

"Dog walkers?"

"Yup." Gina laughs. "I've already heard about Snoop. You name it, I have it."

Alice merely smiles, wondering why on earth she would need a dog walker when she has a perfectly good pair of legs herself. And a decorator? What for?

Gina continues bubbling away. "Joe says you're going to be looking for a place in the country too."

Alice nods. "We just haven't decided where. I've been trying to persuade Joe to leave the city for a day so we can drive around Connecticut and get a feel for where we want to live, but he refuses to start looking until we've bought somewhere in the city."

"We have the cutest place in Connecticut," Gina says. "Just north of Highfield, and I'm there pretty much all the time in the summer. You should come up and I could drive you around, show you the towns. There are so many pretty places."

"I'd love to!"

"You know what? We're up there next weekend. Why don't you drive up on Saturday for the day? Come for lunch, both of you."

"What's this?" Joe stops talking, having caught the tail end of Gina's invitation, and looks up at them questioningly.

"Gina's inviting us to their country place next Saturday."

"Great! We'd love to come." Joe squints at Alice. "You're sure you're not cooking up some plan? We're not going to come back from our day in the country having bought a house?"

Gina laughs. "The only thing we'll be cooking is a barbecue."

"Uh-uh." George shakes his head. "You're not getting near my Viking. The barbecue is my job. You can do the salads."

Gina rolls her eyes. "Why, I'm so sorry. I forgot that barbecueing is men's work and the little women can only just manage to daintily tear up some lettuce. Salads indeed. It's a good job I love you."

"I know. I'm the luckiest man in the world."

Alice grins at both of them as she takes Joe's hand under the table, leaning back as the waiter arrives with their scrambled eggs and smoked salmon, toasted bagels, and French toast.

She squeezes Joe's hand and he turns to look at her, smiling as he sees how happy and relaxed she is.

"See," he whispers. "I said you'd like them."

"I know. You were right."

"Hey! No whispering at the table," Gina says.

Joe picks up his glass of orange juice and proposes a toast. "To new friends!"

"To new friends!" they echo, holding up glasses and coffee cups.

"And to new houses in the country," Gina laughs as Alice joins in.

"I'll second that." Alice smiles, and the men just raise their eyebrows and tuck into the food.

13

Alice is in charge of the map as Joe steers their hired car along the Merritt Parkway, Alice growing more and more relaxed as they drive out of the city, through Westchester, and then into Connecticut.

She strains to see through the thick trees that abound each side of the highway, hoping to catch a glimpse of picture-perfect houses, white picket fences, all the things she imagines Connecticut to be, but Joe's driving too fast, and in the end she gives up.

"So you really think they liked us?"

Joe sighs. Alice hasn't stopped talking about Gina and George, so excited at having found a potential new friend, so insecure in case they don't feel the same way. They've already had this conversation four times, and Joe is starting to find it somewhat irritating.

"Yes, I really think they liked us," he says. Again. "We wouldn't be sitting in this car driving down to lunch with them if they didn't, would we?"

"Okay, okay. Sorry. What do you think their house is like?"

"Alice! For God's sake. Stop asking me such stupid questions."

"Okay, okay." Alice turns to look out the window again. "Pardon me for breathing."

Gina is standing barefoot in her kitchen, slicing tomatoes and onions and wiping the tears from her eyes.

"Damn," she mutters as George walks in, coming over to her in concern.

"What's the matter, sweetie? Are you crying?"

"No," she grimaces, reaching for some paper towels. "These onions. Ow! My eyes are stinging!"

"There, there, baby," George croons, laughing as he puts his arms around her and rubs her back. "It'll be okay. I'm here."

"I told you, I'm not crying." Gina laughs through her tears as she attempts to push him away.

"Of course you're not," George says soothingly. "You're being a big brave girl."

"Oh, George!" Gina wipes her eyes and smacks him on the arm. "You're ridiculous."

"So what are you making?"

"Tomato, onion, and mozzarella salad. Do you think we'll have enough food?"

"Of course we'll have enough food. We've got steaks, burgers, tons of meat for the grill, and this looks great in here. What are you worried about?"

Gina shrugs. "I just want to make a good impression. You do think they liked us, don't you?"

"Of course they did. Actually, I'm not so sure about me, but they definitely thought you were great."

"Do you think maybe they'd join us for that benefit at the Met next month, or do you think that's a bit strong?"

George pauses and thinks. "What do you mean strong?"

"I mean I don't want to scare them off."

"I agree. We should take things slowly."

"Yes. Because I don't want it to burn out. I really really like them. I mean, I could see us being really good friends."

"So are you saying we should play hard to get?" George's mouth twitches.

"Oh, ha-ha. No. I'm just saying we shouldn't move too fast before the third date." And they both start laughing.

Joe and Alice pull off the Merritt and follow the instructions George has faxed them. Up a series of winding country lanes, across a railway bridge, and then, as directed, left up Vineyard Lane, past the huge new McMansion, and right at the third (green) mailbox on the right.

They pull up outside a pretty, old shingled cottage, and Gina and George both come running around the side of the house to greet them. George is in baggy shorts and a T-shirt, a baseball cap on his head, and Gina's wearing a tight white T-shirt and an exotic sarong that flicks open as she runs, much to Joe's appreciation.

"How lovely you're here!" Gina, unaware of Joe's admiring looks, gives both Alice and Joe a huge hug. "Did you find us okay? Was it easy? Did you understand George's directions?"

"It was very easy. And it's so beautiful here!" Alice looks up at the huge canopy of trees above them, the sunlight twinkling through onto the gravel driveway. "How do you manage not to stay here all the time? God, if this were mine Joe would never be able to drag me away."

"That's only because you're seeing it in summer." Gina links her arm through Alice's and leads her to the back of the house. "In winter it's hellish. As bleak as bleak can be."

"But don't you get gorgeous snow in winter? And build big roaring fires?"

"Excuse my wife." Joe makes a face. "She has a secret yearning to be Anne of Green Gables."

Gina laughs. "The snow looks gorgeous for about a minute, but trust me, it's not fun when you have to wait for the snow plow to clear the roads to get out, and it all turns to brown slush piled up on the sidewalks for weeks."

"I don't know," Alice says. "It still sounds lovely to me. Oh! Look at this!" The four of them climb onto a large deck overlooking a small, kidney-shape swimming pool. "My God, this is idyllic!"

"Well, it's pretty and it suits us. Come sit down. We made some Long Island iced tea."

They move down to a large table beside the pool, a white umbrella creating some much-needed shade.

"So how long have you been here?" Joe asks.

"We found it three years ago," George says. "Gina got it into her head that we needed a weekend place, and we were fed up with the Hamptons, and quite honestly

I couldn't believe the prices up here, it was so cheap compared with what we were used to."

"So I got on the web." Gina takes over as she pours the drinks into tall, ice-filled glasses. "And I found this."

"Did you need to do a lot of work?" Alice asks, looking up at the house.

"Nope. Didn't touch it," George says. "We were lucky."

"You know, I did our apartment in the city, and I just didn't want to take on another big project. I wanted something that was ready to move in to, and luckily for us the person we bought from did all the hard work and knocked everything through to make it open plan. I was too lazy and too tired to look for a decorator. I didn't want to have to do anything."

"But why would you need a decorator? Couldn't you do it yourself?"

"I'm hopeless at houses," Gina laughs.

"But you've clearly got style. I don't believe that."

"Honey, I'm clothes-obsessed, but when it comes to houses I'm an amateur. Now, how about a swim before lunch?"

The four of them have been swimming,

have had a tour of the house, and have just finished lunch.

Large bowls of wilting lettuce and leftover tomatoes and onions sweating in warm olive oil sit on the table as they talk, telling their stories, turning their acquaintanceship into friendship.

"You mentioned you were thinking of getting something out here," Gina says as Alice helps her clear the table and bring the bowls into the kitchen. "We have a wonderful real estate agent in town, and she's always there on a Saturday. Do you want to go down and see her?"

Alice's eyes widen. "God, I'd love to! But Joe would go mad. All week all he's been saying is don't think we're going to get a house on Saturday."

"Men!" Gina rolls her eyes. "Just leave it to me."

She brings a bowl of watermelon outside and turns to Joe. "Alice was just saying how she loves the country. I thought after this we could take a stroll into town. It's so pretty and we could probably all do with walking off that lunch."

"Sounds great," Joe smiles. He would have acquiesced to pretty much anything Gina had asked of him, her strong tanned thighs having made quite an impression during their swim earlier.

Not that Joe would ever dare make a move on Gina. She may be sexy but even he isn't that stupid — he can already see how well she and Alice get on, and while he might like the thrill of getting caught, that would be one thrill that would be just a little bit too much, even for him.

Not to mention the fact that Gina hasn't responded to him in the slightest. Joe isn't expecting her to flirt outrageously with him, but every time he starts a charm offensive Gina just becomes very matter-of-fact and ignores it.

But a pretty face is a pretty face, and just because she isn't responding doesn't mean he can't appreciate her.

"A walk in town sounds perfect," he says, reaching out and pulling Alice toward him for a kiss as she walks past his chair.

"Mmm." She smiles, sinking onto his lap. "What was that for?"

"For nothing," he says. "Just because."

Gina watches them with a smile. She can't figure them out. Alice is lovely, and she wants to like Joe but she senses he's dangerous. If she didn't know better, she could have sworn he was flirting with her earlier, but surely not? Would anyone be that obvious? To flirt in front of his wife and her husband? She pretended she hadn't noticed, and thankfully he seems to have stopped.

And look at them, Alice snuggled on his lap, the pair of them looking like a couple of honeymooners. Maybe Gina imagined it after all.

An hour later George and Joe stride ahead as Gina and Alice meander behind, stopping to look at every shop window, to walk inside and poke around dusty antique stores, to greet the shopkeepers, all of whom Gina seems to know by name.

At the end of Main Street they walk into an old-fashioned ice-cream store and all have giant ice-cream cones, dripping slowly across the street as they cross to the real estate agent's office.

"Where are we going?" Joe asks sternly, seeing a plate-glass window filled with properties that are obviously for sale.

"It's our hobby," Gina says. "Every time we're here George has to see what's on the market to reassure himself he didn't pay too much for our property."

"And did you pay too much?" Joe turns to George.

"Of course. But as Gina's mother always says, you never pay too much, you only pay too soon."

"That's right." Gina laughs. "And we're still waiting for the market to catch up with us."

"Nearly there," George says, peering through the window and looking at the houses. "Jesus. Look at that, Gina. That dreadful sixties colonial down the road is for sale. Over half a million dollars. Are they mad? If that's over half a million, what does that make ours?"

"It sounds like the market's finally caught up with you." Joe smiles.

"Thank the Lord!" George clasps his hands in prayer as he looks up to the sky. "About time."

"Oh, look." Gina peers through the glass and starts to wave. "There's Sandy." She turns to Joe. "She's the woman who sold us our house, who's now a good friend. She's great. Look, she's seen us." Gina beckons the woman outside. "She's coming out to say hello."

Twenty minutes later they're all squeezed into the back of Sandy's Jeep, on their way to look at a house.

"I can't believe we're going to look at a

house," Joe keeps saying. "I knew this would happen."

"Relax," George keeps instructing him with a laugh. "Sometimes you just have to accept there are things beyond your control, and women and houses happens to be one of them."

Alice smiles happily as she looks out the window. She's already fallen in love with the town. The minute they stepped out of the car and she saw people strolling along the street in shorts and flip-flops, with sand on their ankles and sunglasses in their hair, she knew she'd come home.

Standing in Sandy's office, Alice couldn't speak from fear and excitement. Gina and George had taken over, introducing Sandy, telling her that Joe and Alice were thinking about getting something in the country and that even though they weren't ready to look, they were interested to know what was in their price range.

"But we're not ready today," Joe kept saying. "We're not in the market just yet. Not until we've closed on the apartment in the city."

"I quite understand," Sandy had said, winking surreptitiously at Alice. "You're not ready but you just want to see." She'd spread some details in front of them, all of which were either more than Joe was willing to pay or ugly as sin.

"There is one property that isn't on the market yet but I heard it's about to come on. I wonder . . ." Sandy picked up the phone and made a call, and before they knew it they were squeezed in the back of her car.

"Now don't get too excited," she told Alice. "It's wonderful land but a terrible house. Charles Owens, the owner, tried for years to get Planning and Zoning approval to knock down the house and build a new one, but he didn't get it because the property was too small and there weren't enough setbacks."

"And now?"

"Well, the house itself is on a third of an acre. They've been trying to sell it for years and couldn't, but now the plot of land behind the house is just about to come up, and that's three acres, so if you put the two together you could have something wonderful."

"I have to tell you, Joe," George says, "in this area it's a huge bargain. It sounds like an amazing price."

"And it's well within our budget," Alice says, immediately shutting her mouth, for she had vowed not to say anything at all, knowing that the less she said, the less enthusiasm she showed, the higher the likelihood of Joe liking it, or, at the very least, seeing it as a viable investment.

"Let me ask you something." Joe leans toward Sandy. "This Charles couldn't get planning permission because the plot was too small, so are you saying if you bought both and combined them you'd be able to build something new?"

"That's exactly what I'm saying," Sandy smiles. "It's every developer's dream. I just hope we've got there quickly enough."

"Sandy, they haven't even seen it," Gina laughs. "Give them a chance. They might hate it."

"What's to hate?" says George. "It's three acres of usable land in Highfield. You could build whatever you want."

"Oh," Sandy adds distractedly, "and did I mention there's a pond? Here we are. Now you can see for yourself." She turns left up an old dirt track and they bump along a potholed driveway until they reach a filthy old house, half covered in weeds.

The trees are so overgrown it feels as if the house is hiding in a dark tunnel, and as they climb out of the car Alice feels her heart sink. Damn. She was so excited, so convinced that fate was working in mysterious ways and that this house has been waiting just for her.

Gina looks over and reads her body language instantly. "Come on." She slides an arm around her shoulders. "It's not that bad."

Alice raises an eyebrow as she looks around. "It's not that good."

"Oh, dear." Sandy sighs. "I did warn you it was a bit of a mess."

"A bit of a mess? It's a wreck." Joe laughs, delighted he won't have to put his hand in his pocket after all.

"But remember, we're not here to look at *this* house. You can level this one in a second and build something wonderful next to the pond. Let's walk around and have a look at the land."

They walk to the back of the house, and instantly Alice starts to perk up. At the back is a large fieldstone terrace, completely overgrown with weeds, but the trees are far fewer behind the house, and sunlight is struggling to make it through the leaves.

"Mmm. Well, this is beautiful," Joe says sarcastically, which Alice ignores.

"Would you just forget the house?" Gina says. "Think about the land. Sandy, show us the pond before these two have a heart attack."

Sandy leads Gina, George, and Joe through the woods as Alice pokes around on the terrace. She knows they're not supposed to be interested in the house, knows that Joe would level it in an instant and build a huge monolithic manor house in its place, but the more she looks at the little house, the more she is able to visualize what it could become.

Those horrible sliding doors could be ripped out and replaced with French doors, that terrace could clean up beautifully, and look at where the sun is, see how it's west-facing, imagine how it would look with hundreds of terra-cotta pots spilling brightly colored pelargoniums, lavender bushing out of the beds on either side of the stone steps leading down to what would have once been a lawn.

"Alice!" She jumps as she hears Joe's voice, and runs down the steps to join them, stopping as she sees them standing by the edge of what Alice would describe not as a pond, but as a lake.

The waters are a murky green, algae covering the entire surface, but it is immediately apparent what it could be.

Gina stands behind Joe and gives Alice a large grin and a thumbs-up as she approaches to hear the tail end of a conversation Joe is having with Sandy.

". . . so you could take down all these trees without Planning permission?"

Sandy nods enthusiastically.

"Really? Nothing?"

"Really."

Alice approaches. "So you could decimate all this lovely forest and build whatever you want?"

"Decimate, yes. Build whatever you want, no. It has to go through Planning and Zoning, but with three acres you could almost have a free rein."

"You could put the pool there," George murmurs, leading Joe through the trees. "Tennis court over there. Eight-thousand-square-foot house here."

"And I could make the little house lovely. It could be our guest house." Alice can't help herself.

"What? That old wreck?" Joe turns and looks at her as if she's mad.

"That old wreck could be gorgeous," Alice says defensively. "You know I could make it lovely. Sandy, you wouldn't happen to know anything about the history of this house, would you?"

"Well, oddly enough this house did have a history. There was a famous local author called Rachel Danbury who lived here."

Joe and Alice look at her blankly.

"I know you won't know her, but she was quite famous around here. Her most well-known book was called *The Winding Road*, and it was set here in Highfield. She wrote it in this house, and there was uproar at the time because apparently she wrote about all the locals. Anyone she'd ever had a disagreement with was in the book, thinly disguised." Sandy laughs.

"I'd love to read it," Alice says. "Do they have it in the library?"

Sandy shrugs. "You could try, but I think it's been out of print for years. I was brought up in Easton, and I remember my parents having a copy when I was growing up, but I haven't seen one for years. Try the library, though, and I'll ask around. I'm sure someone's bound to have a copy. It's an interesting house. Seriously. And one that would be a perfect guest house," Sandy concurs.

"And it *is* a great investment," George repeats.

Joe takes a deep breath and turns to

Alice. "I thought we weren't going to buy a house today?"

"Does that mean we are?" Alice holds her breath as Joe turns to Sandy.

"So," he says. "How much should my first offer be?"

14

The sun streams through the window, causing a puddle of sunlight on the bare hardwood floor. Alice quietly throws back the duvet as she slips her feet into slippers and walks softly out of the bedroom, picking up a sleepy Snoop on her way out the door.

Joe is snoring as she makes her way down the stairs and into the kitchen, opening all the doors and windows as she walks the length of the room. Snoop clatters over the floor toward the French doors leading onto the patio and runs outside to the garden.

Alice fills the kettle, puts it on the stove, and goes to stand by the back door, unable to resist a smile as she breathes in the fresh morning air.

It's mid-October, and the Highfield

wreck, as Joe has come to call it, is almost unrecognizable.

They closed on both the house and the apartment by the end of August, and since then Alice has been in Highfield, in the country, almost all the time, trying to make the little house habitable, trying to entice Joe to fall in love with the country, and although he has yet to fall in love, he is astonished at what a transformation Alice has made with just a fresh coat of paint and several dozen cans of floor wax.

The house is now light and bright, each wall a brand-new white. The bathroom is still untouched since the 1970s, an avocado green plastic that Joe detests, but at least it is clean, and as soon as they manage to find a decent plumber, Alice has sworn to rip it out and put in a new bathroom.

The kitchen is large and unmodernized, but Alice loves it. It isn't Joe's domain, and the only item he's expressed a preference for is a Viking stove, and only because it's the best money can buy. Alice loves the scratched marble countertops and the old chipped butler's sink. She loves the old-fashioned country cupboards and huge walk-in pantry.

A landscaper has been in, taken down

dozens of trees around the house, and severely pruned the ones that remain.

The water in the pond has been treated, the pH balance has been restored, and it is starting to look like less of a bog and more like a pond, although there is still quite some work to be done before Alice dares put any fish in.

The exterior of the house has also been painted, the shutters now a glossy black, and window boxes have been added, which Alice has planted with lobelia and trailing geraniums even though summer is practically over and they will undoubtedly be killed by frost within weeks.

Alice slips her feet into Timberlands, fills her pockets with doggie treats ("Never go anywhere without them," Harry said. "You can train anytime, anywhere"), picks up her coffee, and steps out the door into the "yard." How funny, she had thought, to call three acres of woods, and a pond, a "yard."

"Come!" she says to Snoop, reaching down and giving him a treat as he obediently runs up to her, and the pair of them set off across the lawn.

Alice walks slowly, sipping her coffee and smiling as she looks around. The only noises are the birds, a group of bright red cardinals hopping around the lawn, and the occasional rustle of a squirrel.

She reaches the water and sits down on a huge tree trunk that must have fallen down during a particularly bad storm. The water is still filthy, still overhung and dark, but Alice has never been happier in her life.

Finishing her coffee, she walks back up to the house, standing on the patio for a while as she shivers in the chill of the early morning air. Still sunny, October is nevertheless edging toward winter, and the leaves are about to transform into the rainbow of colors for which New England is famous.

Alice examines her handiwork. She's pulled weeds out of the stones one by one, scrubbed the patio of moss and mold, brought in pots filled with flowers to add some much-needed color before winter.

It is almost unrecognizable. Alice perches on the arm of a green Adirondack chair and examines her nails, now short and ragged, testament to everything she has done to turn this house into a home.

She still has a long way to go. Windows need replacing, and chimneys need repairing before winter. The gutters are being fixed next week, and in an ideal world she'd love to build a small extension off the kitchen, but she'll wait. After all, Joe still thinks they're going to build a huge McMansion on the other side of the pond.

But Alice is quite happy. This little house with its crooked floors and rickety stairs is everything she has ever dreamed of, and already, after just a couple of months, she feels as if she has been here forever.

She hears a rustle behind her and turns slowly to see if she can see anything. Last week she had jumped as something moved on the lawn. Looking out, she had gazed in wonder as five deer slowly walked across the garden. She knew she ought to shoo them away — everyone had warned her about the deer carrying ticks, which in turn carried the dreaded Lyme disease — but there was something so magical about seeing deer in their natural habitat, she just watched them in awe until they meandered off.

Four hours later Joe is on his laptop reading the paper online, visiting his regular sites, a cup of strong coffee at his side. Alice is unpacking her books, stacking them on the shelves either side of the huge stone fireplace in the family room as Pachelbel fills the room from the large stereo in the corner — the one item that Joe insisted on buying immediately.

"Hello?"

Alice jumps at the unfamiliar voice and turns to see a woman, about her age, standing in the open doorway of the family room, holding a plate covered with tin foil.

"Yes?" Alice, in her very English way, is both polite and formal, completely unused to strangers walking into her house, even if they are smiling.

"You're Alice?" Alice nods. "I'm Sally. Sandy told me you'd moved in and I wanted to come up and say hi. I made you an apple pie."

"You did!" Alice almost laughs, shocked at how very American this scene is, amazed because this would never, ever happen in London. "How completely lovely of you. Come in, please. Would you like a coffee?"

"I'd love one." Sally walks in, just as Alice hears a squeal from outside. "I hope you don't mind, I brought my daughter, Madison. I think she's just fallen in love with your dog."

Alice smiles and walks to the door to see a little girl, aged about two, running after Snoop, who is slightly bemused, having never seen someone this small this close, nor this eager to catch him, before.

"Say hello, Madison," Sally says.

"Lo," Madison says, not looking up. "Doggie! Madison catch the doggie?"

"Oh, she's lovely," Alice smiles. "Would she like a drink?"

"She's fine. Crazy about animals though. She'll come inside in a minute." Sally places the plate on the counter and turns around with a smile. "So how are you settling in?"

Alice takes a deep breath. "Do you think it's too early to say I absolutely love it?"

"Probably, but we moved here from Manhattan six years ago, and I fell in love with it after about five minutes."

"Six years? So you must know pretty much everything about the town."

"Not everything, but enough. I can probably help you with anything you need to know."

"Mommy." Madison bounds through the door, followed closely by Snoop, who seems delighted to have found a friend. "I have the doggie?"

"No, honey." Sally crouches down and smiles. "You can't have this doggie, but maybe when you're a little bit bigger and can deal with the responsibility, you can have a doggie of your own."

"I have a doggie," Madison says again, nodding to herself, then wanders off to examine the contents of the kitchen cupboards.

"Do you have children?" Sally asks, as Alice pulls some plates out of their wrapping paper and hastily washes them.

"No. Not yet. I'd like them though. Soon."

"Hello." Joe walks into the kitchen, eyebrow raised at the strange woman sitting at the kitchen counter. "I'm Joe."

Alice turns to admire her husband, looking particularly sexy and rumpled in his oldest jeans and a faded polo shirt, barefoot as he pads over to Sally to shake her hand.

"Hi, how are you?" Sally says with a genuine smile, shaking his hand as Alice breathes a sigh of relief. She may not believe Joe is anything more than a terrible flirt, but she sees the effect his charm frequently has, and she bristles instantly when she sees yet another woman fall under his spell. Watching Sally, just as with Gina, Alice fails to detect even the smallest hint of flirtation in her voice. Thank goodness for that, she thinks. A woman I can actually trust.

"You know, the two of you should really come over to our house," Sally says. "We'll introduce you to some of the neighbors. What are you doing next Saturday?"

"Absolutely nothing," Alice says. "We haven't met anyone yet, so there isn't a single date in the diary."

"Great! Both of you come over for a barbecue. Around five, how does that sound?"

"Sounds great," Joe smiles.

"Good. In the meantime you both have to have some of this pie. It's still warm, fresh out of the oven."

"Another cook?" Joe reaches into the drawer for forks as Alice cuts the pie, releasing the delicious aroma of apple and cinnamon into the air. "You two are clearly going to be best friends."

"I hope so," Sally smiles. "Sandy said I'd like you and she was right."

"Oh, good," Joe says smoothly, digging into the pie. "We aim to please."

"So what are they like?" Chris, Sally's husband, wipes his hands on a cloth and walks out of his workroom.

"They seem really nice," Sally says, putting down Madison, who runs instantly into Chris's arms.

"Hi, sweetie." He scoops her up. "Did you have a nice time?"

"I have a doggie," she burbles. "Doggie is Soop."

"Doggie soup? Yeuch!" Chris makes a face and Madison starts laughing. "That sounds gross."

"Not doggie soup, Daddy!" the little girl giggles. "Doggie Soop."

"They have a dog called Snoop," Sally laughs. "That's what she's trying to say."

"So? Are we going to be friends with them?" Chris puts Madison down and turns to Sally.

"You'll like them. She's kind of British and a bit reserved but seems really nice, and he's incredibly charming with a dangerous twinkle in his eye."

"You mean he came on to you?"

"No!" She shoves him. "Not me. But he seems the type to maybe play around. Gosh, would you listen to me? What a terrible thing to say. Anyway, they're coming for a barbecue next Saturday at five, so you can make up your own mind."

15

In the abstract Joe loves having a place in the country, couldn't wait to tell his colleagues, his clients, about their "weekend house," but the country has never really been his cup of tea, and he's been happy to let Alice take over these past few weeks.

Joe loves living in New York, would be quite happy if he never traveled farther north than Ninety-first nor farther south than SoHo, other than for his work on Wall Street. He loves the pace, the people, the lifestyle, and if there is any hindrance at all it is Alice.

He is still trying with Alice, God how he is trying. He has — again — mentally renewed his commitment to her and is trying his damnedest to be the husband he knows she wants him to be, but he's in New York, where there's temptation on every cross street, and he can feel the itch beginning again.

Just the other week he'd been at a client dinner at Le Colonial. He arrived early, went upstairs to the bar, expecting to have a quiet drink, perhaps review some papers, but the music was throbbing and the room was crushed with beautiful people. He watched with amusement, noticing how everyone spent their time looking around the room to see if they were missing something, or *someone,* more interesting, and found himself drawn to a dangerous-looking brunette in a tiny black dress and high leather boots.

He was just enjoying the frequent flirtatious glances, the hint of a smile from her as she realized he was staring, when his client showed up. Ah, well. Better for it to be over before it had begun. Nevertheless, he had gone back up to the bar when the dinner was over, had hoped she would still be there, but of course she had gone.

And Alice? Alice now feels much the same about New York as she did about London. Easier only because she is anonymous in New York, doesn't feel the same pressure to be the perfect trophy wife. But Alice is beginning to spend more and more time in the country, and the longer she stays there, the more work she does to the house, the more she falls in love with it and the less she wants to leave.

Alice has knocked down walls and discovered raised wooden paneling that was hidden sometime in the 1960s. She has ripped up the linoleum in the kitchen and discovered wide old oak planks. She has found the room that must have been Rachel Danbury's office, and finds she can spend hours sitting on the window seat in there, gazing up at the trees, thinking about nothing other than how at peace she feels.

The more she discovers about the house, the more she feels as if she knows the writer. She has yet to lay her hands on a copy of *The Winding Road*, but it's as if Rachel Danbury's personality is embedded within the walls, the very foundations of the house, and Alice is slowly drawn into her spell, falls more in love with the house with every passing day.

There are times, however, when Alice has to go into the city. She does so reluctantly, but Monday to Friday — or Tuesday to Thursday if she can get away with it — go in she does. To the theater with Joe, to openings at the Met, charity benefits at the Frick, restaurants, bars, and clubs. She goes in to have her highlights done at Frederic Fekkai, to shop at Bergdorf Goodman for the requisite black-tie outfits, to lunch with Gina at Jean-George or Le Cirque 2000 — the only thing she truly enjoys about coming into the city.

Alice is astonished at how close she and Gina have become in such a short space of time. "My replacement," Emily had said with a sniff in mock disgust, but to a large extent it's true. Emily is her oldest friend and will always be her best friend, but with the distance now separating them, Emily can't possibly understand what her life is like.

And she and Gina seem to have so many things in common. "We're so lucky," Gina says repeatedly. "You and I have such wonderful husbands. Can you believe how lucky we are?"

Alice smiles each time and agrees, grateful that Joe is back to being the man she married, the man she first fell in love with when she was a teenager. He's home every evening, and phones when he says he's going to. His mobile is always on, and for the first time in years she doesn't lie in bed awake every night, heart pounding as she tries not to think about where he is or what he's doing.

She doesn't dwell on those years of insecurity and panic, on pushing those fears out of her head because the truth might be too terrible to contemplate.

Now, even those nights when Alice is in the country and Joe has stayed in the city to work, she phones and he picks up. He's never unavailable these days, never seems to have inexplicable absences or business trips to unnamed hotels. She phones him late at night, at the apartment, and he answers and tells her how much he misses her.

And on the weekends, when he catches the train down to Highfield on a Friday night or a Saturday morning, and she picks him up at the station in her new Ford Explorer, he puts his arms round her and kisses her deeply, and she knows beyond a shadow of a doubt he really loves her.

16

Joe watches Alice as she stands outside throwing sticks for Snoop, laughing and reaching down to pet him enthusiastically each time he drops a stick at her feet.

There are times, like this, when he feels as if he barely knows Alice anymore. The Alice he knows is quiet and reserved. The Alice he knows is sophisticated and insouciant. But the Alice he's watching now throws her head back with laughter as Snoop chases her around in circles.

The Alice he thought he knew would never have dared get grass stains on her trousers, but then again, the Alice he thought he knew would never have worn old faded jeans, a Gap sweatshirt, and a sleeveless down jacket.

But most of all, the Alice he thought he knew always had an air of mystery about her. She always seemed to be living in something of a dream world. Even when they were together, he never felt that she was quite with him, which was undoubtedly part of her attraction for him.

There was a deep air of sadness surrounding the Alice he thought he knew. This Alice, this Alice who is now rolling on the grass and giggling as her dog tries to lick her face, is permanently and deliriously happy.

This Alice wakes up in the morning and bounds out of bed. She is always busy doing something. If not cooking — something she hasn't done on a regular basis for years — she's waxing a table, or ripping down a wall, or staining a piece of furniture.

The house seems to be filled with music, and Alice, Alice who has always been so quiet and reserved, bubbles away with conversation. She tells Joe of her trips, her visits to the farmer's market in Wilton, the people she met while looking for pots of tarragon and lavender at Gilberties. She tells him of her walks on the beach, of the people she passes and the houses she admires. Her newfound joy is bursting out of the cracks in the walls, squeezing under the windowpanes and touching everyone who crosses her path.

Including, naturally, Joe, who refuses to be swept up in her good humor.

Joe cannot understand where his meek, subservient trophy wife has gone. He sees only flashes of her these days in Manhattan. When Alice comes into the city, accompanies him to a party, or a gallery, or a busy bar, she reverts back to the Alice he knows, the Alice he fell in love with.

In Manhattan, the city he is starting to feel he is getting to know, Joe is very definitely king of his world. He is the quintessential Wall Street banker, with enough money to ensure his life runs exactly as he wants it to run. He knows who he is in Manhattan. He knows his role, he knows Alice's role, and when in the city Alice plays it well, dressing up in her designer clothes and smiling beautifully but blankly at the colleagues and clients with whom he has to socialize.

But out here in Highfield there can be no doubt that Alice is queen of her castle, and despite himself it makes him nervous. The dynamics of their relationship seem to change almost as soon as they cross the border from Westchester into Connecticut.

When Joe thought about a place in the

country, he envisaged a large new house, preferably with a pool, and preferably on the beach. He assumed it would have giant power showers and rolling lawns; otherwise, quite frankly, why bother? He never thought his place in the country would be a tiny crappy cottage filled with nooks and crannies.

Of course he still plans to build the house of his dreams on the other side of the lake, although he really hasn't got time to start researching architects and builders, and Alice doesn't seem the least bit interested in a different house. But when colleagues ask about his country place, he tells them about the beauty of the land and the pond (true), how it was the deal of the century (true-ish, although not quite as good a deal as George had tried to persuade him it was), and that they're about to start building the Chambers mansion (not if Alice has anything to do with it).

Joe doesn't really know what to do with himself out here. He can't see the point in going for walks, has never understood the point of walking for the sake of it, and so each time Alice asks him to join her, he declines.

Like so many other men who work on Wall Street, Joe finds it almost impossible to relax. For him it means slumping in front of the small television in his office with the *Wall Street Journal.*

Joe doesn't like cooking (although he loves eating), and he doesn't like gardening, and he doesn't have any hobbies. He doesn't like animals — although the first time he came upon eighteen wild turkeys meandering up the driveway he had to admit he was awestruck — and he's too lazy and disinterested to explore the local area.

What Joe does best is socialize, shop, and seduce. Socializing has been difficult because other than Gina and George, he really hasn't met anyone else down here, and Gina and George, as lovely as they are, are not here every weekend. Shopping is fine if he bothers to go to Greenwich, and seduction is something from which he's trying very hard to abstain right now.

But the itch is getting stronger. Particularly now that Alice just doesn't seem to need him as much as she has always done. Joe has always been the strong one in the relationship, has grown accustomed to being dominant, has enjoyed being the strong, manly husband, but just as Alice seems to grow more confident and more powerful as they cross the border into

Connecticut, Joe seems to weaken.

He is well aware he does not have the control he is used to in Highfield, and Joe's very sense of masculinity involves control. If he can't control Alice, surely temptation, in the form of a long-legged lovely who laughs at his jokes and thinks he is wonderful, is lurking just around the corner. . . .

"Aren't you going to change?"

"No? Why?" Alice is dropping homemade lemon polenta cookies into a small gift bag to take to Sally and Chris's barbecue.

"Well, for one thing you've got grass stains all over your knees." He doesn't say that she surely can't be thinking of going to a social occasion in a gray sweatshirt and jeans.

"Oh God," Alice groans. "Thanks. Won't be a moment." She runs upstairs and emerges a couple of minutes later in a clean pair of equally faded jeans, with the same sweatshirt and an old pair of loafers.

"Makeup?" Joe says hopefully, as Alice laughs and runs back upstairs. Five minutes later she comes down with her hair freshly brushed, her lips shining with a pink gloss, and the sweatshirt exchanged for a crisp white linen shirt.

"Better?" She laughs.

"Much," Joe says gratefully, although he still would have liked to see her in her straight-legged wool crêpe Michael Kors trousers with her high-heeled Jimmy Choo boots.

"Whoa," Alice laughs and steps nimbly out of the way to avoid a procession of screaming three- and four-year-olds heading toward her, while Joe groans.

"Oh God. Children."

"Of course children. What do you expect of a barbecue at five o'clock on a Sunday afternoon?"

"Haven't these people heard of nannies?"

Alice's mouth drops open in amazement. "God, you're so old-fashioned. Who do you think you are anyway, Little Lord Fauntleroy?"

"But why do these people take their children *everywhere?* What happened to grown-ups having a grown-up evening?"

"Keep your voice down," Alice hisses just before they round the corner to the back of the house where the barbecue is — judging from the noise — in full throes. "First of all, it's not evening, and second, it's lovely to have your children with you. If we had children they'd come everywhere with me. I suppose you think children should be seen and not heard."

"Actually I . . . ow!" Right on cue a nine-year-old bashes into Joe sharply as he runs past, chasing after the others.

"Ha!" Alice laughs. "Serves you right. Now put on your charming face and let's go and meet some of the neighbors."

"You must be Joe and Alice! Hi, I'm Tom O'Leary and this is my wife Mary Beth. We live right around the corner from you on Winding Lane."

"Hi, I'm Chris, Sally's husband, and I know you've met our daughter, Madison."

"Alice! Joe! How lovely to see you again. Tim, this is Alice and Joe who bought the old Danbury house. Remember the sale I told you about?" Sandy beckons her husband over proudly. "So tell me all about the house. I hear you've done incredible things already."

Before Alice has a chance to reply, yet another couple descends on them. "Joe and Alice, right? Welcome to Highfield, we've heard so much about you! I'm Kay and this is my husband, James. We're at number seven. Those three are ours —

Summer is five, Taylor is three, and whoops, where's Skye? Oh, there she is crawling off again. Skye is eleven months."

"Hello, gorgeous," Gina swoops down on Alice and gives her a tight squeeze, releasing her to give Joe a kiss. "Isn't this a lovely surprise?"

"I thought you weren't down this weekend," Alice says, knowing that Gina always pops in or phones to tell them they're in the country.

"We weren't. But I called to get my messages this morning, and Sally had left a message saying there'd be a barbecue, and it's such a beautiful day we jumped in the car after lunch and drove down."

"Oh, I'm glad you're here." Alice squeezes Gina's hand, although the familiar tightening of her chest when she walks into a social situation where she knows barely anyone is missing today.

Of course it helps that everyone seems to be eager to meet them, and everyone is so friendly, which is something of a shock, although an enjoyable one. Alice is used to socializing in London, used to being terribly British and reserved, and standing around with a forced tight smile, never presuming to speak to anyone without an introduction, and never daring just to walk right on over and introduce herself. She is used to waiting for an introduction from the hostess and then waiting for the hostess to provide some grain of common ground that can, it is hoped, form the basis of small talk for a few minutes.

But here everyone just walks up with outstretched hands and welcoming smiles. Steaks and burgers are sizzling on the barbecue with Chris keeping watch, and the women are emerging from the kitchen with bowls of salads and baskets of bread to place on the table.

Beers and sodas are packed together on the table next to a huge bucket of ice, and everyone is cheerfully helping themselves while hordes of children run around on the lawn.

Alice walks into the kitchen. "Can I help?" she asks Sally, used to asking the question in London, and more used to hearing a "No, don't worry," even when the hostess is quite clearly harassed and not coping.

"That would be great," Sally says. "You can chop the tomatoes." And she slides the chopping board and knife over and turns to spoon some salsa into a bowl.

"So everyone here is a neighbor?" Alice asks, looking out through the window to see Joe presumably charming the pants off Kay and James. While friendly enough, if there was anyone here to set her antennae off, it would be Kay. Her figure completely belies the fact that she has had three children, an asset of which she is presumably well aware, dressed as she is in tight blue capri pants and a tiny T-shirt that more than shows off her suspiciously pert breasts. And unlike the other women here, all of whom are dressed much like Alice in jeans and loafers, or flat mules, Kay is standing tall in strappy high-heeled slingbacks.

And despite Joe talking to Kay and James together, Alice can see, even through the kitchen window, that Kay is dangerous. She feels that familiar fluttering, those danger signals that make her feel ever so slightly sick, but she tries to calm herself. Don't be ridiculous, she tells herself. Not only is the woman married, she has three young children as well. Hardly a threat.

And Kay's husband is handsome. Why on earth would she be flirting with Joe? Because Joe is English, and charming, and different? Don't be ridiculous, she berates herself, chopping tomatoes fast and furiously. Joe and she have never been happier.

The last thing she has to worry about now is Joe flirting with other women. He's a changed man. And anyway, surely Kay isn't his type?

"Kay and James seem nice. Do they live here all the time?"

"They do now," Sally says. "They used to be weekenders, but after Skye was born they bought a bigger house down here and now they live here permanently."

"Were they in Manhattan?"

"Weren't we all?" Sally laughs. "Actually that's not true. Chris never lived in Manhattan, but I did. Most of us have lived there before we got married and settled down."

"They seem very friendly," Alice lies, wanting to try to discover something about Kay, wanting to know whether she should be threatened, but not wanting to be obvious. She knows she should be asking Gina, but she doesn't want Gina to suspect that Alice might be suspicious of Joe, and Gina knows her too well already.

"Oh, they are. And their children are just adorable. Kay actually runs the newcomers' tennis team if you're interested."

"Tennis? Oh, no. Not our game."

"Oh, really? So do you have a game?"

Alice laughs. "No. I suppose living in

the center of London we never really had time for sports. Joe loves his gym though, and I'm completely obsessed with my garden."

"We have a gardening club," Sally says enthusiastically. "You should come. We have guests come in to talk to us, and every spring we hold a big plant sale. In fact, next week we have someone coming in to talk about autumn plantings for spring flowers. You should come."

"Mmm," Alice says noncommittally, thinking how horribly suburban it seems. "Sounds interesting."

Sally starts laughing. "I remember saying exactly the same thing when we moved here. I know how awful it sounds, but if nothing else it's a great way to meet people."

Alice blushes. "I'm sorry. Was I being a horrible snob?"

"No more than any of us when we first got here. It just takes time to get into the small-town way of life. It's very different, and we all think we're better than that when we arrive fresh out of the Upper East Side or . . . ?" She looks at Alice questioningly.

"Belgravia."

"There you go. We'll make a Highfield

271

girl of you in no time."

Alice carries the tomatoes outside and helps herself to a beer, trying to ignore her slight alarm at seeing Kay still talking animatedly to Joe, Kay's husband having disappeared to help Chris with the barbecue.

"Darling," Joe says, turning and pulling Alice to his side with a tender smile, causing all Alice's fears to disappear in the wind. "Kay was just telling me about her tennis team. I'm going to join."

Alice starts to laugh, able to relax as she basks in Joe's public display of affection. "Tennis? Since when have you played tennis?"

"I played tennis for years," Joe says defensively. "Although I have to admit my game is a bit rusty. But Kay says they're looking for some more players, and it's a great way to meet people."

"Why don't you come too?" Kay smiles at Alice, and Alice knows instantly that while she may be able to trust her husband, she must not trust this woman. Her mouth is smiling but her eyes are cool and appraising, and her body language — a subject in which Alice has had to become well versed — is directed straight at Joe, a sign of attraction if ever there was one.

"I don't play tennis," Alice explains, trying to keep the wariness out of her voice. "Although I could learn."

"Darling, you'd be hopeless," Joe laughs. "Your hand-eye coordination is dreadful."

"Thanks," Alice says, adding flirtatiously, and entirely uncharacteristically, "You weren't complaining last night."

Kay raises an eyebrow and smiles as she backs off. "I'm going to get some food. Nice to meet you." Kay knows when she has met a fighter. At the end of the day she was only having a harmless flirt, and he is attractive, but clearly the wife doesn't like him talking to attractive, no, make that beautiful, women.

With a toss of her hair, Kay walks up to the table to help herself to salad. She turns around and catches Joe studying her rear, and smiles to herself as she straightens and turns to display her gorgeous, well-toned body, pretending obliviousness at his continuing stare.

Good choice of clothes, she commends herself. She knew it was worth wearing those high heels.

Under normal circumstances Kay wouldn't be his type. Rather too confident

273

for his liking, and brunettes have never really been his style, although there is always the odd exception to the rule. But the longer he spends in Manhattan, the more accustomed he is growing to these strong women who know what they want and are frighteningly direct in getting it.

And quite frankly, she had what Joe has come to think of as "the look." Yes, he knows she's married, and the husband seems like a nice man if a little dull, and there are the three young children to consider, but she definitely looked like she was up for it. Something about a sparkle in her eye, a raised eyebrow, a hint of suggestiveness in what was otherwise a perfectly reasonable conversation about moving to America.

There was something that told him she was bored, and that her husband didn't excite her anymore, and that should a tall dark handsome stranger come along, particularly one who had both charm and an English accent, she might just jump at the opportunity.

A flirtation is all he's thinking about right now. Even though Alice is not the Alice he thought she was, he's still trying to be the faithful husband, still doing his hardest to treat America as the fresh start it was always meant to be.

But God, it felt good to see that sparkle, to see the look again. Christ — he'd almost forgotten how to recognize it. And good to know that he has still got it after all, that he's still as attractive as he was in London (for a while there he was beginning to doubt it). And what harm could it do to play tennis with her? Bet she looks fanfuckingtastic in a little tennis skirt, those long bronzed legs with little bobby socks on.

Joe starts to get excited as he surveys her rear, imagining her in her tennis whites, and he sees her glance at him then pretend not to have seen as she turns and stretches, her full breasts straining under her tight T-shirt.

Not usually his type, but she's one hot little number. He likes the fact that she looks after herself. That she may have had three kids but her stomach looks as taut as a teenager's, and that she's well aware of how good she looks, how sexy she is.

He smiles to himself as he turns away and takes a long swig of cool beer. He'd better find a sports store in Manhattan this week. Buy a couple of rackets and a couple of pairs of tennis shorts. And tennis shoes. God. He hasn't worn tennis shoes in about twenty years.

Hmmm. Looks like life in the country might not be so boring after all.

17

Living in a big city, it's easy to forget just how black the night sky is. As dusk turns to darkness in this small town in Connecticut, Alice gazes up at the stars, mesmerized. Candles have been lit, lanterns switched on, and the children have either dropped off to sleep in various strollers or are transfixed by Shrek on a huge television screen in the basement playroom.

The women have draped brightly colored cable-knit sweaters around their shoulders or pulled thin quilted jackets on to keep out the chill in the night air, but people are now starting to move inside to the kitchen and the family room, the men settling down on the large squashy sofas, the women fulfilling a housewife stereotype by huddling together in the kitchen, scraping plates and loading the dishwasher as they discuss which schools their children are at and whether they are happy there.

"Hey, I didn't see you there." Gina picks up the last of the bowls on the table outside when she notices Alice lying on a rattan lounger.

Alice turns her head and smiles. "Just thinking how incredible it is here. Look at that sky. I don't think I'll ever get used to the darkness in the country."

Gina smiles and perches on the edge of the lounger. "How many times do I have to tell you this isn't the country, it's the suburbs."

"Not for me it's not. You don't find deer and raccoons in the suburbs in England."

"No? What do you find?"

"Rows of semidetached houses mostly, and the odd souped-up Ford Escort."

Gina laughs. "Sounds beautiful."

"Just gorgeous," Alice laughs. "Definitely worth seeing on your next trip."

"So." Gina lowers her voice conspiratorially and leans in to Alice. "What do you think of the neighbors?"

"All of them or any in particular?"

"Just generally. They're nice, aren't they?"

"Sally's lovely. I can't believe what a

wonderful spread they had, and how relaxed everyone is."

"I know. Sally and Chris are great. Who else have you talked to?"

"I spoke to Kay a bit."

"Ah. Kay."

Alice perks up. "Now, why do you say, 'Ah, Kay,' in that tone of voice?"

"What tone of voice?" Gina feigns innocence.

"Oh, come on. Tell me. Is she a bitch?"

"Not a bitch." Gina turns around to check there's no one within earshot. "I just think she's incredibly insecure."

"Insecure? But she's gorgeous."

"I know, but did you see what she was wearing? Those heels? For a Sunday night barbecue? Please! And she flirts with all the husbands."

Alice breathes a sigh of relief. "You mean she's not planning on having an affair with Joe then?"

"Probably. And George, and Chris, and Sam, and pretty much whoever else happens to be male."

"I thought she was flirting with Joe and I got completely paranoid."

"God, no need to get paranoid. George thinks it's funny. Actually I think he's quite flattered, but that's just Kay. She needs to feel attractive."

"Doesn't her husband mind?"

"James? Actually I think he's something of a flirt himself."

"Oh." Alice's face falls. "He didn't flirt with me."

Gina laughs. "Don't take it personally. He doesn't practice when husbands are in earshot."

"Ah. Good. That makes me feel much better. So do you think the two of them actually do anything about it, or is it just flirting?"

"I want to say that I'm pretty sure it's just flirting, but around here you just never know."

"What do you mean?"

"Well, key parties were huge in the seventies around here."

"*Key parties?* What in God's name is a key party?"

"You know." Gina looks at Alice in disbelief. "When everyone put their keys on the coffee table and picked up someone else's keys and went home with them."

"Oh, you mean *swinging* parties."

"Yup."

"Like that movie, *The Ice Storm*?"

"*Exactly!* That was set just down the road from here in New Canaan."

"No! So it really went on?"

"Honey, it was before my time, but that's what they say."

Alice starts to giggle. "I dare you to drop your keys on the coffee table in front of James and see what he does."

"Yeah, right. He'd probably pick them up and then what?"

"Well, he is quite attractive . . ."

"And so is Joe, but that doesn't mean I want to sleep with him."

"You would if your name was Kay."

Gina laughs. "I swear to God, if anybody actually took her up on it she'd run a mile. She just likes the attention."

"Rather like my husband."

"Oh. And I thought I was special."

Alice laughs as Gina stands up and extends a hand to help Alice up. "Come on, everyone will be wondering where we've got to."

"Now that could be another rumor in the making."

"That's true." Gina laughs. "That would really give them something to talk about!"

"So, I hear you bought Rachel Danbury's house." Tom places his cup of coffee on the table and sits down next to Alice.

"Yes," Alice says politely. "Do you know it?"

"I don't know the house, but she was very well known around here in the twenties and thirties."

"So I hear. I keep meaning to get a copy of *The Winding Road.*"

"You should talk to James. James!" Tom calls him over. "You have a copy of *The Winding Road*, don't you?"

"Sure," James nods. "Good old Rachel Danbury."

"Did you know her?"

"I knew of her." James sits down on Alice's other side and leans back comfortably. "And I vaguely remember her being pointed out to me when I was a child. But my grandparents knew her, although after the book they didn't speak."

"Where could I get hold of a copy? I'd love to read it."

"You're welcome to borrow mine."

"Really? I'd love to!"

"I'll drop it in this week."

"That would be lovely!"

"Are you here all week?"

"Well, Joe's back in the city tomorrow, and I'll either join him tomorrow or Tuesday, and then back here on Friday, but you can just leave it on the porch." As she says it Alice smiles to herself, wondering whether Gina was right, whether he'll try to get her on her own, because thus far she's seen no sign of flirtatiousness whatsoever.

"Okay," he smiles. "I'll do that."

Alice is just about to ask him to tell her more about Rachel Danbury, when Joe appears in front of her. "Darling," he says, "I'm catching the five-thirty death train tomorrow morning so we need to make a move."

"Okay." Alice stands up and starts to say her good-byes.

"So what did you think?" Alice lowers her book and waits for Joe to come out of the bathroom.

"It was lovely."

"It was, wasn't it? Aren't they a lovely crowd?"

"Very nice."

"Who did you like the most?"

"Oh God, Alice. I need to go to bed. Can we talk about this tomorrow?"

"You won't be here tomorrow. You're in the city."

"Exactly. Which is why I need to go to bed now."

"Okay," Alice says huffily as Joe switches

off his bedside light and climbs into bed. He leans over and pecks her quickly on the cheek before rolling onto his side and closing his eyes.

"Joe?" Alice whispers five minutes later, but Joe doesn't answer, already half asleep, drifting away in a fantasy involving Kay, a tennis court, and a hot summer's day.

Alice is woken by a combination of the shrill ringing of the telephone and Snoop licking her face and crying to go outside.

"Shit." A quick glance at the clock tells her it's eight thirty-four, and poor Snoop's bladder is probably about to explode.

She runs to the phone, grabs it, and cradles it under her chin as she runs down the stairs, heading straight for the back door and opening it as Snoop runs outside and immediately relieves himself next to the fence.

"Hello. You sound out of breath. Are you having sex or something?" Emily's voice is loud and clear, and distinctly amused.

"I wish," Alice laughs. "Actually it's far more exciting. I'm out of breath due to running down the stairs and letting Snoop out before he pees all over the hardwood floors."

"What a glamorous life you lead," Emily snorts.

"So do you want to know what I can see right now?"

"Dog pee?"

"Aside from dog pee."

"Go on, make me jealous."

"I can see a bright blue sky, hundreds of tall trees, the sun shining and, hang on . . ."

"Hang on why?"

"Hang on because I'm walking round the back of the house. Oh yes, here we are. I can see the sunlight glistening on the water of my own private pond."

"God, you make me sick."

"So where are you? Brianden or London?"

"Well, here's what I can see out my window. Wow! There's a car with a smashed window and glass all over the pavement, and, hang on, yup, a homeless person slouched in a doorway, and is that, could that be, yes, you'll never believe it but there's actually rubbish blowing along the pavement."

"So you're in London then?"

"Apparently, yes. Although God knows why. On a miserable day like today I should be holed up in Brianden with a good book and a lovely roaring fire."

"What about a fiery roaring lover?"

"Would that be young Harry to whom you're referring?"

"I don't know," Alice grins. "*Is* he a fiery roaring lover?"

"I'm not sure he's very fiery, and he doesn't do much roaring really, but he's definitely a lover, and a lovely one at that."

"Does that mean it's true love?"

Emily's voice turns serious. "I think that I probably do love him, but is he the one? That I don't know."

Alice is shocked. "That sounds like a change of tune. What's going on?"

"Nothing. He's lovely, and we're fine, I just don't know whether this is it. Actually I'm not even sure it matters really. I sort of feel that I'm enjoying myself today, and I do believe that everyone comes into our lives for a reason, and that clearly there are lessons I need to learn from him, and it either will work out or it won't, but either way that's fine."

"Em, that doesn't sound like you at all."

"Maybe I'm just growing up when it comes to relationships. I've always leapt in before, and I'm just learning to take each day as it comes. Anyway, more to the point, we were talking last night and both of us could really do with a holiday, and we were thinking . . .”

“Come and stay! You have to come and stay!” Alice practically shouts into the receiver as Emily starts to laugh.

“We were hoping you'd say that. I miss you desperately, and besides, neither Harry nor I have any money, so basically it's either a bucket flight to New York and free bed and board with you, or a package deal to Birmingham.”

“Oh, actually, if that's the choice maybe Birmingham would suit you better.”

“And maybe Harry won't demonstrate his spectacular carpentry skills in your country home.”

“Are his carpentry skills spectacular?”

“Well, I'm sitting on a window seat that he made, looking at my new bookshelves, which he knocked together in an afternoon.”

“And you're still not sure he's the one? Are you nuts?”

“There's more to marriage than window seats and bookshelves.”

“And animal-loving.”

“Yes, and even animal-loving.”

“Not much more.”

“Can we not get into this now?”

“Okay, sorry, sorry. But you realize I will

have to steal you away and quiz you mercilessly while you're here?"

"Yes, yes, I know, it's the price I have to pay."

"Oh, Em! I'm so excited. When are you thinking of coming?"

"Well, what are you doing for Christmas?"

"Christmas? But Christmas is years away! I thought you meant you'd be coming next week."

"But it's practically November already, and Christmas is only nine weeks away. It's almost next week."

"You're right, I'm just getting excited. We can go to the Christmas tree farm and choose a tree together, and we can make decorations, and we'll have so much fun!"

Emily shakes her head in disbelief. "Ali, I know you know this, but I'm no longer twelve years old."

"So? Christmas is going to be wonderful! Oh, I'm so excited."

"Do you want to check it's okay with Joe?"

"Don't be ridiculous, he'll be thrilled."

"We thought maybe we could come in around Christmas Eve and maybe stay until New Year's, but we'd like to spend a couple of days in the city as well, take in a show and hit the sales . . ."

"I thought you said you didn't have any money?"

"I don't, but when Banana Republic calls, Banana Republic calls. So what do you think?"

"I think you've just given me the best Christmas present I've ever had."

"Don't get too excited, we're not there yet. Who knows, we may have a horrible time."

"Absolutely not possible. Tell Harry I can't wait to see you both. Bugger, who's that?"

"Who's what?"

Alice crosses her arms as a big black Suburban rolls down the driveway. "I'm standing here in my pajamas," she whispers to Emily, "and someone's here in a monster of a car and I have absolutely no idea who it is and I can't just run inside without looking like a complete idiot."

"What kind of pajamas? Thick winceyette or sexy floaty see-through chiffon ones?"

"Sexy floaty see-through chiffon ones? Who do you think I am, Barbara Windsor? I bloody hope they're not see-through, although they are thin cotton." Alice folds one arm protectively over her chest as she tries to see through the tinted windows of the car as it rolls to a halt.

"I'd better go," she says to Emily, as James climbs out of the car with book in hand and a large smile on his face, unable to believe his luck in catching the lovely Alice in such revealing pajamas. He knew she had a great body, but he didn't think it was quite this great.

"I'll talk to you later," Alice whispers, with a fake smile and a wave to James. "Lots of love."

Five minutes later Alice manages to escape upstairs for her dressing gown, coming back down feeling far less vulnerable as she puts the kettle on to make coffee for James.

"I hope I haven't called at a bad time," James says, leaning forward on the stool to rest his elbows on the kitchen counter. "I was worried I would forget so I put the book in the car this morning and thought I'd drop it in early on my way to work. Where's Joe?"

"Oh, he took the five-thirty train this morning."

"That is such a killer. I can't understand these men who make that commute. Particularly when they leave such lovely wives at home."

Alice chooses to ignore that last statement. "So where do you work?" she asks politely.

"Do you know Sunup?"

"The garden center?"

"Yup. The nursery. That's mine."

"Really? I had no idea. I'm in there all the time. I've never seen you there."

"Unfortunately, this time of year I'm mostly doing admin work, hidden away in my office, but next time you're in you'll have to knock on the door and come say hello."

Alice thinks back to what Gina had said and smiles to herself.

"You don't look like a gardener," she says.

"Oh, really? What are gardeners supposed to look like?"

"Aren't they supposed to have mud-encrusted boots and dirt under their fingernails?"

"You should see me in the summer. That's exactly what I look like for seventy percent of the year. Kay hates it."

Alice decides to change the subject. She moves the book over and looks at the cover, opens it and flicks through the first few pages. The inscription reads: "To Jackson, for holding my hand down the road."

"What does that mean?" Alice looks up at James, who watches her closely as she reads. "Was Jackson her husband?"

"You should read the book, it will tell you everything. It's basically her autobiography very thinly disguised as fiction. Her husband in the book is completely based on her real husband, and just in case you're interested, my grandparents in the book are Jean and Eddie."

"Your grandfather's name was Eddie?"

"No. He was actually Andrew Rollingford the Third, but in *The Winding Road* he appears as Edward Rutherford the Third."

Alice laughs. "Oh. Rather too close for comfort I would think."

"That's the point. It was completely obvious who everyone was."

"Did anyone sue?"

"Believe it or not, once upon a time America wasn't the litigious society it is today."

"In other words people didn't drive into a tree and sue the tree for dangerous planting?"

James laughs. "Exactly. So no, nobody

sued, but nobody spoke to her for years either, which in a small community like this was just as bad, if not worse."

"So what did she do?"

"Eventually she moved farther north, out to Old Saybrook."

"She ran away? I'm surprised."

"Surprised? Why?"

"I know this sounds bizarre, but living here in the house, knowing that she lived here, sometimes I just sort of feel that I know her, know what she was thinking."

James raises his eyebrows.

"Oh God. I told you it was bizarre. I suppose it's just that I've been restoring the house, and every time I discover something, like that wainscoting on the wall that was hidden since the sixties, I think, yes. Rachel Danbury would have liked that."

"No. That makes sense. But enough about Rachel Danbury. I'd love to hear more about you. It's not often we get such a glamorous and beautiful neighbor, not to mention one with such a wonderful accent. How on earth did you come to be living out here?"

Glamorous *and* beautiful. Alice cannot help but smile. Flirtatious? No, not yet, but she can tell from the way he's looking at her that he definitely finds her attractive, and even though Alice would never ever flirt with anyone, nor encourage anyone to think she might possibly be interested in any kind of liaison whatsoever, there's no harm in enjoying a coffee with an attractive man who finds her both glamorous *and* beautiful. After all, if Kay had popped in to find Joe sitting here, Alice has no doubt the pair of them would have had coffee.

At the very least.

"It's a long story," she smiles. "Would you like some cake to go with your coffee? It's a homemade coffee crumb."

His eyes widen? "A homemade coffee crumb? My goodness, you cook too. Is there anything you can't do?"

"Don't tell anyone" — Alice grins and lowers her voice — "but I'm a terrible ironer."

"I think that's allowed," James says with a wink. And Alice, despite herself, is surprised to feel her cheeks redden as a hot flush springs upon her face.

"So how was your day?" Alice curls her feet underneath her and sinks back into the cushions as she puts her book down.

"Exhausting." Joe leans back in his chair and closes down his computer screen. "I swear to God that five-thirty train is a killer. Thank God I'm in the city tonight. Early night for me."

"You say that every night and then you force yourself awake for *Seinfeld*."

"Not tonight. Tonight I'm planning on being asleep by ten. So what have you done today?"

"Not much. Snoop and I went to the beach this morning, I dropped a note into Sally and Chris's mailbox to thank them for last night, and I found a lovely old breakfront at the consignment —"

"What's a breakfront?"

"A dresser. For the kitchen. To put plates in. They call it a breakfront over here, although I had no idea what the woman was talking about at first. Anyway I'm going to paint it and stencil some roses on."

"Sounds lovely." Joe is distracted.

"And I had coffee with James this morning."

"James who?"

"James, Kay's husband."

That got his attention. "What? What do you mean?"

"I mean he dropped the Rachel Danbury book off and he had coffee here, told me some of the local gossip."

"Oh? Anything interesting?" Joe waits to

hear if Kay will be mentioned, but Alice merely talks about Rachel Danbury for a while until Joe grows bored.

"All right, darling, I have to go now, I'm incredibly busy." Joe signals to a colleague who's waiting patiently for Joe to pack up and come out for a drink.

"Where are you off to?"

"A client meeting. I should be back at the apartment by nine. Are you coming in tomorrow?"

Alice sighs. "Yes. I should be in the city by lunchtime."

"Great. Don't forget we've got that charity thing at the Met tomorrow. What are you going to wear?"

Alice snorts. Back in London Joe wasn't the slightest bit interested in what she was going to wear, as long as she looked beautiful. "Don't worry," she says, knowing how much it bothers him that she spends most of her time now in jeans and boots. "I won't be wearing jeans and a gray sweatshirt if that's what you're worried about."

"Don't be silly, I know you wouldn't, that's not what I meant." But he breathes a sigh of relief. "Black suits you," he adds, just in case she was thinking of chinos.

"I know, I know, and everyone in New

York wears black. I thought maybe a Ralph dress."

Joe has no idea what the dress is like but he hears Ralph Lauren and relaxes. "Perfect," he says. "You'll be the belle of the ball."

18

Joe buries his face in the towel, wiping the sweat from his eyes, and grins up at Kay. "Great game."

"You played well today too." She smiles, undoing her ponytail and shaking her dark hair onto her shoulders, then turning to wave good-bye to their doubles partners.

"We'll meet you up at the clubhouse," they shout, as Joe and Kay nod their assent and wave them off.

"I'm surprised I played so well." Joe stands up and starts to gather his things, zipping his rackets into their covers and tucking his tennis balls into his bag. "Given that there were so many distractions."

"There were?"

"Those, for starters." Joe looks pointedly down at Kay's smooth legs and raises his eyes slowly to meet hers, daring her to flirt with him, to take this further, hoping that she'll take responsibility for whatever might happen between them in the future.

Kay smiles seductively and walks off with a flick of her hair. "We aim to please," she says with a pout over her shoulder as she crosses the court. "I'll see you at the clubhouse."

This happens every time they play tennis. For the last few weeks they've gradually become more and more flirtatious, and he's quite sure she's up for it, yet every time he dares her to take it further, she just smiles and seems to back down.

Not that he's even sure he wants to take it further. Naturally he'd like to have sex with her, what red-blooded male wouldn't, but Joe is not stupid, and Highfield is a small town, and he is fully aware of how people like to talk. His father may have dirtied his own doorstep with his regular affairs with neighbors, but Joe has never been particularly turned on by the prospect of being discussed by everyone in town.

However, too much freedom can be a very dangerous thing, and Joe is finding that the more time he spends in the city without Alice, the more he feels like the bachelor of days of old, and the less point he sees in remaining faithful.

And, Christ, the women here are something else. The women he knew in London were beautiful, but not a patch on the women he sees every day walking down the streets of Manhattan.

Groomed beyond perfection, their hair is glossy, their lips are shining, their bodies are taut, and their heels are high. In other words, they are exactly his type. And you can hardly blame him for being tempted, he figures. After all, it's not as if Alice is keeping up her side of the bargain. Alice, who was the perfect companion in London, is now slopping about in old clothes and Timberland boots. Every time she accompanies him to a restaurant or a charity event, he holds his breath, terrified she'll make a sartorial error of judgment and turn up in jeans or a plaid shirt.

So far she's managed to make the effort, but even so, he can see the other women looking at her, assessing her clothes, dismissing her when they realize it's not this season's Givenchy or the latest Galliano. Joe has had to drag her to Bergdorf Goodman and practically *force* her to try on a confectionery of clothes.

Alice, who used to be so excited by

shopping, now appears as if she couldn't care less.

In fact, Alice, bewitched by her love of the country, her charming little house, her fulfillment of a lifelong dream, is discovering that she is no longer under Joe's spell. Of course she still loves him — he is her husband, after all — but she no longer has to pretend to be something she's not in order to please him, to please his friends.

The insecurity and need to be loved, to be accepted, has left her somewhere along the journey from London to Connecticut, and her newfound happiness is not the only fundamental change in Alice. Alice has a confidence that was missing before. She finally looks like a woman who is comfortable in her skin.

Even the fact that Joe is in Manhattan by himself for a part of each week (gradually becoming a longer and longer part as each week goes by, for the more time Alice spends in the country, the more reluctant she is to leave) no longer fills her with fear.

The days when she would accuse him of having affairs, felt sick when he wasn't answering his mobile phone, feel like a lifetime ago. Now she barely thinks about Joe when he isn't around, phones him only when she remembers or when she needs him to pick up a lamp or a cushion from Gracious Home.

And Joe, used to Alice needing him, is starting to feel neglected. The women he passes in the streets assess him coolly, smile invitingly, and occasionally start up a conversation. Up until now he has smiled in return and entered into a brief conversation if pushed, but has never taken it further.

Despite his vows, Joe is not sure how much longer he can remain abstinent. The women are perhaps that bit too beautiful, too persistent, and his wife that bit too absent.

Alice has fallen in love again, with her life in the country. Isn't it only fair that Joe should find a new interest of his own too?

"Hello? Is anyone home?"

Alice puts *The Winding Road* back on her bedside table — is she ever going to have time to read this book? — and clatters down the stairs to find Sandy standing in her living room, Snoop leaping up to try to give her a kiss hello.

"Oh, I'm sorry. Is this a bad time?"

"Don't be silly. Come in and sit down." Alice gestures to the kitchen stools, delighted to have some company. As happy as she is, when Joe and Gina are in their respective apartments in the city, Alice is beginning to find that she is growing lonely on her own. Her days are filled with projects — painting, restoring, shopping — but when the projects are over she is forced to admit that she could do with some friends.

"But I thought you *were* meeting people?" Emily had said on the phone when Alice confessed her loneliness.

"I am, but at this moment I'd say they were still acquaintances."

Emily had shrugged. "You can't expect instant friendships, it takes time. But it will happen."

Alice tries to go out every afternoon. If not shopping, then to the park or down to the beach to give Snoop a long walk. She does talk to people, Snoop being the perfect conversation-starter, but having a quick chat with someone about her dog is not the easiest way to segue into inviting someone over for a coffee and instant friendship.

Sandy sits down on the stool and places a folder on the kitchen counter. "I brought these for you. Newcomers' Club."

"Newcomers what?" Alice picks up the folder, intrigued.

"It's the Newcomers' Club. Almost

every town has one, and I know it sounds cheesy, but you wouldn't believe the number of people I know who met their oldest and dearest friends at the Newcomers' Club when they first moved here."

"But what is it?"

"It's an organization for people who have recently moved here, and every week there's something going on for people new to the neighborhood. Look." Sandy picks up the current issue and flicks through. "See here? Next Friday is the Dinner Club. Every month we meet up and go to different people's houses for dinner. There's a different theme each month, and everyone brings a different dish. So next week it's Spanish, and Julie and Brad, who are hosting, will make a paella, and the rest of us are bringing assorted tapas."

"It sounds lovely," Alice lies, thinking it sounds unbearably parochial.

"I know, I know," Sandy laughs. "Sally told me what you'd say. And when I first moved here I thought I'd never do something as dreadful as join Newcomers, but how do you think I found friends?"

"Really? But *normal* people? People you would have been friendly with otherwise?"

Alice is still dubious.

"Absolutely. How do you think I met Sally and Chris?"

"You're not going to let me say no, are you?"

"Actually . . ." Sandy makes a face. "Not only am I not going to let you say no, I need a partner to help me run HomeFront, and I've decided you're the woman."

"Well, thank you. I'm very flattered," Alice says in an extremely dubious tone, "but what exactly *is* HomeFront?"

"Every month we do something to do with the home. Like a few months ago we visited an interior designer's house and studio, and she gave a really interesting talk about putting a room together. And then one time we visited a paint effect expert who gave us a demonstration on how to crackle-glaze a table."

"Oh God." Alice can't help herself. "That sounds exactly my kind of thing."

"Exactly! See, it's not awful. I thought you'd like it, so how about getting involved in running it with me?"

"Do I have to stand around and make small talk with people I don't know? Because I'm not very good at that."

"Rubbish. You look like you're perfect at

that. But this is the bit where I get presumptuous."

"Go on."

"Next Tuesday we're having a florist who's going to give us a demonstration of really fun flower arrangements for dinner parties. It was going to be at someone else's house, but she's busy, and I'm having my living room painted so I can't do it at mine . . ."

"So you want to have it here?"

Sandy grimaces. "Could we?"

"Of course! Although it's pretty small. How many people do you think will come?"

"At the moment I've had four replies, but I would think around twelve probably."

"That sounds fine. And what do I need to do? Drinks? Food?"

"Oh no, maybe just some sodas and snacks, but don't go crazy. Oh, I'm so glad you're going to do this, and you'll meet so many nice people."

"You know what, Sandy, it's exactly what I need right now."

"Good. That's what I was hoping. And if you hate absolutely everyone there I promise I won't make you do it again."

At six o'clock on Tuesday evening Alice's house is gleaming. Bowls of roses perch prettily on polished cherry tables, and Alice, who couldn't possibly have people over and serve them merely bowls of chips and peanuts, has spent the morning preparing elaborate hors d'oeuvres.

Her pork and ginger wontons are fanned out on a large platter, sticks of chicken satay are waiting in the fridge, and homemade California rolls are sitting next to bowls of soy and small pyramids of wasabi.

Snoop has been banished to the bedroom — the wontons on the coffee table are far too much of a temptation for him — and Alice has lit perfumed candles that are just starting to fill the air with the smell of oranges and cinnamon.

Now that November is under way, it's cold enough for a fire, but the fire gives off so much heat so quickly, Alice doesn't want twelve women to suffer heatstroke. Instead she lights three huge candles and puts them in the fireplace instead.

At 6:15 Sandy is the first to arrive. "Good Lord," she says, walking in carrying a large cake box. "It looks beautiful in here. I still cannot believe what you've done to this house."

"Thank you." Alice feels a rush of pleasure as she looks around at her home.

"I swear, I would never have believed this house could look the way it does today when I first showed it to you." She smiles at her. "You're clearly so much more than a pretty face."

"I should hope so!" Alice is indignant, but pleased. "So how many people are coming?"

"Ah. A few more than I thought. I think there'll be seventeen, and there are a couple of people who usually come but who didn't reply, so it's going to be a bit cozy but . . . oh my goodness!" She tails off as she notices the food. "Alice, look at all the trouble you went to. Look at all this delicious food! Where did you get it? Oh my." Sandy puts a hand on her chest. "Now I feel guilty. I'm supposed to be your partner, and all I did was bring a cheesecake and you've provided a feast. Oh no."

"Oh, don't be so ridiculous. I made it all this morning in about an hour."

"You *made* it? All this?"

"Yes."

"Even the sushi?"

"Yes. Trust me. It's much easier than it looks. In a former life I used to be a caterer, so this was nothing."

"Now isn't that interesting? You meet people here and think that they're wives and mothers and you never think about the possibility of them having a career as well, then all of a sudden you discover they had these fantastically interesting lives before moving here. You're obviously one talented lady."

"Or one lady with far too much time on her hands."

"Well, that will change now that I've got you into Newcomers. You're going to have so many friends you won't know whether you're coming or going."

Emily laughs so hard that for a few seconds there Alice worries she's having some sort of seizure.

"I cannot believe that you, my darling sophisticated Nobu-visiting glamorous friend, hosted a flower-arranging night yesterday evening. And what's more it's part of the . . . what's it called again?"

"Newcomers' Club, and it's not that funny." Alice pouts.

"Oh, Ali, who would have thought? One minute you're posing for *Tatler* as one of London's most beautiful hostesses, and the next you're living in the country and learning about flower arranging with a load of housewives."

"Actually there were some really nice women there, although" — Alice's voice drops guiltily — "the flower arranging was a bit crap."

"Not Jane Packer then?"

"God no. Barely even bloody Interflora. She did some horrible thing with purple lisianthus, bright pink gerbera, red berries, and yellow carnations."

"Well, I have no idea what lisianthus or gerbera are, but the colors sound a bit too colorful."

"Exactly. I was tempted to stand up and take over."

"You should have done."

"Don't be silly. I'm British. I'd never dare do something like that. Although" — Alice laughs — "two of the women asked her how to do the arrangement on my coffee table, and I think she was a bit pissed off when I admitted I'd done it myself."

Emily smiles. "They probably didn't know what hit them."

"Well, everyone said lovely things about the house. I think the only reason we had such a big turnout was because everyone wanted to see the Rachel Danbury house."

"Oh yes. You said it was the writer's

place. Have you started her book yet?"

"I've only managed the first couple of pages. Every time I try to start something distracts me. I really must make the time."

"What about bedtime?"

"This country air knocks me out. By the time I actually go to bed I'm so exhausted my head hits the pillow and bam! I'm out."

Emily pauses. "Alice, I know this sounds like a silly question, but where's Joe?"

"What do you mean, where's Joe?"

"I mean you just never seem to talk about him anymore."

Alice shrugs. "What's there to say? He's in the city during the week and down here on the weekends."

"So do you miss him when he's in the city?"

Alice thinks for a minute. "I definitely miss having company, but I'm so busy here I don't really think about it much. I'm sort of getting used to being here on my own, although," she adds quickly, "it is lovely when he's back here on the weekends."

Alice feels obligated to say that, even though it is patently untrue. She is growing accustomed to living in Highfield on her own. She buys the food she wants to eat, watches the television programs she wants to watch, and sleeps with as many blankets and comforters as she can pile on the bed.

She takes Snoop out for long walks, potters around antique shops and consignment stores, and spends hours happily restoring the house to its former glory.

Joe arrives on Friday nights. He rings her from the train, expecting her to drop whatever she's doing and jump in the car and come and pick him up. He expects there to be a home-cooked meal waiting for him on the table, and he immediately retires to the study — the study that Alice has recently taken over — and regularly berates Alice for leaving her papers on the desk, or messing up one of his piles, or not using the computer properly.

Alice is always ready to crawl into bed by ten, but Joe stays up watching television until hours later. He insists on keeping a window open in the bedroom, even though Alice is permanently freezing, and won't sleep with anything more than one comforter, so Alice wakes up shivering, and has to sleep in a sweatshirt *and* a camisole.

On Saturday mornings, when he disappears to play tennis, Alice feels as if she can breathe again, tensing up only when he walks back in and takes a shower, leaving soaking wet towels all over the bathroom floor, acting as if he owns the place (which of course he does, although Alice has long thought of it as "her" house and of the place in the city as "his" apartment — a deal she thinks perfectly fair).

By Sunday afternoon Alice can see that Joe is going stir-crazy. He refuses to join her and Snoop on their long walks and, other than watching television or surfing the Internet for hours, cannot seem to think of ways to fill his time.

Clearly he needs friends, needs a diversion out here, and Alice has taken to sending him into town on last-minute errands, or sending him over to Mary Beth and Tom's to borrow a drill, hoping they'll somehow keep him busy for a while.

The only times he seems to enjoy himself are when Gina and George are also down for the weekend, although now that winter is approaching they spend less and less time in the country.

"Oh, please come down this weekend," Alice has pleaded laughingly on the phone.

"But it's freezing!" Gina will say. "You keep forgetting that it's our summer house. Not our freeze-up-and-die house."

But those weekends spent with Gina and George, Joe is like a different person. He discusses the world of finance with George, flirts innocently with Gina, his truculence and apathy toward Alice replaced with genuine warmth and affection.

Those weekends Alice reverts back to the Alice of old. She basks in Joe's attention and takes solace in the familiar feeling of needing to be needed. And Joe in turn welcomes back his old Alice, for Gina is nothing if not glamorous, and — much to Joe's pleasure — Alice does tend to make more of an effort if they are spending time with Gina and George.

So when Alice tells Emily that she looks forward to Joe coming back on the weekends, it's not entirely untrue. As long as Gina and George are there as well, she knows she'll have a lovely time.

"Enough about me," Alice says briskly to Emily. "Less than six weeks to go before you get here. I'm so excited! I can't believe you're coming!"

"God knows, neither can I. And let me tell you, we really need this holiday."

"Is Harry excited?"

"I think so."

"You *think* so? Don't you *know?*"

"Of course he's excited. I haven't seen him much this week. I needed a bit of a break."

Alice's heart jumps into her mouth. "Oh no. You're not going to break up, are you?"

"Oh, I shouldn't think so. We've just been seeing so much of one another he was starting to drive me a bit mad and we agreed to give each other a bit of space."

"Please don't break up with him, Em. He's so lovely."

"I know, I know. I'm sure it's just a temporary blip, and by the time we come out to see you we'll be deliriously happy again."

"You're definitely both coming then?"

"Not only have we booked our tickets, they're nonchangeable and nonrefundable, so I'd say yes, we're definitely both coming."

"Oh, good. And you swear you think everything will be fine by then?"

"Absolutely. We're going out for dinner on Saturday to have a talk, and I know everything will be fine after that."

"What are you going to talk about?"

"I think we just need to take things a bit more slowly, that's all. I suppose I've been feeling a bit . . . well . . . trapped. Does that sound crazy?"

"Not in the slightest. If it's any consolation, it's pretty much how I feel every weekend when Joe's at home."

"Now that doesn't sound good."

"Nah. Tell me about it. Oh God. Here I

am complaining again. Actually I don't feel trapped, he just drives me a bit mad sometimes because he gets so bored, he just doesn't know what to do with himself out here and he expects me to spoon-feed him a life."

"And do you?"

"Nope. I'm far too busy. Speaking of which, my darling, I have to go. I'm off to my Gardeners' Club."

Emily starts laughing again. "Oh God. Now I really have heard everything! Alice Chambers, you are extraordinary." And with that they say good-bye.

19

Alice still cannot quite believe how involved she has become in the Newcomers' Club, and worse, how much she's enjoying it. It is quite as horribly parochial and hokey as she had suspected, and she loves every minute of it.

December has brought a round of "cookie exchanges" — something she couldn't quite believe really existed. All the women invited have to bake a dozen cookies, bring them to a women-only soirée together with the recipe, and leave at the end of the evening with an assortment of home-baked cookies and accompanying instructions.

The social life in suburban America seems to revolve around women. At first Alice found it odd that so many women socialized without their husbands, that when she and Joe went to parties the men would stay in one room and the women invariably in the kitchen.

Alice would whisper to Gina that she would refuse to sit in the kitchen with the women on the grounds that she is a postfeminist child of a feminist, but as time has passed Alice has found herself comforted by this new-found female solidarity, and she is increasingly grateful for this companionship that she once would have found so myopic and cloying.

Even those days and nights when Joe is in the city, Alice is never short of invitations, from lunches and dinners to movies and coffees in town. She is just as busy as she used to be in London, and yet everything is so much more relaxed than it ever used to be. Out here she never squeezes her feet into Jimmy Choos or slides one stockinged leg over the other while sitting at smart restaurant tables. Nowadays her wardrobe is almost unrecognizable, and dressing up consists of a pair of black Gap trousers and an Eddie Bauer cable-knit sweater.

Her smart clothes, and of course she still has smart clothes, are in the apartment in the city. Her Chanel and Hermès handbags are lined up in her walk-in closet, her

Ralph Lauren cashmere sweaters stacked neatly by color, her Christian Louboutin heels next to her JP Tod flats.

She has learned that jeans will not do for their lifestyle in Manhattan, and, perhaps *because* she goes into the city so rarely, she has finally learned to treat the clothes and the accompanying lifestyle much like a game, has learned to enjoy dressing up and living the fast lifestyle that she once took for granted.

As Christmas approaches, Alice has spent more time in the city, buying the gifts she knows her friends and family will love. For Joe she has bought a Patek Philippe watch, one he has coveted for some time. Gina and George will be thrilled with their matching Burberry scarves, and for Emily she has a beautiful intricately beaded bag that she found in SoHo and knew Emily would adore. For Harry she has a small but perfectly formed toolbox, containing everything the carpenter on the go could possibly need.

Now she just has to wait for them to get here.

The doorman buzzes the apartment at 5:10 p.m. to let Alice know that Emily and Harry are downstairs. She had wanted to go to JFK and pick them up, but Joe, who was still in the office, said not only would the traffic be terrible, the place itself was a zoo and she'd never manage it on her own.

Instead she sent a car to collect them and told Emily and Harry to look out for a uniformed man with their names on a large square of cardboard.

Minutes after the doorman buzzes, Alice hears a familiar knocking on the apartment door. Dashing to the door, she runs straight into a grinning Emily's arms.

They hug each other tight for what feels like hours, Harry standing back and watching them with a smile, stepping forward to give Alice a brief hug only when the girls have pulled apart. But with each step into the apartment Alice and Emily grin at each other and hug again.

"Anyone would think you two were long-lost lovers." Harry laughs, after the fourth hug in as many minutes.

"You're just jealous," Emily says. "And anyway, she's my best friend in the whole wide world and I've missed her." She turns to Alice, who is trying not to let the tears trickle down her cheeks. "Do you know how much I've missed you?"

"About a half as much as I've missed you?"

"Yeah. Probably about that much. So this is home?"

"I suppose. Harry, come and I'll show you where you're both sleeping. You can put your bags down, and then what do you feel like doing?"

"We have to go out!" Emily says. "I can't believe we're *here,* in New York! What should we do? Where's Joe? When are we going to see the other house? Where can I find the best bargains?"

Alice bursts out laughing. "One question at a time. First, Joe's at the office and meeting us later for dinner."

"I see some things never change." Emily raises an eyebrow, which Alice chooses to ignore.

"We're going to the Gramercy Tavern for dinner, so what we do first is entirely up to you. I didn't organize anything because I didn't know how tired you'd be, but tomorrow I thought we could go shopping in the morning, and then I've booked tickets for *Hairspray,* and then I thought we could either go down to the country tomorrow evening or stay in town and go down the following day."

"Christmas Eve. Have you got your tree or are we still going to the Christmas tree farm to pick our own?" Emily laughs.

"Actually a man turned up in the driveway last week with a truck full of Christmas trees so I just picked one. I know it's not quite as romantic."

"But eminently more practical, I would think. At least tell me you haven't decorated it yet."

Alice grins. "Nope. I've saved the joys of decorating for the four of us on Christmas Eve. Oh, and we've also been invited to Sally and Chris's for New Year's Eve."

"Us as well?"

"Of course you as well. Sally can't wait to meet you. Unfortunately it won't be very festive on Christmas Day, it's just us, but I'm doing a proper lunch."

"The whole bit? Turkey and trimmings?"

"Of course! Actually they don't do that here, they do all that stuff at Thanksgiving, but Christmas isn't Christmas without a turkey."

"And chipolatas?"

"Of course!"

Harry turns from the window and smiles at Alice. "Emily kept saying you'd turned into a country bumpkin, and here you are looking just as glamorous as the last time I saw you. I was expecting wellies and an anorak."

"I said she'd turned into a bumpkin,"

Emily tuts. "Not Worzel Gummidge, for God's sake. But meanwhile" — she turns to face Alice — "I have to say I agree with Harry. I thought you said you never wore makeup anymore and you lived in jeans. Look at you, Miss High Heels and Cashmere Sweater."

"I swear to God I only dress like this in Manhattan. Just you wait."

Emily walks over to join Harry at the window, and they both look up at the sky. "So what do you think?" Emily turns to Alice. "Is it going to snow? You said last week they were predicting it might snow. Are we going to have a white Christmas?"

"They said it might, although it's more likely to happen after Christmas Day. All the locals say they dread the snow, and I can't tell them that I go to bed every night praying for it. Now. On to more practical issues. What do you want to do before dinner?"

Harry suppresses a yawn. "I know I'm being a wimp, but I'm bloody exhausted. Would you mind if I had a sleep?" He's clearly struggling to keep his eyes open, and Emily is quick to hustle him into the bedroom.

"Good," she whispers when she comes back out. "I've been dying to see you by myself. Shall we go out and get a coffee? I can't believe I'm in New York with my best friend! Come here and give me another hug!"

"Two grande skim lattes." Alice squeezes in next to Emily in the corner table in Starbucks.

"Thanks, Ali. So you promise that bag shop will still be open on the way back?"

"I promise. Don't worry, you'll still be able to indulge your compulsive shopaholism. Bags." Alice shakes her head. "I don't know. You've only been in New York a minute and already you're itching to spend money."

Emily sighs. "I know it's dreadful. I'm clearly a horrible person."

"So tell me everything. Tell me how it's all worked out with Harry. You seem happy again. I know you told me on the phone, but it's always so rushed and we never seem to talk properly. So tell me now."

"He *is* lovely . . ." Emily starts. And stops. "I mean really, he's just the nicest man I've met."

"There's a but coming, isn't there?"

Emily grimaces. "There's always a but. The but is . . . actually it's not even him, it's me."

"He's too nice, isn't he?"

"Oh God, Ali, that's why I love you and that's why I need you. You know me better than anyone else. Why, oh why, am I so ridiculous? Why is this a problem? But yes, that's it. He's just too bloody nice to me and I'm bored." With that Emily's eyes widen, and she claps her hands over her mouth. "Oh, shit. I can't believe I just said that."

"I can't believe you just said that either. Emily, most women I know would kill to find a man like Harry. He's kind, he's funny, he loves animals, and he adores you. *I'd* kill to find a man like Harry, for Christ's sake."

"So how *are* things with Joe then?"

"Uh-uh. You're not changing the subject that easily. I'm serious, Emily." Emily folds her arms across her chest like a disgruntled teenager and looks down at her shoes. "He's wonderful. How can you be bored?"

Emily makes a pained face. "I know this sounds terrible, but I'm sure if he was a bit more of a bastard I could fall in love with him."

"You're serious, aren't you?"

"I know, I know. It's dreadful. I am a disgusting person, but if he's ever a bit off with me, or doesn't call when he says he's going to, or I think he might be flirting with someone else, then suddenly I'm interested again."

"Emily, that's sick. That's all your *stuff*. You should go and see someone."

"Someone like a therapist?" Alice nods as Emily shakes her head with a shrug. "Nah, couldn't afford it even if I wanted to."

"But, Em, you can't possibly pass up what will probably turn out to be the greatest man you'll ever meet because of your own crappy baggage."

"I know," she says sadly. "That's why I can't break up with him. Because I do think he'll probably be the greatest man I'll ever meet, and because I keep hoping that one day I'm going to wake up and be madly in love with him."

"You know, Em, marriage isn't everything we're led to believe it is."

"What do you mean?"

"I mean we're told it's supposed to be this huge great overwhelming passion, and that we're supposed to look for our soul mate, our other half, but it's actually pretty damn mundane."

"Mundane?"

Alice sighs. "Well, yes, mundane. It's just that after a while all the excitement goes, and what you really want to be left with is someone who is a really good person and who adores you, and who you can grow old with. I know the bastards are exciting, but they don't make good husband material. Trust me."

Emily doesn't ask her how she knows. She doesn't need to.

"You know what, Em? Sometimes I wish I hadn't fallen quite so head-over-heels with Joe. Sometimes I think I might have been better off with someone more like Harry."

"But I remember when you first got married. Okay, it might have faded a bit now, but you were so in love you could hardly see straight. I want to feel like that, I *should* feel like that with the man I'm going to marry."

Alice shakes her head. "No! That's not what it's about. That heady exciting stuff just blinds you to what's real. And what's real is Harry. I think he's perfect for you. I think he'd make you happy, you could forge a loving and lasting union with him."

"But I'm bored," Emily whispers furiously. "I'm bored, Alice. Everything's so predictable, I never get excited by anything anymore. You can't tell me that's a good thing. And if you do I won't believe you. If you were to tell me that, then I'd have to assume you made a terrible mistake in marrying the love of your life."

Alice is silent.

"So?" Emily persists. "Did you make a mistake?"

"Of course not," Alice says quickly. "That's ridiculous. I love Joe and he's a wonderful husband, but men like Harry are few and far between. I just don't want you to break up with him then spend the rest of your life regretting it."

"Who said anything about breaking up?"

"It sounded like you were on the verge of shoving him out the door."

"No. That's the problem. I've thought about it so many times, but every time I do something stops me because he is a lovely guy and, as I said" — she shrugs — "I keep hoping I'm going to fall in love with him."

"Do you think it was wise, to bring him here?"

"Yup. I have a feeling this holiday may well turn out to be make-or-break."

"Oh, thanks." Alice rolls her eyes. "And here was I planning a lovely, relaxing Christmas in the country, and now I discover it could be tears all round."

Emily laughs. "Nope, there won't be

tears. Actually we had a lovely flight, so who knows, America could be just what we need to get our relationship back on track and fall in love. Although . . ."

"Although what?"

"Although there kind of is . . ."

"What?"

Emily grimaces. "Well, the thing is I've kind of met . . ."

"Oh, no." Alice's voice is stern. "You've met someone else?"

Emily seems to shrink in acknowledgment.

"Emily, that's awful."

"It's not as awful as it sounds. I mean, I haven't done anything. Actually I don't even know if he's interested, although I think he might be. But I've found myself incredibly attracted to this man, and that's what's really set this whole thing off."

"But, Emily, just because you're with someone doesn't mean you stop being attracted to other people. It's a question of choice."

"For you maybe, but you've been married for over five years. We haven't even reached a year, so don't tell me it's normal to really fancy other men."

Alice sighs. After all, Emily does have a point. "So who is he?"

"He's the new features editor at that men's magazine I've been writing for."

"And?"

"And we had a business lunch about three weeks ago."

"And that's it? You're questioning your relationship because of a business lunch?"

"Well, no. I mean, yes, that's where we met, and Alice, I swear to God I felt something unlike anything I've felt before."

"Em, I'm sure I've heard you say this before. In fact, I'm sure I heard you say this about Harry when you first met."

"No, Alice. This was different. I know it sounds crazy, but if there is such a thing as a soul mate then I think he might be it. I just had this unbelievable reaction when we looked at one another, and we were in the restaurant for hours, just talking about everything."

"I suppose you felt as if you'd known each other all your lives?" Alice can't keep the cynicism out of her voice. She loves Emily but she knows her better than anyone, and knows this isn't the first time she's felt like this, and probably won't be the last. And more to the point, she likes Harry, and she doesn't want Emily to screw up what could be, what probably is, a wonderful relationship, and certainly the best relationship Alice has ever seen her in.

"Alice!" Emily is hurt.

"I'm sorry. I didn't mean it. So go on. You were talking about everything."

"Well, yes. And I did feel as if I'd known him for years." Even as she talks her eyes start to sparkle, her voice becomes more animated. "He is just amazing. And *gorgeous*, Ali! I swear, he looks exactly like Ben Affleck."

"But I think Harry's pretty gorgeous too."

"No, Colin is gorgeous."

Alice starts to laugh. "He's gorgeous and his name's *Colin?*"

Emily bristles. "What's wrong with Colin?"

"Nothing, nothing. I just didn't expect someone who looks exactly like Ben Affleck to be called something as, well, as ordinary as Colin."

"Well, he's gorgeous, and funny, and incredibly bright, and well, just amazing really."

"So that's it? You had lunch?"

"Yes. And then a few days later I went to a preview and he was there and we spent the whole night talking."

"Just talking?"

"God, yes. We were in a restaurant. But,

Alice, I swear there was this amazing chemistry between us."

"But you promise you didn't do anything?"

"No. I mean, he kissed me good-bye, but no tongues or anything. Just a peck on the lips. But the *lips*, Alice! Don't you think that means he likes me?"

"Emily," Alice says sternly, "I'm not getting into this with you. I'm not playing the game of he said this so that must mean he likes me, or he looked at me that way which must mean he thought about me all week. It's not fair to Harry."

"But, Alice, you're my best friend," Emily groans. "I haven't told a soul and I've been dying to tell someone."

"No, Emily. I love you but I don't want to see you make a terrible mistake. I'll always support you, whatever you do, but please don't put me in a position where I have to support infidelity."

"But I told you, we haven't done anything."

"Yet."

There's a long silence while Emily digests what Alice has said. "Okay," she says finally. "I do understand. And you're right, it's not fair to Harry, which is what I feel so terrible about. And anyway, I did find

out that Colin's in a five-year relationship . . ."

"A *what?*" Alice shouts.

"Relax! Relax! Apparently he's really unhappy and he's tried to leave loads of
times . . ."

Alice shakes her head in dismay. "Emily,
you're old enough to know better. Someone's going to get very hurt, and not just
Harry."

"You're right, you're right. The point is
that probably nothing will happen and it's
just that it's made me remember what it's
like to be single again and to have that excitement."

"And that's okay," Alice says. "It's okay
to miss being single, just as long as you
don't do anything about it."

"I know, you're right. You're right. While
we're here I swear to you I'm going to do
everything I can to give Harry my best
shot, and as long as I'm with Harry I won't
do anything with Colin, okay?"

"Not even lunch?"

"But nothing happened at lunch!" Emily
protests. "And he's my features editor, I
have to meet him."

"You can meet him, but not for lunch.
Just meet him in the office where there are
other people around. If you decide that

Harry's not going to work out and you and Harry split up then you can do whatever you want, although I have to tell you, a five-year relationship, unhappy or not, doesn't look good."

"But apparently his girlfriend is a real bitch."

"*Emily!* Joe and I have been married for five years. Imagine, that could be me you're talking about. Five years is a long time. Marriage or not, it's a serious commitment, and Harry or no Harry, I would think very carefully before pursuing this."

"Okay. You're right. If I promise to stop thinking about him, will you start being nicer to me?"

"Oh, Emily," Alice laughs despite her exasperation. "You know I love you even though I don't always understand you." She looks at her watch. "Come on. Do you still want to go and look at those bags?"

Harry groans and half opens one eye. He has been in a deep, deep sleep, lost in a dream about pulling up endless weeds in his garden that had grown and morphed into a huge country field.

"Come on, lazybones." Emily is sitting on the edge of the bed, shaking him as she leans over to kiss his cheek. "Time to get up and get ready for dinner."

"Oh God," Harry mumbles. "I feel like I've been drugged. I think I'm just going to stay here and go to sleep."

"And leave me as gooseberry? I don't think so. Come on." Emily drags the duvet off him as Harry buries his head in the pillow. "Come and have a shower with me?"

Harry smiles. "A shower with you?" He flings his legs over the side of the bed. "Now why didn't you say that before?"

20

Joe hurries into the Gramercy Tavern, is greeted with a warm smile by the hostess, and weaves his way through the tables until he reaches Alice, Emily, and Harry.

He leans down to give first Alice a kiss, then Emily, finally extending a hand to shake Harry's warmly as he scrapes the chair back and sits down.

"Harry, good to see you again."

"Good to be here, Joe."

"Good journey over?"

"Great actually."

"Did you fly BA?"

"No. United. The deal was too good to pass up."

"So how's life back in rainy old London?"

Emily rolls her eyes. "Raining. And how's life here in fabulous New York?"

"Fabulous," Joe echoes with a smile.

"No, really." Emily pushes. "Do you love it as much as Alice?"

"I'm not sure anyone could love it quite as much as my darling wife." He smiles affectionately at Alice. "But all in all I'd say it was a pretty good move." He turns and signals the waiter to come over, ordering a spicy Bloody Mary before turning back to the table.

"So what do you miss most about London?" Emily continues.

Joe stops to think. "I miss being able to jump on a plane and hop over to Europe for the weekend."

"But," Alice interjects, "we do have the Caribbean, which isn't exactly bad."

"True, but it's not quite the same thing."

Emily nods. "I'm afraid I have to agree with Joe there. Sorry, but you can't compare the Caribbean to Europe. Anyway. Go on."

"So Europe. And obviously I miss my friends. I miss how familiar everything is in London. I'm very comfortable in New York, but I don't know the people in the corner shops the way I do in London. I miss the television."

"You have to be joking!" Emily exclaims as a waiter silently drops a menu into her

hands. "America has much better television. What about *Frasier*? And *West Wing*?
All the best TV's from here."

Joe shakes his head. "No. You think that
because only the best of the best gets
picked up by Britain. You wouldn't believe
the amount of crap that's on here."

"Don't you get hours and hours of those
made-for-television dramas starring the
Bionic Woman?" Harry grins as Alice
starts to laugh.

"I can't believe you just said that! Twice
last week I was flicking and both times I
passed films starring Lindsay Wagner!"
splutters Alice.

"And was she coping with cancer or a
dying husband?"

"I didn't watch for long enough, but
there was definitely some kind of major
tragedy going on. Lots of hankies and worried expressions during phone calls.
Actually I had the thing on mute as I was
on the phone, but more to the point" —
Alice peers at Harry — "how come you
know so much about dramas starring the
Bionic Woman?"

"It's a little-known secret, but I lived in
San Diego for a couple of years when I was
a teenager."

"I didn't know that!" Emily is shocked.

"How come?" Alice is curious.

Harry shrugs. "My dad's American, and they wanted to make a go of it over here so they dragged me over when I was thirteen, but it didn't work out. We went back to England when I was fifteen, and" — he shrugs again — "we've been there ever since."

"I was going to say you don't have a trace of American accent."

"Wasn't here long enough."

"But," Alice muses, "it does explain those perfect teeth."

"Why, thank you." Harry bares his teeth in a rictus. "I bet you say that to all the boys."

By ten o'clock Emily looks like a zombie. Harry, having managed to have a nap in the afternoon, is slightly more alert, but the fact that it is three o'clock in the morning English time, combined with the fact that the pair of them are well into their thirties, does not bode well, and Harry has to practically carry Emily out of the restaurant.

"We're supposed to be going to a party," Joe whispers miserably to Alice as he heads to the corner to look for a cab.

"Oh, shit. I forgot. But they're in no

state to go anywhere other than bed."

"Look, we'll give them the keys and they can let themselves in, and you and I can go."

"But that's so rude."

"Far ruder to have accepted an invitation and then simply not show up."

"Oh, come on, Joe. You know what these parties are like. There'll be a million people there, there's no way they'll notice whether we're there or not."

"That's not the point," Joe says sternly. "Alice, I know you forgot but you said we'd go, and I want you to come with me. We barely see one another anymore, you're always in the bloody country, and the least you can do is spend time with me when you actually manage to make it into Manhattan."

Alice is not happy. The very last thing she wants to do is go to a superficial party filled with superficial people, but Joe is right. Although she probably didn't spend that much more time with Joe when they lived in London, over there it was his choice: She didn't see him because he was always working, or traveling, or canceling her at the eleventh hour.

Now she barely sees him because she is too busy, too wrapped up in her life outside of the city, and this shift of balance in their relationship makes her uncomfortable, guilty.

Which is why she agrees to accompany Joe to the party tonight.

The minute the cab stops outside the Hudson Alice knows she's not going to have a good time. She can already see the place is jam-packed with beautiful people, the music's loud, and she'd forgotten how much she hates parties.

Joe walks in ahead of her and immediately runs into people he knows, leaning down to kiss the women, shaking the men's hands as Alice stands behind him with a false smile, waiting to be introduced.

"Ted, Kerry, this is my wife, Alice."

"Hi, how are you?" They all shake hands, Kerry with a smile that is just as false as Alice's. A tall skinny redhead, she looks Alice up and down appraisingly, deciding that yes, Alice will pass.

"We've all been waiting to meet you," Kerry shouts into her ear above the din. "For a while we thought maybe Joe was delusional."

"What do you mean?" Alice shouts back into her ear.

"I mean he kept saying he was married

but no one ever saw you. We decided he must have been making you up."

Alice smiles. "Oh no." She extends an arm. "Feel this. Real flesh and blood. So how do you know Joe?"

"Oh, around and about. When you start doing the scene, you find you see the same people over and over. Joe's just become a familiar face I guess."

"The scene?"

"You know. The parties. The benefits. Just *stuff*."

Alice doesn't know. And more to the point, she didn't know Joe was doing "the scene" enough to have become a familiar face. How did he fit it in? Most of the time, when Alice is in the country and they speak late at night, he's about to go to bed. At least that's what he says.

Alice sighs as she feels a familiar tightening of her chest, a familiar feeling that all is not so well in her world after all. She looks up at Joe, who does seem to know an awful lot of people here, and her mind races. Has he been lying? Why would he lie? Is he up to no good? Am I being over-sensitive?

The thought that wins out is this: So what if he goes out to parties when I'm in the country? I can't expect him to go to bed every night at nine o'clock. And just because he's going to parties without me doesn't mean he's having an affair, for God's sake. As Kerry just said, he talks about his wife, so clearly he's not pretending to be single.

I am being oversensitive, Alice decides as she slips her arm through Joe's and smiles up at him, vowing not to let her imagination run away with her again.

"Good morning. You're up early." Alice leans against the doorjamb to tie the laces of her tennis shoes as Snoop leaps up and down at her heels.

Harry peers over the top of the *New York Times*. "I've been up since five. Bloody jet lag. But more to the point, you're up early too. What time did you get in last night?"

"Not too late. Just after midnight."

"And how was the party?"

Alice shrugs. The party had ended up being like a million other parties she'd been to since she got here, all of which she hated.

Packed with skinny people in designer clothes, all repeating the same conversations: gossiping about people they had in common (none of whom Alice knew), or the women trying to befriend her by asking where she got her hair done or whose lipstick she is wearing. The men stand together, rather like the teenage discos Alice remembers from her teenage years, and talk markets, property, and sports.

"The party was fine. Fun. If you like that sort of thing."

"And *do* you like that sort of thing?"

"To be honest I would have been much happier in bed."

"We were definitely much happier in bed."

"Ooh. Too much information, thank you."

Harry grins. "That's not what I meant, thank you. So where are you off to at the crack of dawn in your exercise gear? Working off last night's supper at the gym, I take it?"

"You have to be joking. Didn't Emily tell you I'm allergic to gyms? Snoop and I are actually off for our morning walk in Central Park. Want to come too?"

"I'd love to. Hang on, I'll get my shoes."

"Bring a jacket too. It's supposed to be cold today."

Harry glances out the window. "But look at that sky. It's a perfect blue and the sun's shining."

"Doesn't mean a thing. The sun's always

shining here, but it's deceptive. I'm telling you, bring a jacket."

"Okay, okay. The lady knows best."

"Good. Now that's what I like to hear. Take this too." Alice grabs two woolen hats from the bench just inside the door, flings one to Harry, and pulls the other down tight over her ears.

"I don't think it will suit me." Harry raises an eyebrow as Alice makes a face at him.

"I think you'll find you'll be thanking me later. Come on. Snoop needs to pee."

"Jesus," Harry hisses as they step out the door. "It's freezing."

Alice laughs. "Don't say I didn't warn you."

"Are you always this smug?" Harry frowns.

"Are you always this much of a wimp?"

"Point taken. So how far's the park? Are we nearly there?"

"God, you *are* a wimp. Come on, let's jog. It'll warm you up."

"I'm impressed." They reach the park and Alice slows down to unwind her scarf. "You're fitter than you look."

"And you're just as fit as you look.

Anyway, what do you mean I'm fitter than I look? There isn't an ounce of fat on me."

"I know. All that gardening and carpentry must keep you fit."

Harry raises an eyebrow. "You remember?"

"Of course. You think I invited you down to the country just because I like you?" Alice laughs.

"Damn. I knew there was a catch. So will I be building bookshelves? Or planting bulbs?"

Alice turns to him. "Aha! I knew you weren't as good as I thought, or you'd know that it's far too late to plant bulbs."

"Actually I knew that. I was just testing you." Harry grins and holds out a hand for Snoop's leash. "So let's see how your training's been coming along. Got any treats?"

"Of course!" Alice reaches a gloved hand into her pocket and passes a bag of treats to Harry. "You trained me well."

"And hopefully you've passed it on to the lovely Snoop. Snoop? Sit!" Snoop obediently sits down and looks at Harry expectantly.

"Good boy!" Harry slips a treat into his mouth and pats him on the head.

"Down!" Snoop slides down to the ground, still looking at Harry, as Harry looks impressed and gives him another treat.

"Stay!" Harry turns and walks away for a few yards, turns around, and sees Snoop in exactly the same spot, lying there immobile. "Alice Chambers, I am very, very impressed."

"Watch this," Alice grins. "Shake hands, Snoop." She laughs as Snoop obediently raises his right paw and places it in her hand. "And the other hand." Snoop puts his paw down and raises the other one, and Alice swears he's smiling as he does it.

Harry walks back and makes a big fuss of Snoop. "Good boy!" he says, ruffling his fur. "What a good boy! And what a good girl!" He turns to Alice and uses exactly the same tone of voice, proffering a treat to her lips as she grimaces in disgust, then starts laughing, pushing his hand away.

"Good girl, Alice!" Harry continues, laughing as he tries to push the treat in her mouth. "Who's a good girl!" Snoop starts barking, wanting to join in the game as Alice shrieks, laughing as she tries to get away from the revolting-smelling treat in Harry's hand.

"Get off!" she shouts, still laughing. "Leave me alone. Yeuch. That's disgusting!" Harry finally gives the treat to Snoop.

"But you've trained him well. Seriously. I am impressed."

"Of course. What do you think I do in the country all day? Watch television?"

Harry shrugs. "Only, I assumed, the made-for-TV dramas."

"Ha-ha."

They carry on walking in silence for a while, down to the water, where they sit on a bench to watch the ducks.

"Aren't they supposed to fly south for winter?" Harry says after a few minutes.

"I thought so too. I think these are the ones who couldn't afford the holiday."

"Hmm." Harry nods. "Couldn't they have gone EasyJet?"

"I'm not sure they cover America."

Harry smiles and turns to Alice. "You know, you've changed so much."

"I have? But you hardly know me. How can you tell?"

"You're just glowing, Alice. I mean, you're right, I don't know you well at all even though I feel like I do because Emily has always talked about you so much. I felt like I knew you before I even met you, but I remember being surprised when we met because even though I liked you, you seemed so, God, I probably shouldn't say this, but you just didn't seem happy."

"Really? How odd. Even at Brianden? We all had such a nice time. Didn't I seem happy then?"

"It's not that you were sitting around crying or anything, you just seemed to have this air of sadness, and it's gone now, Alice. You just look completely different."

"That's because it's first thing in the morning and I'm not wearing any makeup."

"No, although I'll admit you do look a bit rough . . . ow!" Alice elbows him sharply as she makes a warning face. "Okay, okay, I was joking. But seriously, it's got nothing to do with makeup or what time of day it is, your whole, aargh . . ." He grimaces and hides his head in his hands.

"What? Are you going to say something horrible? Is that why you're making a face? Go on. Tell me."

"This is going to sound so cheesy, but . . . your whole aura has changed."

"You're right. It does sound cheesy."

"I'll just shut up then."

"No. Don't. It's nice talking about me."

Harry shakes his head. "I can't believe you just said that."

"But it's true!" Alice lies. "It's my favorite subject."

"Anything else you'd like to add about yourself then?"

"Oh no. It's much more fun to listen to what other people think about me. Come on. Let's keep walking." Alice stands up because, despite the jokes, she's suddenly not comfortable with this conversation, with the intimacy that has sprung up, and although she has tried to hide her discomfort with humor, it is far easier to stand up and keep walking, to change the subject altogether.

"So," Alice says briskly. "Let's go and get some coffee and bagels to take back to the apartment. We've got a million things to do today, and then you two have to decide whether you want to go down to the country tonight or tomorrow."

"Oh, right." Harry stands up. "I'm pretty easy really. Which would suit you better?"

"Well" — Alice looks up at the sky — "as long as it doesn't snow we're fine either way."

"And what can you tell from looking at the sky? Snow today or no snow?"

"I think no snow today."

"How can you tell?"

"I can't. I just like to look as if I know

what I'm talking about."

"Ah." Harry nods sagely. "In that case I'd have to agree with you. Definitely no snow today."

Back at the apartment they are met with silence. The *New York Times* is exactly where they left it, the bedroom doors still firmly shut.

"My God, they're lazy," Alice laughs, putting the coffee and bagels down on the table. "Let me just put these out then we'll wake them up."

"What can I do?"

"How about plates and knives?"

"Okay."

"Oh, and cream cheese in the fridge."

"Got it."

"Right." Alice spreads everything out. "Let's go and drag them out of bed."

"Darling," Alice whispers to a naked, sleeping Joe. "Breakfast is on the table."

Joe turns and smiles sleepily. He's been awake for a while, so warm and comfortable in bed he let himself doze on and off. Oddly, he found himself thinking about Josie. He hasn't thought about her in a while, hasn't spoken to her or had any contact, other than seeing her name at the top of a group e-mail from time to time, but this morning he started to remember the feel of her skin, the smell of her hair.

He was just getting excited when he heard Alice come into the bedroom. Ah, lovely Alice. Just what the doctor ordered. He rolls over to her and slides his hand under her sweatshirt, stroking the underside of her breast and smiling.

"Come on." She pulls away from him and throws back the covers. "Breakfast is on the table."

Damn. Alice gets up and disappears out the bedroom. Clearly she is not in the mood, and clearly he doesn't have time to take care of what is now a major erection. Damn, damn, and damn. Slowly Joe heaves himself out of bed and into the bathroom for a quick, cold shower.

"What a lovely time we've had!" Emily sighs as she turns around to see the New York skyline recede behind her. "Isn't New York wonderful? I could stay here forever."

Yesterday morning had been spent shopping, then lunch at a diner in the village, theater in the afternoon, and dinner in Tribeca. Emily is exhausted and exhilarated, and sorry that they're leaving already.

"Well, they certainly loved you," Harry smiles. "My darling Emily who single-handedly helped the economy back on its feet."

Alice smiles but Emily is stony-faced. "How can you say that, Harry? Everything I bought was either from the market in Canal Street or cheap little shops in SoHo."

"It's not quality, Em, it's quantity," Harry says. "I don't know how we're going to get everything home."

"We'll buy another bag," Emily grumbles.

"I thought you didn't have any money?" Harry says.

"Oh, for God's sake, Harry. Why don't you just lighten up?" she snaps. "We're on holiday. You're supposed to have fun on holiday."

Alice and Joe sit there uncomfortably. Alice wants to tell Emily to relax, that she is being oversensitive, but she has learned not to get involved in other people's affairs, and so she stays silent.

Eventually Joe breaks the awkwardness. "I hope you brought your tool kit, Harry. I think Alice has got some jobs for you."

"Damn, I knew I left something behind." Harry smacks his forehead.

"Oh, well," Joe smiles. "You can borrow mine."

Alice splutters with laughter. "You don't have a tool kit."

"I do have some screwdrivers though," Joe blusters.

"*I'm* the one with the tool kit, thank you," Alice says, turning to Harry, "and I'd be happy to lend it to you."

"And who said there was such a thing as a free holiday?" Harry tuts, looking out of the window.

"I can't believe we're here," Emily squeals as the car turns into the driveway in Highfield. "I mean, I thought Brianden was in the country, but it's nothing like this. This is like something out of a film. Look at these woods, all these trees."

"Isn't it beautiful?" Alice smiles, already more relaxed now she's home. They roll down the driveway and pull up in front of the house.

"This is it?"

"Er . . . yes."

"It's lovely," Emily says, and it is, but somehow she'd expected something much grander. She knows Joe is planning on building a far bigger house somewhere else on the land, but she also knows that Alice is quite happy with this, and even though it's pretty, if you like that old Americana type of style, it's not at all what she expected.

"The boys will take the bags. Come on, Em, I'll give you the tour."

They walk around the ground floor, Alice pointing out what's been painted, what restored, what work she's planning to do, and then upstairs to see the three small bedrooms, the guest room chic and welcoming with its blue toile bedspread and matching curtains, small check pillows thrown casually on the bed.

And then downstairs again, out of the French doors and into the garden, strolling down to the pond, where they huddle on a wooden bench that sits under a huge old maple tree.

"Just listen," Alice smiles.

"What? I can't hear anything."

"Exactly! Isn't it the most peaceful place you've ever been?"

Emily smiles. "It is. I'd probably go out of my mind living here, but I can see how you would love it."

"But you have Brianden. That's the country."

"Yes, but it's the Cotswolds. It's different. And I'm only there on weekends, and I spend most of my time elbowing past American tourists looking for a bargain in the antique shops. It's always pretty busy there, but this is so quiet."

"I know. My favorite place in the world."

"I can't believe you've done it, you know." Emily turns, her face now serious.

"Done what?"

"You've made your dream come true. You always wanted this. Always wanted to live in the country and have a simple life, and look at you now."

"You know, I wake up in the mornings and sometimes I feel as if I have to pinch myself," Alice laughs. "It just feels ridiculous that I'm this happy."

"Oh, Ali, it's lovely." Emily reaches out and puts her arms around Alice, squeezing hard. "I'm so happy for you."

They hug tightly for a few seconds, then pull apart and stand up. "Come on," Alice says. "Let's go and see what those boys are up to."

Back at the house Harry is building a fire and Joe is sitting at the computer in his study.

"Joe," Alice hisses under her breath in the doorway. "We have guests. Can you not disappear and be so rude?"

"Relax, Alice. I'm just checking my e-mail. I'll be out in a second."

Alice sighs and closes his door again. *Plus ça change, plus c'est la même chose,* she thinks. The more it changes, the more it stays the same.

21

"Happy Christmas!" Harry runs a hand through his tousled hair as he walks into the kitchen to see Alice slathering butter on a giant turkey.

"Aren't you the early bird?" Alice grins. "I take it everyone else is fast asleep."

"Emily's out for the count, and I didn't hear a peep from your room" — Harry peers over Alice's shoulder at the bird — "although I admit I didn't listen for very long. What time is it anyway?"

Alice gestures up to the old clock on the kitchen wall. "Seven-ten. Almost, but not quite, the crack of dawn. This feels like it's becoming a habit, you and me in the kitchen first thing."

Harry smiles to himself, remembering Brianden. He yawns and stretches his tracksuit-clad legs out in front of him. "Do you want me to take Snoop out for a walk?"

Alice smiles and shakes her head, sprinkling a liberal amount of salt and pepper on the turkey then walking over to the fridge for rashers of bacon to lay in strips on the turkey's breast.

"Snoop's already been out. But thanks."

"And you're calling *me* the early bird?" Harry laughs. "What time did *you* get up?"

"Around six."

"Six o'clock? That's the middle of the night!"

"That's what I used to think when we were in London, but here there's so much more to do. I just seem to be so much busier that there are never enough hours in the day. If I didn't get up early I wouldn't get anything done."

"Speaking of which, what can I do to help?"

Alice pauses, about to say what she always says, which is nothing, I'm fine, but she could do with the help, and there's no harm in admitting she's not Superwoman after all.

"Tell you what," she says. "There's fresh coffee in the pot so help yourself, then you can peel potatoes."

"Sounds great. There's nothing like

man's work to really make me feel useful."

Alice shrugs. "Well, you did ask. You could peel the parsnips if you prefer. Or help make the stuffing."

"Ah, stuffing." Harry raises an eyebrow. "That does sound like man's work."

"Oh, ha-ha. We'll have none of that talk in this house, thank you."

Harry walks over to pour himself a coffee, grabbing Alice's cup on the way and refilling hers. As he pours he peers out of the window into the darkness. "Bummer. I see there's no snow. I don't even remember the last time I had a white Christmas."

"I know." Alice smiles. "You'd think that out here in Connecticut you'd at least have more of a chance. I suppose you have to go farther north, Vermont probably, to get the snow."

Harry laughs. "I suppose it would have been too good to be true to wake up on Christmas Day and find a blanket of snow. Already it feels like I'm waking up in someone's fantasy."

Alice turns to him. "What do you mean?"

Harry starts to peel the potatoes. "I mean this house, being in this part of the world. It's just the most perfect romantic life, so perfect it's almost ridiculous."

"Harry, do you know I'm so glad you said that. That's how I feel every single day when I wake up here, but no one else seems to understand it."

"Listen, I'm a real country boy at heart. I completely understand it. But that's what I meant about the snow, it would be so corny it would be laughable."

Alice laughs. "Yes," she says. "I do see what you mean."

"Alice? What should I do with the peelings?"

"Just chuck them in the bin."

"What about using them for compost?"

"I don't have a compost heap, unfortunately."

"I could start one for you if you want."

Alice stops laying on the bacon and looks at him with a smile of disbelief. "Harry, I would love that. God, is there anything you can't do?"

"Nope." Harry picks up another potato. "I'm completely perfect in every way."

Alice doesn't smile. She looks quickly down at the turkey, a hot flush rising in her cheeks. She remembers how she and Emily once joked about ending up with the wrong men. Why does it suddenly not seem quite so funny anymore?

★ ★ ★

By the time Emily and Joe make it down to the kitchen, the oranges and lemons have been zested, and the zest, the cranberries, the sugar, and a liberal amount of port are reducing their way down to a delicious cranberry sauce.

The breadcrumbs have been mixed with the onions, sage, and chestnuts, and half is stuffed carefully between the breast of the bird and the skin, the rest waiting to enter the oven in a pan.

The parsnips and potatoes have been peeled, a butternut squash soup has been made, and the Christmas pudding — courtesy of Marks & Spencer and smuggled in Emily's suitcase — is merrily steaming away.

Harry has built a roaring fire, and he and Alice, after arguing about the music (Nat King Cole, they both agreed, would be far too cheesy), have finally settled on Enya. Not very Christmassy, but very relaxing.

"Morning," Emily yawns. "Have I just stepped into *It's a Wonderful Life*, or is this for real?"

Alice laughs. "It's for real, all right. Coffee's in the kitchen. Are you hungry?"

"Please don't tell me there are home-made blueberry muffins, or I may throw up," Emily grimaces.

"Does that mean you don't want them?"

"You have to be kidding. Of course I want them. I just can't believe what a regular Martha Stewart you are."

"Oh." Alice's face falls. "I was rather hoping I'd give Nigella a run for her money."

"Darling, unfortunately you have neither the sultry dark locks nor the requisite curves." Joe laughs.

"But surely a few more homemade blueberry muffins could solve that."

Emily shakes her head. "Nope. You either got it or you ain't. I, on the other hand, could definitely fill Nigella's shoes. Hell, I could fill her dresses."

"And thank God for that." Harry stands up and puts his arms around Emily, leaning down to kiss the top of her head. "Nothing's more of a turn-off than a skinny woman."

"And you wonder why I'm still with him." Emily laughs, turning her head to kiss Harry as Alice looks away.

"Oh, thanks," Harry says, with mock hurt.

"Oh, don't be such a baby," Emily laughs. "Now. About those blueberry muffins . . ."

"Actually there aren't blueberry muffins. But there are bagels in the drawer and probably some cinnamon raisin bread too. But, Em, we've got a huge lunch. Don't eat too much or you'll lose your appetite."

"And since when have you ever known me to lose my appetite?"

"Good point." Alice laughs. "Eat as much as you like."

"I feel sick," Emily groans as she stumbles to the sofa and collapses, holding her stomach.

"Oh, thanks a lot!" Alice laughs. "After all the trouble I went to and all you can say is 'I feel sick'?"

"You know I don't mean it like that," Emily says. "It was the most delicious meal I've ever eaten, but I'm so stuffed. I can't believe I ate that much."

"I can't believe you ate that much." Joe joins her on the sofa and looks at her with respect. "You should win an award."

"Oh, don't. You're making me feel like a pig."

"Well, I didn't want to say anything but . . ."

"Pig!" Emily picks up a cushion and bashes Joe over the head with it.

"Ow! I didn't mean it!"

"Children, children," Alice cautions from the doorway, where she stands with a pile of stacked dishes.

"Shall I put these in the dishwasher?" Harry calls from the kitchen.

"Yup, that would be great," she calls back. "Just stick everything in the dishwasher."

"Alice, leave everything," Emily commands from her sunken position on the sofa. "Let me clear up. Just give me a few minutes to recover and I'll do it."

"Em, it's fine. Everything's going in the dishwasher. I can manage."

"No." Emily stands up. "I won't hear of it. You went to all that trouble, there's no way I'm going to let you clear up as well. Come and sit down on the sofa. I'll go in and clean up with Harry."

Alice is about to protest, but Emily comes over and takes the dishes out of her hands, and she acquiesces, walking over to the sofa to join Joe.

"It's nice having them here, isn't it?" she says, snuggling into Joe, who gives her an absentminded kiss before picking up the remote control and turning on the television, flicking from channel to channel in a quest to find something that will hold his interest for longer than ten seconds.

"Yup."

"Did you like lunch?"

"It was delicious, darling."

"Was the soup okay? Not too spicy?"

"The soup? No, darling. It was all delicious. Well done." He pauses on a shot of a big-breasted blonde in a bikini, splashing in the water.

"Joe!" Alice admonishes, laughing.

"What?" His face is the picture of innocence.

"You know what. We're not watching this. Actually, why do we have the television on at all? It's Christmas Day. We shouldn't be watching TV. We've got presents to open."

"I'll turn it off when the others come back in, okay? Deal?"

"Okay," Alice says reluctantly. "Deal."

Emily squeals with delight. "I love it! I love it!" She hooks the beaded bag over her arm and swoops down on Alice to give her a huge hug and kiss. "Oh, Alice, thank you so much! I love it! Thank you, thank you, thank you!"

"You're very welcome," Alice says, beaming with pleasure. "Now Harry's turn."

"Nope." Harry shakes his head. "Your turn, Alice. Emily and I both bought separate presents for you. I hope you don't mind."

"Yes. Not being married and everything, we decided not to do a single unit present. Anyway, we couldn't agree on what to get you."

"Oh, you're both ridiculous," Alice says, feeling a childlike thrill of delight at having so many presents to open. "Which one first?"

"Mine first, mine first!" Emily says, thrusting a small box into Alice's hand. Alice carefully unwraps the paper, opens the box to find layers of tissue paper, and finally manages to pull them apart to discover a bed of cotton on which nestles a delicate rose quartz crystal on a fine silver chain.

Alice gasps. "It's beautiful!" and Emily grins.

"Isn't it? I saw it and thought you'd love it, and rose quartz is supposed to bring love into your life."

Joe raises an eyebrow.

"Sorry, Joe. I didn't mean a new love, it's just meant to make everything more loving, I think. Not you, just, oh God." Emily stumbles. "I think it's just meant to make your life nice. Okay?"

"Oh, Emily, stop being so silly. Whatever it's supposed to do, it's lovely. Help me put it on." Alice bends her head forward for Emily to do up the clasp.

"Oh, and the woman in the shop said you have to program it first," Emily adds as an afterthought. "You have to clean it by dropping it into water and vinegar, then leave it in direct sunlight for a day, then stare at it while you clear your mind and envision a pure white light going through it. Then it's yours, and clean, but you mustn't let anyone else touch it or it will become impure."

"Emily?" Joe says quietly.

"Yes?"

"When exactly did you lose your mind?"

"Oh, fuck off, Joe." Emily blushes. "Apparently it really works."

Alice runs out of the room to look at herself in the mirror. She takes the stairs two at a time then walks into the bathroom, fingering the crystal as she looks at her reflection. "Bring love into my life," she whispers, thinking of Joe sitting downstairs. Not that he's cold or distant particularly, and God knows he hasn't done any of the disappearing acts he used to do in

London, and he still tells her he loves her, but somehow Alice feels they have less of a partnership than they had before. Their interests seem to be moving further and further apart, and Alice wishes they could find some common ground that would keep both of them happy.

Time has given her a different perspective on her marriage. Time, and the space she has when she is on her own in Connecticut while Joe is working in the city. She realizes now how much she suppressed her own wants and desires when they were in London, where she always tried to mold herself into the wife that Joe expected her to be.

She's still happy to dress the part occasionally, knows that when she goes into the city she still has a role to play, and she is willing to make that compromise because, after all, what is marriage if not compromise? But she is not willing to put Joe's needs before hers anymore. At least not all the time.

And in turn she is hoping that Joe will make some compromises of his own. Yes, he comes out to the country every weekend, but she can't help but feel tense when he is there, because she knows he doesn't enjoy it, feels like a fish out of water. He seems happier now that he is playing tennis on a regular basis and is presumably starting to find friends of his own, but given the choice, she knows he would gladly sell up here and never set foot north of Ninetieth Street again.

The fact that he comes to the country at all is, she realizes, Joe's way of compromising. She just wishes he wouldn't be so obviously unhappy about it.

"Let us be more loving," she whispers, looking at the rose quartz crystal in the mirror. "Let us find our love for one another again. Help us be happy." And tearing herself away, she goes back downstairs.

"Your turn now," Alice says to Harry, picking up the biggest box and handing it to him.

"Oh, Christ!" Harry says. "This one's for me? I've been looking at this all day assuming it was for Joe. It's huge. What is it?"

Joe smiles. "Open it and see." But of course he is as much in the dark as Harry, Alice being the one assigned to buying presents.

Harry opens the card. "To Harry, Merry Christmas, love Joe and Alice xx," then tears open the paper, revealing the toolbox. He starts to grin.

"Ah-ha!" He laughs. "You did say there was no such thing as a free lunch."

"I did, didn't I?" Alice laughs. "And you thought you'd get away with it because you hadn't brought any tools with you."

"But this is fantastic!" Harry says, opening the toolbox and carefully examining everything inside. "What a fantastic tool kit. Look how cool it is. Look, look at these." He brings everything out, one by one, to show the others as Alice smiles to herself, delighted at Harry's delight.

"But I've got you something ridiculous," he says, mortified at how much Alice and Joe have spent. "Not to mention cheap and nasty. Oh God, I'm not going to give it to you."

"Don't be ridiculous," Alice says. "You didn't have to get me anything at all. Meanwhile" — she extends her hand as Harry tries to hide the present — "hand it over."

"Okay." Harry reluctantly hands Alice a small box and Joe what is quite obviously a book.

Joe rips the paper off. "*The History of Porsche*," he says delightedly. "Thanks, Harry. What a great book."

"My pleasure," Harry smiles. "Go on, Alice. Open yours."

Alice opens the paper, then the box, and finds an alarm clock shaped like a dog, a dog that looks exactly like Snoop.

She laughs delightedly. "I love it!" she says.

"Wait," Harry smiles. "You have to hear the alarm." He takes the clock and turns the dials on the face until the alarm goes off, a person barking in a thick, almost indecipherable, Japanese accent.

"What the . . . ?" Joe starts laughing.

"What is that?" Emily giggles.

"I know. It's made in Japan. Isn't that bizarre?" Harry grins. "It just made me laugh, and of course I couldn't miss the resemblance to Snoop."

Alice laughs. "It will have pride of place on my bedside table. Thank you." And she leans over to give Harry a kiss.

"Come on, guys," Emily says. "What about your presents to each other? Your turn now."

Alice and Joe exchange gifts and open them at the same time. Joe is thrilled with his watch, and Alice is embarrassed to open a large orange Hermès box, to find a beautiful russet Kelly bag within. It's a classic, it's smart as hell, and it's just about the very last thing Alice wants right now.

What did she want? A KitchenAid mixer would have been fantastic, not to mention a fraction of the cost of the Kelly bag. Or a new pair of gardening clogs and gloves. Or perhaps a set of thermal underwear to keep her warm.

"Wow!" Emily says, well aware of the beauty, and cost, of a Kelly bag.

"Nice bag," says Harry, who has no idea.

"Do you like it?" Joe says, used to Alice gushing with joy in the past over presents such as these, somewhat mystified by her silence.

"It's beautiful," Alice smiles, getting up to kiss him and making a pretense of admiring the bag. "I love it." As she sits down again she reaches up and fingers the quartz crystal. Help him know who I am and love me for it anyway, she thinks. Help us understand one another. Help us. Please.

The rest of their days pass all too quickly. They bundle up in gloves and hats, go for long walks along nature trails or take Snoop to the beach — bleak and deserted in the middle of winter.

They drive up to Mystic and wander through the Seaport, stopping at the touristy shops, laughing at how gullible they are but buying fishy mementoes nevertheless.

They have antiqued in New Canaan, all four of them horrified by the extravagant prices for reproduction furniture, the originals of which are available at a fraction of the price at any number of shops along the Kings Road. "Are they mad?" Joe kept repeating. "Three thousand dollars for that repro bit of shit?"

They have been on holiday house tours — days when handfuls of people in various towns open their houses to whoever would like to poke around in them — and have oohed and aahed at magnificent modern houses on the water, at charming converted barns in the middle of the woods. "Isn't this extraordinary?" Alice had nudged Emily. "That people just open their houses to strangers?"

"No, not at all. I'm thinking of doing it at home actually. I thought I might stick a sign up in Camden High Street and open my flat up one Sunday. What do you think?"

Alice bursts out laughing. "I think you'd have all the local winos moving in."

"Surely not," Emily says with a serious face. "You don't think they'd just walk around, admire my Habitat throws covering my scruffy old sofa, then leave?"

They go to trendy South Norwalk — SoNo — and make comparisons with Covent Garden, Alice and Emily even going so far as to buy handfuls of beads in the bead store — and spend an afternoon making necklaces and earrings, which they insist on wearing for the next two days and then remove, never to be worn again.

Alice and Emily leave the boys behind one afternoon and drive up to the Danbury Mall, both of them astonished by the reductions in the end-of-year sales. "But I had to buy it," Emily explains to a surprised Harry, surprised because he is still under the illusion that Emily has no money. "It was half price. As far as I'm concerned that's practically free."

They alternate between cooking at home — each of them taking turns (Alice inevitably produces homestyle stews and casseroles, Emily has so far made pasta twice, Harry has made roast chicken, and Joe has organized Chinese takeout, which was voted most inspired meal of the trip) — and going out to restaurants as far afield as Southport and Monroe.

The rose quartz crystal, which Alice surreptitiously and secretly "programmed" on December 26, and which she has not taken off apart from at night, appears to be working. Joe's workload seems to have eased off, and he has spent far more time than Alice would have thought possible with the rest of them, genuinely appearing to be having fun.

In fact, he has disappeared only twice, for last-minute tennis matches, and has been as loving and attentive as Alice had wished for. Alice has not been this happy for a long time, and having Emily (particularly Emily) and Harry here cements that happiness for her. She has her dream home, her dream life, her husband, and her best friend here. What more could she possibly ask for?

22

The house is completely silent as Alice walks in the front door, her arms filled with brown paper bags of groceries.

She dumps the bags on the kitchen table, pausing as something catches her eye outside. Leaning forward to see better, she watches with a smile as Harry bends down to reward Snoop with a treat. Snoop, who clearly adores Harry, trots off next to him as they both head down to the pond. "Traitor," she whispers under her breath, but the smile doesn't leave her face.

She unpacks and puts away the food, stokes the fire, then pops her head around the study door to find Joe tapping away at his computer.

"Do you need anything?" she says.

"No, darling. I'm just doing some work. Won't be long."

"But, Joe, it's New Year's Eve."

"I know, darling. I'm sorry, but that's why I won't be long. Promise. I'll be out in about fifteen minutes."

Alice sighs. "Where's Emily?"

"Don't know. Try upstairs."

Alice closes his study door again and walks softly upstairs, knocking on Emily's door.

"Em? Are you in there?"

Silence.

She pushes open the door as Emily stirs and opens her eyes. "Bloody jet lag," she mumbles, still half asleep. "I can't believe I've been here a week and I'm still exhausted."

"Oh God, I'm sorry. Did I wake you? Bugger. Look, you go back to sleep, sorry. Sorry." Alice starts to close the door.

"No," Emily says. "Come back. I was just waking up anyway." She pats the bed. "Come and talk to me."

Alice kicks her shoes off and lies down on the bed next to Emily, rolling onto her side to face her friend, resting her head on her arm, and smiling at her.

"So were you having dangerous dreams?" Alice says.

"I know they were weird but can't remember them."

"So not about" — she drops her voice and silently mouths — "Colin?"

"No!" Emily says. "Shhh. Where's Harry?"

"Outside playing with Snoop."

"He misses Dharma."

"Em, I know you don't want me to say this, but he's just so lovely. How can you not fall madly in love with him?"

Emily sighs. "I don't know. I just don't know. Anyway, if you think he's so lovely, you can have him."

"Thanks," Alice snorts. "But no thanks. Like I haven't got enough to deal with."

"Joe seems to be on pretty good form."

"I'm sure his computer would agree."

Emily frowns. "What do you mean?"

"I mean all he seems to do when he's down here is read the papers or sit at his bloody computer for hours doing God knows what. He says he's working but half the time when I open the door he gets rid of whatever he's looking at, so for all I know he's playing bloody Solitaire."

"Maybe he's addicted to Internet porn," Emily grins.

Alice rolls her eyes. "I tell you, nothing surprises me anymore. Anyway, you should get up because we've got the party later on and we have to make ourselves beautiful."

"Okay. So what are you wearing for the party? Are they smart or casual?"

Alice shrugs. "I think I'll probably go for black trousers and a black sweater."

"When in doubt keep it black?"

"Absolutely. What about you?"

"I bought a sparkly leopard-print top last week in SoHo. I thought I could give it its first outing tonight."

Alice laughs. "You'll certainly give the locals something to talk about."

"Will they all hate me?"

"Nah. Only the women. The men will probably spend all night lusting after you. Especially James."

"James?"

"The local lech. All mouth and no trousers."

Emily smiles. Exactly what Alice has always said about Joe.

"Is he nice?"

"Do you care?"

"Just curious."

"He is nice, actually. Just a terrible flirt but only when your other half isn't around. But his wife's a bit of a nightmare. She and Joe play tennis together, and she's also a horrible flirt whom I don't trust at all. She's charm personified to Joe and rather cold and flinty to me."

"Sounds awful."

"She's the only person I've met here who I don't really like. But hey, you can't like all of the people all of the time. Now come on. Up you get. I'll see you downstairs."

"Wow!" Joe looks up and gives a long whistle as Emily walks down the stairs and gives a twirl in front of the Christmas tree.

"Why, thank you," she says. "You don't think it's too obvious?"

"You look sexy as hell," Joe says, taking in Emily's luscious breasts in her semitransparent top and high spindly heels. "Good enough to eat."

"Joe!" Emily, while enjoying the compliment, refuses to flirt with Joe.

"Sorry, sorry. But you do look fantastic."

"And you promise they won't all think I'm a slut?"

"Well, they might, but they'll all fancy you anyway."

"Oh shit. I'm going to change."

"No!" Joe says. "You'll probably be the most exciting thing they've seen since the OJ police chase."

"God. I do have to change. I'm too obvious now."

Alice steps down the stairs in her flat

suede shoes and laughs when she sees Emily.

"Wow," she says. "You look amazing."

Emily looks worried. "Too sexy, do you think?"

"Unbelievably sexy, but who cares?"

"Are you sure?"

"Quite sure. What does Harry think?"

"He was in the shower. Okay. I'll wait and see what Harry thinks."

A few minutes later Harry emerges, hair still damp from the shower. His eyes open wide when he sees Emily.

"Wow," he says.

"You like?"

"You look incredible," he starts. "But do you think it's appropriate for the country? I mean, Alice is in trousers and flat shoes. I think you look amazing, but you might feel a bit out of place."

Alice watches as Emily bridles. "I *feel* amazing," she says. "And this is what I'm wearing."

Joe grins. "Don't worry, Harry, she'll be the hit of the party."

The four of them pull up into Sally and Chris's driveway. Small white fairy lights twinkle between the needles of the white pine trees lining the driveway, and there are candles in all the windows, giving the house a traditional, festive air.

Sally comes to the door in a long black velvet dress, glass of eggnog in hand, and kisses both Joe and Alice hello.

"Great to meet you," she says warmly, putting the drinks down to shake hands with Harry and Emily. "Let me take your coats."

Her eyes widen slightly at Emily's leopard-print extravaganza, but she has the good grace to recover quickly, and with a smile she leads everyone into the formal living room.

"I'll be back in a minute," Sally says. "I just have to deliver drinks and check on the food. Chris is around somewhere, and of course you know Kay and James over there. Chris!" she shouts, "Come and say hello!" With that she disappears.

"Who is that?" Emily whispers out of the corner of her mouth as Kay advances with a large smile and a mile of leg. "Nah, don't tell me. She's got to be the nightmare."

"Yup." Alice plasters a false smile on her face as she nods. "I wonder how you knew? Kay! How lovely to see you!"

"Hello, Alice, I haven't seen you in ages." Kay smiles coldly, enthusiasm reaching her eyes only when she turns to

Joe. "Hi, partner," she says, her lips suddenly forming more of a pout, her eyes twinkling with an uncharacteristic warmth.

"Hi, partner!" Joe laughs, bending down and giving Kay a peck on the cheek. Alice turns to Emily and rolls her eyes as Emily stifles a laugh. "These are our friends Emily and Harry," Joe says. "They're visiting from London."

Kay turns slowly and sizes Emily up and down. "Well," she says brightly, "great outfit," but her voice is full of disdain, and Emily doesn't feel the need to pretend to be polite.

"I could say the same about yours," she says, giving Kay the same look, taking in her tiny Lycra miniskirt and strappy sequinned top.

Kay's face hardens and she turns to Harry, the smile returning. "Well, hello," she says. "I'm Kay."

"How do you do. Harry." He shakes her hand politely, admiring her rather spectacular cleavage.

"God, aren't men pathetic?" Alice whispers to Emily. "Let's go and get something to drink."

"Good idea," Emily agrees, turning to the men. "Back in a minute."

They walk out of the living room,

shoulder to shoulder, heads together as they giggle.

"Isn't she *awful?*" Alice says. "Joe thinks she's 'great fun,' but I think she's dreadful. Did you see the way she looked at Joe? Talk about thinking you're God's gift."

"What about how she looked at Harry?"

"Yeah. She looked like she thought it was Christmas."

They both start laughing.

"And what are you two lovely girls laughing at?"

They stop abruptly and turn to see James. "Ah, James, we were just talking about you."

"You were?"

"We were?" Emily is just as surprised, but not half as delighted.

"Well, we were talking about your wife actually, just saying how wonderful Kay looks tonight."

James raises an eyebrow as he stares at Emily's breasts, thinly concealed in the leopard-print top. "I'd say she had some pretty stiff competition," he says.

"As long as that's the only thing that's stiff." Emily laughs merrily.

"Emily." Alice nudges her sharply, because while she has come to realize that harmless flirting is fine, the double entendres that are so common at home seem to go down like a lead balloon over here.

True to form, James looks slightly shocked.

"Sorry," Emily mumbles. "I didn't mean anything by it. You must be James." She extends her hand, which James takes gratefully.

"I am. And you are?"

"Emily. How do you do."

"Another lovely English girl," he says. "What have we done to deserve this?"

"James?" Kay rounds the corner and joins them as James looks flustered. "What are you doing?"

"Just talking to Alice," he says. "Sorry, honey. What was it again that you wanted?"

"A Cosmopolitan." Her irritation is apparent. "I'll wait for you, shall I?"

"No, no. I'm going now. Nice to meet you," he says to Emily, and scurries into the kitchen for the drink.

"Bit of a weird dynamic," Emily says when Kay has gone back into the living room. "What's going on there?"

"I'd rather not know. Although he's actually very nice once you get past the leching. He owns a garden center in town. But anyway, Em, what did you expect wearing that? I warned you."

"He's attractive, isn't he?" Emily muses, as James walks back past them, a Cosmopolitan in one hand, a beer in the other.

"I suppose so, but in a very henpecked way."

Every few minutes the doorbell rings, and within half an hour the room is packed. Frank Sinatra plays softly from the stereo, a fire blazes in the huge stone fireplace, and glass bowls filled with cranberries and fat red candles flicker light gently around the room.

The hum of conversation grows louder the more relaxed people become, and Sally and Chris push their way through the crowd bearing silver trays piled high with canapés.

Joe is astonished by how many people Alice seems to know. "HomeFront?" he keeps whispering as yet another woman waves at Alice from across the room or walks over to say hello.

"She's from HomeFront," she'll say. Or, "No, that's Caroline who works in the coffee shop," or, "That's Samantha, I met her at the supermarket."

"But you know everyone!" Joe says.

"When did my wife turn into such a sociable creature?"

"My darling husband, if you ever took a break from work" — Alice smiles lovingly — "you would have noticed how sociable I am. Actually I think it's just because I'm happy."

"Are you, darling?" He smiles down at her and puts an arm around her waist, pulling her close as he kisses her softly on the lips and smiles into her eyes. "Good. Have I told you recently that I love you?"

Alice leans into him, savoring the closeness, remembering how much she loves it when he is this affectionate, this loving, suddenly realizing how much she has missed by spending so much time away from him in the country.

Alice smiles up at him. "*Do* you love me?"

"Very very much."

"Good, because I love you too."

"As much as I love you?"

"Oh, I think quite possibly more."

"Well, that's okay then." Joe laughs and kisses her again as Kay watches from across the room, her face hardening. She would have put money on their being unhappy. God knows Joe flirts with her enough over their weekly games of tennis.

But look at them now over there, acting like newlyweds, eyes only for each other. Surely she couldn't have misread the situation that much. . . .

"Everything all right, honey?" James is at her side.

Kay switches the smile back on. "Oh, yes," she says, putting an arm around his waist as he smiles in delight and surprise. "Give me a kiss, you gorgeous man."

"Here?" he says, looking around. "In public?"

"And why not? Are you embarrassed to be seen kissing your wife?" Kay is aware that Joe is now looking over at them. Hell, he isn't the only one who can play that game.

"Why, no. Of course not." James leans down and gives her a quick peck on the lips, but Kay snakes her arms around his neck and pulls him closer, opening her lips as she presses a full-blown smooch upon his mouth.

"Wow!" James pulls back, looks at Kay with delight, then moves in for another go.

"Don't be silly." Kay pushes him away, Joe having turned away. "Not here." Leaving James completely mystified, she turns and walks off.

"Mind if I join you?" Harry stands in

front of the bench as Alice smiles and shakes her head, wrapping her arms around her for warmth.

"Isn't it gorgeous out here?" she says as Harry sits down. "Look how completely black it is. You can't see anything. I just love it."

Harry doesn't say anything, merely reaches into his pocket, fumbling around until he brings out a packet of Marlboro Lights and a box of matches.

"Harry!" Alice says. "You smoke?"

"Shhh!" Harry raises a finger to his lips. "Only when I'm drunk."

"But you're not drunk. You're completely sober."

"No." He shakes his head. "I always act completely sober when I'm drunk. In fact, the drunker I am the more sober I act."

Alice laughs. "But that's ridiculous. Does that mean you're drunk all the time?"

"No. Only when I'm acting sober."

"So how would I know whether you're drunk or sober?"

"Well now, that's the hard part. You wouldn't."

Alice narrows her eyes and squints at him. "You're joking, aren't you?"

"Maybe." Harry smiles. "Do you know I

was just talking to that man James and he offered me a job?"

"What do you mean, he offered you a job?"

Harry shrugs. "We were talking gardening and he said he could always use someone as knowledgeable as me and would I be interested?"

"What did you say?"

"Tempting as it would be to live out here, I had to say no, although" — Harry grins — "I did say ask me again in six months' time. Right now there's too much I'd have to leave behind in England."

"Emily for starters," Alice smiles.

"Well, yes. Emily for starters." Harry looks down as he shakes a cigarette out of the pack, then reaches back into the pack for a smaller, hand-rolled cigarette, which he takes out, raising an eyebrow at Alice who widens her eyes.

"That's not what I think it is!"

"I don't know. What do you think it is?"

"Is that" — Alice lowers her voice to a whisper — "a *joint?*"

"Is that the same thing as *grass?*" Harry whispers back. "Because if it is then yes, it is a joint. Oh, no. That's terrible. What should we do with it now?"

"Oh, shut up." Alice looks away then

back again as Harry holds the flame to the end of the roll-up, inhaling deeply, holding it in, then exhaling with a satisfied whoosh.

"Harry! You can't!"

Harry smiles. "Why not? We're outside. And the last time I checked we were adults. I promise you no one will know." He inhales again then proffers it to Alice, who stares at it in shock, then slowly reaches out and takes it.

"You swear you won't tell Joe? He'd kill me."

"Believe me, Joe is the very last person I'd tell. And anyway, you'd better not tell Emily. *She'd* kill *me*."

Alice inhales, holding the smoke deep in her lungs as she hasn't done since she was in her late teens. She exhales as she feels a lightness take over her limbs and smiles as she sinks back on the bench.

"God, that's good," she smiles as she passes the joint to Harry. "Do you know how many years it's been since I've smoked?"

"About twenty?"

"More or less," she smiles. "Where did you get it anyway?"

"Trade secret," he says. "Involving shampoo bottles, lots of clingfilm, and smuggling."

"Harry, you didn't! No wonder Emily would kill you. I'd kill you if I were your girlfriend."

"But luckily you're just my friend. Here." And he hands the joint back to Alice.

They sit in companionable silence for a while, Alice sinking into the velvety blackness of the night, experiencing every woodland noise as if for the first time.

"God, this is amazing," she keeps repeating, while Harry simply smiles.

"I can't see anything," she says, a smile stretched wide upon her face, the fact that they are both sitting in pitch blackness suddenly having struck her as very funny.

"Your eyes will get accustomed to it," Harry says. "I bet you could find your way around the garden."

"Bet you I couldn't," Alice says.

"Go on then. I bet you fifty dollars you could."

"Done." Alice stands up unsteadily and starts weaving off, giggling.

"One circle of the garden," Harry shouts as he starts to giggle as well. "I'll wait here and shout if you need help."

"What if I come across a coyote?" Alice yelps with laughter from some feet away.

"Shake his paw and say how do you do,"

Harry shouts back, and the pair of them, in their own pools of respective blackness, collapse in fits of giggles.

"Have you seen my wife?" Joe has had long chats with Sandy and Tim, Tom and James, and a few of Alice's new friends, when it suddenly occurs to him that he hasn't seen Alice for a while and it's very nearly midnight, the start of the new year.

"Alice?" He walks into the dining room to find a crowd of people descending on the food, Emily at the far end, plate piled high with fresh salmon, rare filet mignon, and wild rice salad.

"Excuse me, excuse me. Sorry. Excuse me." Joe pushes his way through everyone surrounding the table helping themselves and reaches Emily at the far end, about to sit down on one of the chairs next to James to eat dinner.

"Emily, have you seen Alice?"

"Nope. Last time I saw her Sally was giving her the guided tour of the house."

"Oh. Okay. Thanks." Maybe, Joe thinks, she's still upstairs looking around. He pushes his way back out of the dining room and walks up the stairs, slowly pushing open all the bedroom doors, save of course for the one with a large enamel plaque on it with the words "Madison's Room" emblazoned across it.

Bathroom: empty. Guest bedroom: empty. Master bedroom: empty. Other guest bedroom: Joe pushes open the door as Kay jumps. She's standing in front of the mirrored wardrobe door, reapplying lipstick, and she gives him a slow smile.

"Nearly done," she says, pouting in the mirror, fully aware that Joe cannot take his eyes off her.

Joe stands there watching her, looking at her thighs, that fantastic tight ass. Shit. He made a vow to himself. But he's been so good. He's been faithful for months. And this wouldn't mean anything. Jesus, it would just be satisfying an itch. Alice would never know, has never found out in the past. And Christ, look at her. Look at how she's pouting, imagine what she'd be like in bed, those firm thighs wrapped around his waist.

Joe takes a deep breath and shuts the door behind him, standing still as he watches Kay. She finishes her lipstick, snaps her bag shut, and turns to look at him.

"Well?" she says softly. "How do I look?"

"If I said you looked good enough to eat, would you believe me?" Joe says, already beginning to harden at the prospect of sex with this woman.

Kay simply smiles as she prepares to leave the room, but Joe stops her with a hand on her arm.

"Kay," he whispers, and she stands still, slowly turning to look at him. "Kay," he says again, raising his hand to trace her lips with his index finger. Kay moans softly and closes her eyes, parts her lips slowly as Joe slides his finger between them to feel the wet warmth of her mouth. He groans as she circles his finger with her tongue, and then his arms are around her and they are kissing passionately, furiously.

"Oh God," Joe groans, pulling her with him as they fall onto the bed. He is absolutely consumed with lust, all thought, all reason having disappeared, the only thought on his mind is being inside this woman.

They roll on the bed, both of them moaning, and Joe reaches under her shirt to unsnap her bra as Kay pulls abruptly away.

"No!" she says, sitting up and pushing him away. "We can't."

"What? What do you mean we can't?"

"We shouldn't be doing this," she says miserably.

"Kay, of course we shouldn't be doing this, but you're the most gorgeous woman I've ever met. I think about you all the time. I know we shouldn't be doing this, but I can't help it, I want you so much."

"I want you too," she says, "but we're married."

There's a long silence. "They wouldn't ever have to find out," Joe says, reaching for her again.

"No!" she says, standing up quickly and smoothing down her skirt. "I can't. I'm sorry. I can't do this."

"You're serious, aren't you?" Joe's erection has disappeared as quickly as it appeared.

Kay nods, embarrassed.

"But you've been giving me the come-on for months. All that flirting, all those comments. Where did you think it would lead, for Christ's sake?"

Kay shrugs. "I'm sorry. I didn't mean anything, I was just, I don't know. I guess I was just enjoying the attention."

Joe shakes his head in disgust. "You are just a prick tease after all, aren't you?"

"I would appreciate you not using that kind of language in front of me," Kay says primly, turning the door handle and walking out.

"God almighty," Joe mutters under his breath. "What a fucking tease." After a few minutes he sighs and rejoins the party. And more to the point, he still hasn't found his bloody wife.

"Help!" Alice stumbles into a pit in the grass and falls down laughing. The more she laughs the funnier it seems, and she becomes absolutely hysterical as she lies on the grass shaking.

"Where are you?" Harry, giggling himself, is stumbling through the darkness toward her, and suddenly he trips over her ankle and falls flat on his face.

"Are you okay?" Alice manages through her heaves. Harry reaches out until he can feel where she is and lies on the ground next to her, the pair of them almost apoplectic with laughter.

"Oh God," Harry sighs when they finally manage to calm down. "That is good stuff."

"That really is good stuff." Alice sighs, smiling up at the stars. "Isn't this a beautiful night? Look at the stars."

Harry lies back and rests his head on his arms. "There's the Milky Way," he says.

"Where? I can't see it."

"Look, there." He takes her hand and

points it up to the Milky Way so she can see.

Alice gasps. "It's beautiful." They lie there looking up at the stars, in silence, holding hands.

The only sound Alice can hear is their breathing, the only thing she can see is the stars, and the only feeling she is aware of is her fingers entwined with Harry's and Harry's thumb slowly rubbing up and down on her skin.

They lie there for what feels like hours, both gently stroking the other's hands, neither of them able to think of anything other than how wonderful it is to lie here, outside, holding hands. And then, at exactly the same time, they both roll onto their sides and their lips meet.

And so they kiss. For a long, long time.

"Alice?" It's a familiar voice, from far, far away, too far to bring them back, too vague to take notice of. Suddenly the garden is flooded with light as the outside lights are switched on. Alice and Harry pull apart, and the only thing they are subsequently aware of is Emily's hand flying up to her mouth as she turns from the doorway and runs back into the house with a sob.

23

"Joe. Drive me home."

"What?" Joe is helping himself to a Scotch and doing his best to avoid Kay. He walks into the dining room, she walks out. She walks into the kitchen, he walks out. Right now the living room is out of bounds, and Joe is pouring himself a stiff single malt to soothe the pain of rejection. He turns to see Emily, her face ashen and her coat on, standing behind him.

"What are you talking about? Where are the others?"

"I don't know but I don't feel well. I think I'm going to be sick."

"Oh God, Emily, I'm sorry. Are you sure you don't want to lie down here? I'm sure they wouldn't mind."

"No. I want to go back." She sighs impatiently and lies, "Joe, I have medicine back at the house that I need. Please just drop me off, then you can come back."

"Okay. Hang on. God knows where Alice is. Let me just tell Sally where we're going."

"Fine. Give me the keys. I'll wait in the car."

Emily would never normally dream of leaving a party without thanking the hostess, but this isn't any old party, and she can't be expected to behave as she normally would. She sits in the passenger seat of the car, shivering, cold and numb with shock. If you had told Emily that she would catch her best friend and her boyfriend locked in a passionate kiss, she would have said that it was impossible, it would never happen.

If you had persisted, she would have said that she would go *nuts*.

She would have said that she would stand there and scream at them. Ask them what the fuck they think they're doing. Slap Harry round the face. Hell, she might even slap Alice while she's at it.

And yet here she is, sitting shivering in a car, unable to do anything, feeling completely numb. Even though she saw it with her own eyes, she still can't quite believe it actually happened, and she sits replaying the scene like a film, wondering whether or not it might have been a bad dream.

But no. They might have been far away, but no one could have mistaken what they were doing. Emily saw, even in that split second before they pulled apart, how Harry was on top of Alice, his eyes closed, his hands entwined in her hair as he kissed her. Emily saw Alice running her hands up Harry's strong back, the back Emily knows so well, and Emily suppresses a sob that starts to rise in her throat.

No. She will not cry in front of anyone. She will not cry in front of Joe. She just needs to get away from everyone. Needs to get away from Harry and Alice.

"Joe? Where are you going?" Alice's heart jumps into her mouth as she runs back in to find Emily and sees Joe with his coat on, car keys in hand.

"Where've you been?"

Alice just looks at him. Could Emily have told him already? Is he testing her? She stands still and eventually shrugs. "In the garden."

"But it's freezing!" Joe laughs, and Alice relaxes slightly. He doesn't know. But oh God. Emily. Her best friend. She'd rather die than hurt Emily, and she has no idea what just happened outside. She only knows she now feels sick, and sorry, and lost.

"Where are you going?" Alice says. "Where's Emily?"

"She's not feeling well," Joe says over his shoulder as he walks toward the door. "I'm just going to run her home."

"Wait! I'll come too." Alice runs toward him but Joe shakes his head.

"Don't worry about her. She's fine. Just needs to get some kind of medicine she left at home. You and Harry stay. I'll be back in a minute."

"No . . . wait . . ." But Joe has already disappeared out of the front door.

"Are you sure you'll be okay? You don't look at all well." Joe opens the front door of their house then turns to look at Emily with concern, as Emily manages to force a smile.

"I think maybe it's just jet lag and exhaustion catching up with me. I'm sure I'll feel better once I lie down."

"You sure you don't mind if I go back and leave you alone?"

Oh God. Alone. She's alone again. Emily turns away so Joe doesn't see the stricken look on her face and she nods, not trusting herself to speak.

"Okay. See you tomorrow. Wish you better." And Joe closes the door gently behind him and heads back to the party.

"Shit." Harry says again. For the umpteenth time.

"What are we going to do?" Alice and Harry are standing miserably in the corner of the kitchen. The alcohol consumed by everyone else here seems to be taking effect. Chris has swapped Frank Sinatra for pumping pop, the lights, already darkened, have been darkened even more, and the living room has now become a dance floor with various couples letting their hair down.

"Harry, I feel sick. I don't know what happened out there." Alice, now completely sober, completely lost, is mystified at the kiss and distraught at the look on Emily's face, at how much she knows she has hurt Emily. "I mean, nothing happened. It was *nothing!*" She says it vehemently, perhaps trying to convince herself, and then in a small voice she looks at Harry helplessly. "I don't know what to do."

Harry stays silent. He knows what happened out there. He may have been stoned, but every time he looks at Alice he wants to take her in his arms and hold her.

He never felt this when he knew her in London. Sure, he liked her, and yes, of course he thought she was attractive, but he knew they were worlds apart, and women like Alice were simply not his cup of tea.

Plus of course he was happy with Emily, too happy even to think about other women. But as the months have gone by he's found that his relationship with Emily is making him less and less happy, that they seem to be less and less compatible.

At first he was worried by Emily's increasing apathy toward him, but her distance and moodiness have made him realize that she's not the woman with whom he wants to spend the rest of his life, and he's well aware that it's laziness and habit that are keeping them together.

Part of him hasn't wanted to admit the relationship hasn't been working. And much like Emily, he had viewed this holiday as a last-ditch attempt, a make-or-break. But nothing had prepared him for seeing Alice again. From the moment he first laid eyes on her in America he hasn't been able to stop thinking about her.

He has never realized before how funny she is. How self-deprecating she is able to be. How she doesn't seem to take anything too seriously. But mostly he has been watching her in the house, playing with Snoop, preparing breakfast in the kitchen, and the more he has watched, the more beautiful he finds her.

Just as he said the other day, she does have a glow. It makes him want to follow her around, bask in the happiness she radiates. And Joe seems to be completely unaware of her. Harry can see that he treats her as a trophy wife, is happy to be affectionate to her in public, to show her off at parties like this one tonight, but he barely pays any attention to her.

Christ, he's barely paid any attention to *any* of them. In spite of having guests in his house, Joe has spent most of the time stuck in front of his computer while Alice has done everything.

And until tonight Harry hasn't realized quite how hard he's fallen. He had thought perhaps he just liked her very much, appreciated her as a friend, even though he found himself lying in bed after Emily had fallen asleep replaying things that Alice had said throughout the day, things that had made him laugh.

Tonight, when he went outside for a smoke and found that Alice was already sitting on the bench, his heart leapt, and he knew then that his feelings were real, that he wasn't merely attempting to get on with his girlfriend's best friend.

But even he had been unprepared for what happened. Could anything possibly be more complicated or more difficult, or more out of bounds?

He had been thrilled to find Alice on the bench, but had never expected, never *dreamed*, that anything might happen between them.

And then, lying next to her on the grass, he couldn't help but keep hold of her hand, and when she had responded by gently stroking his fingers with her own, he had known that there would be no going back. Not for him at any rate.

But here she is now, less than fifteen minutes later, telling him it was nothing. Harry feels like everything he has ever wanted, everything he has ever known would make him happy in life, is about to slip out of his grasp, and he doesn't know what to do. He wants to put his arms around her and tell her that it's going to be okay. That as long as they are together nothing else matters.

But of course he doesn't say that. He simply looks at her as she tells him it was nothing. It meant nothing.

"What are we going to do?" Alice says again. "Should we go home?"

"I think I should talk to her first," Harry says. "I'll explain. Tell her we were stoned and drunk and it was just one kiss and it really didn't mean anything."

"No. I should be the one to say that."

Harry shrugs. At this point he really couldn't care less. All he can think is that Alice thinks it meant nothing.

"Or should I? I just don't know. Oh, shit. Do you think she'll tell Joe?"

Harry shakes his head. He'd love for Emily to tell Joe, for Joe and Alice to split up to give him and Alice a chance, but that is the stuff of fantasy, and he knows that isn't going to happen. "No. It's not Emily's style, and you know her far better than I, Alice. She won't tell him."

"No." Alice sighs with relief. "You're probably right. She won't. Oh God, Harry. I'm so sorry."

"Don't be silly," Harry says. "You haven't got anything to apologize for. If anything I should be the one saying sorry."

"No. You haven't got anything to apologize for. It just happened."

"Yes," Harry nods, forcing a smile. "It meant nothing."

"Exactly. Nothing."

Joe walks back into the party, almost colliding with Kay, and he turns in the direction of the kitchen, wishing he could have stayed at home. Bloody awful parochial party, he thinks, pausing to watch the people try to rediscover their younger, funkier selves in the living room/disco.

"There you two are," Joe says, seeing Alice and Harry in the corner of the kitchen.

"How's Emily?" they both say in unison.

"She doesn't look too good but she thinks it's probably just exhaustion. I think she's going to bed."

"I think we ought to go home and look after her," Alice says.

"Good idea," Harry and Joe say together, neither of them wanting to stay a minute longer at the party.

"Great. Let's find Sally and Chris and say good-bye."

Alice knocks softly on the bedroom door.

"Emily? Can I come in?"

There's a silence. Alice tries again. The

men are downstairs having a drink and watching some late-night television, and Alice has decided she must be the one to brave this.

"Emily? Em? Are you awake?"

Still silence as Alice pushes open the door. The room is dark and Emily is in bed, but Alice can tell she is only pretending to be asleep, her breathing is too slow, too measured, and Alice walks over to the bed and sits down.

"Go away," Emily says, rolling over. "I don't want to talk to you."

"Oh, Em." Alice's eyes fill with tears. "We have to talk about this. It was nothing. It's not what you think."

Emily rolls back over and sits up looking at Alice in disbelief. "You mean I didn't actually see my best friend of thirty years rolling around on the grass locked in a passionate embrace with my boyfriend?" she spits viciously.

"It wasn't passionate. And we weren't rolling on the grass." For a second Alice thinks back to what they were doing. And she's not lying, it wasn't passionate. It was gentle, and soft, and lovely. It felt as if she'd come home.

She pushes this thought aside. "Em, we were both completely stoned and we were lying there looking at the sky and then it just happened. I promise it didn't mean anything. Em, I didn't even know what day of the week it was, let alone who I was kissing. And it only lasted a second. I swear to God if you'd come out a second later it would have been over."

"Well, we'll never know that now, will we?" Emily says. "Of course it only lasted a second. You were caught, remember?"

"Em, please. I love you more than anyone else in the world, and I would never do anything to hurt you. . . ."

"But, Alice," Emily says softly. "You just did. You kissed my boyfriend."

"Emily, it was a kiss. I didn't sleep with him, for God's sake, it was a nothing kiss, and you of all people know how meaningless a kiss can be. Remember when we were young, remember those kissing competitions we'd have with the boys? God, a kiss is nothing. And second" — she refuses to give Emily a chance to interrupt — "second you're acting as if Harry is the big love of your life when you're already planning on replacing him with Colin."

Emily gasps. "I can't believe you just said that."

"Oh God, Emily, I'm sorry, but you

can't pretend that Harry's the one when he clearly isn't."

Emily's voice is as cold as ice. "How dare you presume to draw conclusions about my relationship? And whether Harry is the one or not — as it happens, I hadn't even reached a conclusion about that — what gives you the right to pounce on him? Not forgetting, by the way, your own marital status."

Alice looks down at the floor. "You didn't tell Joe, did you?"

"No, of course I didn't tell Joe. I may be stupid enough not to realize that my best friend and my boyfriend fancy one another, but I'm not that much of a bitch."

Alice keeps looking at the floor, as Emily looks up at the ceiling.

The minutes tick by.

"Look, I really don't want to have to talk about this anymore," Emily says.

"But what are we going to do? We can't leave it like this. I feel sick. I don't want to lose you, Emily. I love you."

"Well, you should have thought of that before." Emily sighs. "I just feel so incredibly hurt, and the only reason I haven't left this house altogether is because we're in the middle of bloody nowhere and I haven't got anywhere to go."

"You're leaving tomorrow anyway," Alice says. "You couldn't leave now. I wish you'd talk about it, Emily. I can't let you leave with this awful feeling between us."

"Perhaps you should have thought of that before you kissed my boyfriend." Emily stares at her with cold eyes as Alice flinches. "I'm tired," Emily continues. "And I need to be on my own. Please go now."

Alice stands up, the tears welling again. More than anything in the world she'd like to be able to turn back the clock, and failing that, she'd like Emily to put her arms around her and tell her she forgives her.

Neither looks likely to happen.

"Do you think" — Alice pauses in the doorway and looks back at Emily — "do you think you'll be able to forgive me? Not tonight I mean, but ever?"

"I don't know," Emily says. "Please just leave me alone now. Maybe we can talk again in the morning."

24

The only person to sleep well in the house that night is Joe. Alice lies awake crying as quietly as she can, terrified she's lost Emily forever. Emily lies awake clenching her jaw with anger, unable to believe what happened tonight, and Harry lies on the sofa downstairs, thinking mostly about Alice.

He gets up from time to time, makes himself a cup of tea, pauses to give Snoop a cuddle, attempts to watch television at around three in the morning, but sleep manages to elude him for most of the night.

Harry can hardly believe what happened last night. Can hardly *dare* to believe it. He walks over to the bookshelf and picks up a picture of Alice, the Alice of old with glossy blond hair and perfect makeup.

Harry smiles. She is so different now,

and he knew, well before yesterday, that he had fallen for her, but kept hoping it would pass. He found himself thinking of Alice when he was supposed to have been thinking about Emily, and although he allowed himself to indulge, he did, truly, think that it was a slight crush that would disappear as quickly as it had arrived.

Until last night.

Until they kissed. Until Harry knew what it was like to hold her, to smell her, to feel her hair wrapped around his fingers.

At seven-thirty the next morning Harry hears someone coming down the stairs, and he sits up, hoping it's Alice, hoping they'll have a chance to talk about what happened, but it's Joe.

"Morning, Harry. What are you doing on the sofa?"

"Oh. Um. Emily had a headache and I thought it was best to leave her."

"Did you manage to sleep at all?"

"No. It wasn't the most comfortable."

"Not for a man your size, no. I'm not surprised. Alice is coming down in a sec. She'll make some coffee before I take you to the airport."

"Oh. Right. Great."

When Alice does come down she can barely look at Harry. She mumbles good morning and smiles at him, but she doesn't look into his eyes, and busies herself in the kitchen getting the breakfast things together.

Emily stays upstairs.

"Is she coming down?" Alice whispers to Harry when Joe is out of the way. Harry shrugs.

"You mean you haven't spoken to her?"

He shakes his head. "She won't talk to me."

"But you're flying home together. She'll have to talk to you."

"You would think so, but we'll have to see. What about you? Has she spoken to you?"

Alice shakes her head. "Not really. She basically said she'll have to think about things."

"I'm really sorry," Harry says, sorry for causing Alice pain, sorry for hurting Emily, sorry for creating such a mess.

Alice sighs. "It's not your fault. I'm sure it will all blow over. Eventually."

Emily comes downstairs just as they have to leave. Alice gives her a hug but Emily stands still, refusing to put her arms around Alice, just bowing her head until Alice lets her go.

"I'm sorry," Alice whispers, and Emily acknowledges it with a faint nod of her head.

"You look terrible," Joe says to Emily, concerned. "Are you sure you're feeling all right?"

"I'll be fine," Emily says, forcing a smile for Joe. Harry and Alice shake hands, Alice jumping as soon as her skin touches his, the force like an electric shock, and still she is unable to look at him.

They are barely up the driveway, Emily and Harry and Joe, before Alice has pulled a pad of writing paper from a drawer and is writing Emily a long letter, trying to express on paper what she was so inadequate at saying last night.

She writes for a long time. She tells Emily how much she loves her, how thirty years of friendship is far more important than a thirty-second kiss, and how she doesn't think she'll be able to carry on without her forgiveness.

She seals and stamps the letter before she has a chance to change her mind, and by the time Joe returns with an empty car, the letter is already sitting in the mailbox, waiting to wing its way to Emily.

By March, Alice has written fourteen letters to Emily. At first apologetic, after a while she decided she had apologized enough, and now she fills the pages with long, rambly tales about what she's been doing and the people she's been seeing. Emily would never admit it, and she is not yet ready to either forgive or forget, but she is starting to look forward to receiving these letters, and as each one arrives a little bit of the pain starts to seep away.

Alice has tried to phone, but Emily has taken to screening her calls and refuses to answer if it's long distance, so that Alice has to leave an uncomfortable message on the machine. Emily never calls back.

Via the letters Emily knows almost everything about Alice's life. Alice knows nothing about Emily's. She doesn't know that Emily and Harry shared a cab home from the airport only because it was cheaper, and after a perfunctory good-bye they have never seen each other again.

Alice doesn't know that Harry tried to phone Emily to explain, to apologize, to say good-bye properly, but that Emily wouldn't take his calls either, and eventually he stopped trying.

Emily sought solace in Colin, jumping into bed with him rather more quickly than Alice would have advised, and although the relationship doesn't seem to offer much more than sex, at least, Emily figures, it is giving her something to think about other than the betrayal by her ex-boyfriend and ex–best friend.

Oh. And the sex is pretty fantastic too.

Harry, on the other hand, still has students lusting after him in his dog-training classes, but post-Emily has made a decision not to get involved with any students again. He still thinks about Alice, thinks about her smile, her laugh, but he knows there's no point, and he tries not to think about her very much. She's happily married, after all. Happily married, in America, and she told him it meant nothing.

What would be the point?

But Alice isn't quite so happy right now. Joe has stopped playing tennis — now that the potential seduction of Kay is no longer an option — and consequently can't see the point in coming up to Highfield at all.

The last time he was down — three weeks ago — it was to meet with, and engage, an architect with whom he intends to build the McMansion of his dreams. Joe excitedly showed Alice the plans — an eight-thousand-square-foot monolithic monstrosity complete with swimming pool, tennis court, and basement cinema.

Ridiculous, Alice thought. What on earth was he thinking? She felt quite ill looking at the plans, and prayed that fate would somehow intervene to stop him from taking down these lovely trees and building such a horrendous house.

With Joe hardly ever there, Alice has busied herself with the house. She found a picture in the library from an old local newspaper — Rachel Danbury sitting on the terrace — and she is doing her best to copy the plants, to restore the terrace to what it was. She has copied the pergola that was once on the side of the house, a pergola that can just be seen in the picture, and is planting wisteria on one side and clematis on the other. The plants she knows Rachel Danbury would have wanted, and the harder she works the more she feels at peace.

Sometimes, when Alice is taking a break on the terrace, she feels almost as if the late writer is looking down on her and smiling, grateful that there is someone working on the house she had so clearly once loved.

"It's my pleasure," Alice has whispered,

more than once, those moments when she feels she is watched. "The least I could do."

She misses Joe, but understands how busy he is, although she thinks it's a shame he's given up on the tennis — he seemed to enjoy it and it was lovely having him down here on the weekends.

These last few weekends, weekends when Joe has professed to be working, he has been living his old bachelor lifestyle. After almost a year of abstinence, Joe can't see the point in no longer indulging. The only thing that turns Alice on these days is that bloody house, and Joe's fed up with his dowdy wife who doesn't pay him any attention anymore, nor make any effort for him.

Joe needs to feel attractive again. Needs a thrill and excitement that Alice could not possibly give him.

His first indiscretion occurs at Blue Fin. He's having dinner with a friend when he notices a sexy blonde staring at him from across the room. He holds her gaze a few seconds too long, turns back to his friend to laugh at what he has just said, then immediately swivels his eyes back to the blonde. She's still looking at him. And this time she smiles.

Her name is Alison, and they go out for dinner two days later and back to her apartment for a fabulous fuck an hour after that. Joe leaves with her number and a huge grin on his face. So many women, so little time. He'll never call her again, not when there are so many others from whom to choose.

His second indiscretion is a hot little Brazilian called Carla. It lasts two weeks, two weeks of blissful, all-night sex, until Joe realizes she wants more, and walks out of her life and on to the next.

His third indiscretion is slightly different. It's three o'clock on a Friday afternoon and Joe is, for the first time in what feels like ages, getting ready to go down to the country for the weekend. He's about to pack up his stuff when a Bloomberg comes through on his screen.

It's from Josie Mitchell.

"I'm in New York," he reads. "Left Godfreys, now at Deutsche. How about a coffee sometime? Josie."

Immediately he starts to smile. Good God. Josie. Now there was a real woman. He hasn't thought about Josie for months, but seeing her name on his screen brings all the memories flooding back, and Joe grins, remembering what she was like in bed.

He Bloombergs her back. "How about five today? Pick a Bagel at the World Financial Center. See you then."

"Okay. See you then."

Joe perches on a seat at the window, sips a steaming hazelnut-flavored coffee, and looks out of the window to see if he can see her coming. It's 5:10 and he hopes he hasn't been stood up. After all, he is supposed to be on his way to Highfield right now.

And then the door opens and he sees her. Glossy, gleaming, and as gorgeous as he remembers her. A slow smile spreads upon his face as he stands to give her a kiss.

Josie turns her head so his lips barely graze her cheek. "Hello, Joe. Whaddayaknow."

25

If you happened to be in Manhattan's financial district at the end of a sunny March afternoon and found yourself walking past a certain bagel shop at around six p.m., and glanced in through the large plate-glass window, you would stop for a second and smile, reassured to see two people so obviously meant for each other.

Joe and Josie certainly look like two people fallen very much in love. They have been cozied up in the corner for nearly an hour now, the first part of which was awkward and strained, but now they are on more familiar, flirtatious territory, and Joe is feeling an excitement he hasn't felt in far too long.

Josie was intending to be cool. She intended to show Joe just what he was missing, just what he left behind when he walked out of her life without so much as a phone call afterward to see how she was.

She had wanted to laugh with a cool toss of her hair, to deflect his advances with just the right amount of graciousness, and perhaps a hint of scorn to make her feel better.

But she's missed him. She didn't even realize quite how much until she saw him again. She's sitting here now, listening to him tell amusing stories about his weekend country wreck, and she's gazing down at his hands, those fingers that are so familiar to her, that used to know every inch of her skin so well, and her own hand, resting only a few inches away from his, is almost hurting from the strain of not reaching over and touching him.

Damn. It wasn't meant to be like this. She's half listening to him, smiling in all the right places, but her mind is back in her apartment in London, back in her bedroom, back in the days when she would watch him climb out of bed and pull her up to join him in the shower before he went home to his wife.

There's a silence and Josie looks up. Joe has stopped talking, is waiting for her to respond, but she has no idea what he's been talking about, what he has asked.

"My wife's in the country," he says finally. "I'm supposed to be on the seven o'clock train."

Josie nods. She's not sure what she's meant to say, although her heart beats just a little faster at the word "supposed."

Joe takes a deep breath. "My workload is rather heavy at the moment. I was thinking that perhaps I oughtn't to be going to the country. . . ." He stares into Josie's eyes. "I was thinking that perhaps I ought to stay in Manhattan this weekend."

Josie just looks at him, her blank expression belying her racing mind.

There are two types of unfaithful married men. Those who are genuinely unhappy in their marriage, but are too lazy or too scared to leave. Perhaps there are children involved, perhaps they are just too cowardly, but either way it is easier for these men to stay married and have affairs, and one day they may or may not meet someone for whom they feel so strongly it becomes impossible for them to keep going home to someone else they do not love.

And then there is the second type, who are far more dangerous. These are the men who are very happily married. Men who love their wives, depend on them, but are addicted to having affairs. Men like Joe Chambers.

Josie thinks Joe falls into the former type, but mistresses always do, otherwise what would be the point? Here he is, nearly a year after she last saw him, and he's offering to spend the weekend with her. Yes, he's still with his wife, but surely not happy, and clearly the attraction between them is as strong as it has always been. And perhaps Josie is right. For years Joe was happy with Alice, but now their marriage seems to be on distinctly shaky ground, and Joe has moved adeptly from the latter type of unfaithful man to the former. As Josie had hoped.

"Alone?" Josie says eventually, raising an eyebrow.

Joe looks down at the table, at Josie's hand resting so close to his own, and he slides his hand over to hers, gently stroking her thumb with his own. Josie closes her eyes for a second, savoring the feeling, wondering how she could have gone so long without him, and when she opens them Joe is smiling.

"We could have dinner," he says. "I know a great Italian place near my apartment."

"How do you know I don't already have plans?"

"I don't. I'm hoping."

"Just dinner?" Josie knows it's not just dinner, it's never been just dinner, but his fingers are now entwined with hers and she doesn't have the strength to resist.

"Let me call my wife," Joe says slowly, reluctantly removing his hand as he reaches for his mobile phone. He stands up and walks outside, presses the earpiece into his ear as he paces up and down just outside the bagel shop.

"Hello?" Alice is lost inside the Rachel Danbury novel when the phone rings, and her voice is distracted.

"Hi, darling, it's me."

"Are you at the station?"

"No, darling. Look, I've got some bad news. I'm afraid that Brazilian client I was telling you about wants some more work done to the roadshow presentation this weekend, and wants me to take him out tomorrow night and show him some of the sights, so I'm going to have to stay in town."

"What Brazilian client?"

"Darling," Joe affects a patronizing laugh. "I did tell you. My meeting today. You never remember anything."

Alice doesn't deny it. She's finding it

harder and harder to pretend to be interested in Joe's work. Lately, stories about clients, and presentations, and emerging markets are tending to go in one ear and straight out the other. "Sorry." She shrugs. "I'm sure you did tell me. So you're not coming down?"

"Do you mind, darling? I know it's been two weeks, but you're coming up this week, aren't you? We've got that charity benefit on Wednesday."

"Oh, yes." Bugger. She'd forgotten.

"Will you be okay?"

"I'll be fine," Alice says, irritated that he's letting her down again, but relieved that he won't be around on Saturday, whining that he's bored, insisting that she comes shopping with him to Greenwich when she'd much rather be mooching around the house or doing local errands. "Couldn't you come down on Sunday?" Alice ventures. "Just for the day?"

"Maybe," Joe says appeasingly. "I'll have to see. What are your plans this weekend?"

"Not much," Alice says distractedly, wanting to get back to her book. "I'm reading the Rachel Danbury novel and I can't put it down, so I'll probably get nothing done at all." She laughs.

"You're probably thrilled I'm not coming then," Joe says, relieved to hear her laugh, relieved she hasn't given him a hard time. "You can read and garden as much as you want."

"That's true. But do try for Sunday, Joe. You are my husband, I would like to see you from time to time."

"I know, darling. I will. Promise. Listen, gotta go, but I'll call you tomorrow. Love you."

Alice smiles. "I love you more."

"I know." Joe flips his phone shut and walks slowly back inside to where Josie is sitting, so temptingly, in the corner.

Alice sighs as she puts the phone down. As much as she loves it here, there are times when she feels lonely, and as much as Joe drives her mad when he's here — his fish-out-of-water act began to grate many, many months ago — she nevertheless looks forward to his company on the week-ends.

But at least this weekend she has her book, and it's true, she hasn't been able to put it down, so engrossed has she become in its pages. Curling up on the sofa, she picks up the book again and loses herself in a Highfield that's long since disappeared, a Highfield that was a true country village, a community of writers and artists, back in 1947.

At eight-thirty Alice realizes that not only is she starving, there's also a chill in the air and her feet are like blocks of ice. She lets Snoop outside while she puts a pan of boiling water on the stove and pours in some pasta, throwing together a spinach salad while it boils.

Alice sits at the kitchen counter to eat, the book open in front of her as she continues to read, and after supper, when she's washed up and the kitchen is sparkling, she and Snoop head upstairs.

Alice takes the book to bed and switches on the bedside lamp, reading in the soft apricot glow as Snoop lies outstretched on the duvet beside her.

At 11:45 she's still reading, but the yawns are coming thick and fast and reluctantly Alice closes the book and reaches sleepily for the phone. Surely Joe is back by now, she'll just phone to say good night. She holds the receiver to her ear and listens to the phone ringing until the machine picks up. She calls his mobile but that's switched off too. With a sigh she flicks off the light and closes her eyes.

Within minutes she's fast asleep.

At 11:45 Joe and Josie have just finished what Joe could only term a marathon session. He's exhausted, exhilarated, and, despite his thirty-eight years, almost ready to do it all over again.

He lies on his side and grins at Josie, reaching across to brush away the hair that's fallen into her eyes.

"Wow," he says softly.

"Wow." She smiles in return.

"Would you be insulted if I told you I'd forgotten how fanfuckingtastic you are?"

Josie shrugs. "Would you be insulted if I told you I'd forgotten how infuckingcredible you are?"

Joe laughs. "Josie, I've missed you. I swear to God I've thought about you, but I just didn't want to screw up your life anymore."

Josie sits up. "But you didn't screw up my life. I knew the score."

Joe sighs. "I know. But you were different somehow."

Josie squints at him. "Different because I'm a ball-breaker?"

"If that's ball-breaking, you can break my balls anytime."

"Ouch. Sounds painful."

Joe laughs. "On second thought I think it might be. But seriously, Josie, I didn't want to hurt you."

"I know," Josie says. It's not necessary to ask how she was different. It's enough to hear him tell her she was. Nor is it necessary to say he hurt her anyway. Not necessary to tell him how much she cared, how devastated she was when he just disappeared. He's back now. That's all that matters. "You didn't. Hurt me, that is."

"Are you sure? Because I wouldn't do anything to hurt you. You know that."

"I do," Josie says, and even though she doesn't, she wants to believe that's true. Josie wants to ask him what happens now. Wants to know whether this is a one-night stand or whether they'll resume where they left off, but she doesn't want to scare him off, not when she has him back, and she knows, she remembers, how Joe loves the thrill of the chase, and she knows she mustn't show him how she really feels. "You'd better go," she says, leaning over to kiss him, enjoying the look of surprise on his face.

"Go? You're not serious. Why? I'm on my own this weekend, remember? I can stay."

"No you can't," Josie says, even though

she wants him to stay more than anything in the world, wants to wake up in the morning and roll over to see him sleeping beside her. "I have things to do and it's better if you go."

Joe shakes his head in disbelief, but climbs out of bed and starts to gather his things. Josie pulls on a robe and walks him to the door and slides her arms around his neck as she kisses him good-bye.

"Oh God," Joe moans. "Please let me stay."

"No." Josie smiles to herself, knowing that however hard this may be, it's the right strategy if she wants to keep him. "You have to go."

"What about tomorrow?" Joe says hopefully, standing in the hallway. "Can I see you tomorrow?"

"Call me," Josie says as she shuts the door. "Call me and we'll see."

Joe falls asleep as soon as his head hits the pillow. He wakes in the morning at eight o'clock and the very first thing he thinks about is Josie, or more specifically, sex with Josie. Jesus, it was good. He has to see her again. Today. Now. As soon as possible. He picks up the phone and calls her.

Josie, just in from the gym, stands in her

kitchen cradling her coffee and looks at the caller ID that's flashing on her phone. Joe. She stands there and lets the machine pick up.

"Josie? It's me. Joe. Just phoning to see how you are. Give me a call when you get in. Talk to you later. Bye."

Half an hour later Joe calls again, but this time he doesn't leave a message, just puts the phone down as the machine picks up.

By three o'clock in the afternoon Joe has tried Josie nine times. Josie is having to physically sit on her hands to prevent herself from answering the phone, but hard as it is, she knows she's doing the right thing.

At eight o'clock that evening Josie calls him back.

"Hello?"

"Joe? It's Josie."

"Hi! How are you?" His voice is casual, and Josie smiles. He has no idea she knows he's been trying her all day.

"Fine, thanks. How are you?"

"I'm great. Busy."

"Oh, yes? What have you done today?"

"Working. Gym. Some errands." All with his mobile phone, from which he continued to try to reach Josie. "Listen, what are you up to now?"

"Now?" Josie had already worked out her speech. She would tell him she was off to a dinner party, therefore not only could she not see him, she would also be implying she had an active social life, was in demand by other people.

"Yes, now."

"I'm going to a dinner party," Josie says, as planned.

"Oh. Couldn't you get out of it? I've been thinking about you all day, I'm desperate to see you."

"Um." She knows she ought to say no, but the words are out of her mouth before she can stop them. "I suppose I could get out of it."

"Great!" Joe cannot hide the enthusiasm in his voice. "How about going out? There's a party going on downtown tonight. Why don't I pick you up in an hour?"

"Sounds good. I'll see you in an hour."

"Wow!" Joe does a slow wolf whistle as Josie steps out of the lift in a pink print Diane von Furstenberg dress, wrapping sexily around her tiny waist, the skirt opening slightly every time she walks.

"You like the dress?"

"I love the dress. In fact, are you sure

you want to go out?"

"Oh, I'm sure," Josie smiles as Joe slips his arms around her waist and kisses her slowly.

"Still sure?" Joe smiles into her eyes.

"Still sure," Josie smiles back. "Plenty of time for that later."

The party is in a huge loft in Tribeca, in a desperately trendy building that used to be an icehouse. The doorman wearily directs them up to the sixth floor, where they can hear the noise as soon as the elevator door opens.

The music's thumping and the lights are so dim it's difficult to make out the mass of people. It's the kind of party Alice would hate, the kind of party that Joe adores. It makes him feel as if he's regressed back to his twenties, with his whole life still ahead of him, as if anything is possible.

Everywhere they look there are people laughing, talking loudly above the din, dancing wildly as the music gets louder and louder. Joe and Josie push their way through to the makeshift bar and each do two tequila shots.

"I feel like I'm eighteen again," Josie shouts into Joe's ear after biting into the wedge of lime that he's holding out for her.

"I know," Joe shouts back. "Isn't it great?"

"Wanna dance?" Josie raises an eyebrow, and Joe nods as she takes his hand and leads him over to the space that's rapidly filling up with writhing bodies.

The music changes to salsa, and Josie laughs as she grabs Joe's hand and tries to teach him how to salsa. He picks it up quickly, and the two of them dance together for a while, each enjoying the buzz from the tequila, the music, the very fact that they still find one another as exciting as they remembered, if not more so. That they are behaving like a couple of teenagers out on a first date.

Effectively this *is* a first date for Joe and Josie. Their affair in London was always conducted behind closed doors, for fear of someone seeing them. Joe was far too well known in London to risk being caught with Josie in a situation like this.

Here in New York Joe is feeling a freedom he never felt in London. He is truly exhilarated to be with Josie again, to be having great sex again, exciting sex, to experience the thrill of the extramarital fling. And in New York Joe still feels anonymous, safe. Can risk dancing groin to groin with Josie in public. Can risk throwing back tequila shots safe in the knowledge that home, or Josie's home, is a cab ride away. Can risk looking deep into Josie's eyes and stroking her hair as he leans forward and slides his tongue into her mouth as she gasps at the newness and familiarity of it all.

"Honey, I'm tired," Gina shouts into George's ear. "Can we go now?"

"Sure," George smiles at his wife. "I thought you'd never ask."

Gina and George wind their way through the crowd, when suddenly Gina stops. "Look!" she says excitedly, and then she freezes. George turns to look at her to see if she's okay, then turns to see what she's looking at, what has caused her to stand as still as a statue.

He turns and follows her stare and sees, just in front of them, Joe Chambers.

Joe Chambers passionately kissing someone who resembles Alice, but who very definitely is not Alice.

Gina had thought she was Alice, was about to throw her arms around her, until Joe pulled away and Gina saw she'd been fooled by the slim body and blond hair. The face is not Alice's, and Gina stands there foolishly, not knowing what to do.

She wishes she'd never seen anything, wishes she could turn back the clock to just a minute ago, wishes she could have pushed past different people, taken a different route out, but as she stands there thinking these thoughts Joe, clearly sensing eyes on him, turns his head.

"Fuck," he whispers as he sees Gina and George, takes in the shock in their eyes. "Oh, fuck." The four of them stand there looking at each other, nobody knowing what to say, Josie not knowing what's going on, until Gina finally clears her throat.

"Hello," she says icily, nodding at Josie. "I'm Gina. Alice's best friend. Oh, do you know Alice? She's Joe's wife."

Josie merely looks at her. What can she say?

26

"I have to tell her." Gina is pacing the floor of their living room, a crystal glass of single-malt whisky in hand, while George watches her miserably from his position in the wing chair next to the fireplace. "Bastard!" she hisses yet again.

"Honey, I don't think you should tell her. All you'd be doing is hurting her."

Gina stops pacing for a moment and looks at George in disbelief. "But she's one of my closest friends, and isn't it hurting her more to have him betray her like this?"

George shrugs. "For all you know they may have an arrangement. Maybe she knows. Maybe she suspects but doesn't want to know. I mean, come on, Gina, look at Joe. I very much doubt this is the first time he's had an affair."

Gina sighs and sits down, shaking her

head. "I just feel so awful. I just keep thinking of Alice stuck in Highfield all by herself, thinking her husband's working hard when he's probably out having all these affairs. It's horrible for her." She looks up at George. "You know if you ever did that to me I'd kick you out immediately."

George nods with a smile. "Yes, honey. I know you'd kick me out immediately, which is why I would never do something like that."

"I hope that's not the only reason why."

George opens his arms. "Come here and give me a kiss."

Gina walks over and puts her arms around him, laying her head on his chest. "Oh, George," she says sadly. "What are we going to do?"

"Nothing," he says. "It's not our place to do anything."

"Are you sure?" Gina says. "Because if you're sure, I won't say anything."

"Trust me." George strokes Gina's hair. "I'm sure."

"Will she tell her, do you think?" Josie turns to Joe in the cab, notes his distracted expression, but Joe just shrugs and looks out of the window.

441

He looks calm. Distracted but calm, even though his mind is racing. How could he have been so careless? How stupid was he to have kissed Josie in a public place? And worst of all, this was his first affair in months, and hell, this doesn't even count, Josie being an affair of old.

God, if he had known he was going to get caught, he would have got up to far worse than this. Of all the bloody bad luck, to have got caught in his first affair since they'd moved. A whole year, for God's sake.

And to have been caught by Alice's friend. Gina wouldn't look at him at all, just introduced herself in that icy voice then stalked off. Shit. Is she going to tell her? Oh God, please don't let her tell Alice. Should he maybe phone Gina, try to explain, come up with some plausible reason why he was kissing a woman in a downtown loft while his wife was fast asleep in the country? Yes. That's exactly what he'll do. Say he was drunk, say he was with friends and this woman made a pass at him.

Joe looks at his watch. Too late now to phone. And anyway, Gina's hardly going to call Alice in the early hours of the morning. He'll call first thing tomorrow, make sure he comes up with a plausible enough story. Joe exhales loudly and starts to relax.

"Joe, are you okay?" Joe turns to look at Josie, and he nods.

"I'm sorry, Josie. It was just a shock. Look, I think I should just drop you off and go back to my apartment. Do you mind? I'll call you tomorrow."

"I think that's a good idea," Josie says brightly, her heart sinking to her knees. "And don't worry about calling tomorrow, I'm actually off to a luncheon party in Purchase. I won't be around much."

"Thanks." Joe smiles at her, then takes her hand and kisses it. "That's what I love about you. You always understand."

Josie just smiles, then turns her head to look out of the window so he doesn't see the pain in her eyes.

"Gina? It's Joe."

"Hello, Joe." Her voice is still cold. She prods George, who is lying next to her reading the *Times*, and raises an eyebrow. George lowers the paper to listen to the conversation.

"Gina, I need to explain."

"I think it was perfectly clear actually.

And anyway, you don't need to explain anything to me."

"But I do, Gina. It wasn't what you think."

"It doesn't matter what I think. It's none of my business. What you get up to when your wife isn't around is none of my business, Joe."

"Gina, I don't get up to anything when Alice isn't around."

"Really? That's not what it looked like to me."

"And that's exactly why I'm phoning you. To explain. Because I know what it looked like and I know what it wasn't."

"Okay. Shoot. What wasn't it?"

"It wasn't what you think."

"Oh? And what do I think?"

"You think I'm a bastard and you think I'm cheating on Alice."

"I'm glad that you were the one to say that and not me."

"Gina, I swear to God I love Alice. I love Alice more than anything, and I would never do anything to hurt her."

"So what exactly do you call what you were doing last night?" George is shaking his head furiously at Gina, but she's turned her back on him. George sighs and picks up the paper again, flicking to the back of the Style section to see if he knows anyone who got married this week.

"I admit, you caught me kissing some bimbo, but you know what? I had no idea who she was, I was out with friends and we'd all had a bit too much to drink, and this girl just started coming on to me. I suppose I was lonely, I missed Alice, and I was flattered that this young girl was flirting with me. It was stupid, I know how stupid it was, and if it's any consolation at all nothing else happened last night." At least this last bit was true.

Gina sits silently, holding the phone to her ear. It sounds plausible enough, and he sounds sorry enough. Maybe it really was nothing. Maybe he's not that much of a bastard.

"Gina? Are you there?"

"Yes. You know you don't have to explain anything to me." Her voice is softer; Joe knows she's on her way to forgiving him.

"I know. But I needed to. I just felt sick afterward, not because I saw you, but at the thought of hurting Alice. Gina, I love Alice so much, I swear to you I wouldn't ever hurt her."

"I believe you," Gina says with a sigh eventually. "Okay. Let's try and put all this behind us."

"Thank you, Gina. Really. Thank you."

"You're welcome. You know, I still don't approve, but I can understand how these things happen, and if it really was a one-time thing then I'm prepared to leave it at that."

"It really was a one-off. In fact I'm going down to spend the day with Alice now."

"Good. I know she misses you when you're in town all the time. Send her my love. Tell her I'll speak to her tomorrow."

Joe puts the phone down with a huge sigh of relief. Thank God he managed to pull it off. Thank God Gina isn't going to say anything to Alice. He picks up again and dials Alice. "Hi, sleepyhead."

"Hi! And I'm no sleepyhead, thank you. I've been up for hours."

"No surprise there. What have you been up to?"

"Reading mostly. And today I'm out pruning."

"Sounds fascinating."

"Oh, ha bloody ha."

"How do you fancy lunch at the Homestead Inn?"

"You're coming down?"

"Yup. I miss you. I thought we could go out and have a lovely lunch, and then maybe spend a leisurely afternoon in bed."

"Sounds infinitely more exciting than pruning."

"I'm so glad you think so."

Alice smiles, thrilled her husband is actually coming down and actually wants to be here with her. "I'll see you later," she says. "Snoop and I are going for a walk."

Joe insists Alice change for the Homestead Inn — "Darling, filthy old Levi's, a baseball cap, and gardening clogs aren't exactly the done thing in Greenwich" — and frowns when she comes downstairs a few moments later in a pale pink cashmere twin set and black trousers.

"What's the matter?" Alice says. "Isn't this smart enough?"

"The clothes are perfect," Joe says. "But what have you done to your hair?"

Alice laughs. "I'm going natural again. You've forgotten how curly my hair is naturally. Frankly I can't be bothered to straighten it anymore. Don't you think it's better curly?"

Joe frowns. "Well, it's certainly different. But you've got to get your roots done, darling. It looks terrible."

"Ah. Well, I thought I might try growing out the blond actually."

Joe shakes his head. "No, love. If you

want me to be honest, you look far more beautiful with blond hair. Curly I can handle, just, but back to your natural mousy color? No. I don't think so."

Alice shrugs. She's not willing to have an argument over something so petty, particularly when he's come all this way just for the day and he's treating her so nicely. "I probably won't grow it out," she lies. "I'd just forgotten what I looked like with natural hair and I just wanted to remember what my color was."

"Just make sure you get an appointment this week," Joe says. "Remember we've got that charity benefit. Maybe Carlo can fit you in that afternoon."

"Maybe," Alice says, knowing she won't even bother phoning her hairdresser. She's fed up with sitting at the hairdresser's for hours every six weeks to get her highlights redone. She just can't be bothered anymore, and her natural color isn't so bad. Mousy, yes, but so much easier. "I'll phone him tomorrow," she says, to keep Joe happy, and he nods approvingly before whisking her off to lunch.

During dessert Joe takes Alice's hand then surprises her with a silver bracelet he's picked up en route (thank God for Sunday shopping).

"It's beautiful!" Alice smiles with delight. "But what's it for?"

"Why does it have to be *for* anything?" Joe says, leaning forward and doing up the clasp for her. "It's just because I love you."

"Are you sure you're not guilty of something?" Alice laughs, and Joe smiles even though he suddenly feels very cold.

"Guilty of what?" he says, trying to keep his voice as normal as possible. Surely Gina wouldn't have told her, not after their conversation this morning.

Alice smiles and kisses him. "Guilty of being a lovely husband. Thank you. It's beautiful. It's been months since you've surprised me with a beautiful present. You used to do it all the time in London. I'd forgotten how much I'd missed it. Thank you." Alice has also, rather conveniently, forgotten how she used to feel when Joe turned up with these presents, forgotten her suspicions of old, forgotten the fear that used to follow her around like a large black rain cloud.

Joe is more loving today than he has been in months. They come back home and do spend the afternoon in bed, laughing together as they make love, Joe experiencing a renewed vigor he thought had disappeared altogether when it came to Alice, helped largely by visions of Josie whenever he — frequently — closes his eyes.

"Wow!" Alice flops back on the pillow, exhausted, and smiles at Joe. "That was some afternoon."

"It certainly was." Joe leans over and kisses her on the lips, then climbs out of bed.

"Where are you going?"

"Shower. Then I have to make some business calls. I'm sorry, darling. Do you mind?"

Alice shrugs, then shakes her head. Of course she minds. But since when does a leopard ever change its — or his — spots?

Joe makes sure his office door is closed then dials Josie's number.

"Hi. It's Joe." His voice is soft, just a tone above whispering as he leaves a message on her machine. Alice is still upstairs in bed, but you could never be too careful. "Listen, I'm in the country, had to come down and be the dutiful husband, but I'm going out of my mind with boredom. I'm coming back up this afternoon and I can't stop thinking about you. I have to see you. I'll try you again later but I want to see you tonight."

He switches his computer on then goes into his Hotmail account and writes Josie a long, explicit e-mail, telling her exactly what he plans to do to her this evening, then phones her again, putting the phone down when the machine picks up. Damn. Why doesn't he have her mobile number? He wants to talk to her. He needs to talk to her.

Josie sits at her kitchen table eating a dry toasted bagel and listens to Joe leaving the message. She wants to pick up the phone, talk to him, tell him she'll be here, but she told him she was at a luncheon party, so she must pretend to be out. But all she wants to do is be with him, and even though she knows she needs to be unavailable to win him, she knows there's only so much willpower she can muster. She won't pick up the phone now, but she knows she'll be there for him tonight. And tomorrow. And whenever he phones and says he wants her.

At ten o'clock Joe unbuttons the top button of Josie's shirt and continues to unbutton as she slides her tongue into his mouth and he gasps. He strokes her soft skin, then slips a bra strap down, tracing

451

his fingers along her collarbone and down to her breast.

Josie sighs as his head moves lower, kissing the path his fingers have just traced. She closes her eyes and sinks back on the bed as Joe moves lower. Thank you, God, she mouths silently, over his shoulder. Thank you for bringing him back to me.

At ten twenty-five Joe's phone rings.

"Fuck!" he hisses, as he stops moving inside Josie.

"You left it on?" she whispers, her hands still clasping his back, wanting him to carry on. "Don't stop," she encourages, trying to ignore the persistent ring.

They wait, and eventually the phone stops. Joe is relieved to find he is still hard, and he starts moving inside Josie again as she gasps.

And the phone starts to ring again.

Alice clasps the phone to her ear. He said he'd be at home, but there's no reply. And his mobile is ringing. If he was asleep he would have turned it off, but it's just ringing and ringing.

Fear clutches her heart, and nausea threatens to rise. She punches the number out again. And again. And again. And again.

"Fuck!" Joe's erection shrinks to nothing, and he pulls out of Josie and walks to the phone. Of course it's Alice. Who else could it be? But why is she phoning him, and what is she thinking of, ringing over and over and over again?

He doesn't know whether to answer or whether to turn the phone off. Why is she ruining his night like this? Furiously he presses the power off button and watches the phone fade to nothing.

Josie pads out to the living room, naked, and stands over him. "Is everything okay?"

Joe nods, still furious, too wound up to speak.

"Your wife?"

He nods again. Why is she hounding him, for God's sake?

Josie sees how tense he is and rests a hand on his shoulder. She walks around to face him then kneels in front of him, cradling his head and kissing him.

"It's all going to be okay," she says, but his shoulders are still tight, his body still stiff and unyielding. "Trust me," she says, her lips moving down his chest, his stomach, then onto his twitching cock.

Joe tenses, then relaxes. Yes. This feels right. Josie is right. It's all going to be okay. He gives in to the feeling of pure physical pleasure and forgets about Alice. All that matters is right now, feeling Josie's warm wet mouth.

Alice gets up and goes downstairs, putting the kettle on to make chamomile tea. Snoop raises his head as she gets up but doesn't have the energy to follow her, so Alice sits alone at the kitchen counter, trying to release the grip of fear on her heart.

Stop being so ridiculous, she tells herself. Your mind is racing because of that bloody book. He probably just forgot to turn the phone off. He's probably fast asleep and the phone is ringing in the hallway. But why did it suddenly switch off midring? Doesn't that mean he turned the power off? Not necessarily. Maybe the battery went dead. A million possibilities race through Alice's mind, and even though the fear abates somewhat, she still feels unsettled.

Two hours later she takes a Valium, and gratefully, half an hour after that, she finally gives in to sleep.

27

Now that Joe has gotten away with it again, he knows he can continue getting away with it. He and Josie have fallen into a routine, much like the routine of old in London, only this time he doesn't have to keep thinking up excuses as to why he's home late.

It's just perfect, he thinks for the umpteenth time, as he heads over to Josie's apartment, smiling at this beautiful spring day.

A wife in the country and a mistress in town. Why didn't he do this years ago? He smiles to himself. Alice had always wanted to live in the middle of nowhere. He could have stashed her in some Cotswolds cottage and played the quintessential bachelor in London. But no, he was too well known there, someone would have talked, word would have gotten out.

But here it's a different matter altogether. Josie is proving to be the perfect mistress. She looks great, she thinks he's perfect, and she's willing to do anything he wants. Plus, she understands the rules of having a married lover: Never put pressure on him and never question him about his wife; never phone his house and do something dangerous like put the phone down should his wife answer, and never expect anything more than you already have.

He couldn't have orchestrated a better situation had he tried. In fact, Josie's so easy to be around he's finding he's spending almost every night with her. He's learned to call Alice at around nine to preempt any late-night phone calls when she might question his whereabouts — the last time that happened he managed to say he was fast asleep with earplugs and had forgotten to turn off his mobile phone — and phone her first thing in the morning just so her suspicions aren't raised.

He's even started going out properly with Josie — to dinner, to benefits, to parties, Alice rarely venturing into the city anymore — even though he's careful not to indulge in any public displays of affection since the last close shave. He introduces Josie as a work colleague, and even though everyone suspects, no one knows for sure. Naturally his own colleagues in the office have a stronger suspicion than most about what's going on — they had all heard the original rumors about why he was transferred to New York, and they know that Josie was the woman involved, but Joe is too senior for people to question him, or tease him, or make jokes to his face, and so he carries on regardless.

And although he's loath to admit it, Josie is, in many ways, proving to be a far better companion than Alice. For starters, she's in the business, can easily hold her own with clients far more important than he. She truly understands how he feels when a deal doesn't come off, or when there are problems at work, and knows how to make him feel better about it.

Alice tries, but Alice has always said that she has a mental block when it comes to numbers, and money, and finances, and Joe has stopped bothering to explain things to her, irritated by her blank expressions of sympathy.

And Josie looks great. She's learned what Joe likes and subsequently dresses to please him. She wears tight white shirts and tailored suits, the skirt covering the stockings and garters he loves. She clickclacks on spindly heels, unlike Alice, who always used to complain that heels hurt her feet, and who now rarely removes her Timberland boots or gardening clogs.

Josie has the mane of glossy blond hair that is always a prerequisite for anyone Joe is involved with, and he finds himself looking at Alice's two inches of mouse and wild curls with increasing distaste.

He's trying very hard with Alice. Trying to encourage her to be who she used to be, the woman he can proudly introduce as his wife. But where once upon a time Alice treated Joe like a god, listened to everything he said, did anything and everything to please him, since coming to America Alice doesn't seem to care anymore.

"But I'm happier like this." Alice grins up at him from her position cross-legged in front of the fire, her hair scraped back in a messy ponytail, blowing the loose curls away from her face. "Aren't you happy that I'm happy, darling?"

Joe smiles and lies that of course he's happy. But look at her, for God's sake. Her nails are short, her hands are now coarse and workmanlike. She doesn't wear her rings anymore because she's worried about damaging them while working in the garden, and her makeup is clearly gathering dust in a closet somewhere.

Alice looks exactly as she did when he first met her. He had known then how malleable she would be, how much potential she had, and how she would have done anything to please him. He cannot understand why he's having such a hard time transforming her again, six years later.

Joe buys Alice a weekly present. A voucher to a spa; a pair of Prada shoes; the latest Vuitton bag that everyone in the city is dying for. He presents them to Alice hoping she will use them, hoping these beautiful things will encourage her to dress up again, to look beautiful, to make an effort for him, but she merely thanks him, lies about how much she's always wanted whatever it is, and then puts it away in a closet in the bedroom.

Alice comes to the city because she has to, not because she enjoys it. She tries not even to stay overnight anymore. She takes the train up to Grand Central in the morning and is usually back in Highfield by five. He knows she's beginning to hate it more and more, she only comes in because she thinks it keeps him happy, but he's beginning to resent having to make the effort.

After all, he has a more than adequate

companion in Josie.

As for Alice, she knows how things have changed. She can sense that Joe is distracted again, distant, but it doesn't upset her now. There are times, like last night, when Alice lies in bed panicking about her marriage. She lies there knowing she's married to the wrong man, knowing they're not making each other happy, knowing they want completely different things in life, and she feels sick and scared, and tries to push the thoughts away.

The nights she has these fears seem to go on forever, but at some point she always manages to fall asleep, and always, when she wakes up and the sun is streaming through the window, she feels better; knows that those night fears were just that — fears, and not a reality.

And meanwhile she has been busier and busier. HomeFront has become one of the most popular classes in the Newcomers' Club, and Alice and Sandy are now running something almost weekly.

Just this month they are organizing a trip to the White Flower Farm in Litchfield, a visit to a pottery kiln, and a class on the secrets of aging new terra-cotta pots for the patio.

She and Sandy meet up regularly, classes aside — walks with the dogs, coffee in town, popping in to one another's houses to finalize plans for the next HomeFront meeting — and she has discovered a new friend in her neighbor Sally.

Suddenly Alice finds that she's not lonely anymore. There are always people dropping in, Sally brings Madison to play almost daily, and now when Alice goes into town to do some shopping or run some errands, she invariably bumps into at least two people she knows.

James has become accustomed to seeing her at Sunup nursery. He's even stopped flirting with her and has become, if not a friend, then certainly someone she enjoys spending time with.

He has helped her plant a small vegetable garden, teaching her how to fence it in with eight-foot fences to keep the deer out, and has helped her discover what will and won't do well in Zone Six.

And now that spring has finally sprung, Alice's garden is a mass of color. The forsythia bushes splash a bright yellow just past the terrace, and the hundreds of narcissus and tulip bulbs she planted in the autumn are in full bloom.

The bed in the front, the bed that Alice

has ignored, presuming the groundcover was weeds, is now covered in tiny purple flowers of vinca, with the yellow flowers of lamium just starting to push through the pachysandra.

Bleeding hearts are weeping small pink flowers everywhere she looks, and Alice is finally getting to know her garden, finally learning about the plants, the soil, which plants will grow and which won't.

And it is a learning curve. Unlike England, with its mild temperatures and steady rainfall, Connecticut has freezing winters, often with thick snow, and boiling summers. Alice has learned the hard way that the plants she grew so well on the terrace in her London house — olive trees, French lavender, potted citrus plants, and dwarf herbs — didn't have a chance out here.

Instead she has had to learn to love rhododendrons, azaleas, hydrangeas. After the disaster with the lavender that died a horrible death over the cold winter, she has edged her borders with Six Hills Giant catmint instead, has planted busy lizzies under the canopy of blue spruce at the back of the garden, has learned to appreciate plants like bayberry and juniper in place of her beloved bays and cypresses.

Alice has become a woman obsessed with her garden, much to the amusement of Sally, who planted a few yew hedges, a couple of rhododendrons, and that was it.

"I guess it's because you're English." Sally smiled, sitting on the terrace one day drinking coffee with Alice. "You're all obsessed with gardening, aren't you?"

"Not all. My best friend Emily — you remember Emily, don't you? She doesn't know the first thing about gardening and doesn't want to. We always used to joke that we ended up with the wrong lives. There I was living this fast glamorous life in London and dreaming about living in the country, and she was the one who bought the house in the Cotswolds when she should really have been married to someone like Joe."

"She's not married, is she? That man, what was his name? Harry? He was just her boyfriend, wasn't he?"

Alice nods. Even the mention of his name brings the guilt flooding back. That night, the night of Sally and Chris's party when Harry kissed her, is something she tries very hard not to think about.

She tries hard not to think about how much she hurt her best friend, and she tries even harder not to think about how she felt, lying on the ground, wrapped in Harry's arms. She doesn't think about it because when she does she can remember it so clearly, it was as if it happened yesterday. She can feel every blade of grass, every millimeter of stubble on Harry's face, smell his warm skin as if he is right in front of her.

And it's too painful. It fills her with a longing she's not used to, a longing she doesn't know what to do with.

Alice jumps up. "Come on, Madison," she says to the little girl. "Why don't you throw the ball for Snoop?" And all three of them run down the steps to the lawn, laughing as Snoop leaps up and down on his hind legs.

Valium always makes Alice feel slightly groggy when she wakes up, and for a split second she forgets why she took the pills in the first place. Then she remembers.

But as always, now that the sun is shining she feels better. Not perfect, but better. She goes downstairs and as she passes the office, a thought occurs to her. If he were up to no good — although today she's sure there is a perfectly reasonable explanation for his mobile phone last night — but if he *were* up to no good, surely there'd be some evidence somewhere?

She pauses outside the office door. No, she couldn't possibly turn into one of those snooping wives in the films. Isn't the first rule of snooping that if you snoop, you're inevitably going to find something you don't want to find? But there is a force pulling her into the office, a force out of her control, and on autopilot Alice gently pushes open the door and looks around.

Receipts. There are his receipts. Alice sits down behind the desk and starts going through the receipts. Nothing unusual. She examines each and every one, fascinated at this hidden life her husband leads, all these restaurants where he entertains clients. She doesn't even know what she's looking for. Nothing, hopefully. She finds restaurant bills, and dry-cleaning receipts, and gas receipts. Nothing suspicious in the least.

She starts to relax, but then notices the computer. After turning it on, she clicks until she's online, then looks at the last few sites that have been visited. Gardenweb.com. She smiles to herself. That's hers. Google.com. Hotmail.com. All hers.

She goes to Hotmail to check her e-mail, and it occurs to her that she could check

Joe's e-mail. His password is the same for everything: champ. She types in his name, then his password, and goes to his inbox. Part of her feels terrible for doing this, but she can't stop. She's come this far and she can't stop.

She clicks on the messages and scans the names of the incoming e-mails, looking to see if there's anything that might be suspicious, but no. Everything looks fine. Her heart is pounding but she's relieved, and she turns the computer off, shaking her head at her stupidity as she goes to make a pot of coffee.

That evening, as usual, Joe phones to say he won't be coming down. Alice doesn't have the strength to be angry. She just nods and puts the phone down, and sits numbly on the sofa staring into space for most of the evening.

On her way up to bed, she remembers the office, his e-mail, and knows there must have been something she was missing, and she finds herself walking back into the office, her head emptied of all thought.

Alice sits down feeling numb and switches on the computer, knowing where she's going, knowing what she's looking for, but no longer caring. Fed up with the pretense, fed up with being taken for an idiot.

Into his Hotmail account she goes. Into a folder she had ignored earlier. A folder marked Private. And there they are. Three new e-mails from JosieJo. And she knows instinctively that JosieJo is far too playful a name to be business. Her heart beats painfully, but even as she clicks on the messages she knows she can't stop. She knows what she's going to find, and this time she needs to know.

Slowly she reads all three messages. Short, perfunctory, but clearly not work e-mails. Still. Not quite enough evidence. She moves back up to the Sent box, where she finds what she both is, and isn't, looking for.

Sent. To JosieJo. This morning at 9:23 a.m. Subject: Tonight. She reads the e-mail five times, each time feeling sicker and sicker. Her hand starts to shake as she reads the explicit language, realizes that this is someone her husband is sleeping with, realizes this e-mail isn't just graphic, it also contains an intimacy that implies this is someone he's known for a long time. Someone who isn't just a quick fuck, not something she, Alice, could pretend isn't happening. Not small and unimportant enough to brush under the carpet knowing that it doesn't pose a real threat to her marriage, that it doesn't really mean anything, that she should pretend it doesn't exist.

She knows, and she needs to know. Right now, as sick and scared and horrified as she feels, she wants to know. For the first time ever, she *has* to know.

When Joe calls her later that night Alice doesn't pick up the phone. She sits where she has been sitting for hours, in the armchair, cradling a vodka, too numb to speak.

The only thing that keeps running through her head is "What am I going to do? What am I going to do?" Over and over and over.

And still it doesn't feel real. Still she thinks that perhaps it was a bad dream, perhaps this is like the night fears, she will fall asleep here, sitting in this armchair, and when she wakes up she will discover it isn't real.

It's only when she hears his voice on the machine that she finally breaks down, finally gives in to the tears, because she knows that this is it. She knows how different they are, how far apart they've grown, and now she can't pretend any longer.

She knows beyond a shadow of a doubt that this is the end of their marriage. She'd never considered the prospect of being on her own at thirty-six, had never thought that her life as she knew it would so suddenly and so finally be over.

"Bastard!" she screams at Joe's voice as he smoothly tells the machine he loves her and says he's going to bed.

She waits until he hangs up then goes straight over to the phone, picks it up, and dials the apartment in Manhattan. No one is less surprised than she when the phone rings six times before the machine picks up.

"Bastard!" she whispers, putting the phone down and sinking to the floor in tears. Snoop runs over and puts his front paws on her shoulders, trying to lick her tears away, trying to make it better, and Alice puts her arms around the little dog and sobs for hours.

When Joe phones on Saturday morning, Alice is prepared. She cried last night until there were no tears left, and then made herself a cup of tea, pulled a jacket on, and went outside to the terrace to lie on a lounger, looking up at the stars to think about what to do.

Alice was shivering, even though the night was warm, but the vastness of the sky and the brightness of the stars were soothing, and as she lay there, her mind a jumble of thoughts, she began to realize that their marriage had probably ended a long time ago.

She thought back to their life in London, a life that seemed a million years away, and remembered how very unhappy she had been. Her life's mission had been to make Joe happy, but in doing so she had suppressed her own desires so much she had forgotten who she was.

She runs their life together through her mind almost as if watching a videotape. From the wedding that wasn't what she wanted, to the clothes he insisted she wear, to the Christmas tree he patronized and laughed at.

And she knows that this woman, this JosieJo, isn't the first. Lying here remembering, she's forced to admit she has always turned a blind eye, hasn't believed it because she hasn't wanted to believe it.

But of course she knew. All the late nights, the unexplained absences, the business trips staying in hotels and refusing to give her the number. The couple of times the phone had rung at home and been immediately put down. Alice, whatever Joe might have thought, isn't stupid, has never been stupid.

She just didn't want to know.

At five o'clock in the morning she calls Emily. It would be ten a.m. in England, and on a Saturday Alice knows Emily will most likely be in bed having a lie-in. They still haven't spoken properly, but Alice still writes, and now that Alice needs her, she knows that Emily will be there for her, that however much Emily professes to hate her, this is too big to ignore.

The answering machine picks up.

"Em? It's me. Alice. I need to talk to you. I . . . Joe's having an affair. . . ." She blurts it out, and as she says the words out loud a sob escapes her throat, closely followed by more. "Oh God," she hiccups into the machine. "I thought I was all cried out. I'm sorry, I didn't mean to —"

"Alice?" A shocked Emily picks up. "Alice? What's the matter? I heard you on the machine. I was in bed. What is it? What's wrong?"

"He's having an affair."

"Oh God." Emily is immediately sympathetic, immediately Alice's best friend again, there to support her and help her through. "Oh, Ali. I'm so sorry. When? I mean, how? How do you know? Are you sure?"

"I found e-mails. Oh God, Em. I just feel sick."

"Start at the beginning," Emily croons. "Tell me what happened."

And so Alice tells her about the unanswered phone calls. Tells her about growing apart. And finally about the e-mails.

"It's over," Alice says eventually. "We've just grown farther and farther apart. He looks at me sometimes and I think he hates me."

"Don't be silly, of course he doesn't hate you."

"I swear to you, Em, I think he does. I know he loved the me he tried to turn me into, the blond glamorous Alice who looked so good on his arm, but I swear he hates the real me. I catch him looking at me sometimes and there's such disdain in his eyes."

"You mean you're not blond and glamorous anymore?" Emily's intrigued.

"I have almost three-inch roots of natural glamorous mouse color, I can't be bothered to go to the hairdresser and have my hair straightened so it's curly again, and I'm spending my life in the garden so I basically wear filthy old jeans and boots."

Emily can't help herself. She starts laughing. "Alice, I don't want to say anything, but the picture you're painting isn't exactly the kind of woman I can see Joe going for."

"But that's the point. Em, I'm so happy living here. I just love it so much, and I love not having to dress up and play the stupid part of some stupid society trophy wife. I love being in the garden and not wearing makeup and not caring about what I look like. And I've been up all night thinking about things, and I can't see how this could work. Even if I could forgive him, even if we could put things behind us, I can't see how our marriage could survive."

Emily doesn't say anything. Just waits for Alice to continue.

Alice sighs. "Em, I can't do it anymore. I can't pretend to be something I'm not, and Joe can't pretend to love the real me when it's not what he wants."

"Have you spoken to him?"

"No. He phoned last night and left a message saying he was at home and going to bed, but I called back immediately and I knew he wouldn't be home."

"And he wasn't?"

"Of course not."

"So now what?"

"He'll call this morning and pretend he's had a great night's sleep, and I'm going to tell him I know."

"On the phone?"

"Yes. And I'm going to ask him to come down here and get his things." Alice hadn't planned to say that, hadn't even thought about that, but the words came out, and now she knows it's the right thing.

"Jesus, Ali. Are you sure?"

"Yes," Alice says slowly. "This is it. He has to go and I need to be on my own."

28

The rocking motion of the train somehow seems to help calm Joe's racing mind, still the panic in his heart.

He still can't believe he was so stupid as to leave e-mails on his machine that Alice could find, and more to the point he still can't believe Alice went looking.

He phoned her this morning, on his way back to Josie's from the deli, armed with bagels, lox, and fresh coffee, mobile phone cradled under his shoulder as he made his regular Saturday morning call to Alice.

"Hi, darling," he started. "I tried to call last night but you didn't pick up. Did you have an early night?" There was a silence from Alice, and he knew, instantly, that something was wrong.

"Alice? Darling? Are you all right? Are you there?"

He heard her sigh.

"What is the matter, Alice?"

"Joe, we need to talk."

His heart started pounding. "What about?"

"You need to come here. I'm not going to do this over the phone. I want you to get on a train and come to Highfield this morning."

Joe stopped walking and stood stock-still. "What are you *talking* about, Alice?"

"You can get a cab from the station," Alice continued. "But I'm going to assume you'll be here by lunchtime."

"Alice . . ."

"No!" Alice cuts Joe off with a shout. "Joe, I know. Okay? I know. I found the e-mails. I know about Josie. I know about all of it. I will talk to you when you get here." And she puts the phone down, without giving Joe a chance to defend himself.

Joe stands immobile, the color draining from his face as his feet feel rooted to the spot. "Shit," he whispers. "Oh, shit."

He doesn't go back to Josie's, can't handle talking about this, explaining it, seeing her. He knows he just needs to get to Highfield, to reassure Alice, to think up some excuse, some plausible reason, something to help her forgive him.

And here he sits, on the train, trying to think of an explanation. The best he can come up with is that Josie is a flirtation, that nothing real has happened, that it's like virtual sex and he's only indulging because Alice is never around, and he's lonely.

It could be true. After all, Alice is never around, and he's a normal red-blooded male. Naturally he'd never do anything to hurt Alice, but he'll tell her that all he was doing was indulging in a little flirtation that may have gone too far. Of course he isn't having an affair, he'd never do that to Alice, and even as he thinks up his excuses his expression becomes contrite, apologetic, and he knows that he can win Alice over as he has always done.

Joe walks in and finds Alice sitting on the sofa. Snoop beside her, his head resting on her lap, his eyes closed. Snoop raises his head when he hears the front door open, looks at Joe with baleful eyes, then drops his head again as Alice continues stroking his ears.

Alice doesn't say anything. Just looks at Joe, and Joe realizes how strange it is to see

Alice, who is always on the move, doing nothing. There is something so unsettling about this that he doesn't know quite what to say, and then he wonders if he may have misjudged the whole situation. He realizes with a jolt that he doesn't know Alice anymore, doesn't know who she is, what she's thinking.

Joe is used to being the one in control, but he cannot control Alice any longer, and with a shock his confidence disappears and he falters just inside the doorway, not knowing what to say.

And then he sees the bags. On the other side of the front door are two suitcases, not yet zipped, and inside he can see the few clothes he keeps here, his office files, some books, his toiletries.

Oh, shit.

Joe sits on the sofa opposite Alice, and suddenly he feels like a little boy. He feels guilty, and scared, and he doesn't know what to say. For the first time in Joe Chambers's life, words have failed him completely.

And so they sit, these two people separated by so much more than a mere coffee table. Alice continues to stare into space, and Joe looks at the floor, the silences punctuated only by Joe sighing or a large yawn from Snoop.

Alice is the first to speak. She has gone over and over this moment, imagined herself screaming at him, raging, venting all her fury and humiliation, but now that he's here all she feels is a deep sadness. He looks so lost sitting opposite her, unable to meet her eyes, that she almost feels sorry for him, but most of all she feels sorry for her marriage.

He belongs in another world, she thinks, looking at his clothes, his watch, his shoes, knowing how important these things are to Joe, how vital it is to be seen wearing the latest status symbols, with the trophy wife, or mistress, at his side.

And she realizes that she is about to break the habit of a lifetime. At thirty-six years old Alice finally knows who she is, and Alice finally *likes* who she is. Having spent her entire life trying to please other people, Alice now knows that the only person she wants to make happy is herself.

She expected to feel so angry, but the anger left her some time during the night, washed away with the tears, and she's too tired to shout, or even to discuss. She doesn't want to hear an explanation, or an apology. It's too late for that. Perhaps he will say that it's not what she thinks, that he hasn't done anything wrong. Perhaps he will blame her, saying that she is never around, she hides away in the country and who can blame him for a harmless flirtation? Perhaps he will admit to a full-blown affair and either tearfully apologize or tell her it's over.

That would be the easiest, Alice thinks. If he were to admit it, and tell her he was leaving her. Of course she'd be devastated, but she knows, as surely as the sky is blue, that the marriage is over, and now she just has to find a way to say it out loud.

"This isn't working, Joe." Alice is the first to speak, both her voice and the words sounding unnatural and strange in the echoey silence.

Joe looks up. He had expected many things, mostly to have to calm her down, reassure her, explain, but he hadn't expected this, and this is the one scenario for which he has no plan, no explanation, no defense.

"What do you mean?"

"I mean this. Us." Alice closes her eyes. "Oh God, I sound like such a bloody cliché, but our marriage. It's not working."

"Alice, I know what you think, I know what you must have thought when you read those e-mails —"

Alice stops him. "No, Joe. It doesn't

matter what I think."

"But it does, Alice. I need to explain. Josie is just —"

"No! Joe, you don't understand. I don't care." And Alice is as shocked as Joe when those words emerge. Joe because he has always thought that Alice loved him more than he loved her, and Alice because she realizes the truth in her words. She no longer cares.

"But . . ."

Alice shakes her head. "No, Joe," she says sadly. "I don't need an explanation. I don't care enough to hear what you have to say. Admit it. Neither of us have been happy for a long time. Maybe this was supposed to happen, to help us realize how far apart we've grown."

Joe is silent. He could have dealt far more easily with tears and anger and recriminations. He could have dealt more easily with soothing her wounds and carrying on as they had always carried on, in the pattern that is so familiar to him, that is all he has ever known.

What he cannot deal with, what he was not prepared to deal with, is the truth.

"Joe. I just can't see the point in pretending. I've been up all night thinking about things, and I love you, but I'm not what you want. Not anymore. And you're not what I want either. I can't bear the way we look at one another, the way we struggle to find things to talk about, and I don't want us to stay together just because we're married and it's a habit, and we don't want to rock the boat.

"I am so happy here." Alice gestures around her. "I love my house, I love being in the country, I love living in a small town and knowing my neighbors. And I know how much you hate it. You hate it as much as I hate being in the city, and neither of us can pretend to be something we're not."

There's a silence as Joe digests what she has said. There's nothing to say. She's right.

"So that's it? It's over?" After a while Joe points to the bags. "I see you've packed my things."

Alice nods slowly. "I want to be able to say it's just having some space, that we need some time, but it's not working and I can't see the point in putting off the inevitable."

Joe looks at Alice for the first time then. He wants to tell her that it could work, that if she reverted back to the old Alice it could work again. See how she's barely mentioned Josie, she's already forgiven him for the affair. It could still work. He opens his mouth to say this, but stops.

She's right. He knows she's right. He changed her once, when she was much younger, much more adoring, was willing to do anything to make him happy. But she won't do it again. They've both come too far to try to turn the clock back to the way things used to be.

"I can't believe our marriage is over," Joe finds himself whispering as tears start to prick his own eyes.

"Please don't start crying," Alice says gently. "I couldn't bear it if you started crying too."

"Can we at least talk about this some more? Maybe when we've had a bit of space? Can I call you?"

"Why don't we leave it for a couple of weeks, let's just try and adjust." Alice is amazed at how calm she is, how normal her voice sounds, but she realizes that she's only able to maintain her composure because she can't quite believe it's really happening.

Joe leaves half an hour later. Packs his suitcases in the trunk of the cab, turns to Alice to try to say something else, but Alice just shakes her head.

"We'll speak soon," she says sadly.

"There's nothing else to say right now."

Joe tries to put his arms around her, but Alice's body language stops him, and instead he leans down and kisses her on the cheek. Alice doesn't respond.

"Take care," he whispers, turning quickly away so Alice doesn't see the tears, even though she hears them in his voice.

Alice watches numbly as the taxi disappears up the driveway, watches the back of her husband's head as his own tears start to fall. He had always thought he was invincible. That he would never be found out. And most of all he had never expected Alice to throw him out.

Joe refuses to talk to anyone for four days. Josie phones but he switches his mobile phone off, unable to deal with talking to her. He calls in sick to the office and works his way methodically through his wine cellar.

A '90 Latour, an '86 Haut-Brion, and a '63 Petrus. Drowning his sorrows, he stops drinking only to sleep or to order pizza.

A few times he picks up the phone to call Alice. The floor of the library is covered with old pictures. Joe and Alice looking tanned and happy, arms around each other's necks as they sit on a sunbed at Cap Juluca, grinning as a passing waiter takes their picture.

Alice looking chic and beautiful, snapped at a restaurant opening for *Hello!*, her blond hair scraped back into a chignon, a low-cut white silk shirt showing off her golden skin.

Joe and Alice together again, sitting on a squashy golden sofa at a friend's house in the country, both of them sipping Pimm's, Joe with an arm around Alice's bare shoulders, Alice so elegant in a black halter neck and diamond stud earrings.

Joe studies these pictures through his drunken haze and picks up the phone, imagining that his beautiful Alice will pick up, that he will somehow be able to phone the Alice in the pictures, bring her back to the present.

But as the days pass and he sobers up, he looks again at these pictures and sees how much Alice has changed.

When was the last time he saw Alice looking as she did in these old photos? When was the last time her hair was ice blond and sleek as silk, her clothes a mix of simplicity and sophistication so stylish as to have several articles written about her in the English papers?

What would those same journalists say if they saw her now?

Joe snorts to himself with amusement as he thinks of them secretly snapping Alice in her garden. "From Gorgeous to Grunge," he imagines the headline. Her muddy jeans, quilted sports coat, and Timberland boots hardly epitomize the aspirations of *Daily Mail* readers.

You can take the girl out of the garden but you can't take the gardener out of the girl, he thinks wryly, dropping the last wine bottle into the waste bin just as the buzzer rings in his apartment.

"Mr. Chambers?" It's the doorman.

"Yes, Brandon?"

"There's a Josie Mitchell to see you."

Joe just looks at the buzzer. Is he ready for this? Can he handle it?

"Mr. Chambers? Are you there?"

"Yes, Brandon. Send her up."

"God. You look terrible."

"Thanks, Josie. You look wonderful, but what else is new?" Joe turns and walks back into the living room, Josie following him as anger finally threatens to show itself in her voice.

"Joe, what the hell is going on? You left to get breakfast and never came back. Your mobile phone's been switched off for four days, you haven't been at work, and you haven't returned any of my calls. And you look awful. What's happened?"

Joe shrugs and smiles. "If you must know, my marriage is over."

Josie's eyes widen, but she doesn't say anything. What, after all, can she say? How awful for you? I'm so sorry? Hooray?

"So that's why I've been at home," Joe continues. "I'm sorry, Jose, I should have called, but it's taken me a bit of time to adjust, and if you must know the truth I've been feeling a bit shit. I mean, it's not every day your wife finds out about an affair and kicks you out."

"Oh." Josie sits down hard on the sofa. "She found out about us?"

"Yup. She found our e-mails. But she didn't even seem to care. She said it hadn't been working for a while and neither of us were happy and there wasn't any point."

"And is that true?" Josie speaks quietly, well aware she is treading on dangerous territory, and not quite sure how to play it, this situation being entirely new to her. It was one thing being a mistress, but quite another being a mistress who split up a marriage. Although she couldn't help but feel a thrill at Joe finally being single and available for her, she could see it wasn't going to be as easy as that. She could see that Joe was far more devastated than he was letting on.

Joe shrugs. "Yes, it's true. The marriage has been a farce since we came to New York. Actually it was probably a farce for a lot longer, according to Alice, but apparently we have nothing in common anymore and there's no point in pretending otherwise."

"How do you feel?"

"Oh, fuck, I don't know. I feel like shit . . . I feel fantastic . . . she's right . . . the marriage wasn't working . . . but it used to work so maybe it could again . . . maybe we just need time . . . maybe I've been a bastard . . . maybe Alice shouldn't have changed so much . . . I'm probably not the type to be married . . . we were wrong for one another . . . fuck knows . . . I don't know."

"Okay." Josie stands up. She'd come over because she was concerned, and angry, but she wasn't prepared to deal with this. She doesn't know how she feels about this herself, and she knows she's probably the worst person to be around Joe right now. The best thing she can do, particularly if her own relationship with him stands any chance at all, is to leave him alone, let him work this out himself. "I shouldn't have come over. I'm sorry. I'm going to go now."

"No!" Joe panics, instantly regressing to a lost little boy. He's lost one woman this past week; he's not prepared to lose another. There are many things Joe can deal with, but rejection is not one of them, and two rejections would be too much. "No," he says in a more gentle voice, walking over to Josie and taking her face in his hands. "Please stay with me," he says urgently, looking into her eyes as she drops her bag on the floor. "I need you, Jose. I want you. Don't leave me."

"Okay," she whispers, as she folds him into her arms. "Don't worry," she croons, stroking his back and whispering into his neck. "I'm here. It's all going to be okay."

"Are you sure you don't want me to fly out?" Emily's voice is filled with concern. "I can, you know. Work's not that busy, and you shouldn't be on your own."

"Oh, Em, thank you. But no. I actually feel as if I do need this time on my own. I need to sort out my head, just think everything through. But thank you. And thank you for being there for me."

These past few days Alice and Emily have spoken four, five times a day. Neither has forgotten the reason for their lack of communication since New Year's Eve, but Emily has forgiven, has forgotten why it ever seemed so important that she risked losing her best friend.

"So are you completely sure you're okay? How do you feel?"

"I don't know. Sometimes I feel relieved, and I know I've done the right thing. We hardly even spoke toward the end, we just had nothing to talk about, and I don't even remember the last time we made one another laugh. I'd go into the city and resent him for trying to turn me into something I'm not, and he'd come down here and hate me for not being what he wanted.

"I feel so happy that I don't have to go into Manhattan anymore and stand next to Joe making boring small talk with the boring wife of one of his clients, and then five minutes later I'm terrified. I can't believe that I'm going to be a divorcée, that I'm never going to wake up and see Joe lying next to me. That there isn't anyone to stand up for me, or step in for me, or take over when things get too difficult."

"I know," Emily says. "That's the bastard about being single. You have to do everything yourself. But on the plus side, you haven't got anyone telling you what to do. You can eat Ben & Jerry's for breakfast, lunch, and supper if you want."

Alice snorts. "If you want what? If you want to grow into the size of a house?"

"Okay, not Ben & Jerry's. How about Baskin & Robbins sugar-free chocolate mint ice cream then? Better?"

Alice laughs. "Much."

"See? You can still laugh. And there's much more you can do besides. You can have lie-ins every day. You can garden twenty-four hours without someone moaning that they want you to cook dinner, or you have to go shopping with them, or you have to go and meet people you don't want to meet for lunch."

"True. I know. Those are all the things I tell myself when I'm feeling good about it."

"And when you're not feeling good about it?"

"Then I tell myself that I'm terrified and I'll never be able to make it on my own. Oh God, Em. I just can't believe it's come to this. I walked down that aisle thinking I was going to be married for the rest of my life. I thought Joe and I would grow old together."

Emily is silent for a few seconds. "Alice, you walked down that aisle knowing who Joe was, what he wanted in a wife. You were willing to turn yourself into what he wanted. That's why your marriage worked."

"I know. It worked as long as I played by the rules. It's just scary, being single again when I thought I had that part of my life sorted out."

"I know. But any time you want to talk, Alice, day or night, you can always call me, and you know I'll come if you need me."

"I know." Alice sighs. "I know."

29

Alice opens the side door and walks into Gina's kitchen, putting the large Tupperware bowl on the kitchen counter as she calls out a tentative hello.

"Alice? Is that you?" Gina's voice drifts down from upstairs.

"Yup." Alice moves over to the bottom of the stairs and shouts up. "I thought I'd come early to drop off the salad."

"Come up. I'm just finishing getting dressed."

Alice walks up as Gina comes out of her bedroom and wraps Alice in a big hug.

"So, aren't you going to put on a concerned face and ask me how I am?" Alice pulls away and raises an eyebrow.

Gina nods and puts on a concerned face. "How *are* you?"

Alice changes her expression into one

that says she is feeling sorry for herself, and shrugs. "Oh, you know. Not bad."

Gina laughs. "Seriously, Alice," Gina says. "Last time I saw you, you were feeling pretty down. You look better even if you don't feel it."

"Seriously, Gina." Alice smiles. "Today is a good day. Sometimes I have good days and sometimes they're bad. That's what's so awful. I wake up every morning with no idea what to expect."

"Have you spoken to him?"

Alice nods as they both walk back downstairs to the kitchen. "He called last night."

"And?"

"And it's just so weird. This is my *husband*. I've been married to him for six years, and there's something so familiar about hearing his voice but something so strange at the same time. I feel this weird dichotomy between knowing him so well and yet not knowing him at all."

"Do you have regrets, or is this it, is it really over?" Gina hasn't told Alice about seeing him with Josie, even now that she knows. It's unnecessary to hurt her more, and Gina doesn't know that Alice will understand her reasons for not telling her.

But Gina was relieved when she first heard the news, relieved that the secret was out in the open, that she wouldn't have to lie or keep a secret from her friend again.

And more than that, Gina is relieved that Alice will no longer be hurt by a philandering husband.

Alice who deserves so very much better.

It has been nearly six weeks since Joe and Alice split up. At first the days seemed to drag, Alice rendered useless by a strange inertia, unable to do anything other than sit on the sofa with Snoop and try to understand that this wasn't something temporary, that her marriage was over and her life would never be the same again.

It wasn't even that she was distraught about *Joe,* but she needed to mourn the loss of her marriage, the loss of her dreams. Alice had always thought she would be surrounded by children at the age of thirty-six. She had expected to be blissfully happy with a husband who shared everything with her, who made her laugh, who showered her with love and affection.

She had expected to have at least three children and a small menagerie of animals. And even though she had had none of these things while married to Joe, she always thought it was just a matter of time.

And now it's too late. Not only did she never have these things with Joe, she thinks it unlikely that she will be able to have these things with anyone else. Not at this late stage in the game.

More than anything else Alice feels a deep sadness and regret that she is becoming yet another statistic, for surely there is no option other than divorce.

Alice doesn't have to ask where, why, or how it went wrong. The gift of hindsight is clarity, and Alice can see just how much she attempted to mold herself into what Joe wanted, and how, sooner or later, it was always destined for failure.

And she has forced herself to consider the near certainty that Josie is not the first indiscretion, and, painful though it has been, she has finally admitted that the signs were always there, she just chose to ignore them.

After reading an article in a magazine about sex addiction, Alice came to the conclusion that Joe couldn't help himself, that he did love her but he was powerless.

She started to understand that there was nothing she could have done to change him, or stop him. And most of all, she understands that he is never going to change.

He is never going to change.

And with that realization comes the knowledge that Alice is going to be okay. That she's been living practically on her own for nearly a year anyway, and that in many ways she is happier.

Life on her own doesn't have to be frightening or daunting, or even lonely. As she starts to accept her new life, Alice realizes she's not in such a bad place after all.

Today — Gina and George's barbecue (the last one of the summer) — is the first time Alice will have seen the neighbors *en masse* since she and Joe split up. During the week Sandy has been around, as has Sally, and Gina has been driving up every weekend to make sure Alice is okay.

Naturally the entire town has heard the news — hence the lack of invitations and the head-turning and whispering wherever Alice goes. It's probably the hottest source of gossip since Rachel Danbury exposed her life to all and sundry, only because nothing exciting ever seems to happen in this little town.

People don't get divorced in small towns like these. They marry for love and they stay married for life. They have between two and four children, drive huge, formidable SUVs, own chocolate-brown Labradors, and are on the PTA committee at school.

The women immerse themselves in the lives of their children and, should they not be terribly happy in their marriages, hide it well in a mountain of diapers and local volunteer work.

The men escape from the problems at work and lose themselves in the television set at home, fantasizing about what might have been when they pass nubile young women on Main Street, on their way to Home Depot to pick up some more decking.

People expect to get married and stay married, so even though Alice and Joe are relative newcomers, news of their split has spread around the community as fast as the bindweed takes hold in Alice's garden, and it is still the hot topic of the month.

And worse, as a newly single woman Alice appears to be suddenly posing a threat to the happily marrieds. The husbands have all been lovely, but Alice is noticing that their wives are looking at her suspiciously, and the invitations that used to flood her mailbox are far fewer.

Highfield is definitely not a place for singles. The separated and divorced are supposed to pack up and move back to the city, to throw themselves back into the dating scene, and not dare to set foot in suburbia until they have found a permanent replacement for their old other half.

But Alice doesn't much care. The true friends she has are still her friends — Gina, Sally, and Sandy — and she wouldn't move back to a city if you paid her. Alice still finds every day as magical as when she first moved here, and she's hoping that the people who are withholding invitations will soon learn she is no threat whatsoever.

Gina, of course, would never see Alice as a threat, and even though one of her gossipy neighbors expressed surprise that Gina was inviting Alice to this barbecue now that Alice is single — Gina told her exactly what she thought about that particular statement — she has been making sure that Alice is okay and has tried to put the rumors to rest.

Nobody knows the exact reason, although Kay has been heard to say rather smugly that he was clearly not the faithful type and in fact made a pass at her after one of their tennis matches, and Kay was pretty sure Alice had caught him with someone.

Kay had no idea whether this was true or not, even though, as we know, this was almost exactly what happened, but her suspicions quickly became fact, and everyone was aghast that he could treat the lovely Alice like that.

"It's a shame," they'd say. "Look at her, so young still and always on her own," and they are delighted that she is here at this Labor Day barbecue that marks the end of the summer season. For many of the locals this is the first time they have seen Alice since they found out. Kay, who now feels even more threatened by Alice, has whispered to her friends that Alice looks dreadful: huge bags under her eyes, gray skin, lost huge amounts of weight.

But as people start to arrive they are pleasantly surprised. Alice, in a long linen skirt and tight white T-shirt, looks tanned and healthy. The sparkle is still in her eye, and she looks quite as happy as she did before.

"How *are* you?" people keep asking after the obligatory hug, and Alice laughs.

"I'm fine."

"Are you *sure?*" they continue. "Is there something we can do?"

"I'm sure." She smiles. "And there's nothing you can do."

Only Kay has the balls, the bad grace, to push it further.

"You know" — she sidles up to Alice, immediately pissed off at how good Alice looks — "I never trusted that husband of yours."

"Oh, no?" Alice starts to turn away, not wanting to know why not, just wanting to move away from this woman she has never liked or trusted.

"No. He had a glint in his eye. Seemed like a womanizer. In fact, I probably shouldn't tell you this, but I feel like you're part of the sisterhood, and I know if it were me I'd want to know." Kay takes a deep breath. "Joe made a pass at me at the Christmas party." She looks at Alice carefully to gauge her reaction, but there was none, so she continued. "Naturally I said no — I mean, I couldn't do that to another woman. I just thought you ought to know though. You did the right thing. Men like that can't be trusted."

Alice shakes her head slowly, trying to hide her shock and disgust at Kay saying anything at all. "I have to say I'm astonished," Alice says smoothly.

"You are?" It wasn't quite the reaction Kay was expecting.

"I am. I just wouldn't have thought you'd be Joe's type at all. He usually goes for sophisticated, beautiful women. I never thought the cheap, tarty type was him. Oh, well," she shrugs. "Maybe he was drunk." And she turns away, leaving Kay with her mouth open in shock.

Gina hustles Alice into a corner. "Did I hear what I think I just heard?"

Alice is shaking with anger. "Can you believe it? What a stupid bitch. Oh God, Gina, do you think he did make a pass at her? That's just horrible. One of our neighbors, for heaven's sake. Was he that priapic?"

Gina gives Alice a hug. "I'm sure she's just making it up. She feels threatened by you, that's all. And please, not that I know what Joe's type is, but you're right, she is cheap and tarty, and I'm sure Joe wouldn't even have looked at her."

"But she was his tennis partner."

"Yeah, and she probably hated the fact that he didn't come on to her. Look at the way she dresses. She's the only woman here in a miniskirt and heels. She thinks all the men adore her and I would think she hated the fact that Joe didn't. I would seriously put money on it."

"You would?" Alice's shaking starts to abate.

"I would. But, Alice Chambers, that was an amazing put-down." Gina starts to laugh. "I'd hate to get on your bad side."

Alice starts to see the funny side too. "I can't believe I said that to her. It's one of those things I usually think of afterward. When I'm lying in bed trying to think of something cutting and witty to say. God knows where it came from."

"Just thank God it did."

Alice's smile leaves her face. "Gina, is *everyone* talking about us?"

Gina grimaces. "I know I ought to lie to you but I can't. Everyone is talking about you."

"Oh God." Alice sinks her face into her hands. "That's just awful."

Gina shrugs. "I know. It is awful but it's natural. It's a huge scandal for this town. The two glamorous Londoners with the great accents who seem to lead a charmed life, and suddenly it's over."

"Do they know why?"

"No one knows for sure. I've heard it's because you couldn't have children and he wanted them. I've heard it's because he couldn't have children and you wanted them. I've heard it's because he found someone else. I've heard it's because you found someone else."

"Me? Me! How the hell am *I* supposed to find someone else? Who else is there? I know practically everyone in this town, and everybody sees me all the time. Who do they think I'm messing around with?" Alice's voice is loud with indignation.

"Shh. Shh. Calm down. *I* know that."

"I hope you told them."

"Of course. Unless you'd like me to start any rumors. Anyone you'd fancy messing around with?"

Alice can't help herself. She grins. "Ooh. We could start some good rumors."

"How about the bitch's husband?"

"Who, James?"

Gina nods with a smile. "That would get back at her."

"No. I couldn't do it. It's too cruel."

"Okay, how about Michael Bolton?"

"Michael *Bolton?* What are you *talking* about?"

"Well, he lives around here. And you've got to admit having an affair with a celebrity would really throw them."

"Even one that looks like Michael Bolton?" Alice is dubious, to say the least.

"A celebrity is a celebrity is a celebrity."

"So, what?" Alice continues. "You're going to say I'm messing around with Michael Bolton?" Alice starts giggling. "Gina, that's terrible. You can't say that."

Gina looks shocked. "Darling, I would

never be that obvious. But I think Kay needs to be informed that you and Michael Bolton were seen having dinner at Cobb's Mill Inn, looking very cozy indeed."

"Oh, well." Alice lets out a fake resigned sigh. "If you must, you must."

"I must," Gina says firmly. "And now I have to check that George is handling the barbecue properly. Come on. Let's go outside and get some food."

An hour later Alice nearly chokes on her burger when Mary Beth comes to sit next to her.

"Tom and I have been meaning to have you over," she says. "We thought perhaps you and Michael would join us for dinner next week."

Alice looks up to see Gina standing behind the barbecue grinning at her. Gina winks as Alice splutters.

"That's very kind of you," Alice says. "Can I check my diary and get back to you?"

"Of course," Mary Beth says, leaning forward confidingly. "I know I shouldn't tell you this, but Michael's version of 'When a Man Loves a Woman' is just my favorite song in the whole wide world."

"Right." Alice looks at her, not knowing what to say.

"Would you tell him for me?"

"Of course I will." Alice finds herself smiling. "If you'll excuse me, I'm just going to get some more food."

"Sure," Mary Beth calls after her. "And we thought Wednesday or Thursday. Let us know!"

"Will do!" Alice smiles as she walks over to Gina and pokes her hard in the side.

"Ow! What was that for?"

"I thought you were joking, for God's sake. I can't believe you told Mary Beth I was involved with Michael Bolton."

"I didn't tell her that. I just said you'd been spotted with him looking very cozy."

"You're mad!" Alice starts laughing.

"Yeah? Just watch." Gina turns Alice around so she can see Mary Beth whisper something to Kay, and Kay turns to look at Alice with shock before scurrying off to tell someone else.

"See?" Gina mutters out of the corner of her mouth. "Told you it wouldn't take long."

"Oh, poor Michael Bolton," Alice says. "I feel terrible, lying about him like this."

"Don't be ridiculous. He's used to it. Anyway, it's what he deserves having that disgusting mullet haircut all those years. Meanwhile" — Gina looks Alice up and down — "he should be so lucky."

"Oh, Gina." Alice leans over and kisses her friend on the cheek. "That's why I love you."

"Good. Now have another hot dog."

"Gina, I'm full. I've already eaten masses."

"Don't be silly, darling." Gina puts another hot dog laden with mustard, ketchup, and fried onions on Alice's plate. "I hear Michael likes his women meaty."

At the end of the evening Alice has spoken to almost everyone at the party. The women have tentatively asked about Michael, and Alice has smiled graciously and said, "No comment," at which they have all laughed.

Only now that she's had a nice time can she admit how nervous she was at her first social occasion on her own. Not that she doesn't go out on her own here — even when she was with Joe she was on her own more often than not — but now that she's truly separated it's different.

She had been nervous about how she would feel, being the only single woman among all those married couples, remembering how awkward and out of place she felt when she actually *was* single, before marrying Joe, whenever she spent evenings with married couples.

But she hasn't felt awkward and out of place. Rather she has been able to relax without worrying whether Joe is having a good time. She has actually enjoyed herself, and even though she worried that all the women would reject her newly threatening status, she found that the sprinkling of celebrity stardust with which Gina adorned her has put paid to any potential bitchiness.

Even Kay came over and apologized, which Alice graciously accepted.

Alice is sitting on the edge of the pool, dangling her legs in the water, when someone comes to sit next to her. It's James.

"Hi, James." She turns to him with a smile.

"Hi, Alice. Listen, I wanted to apologize for my wife. I heard what she said earlier and" — he shrugs — "sometimes she just doesn't think. I don't think she means badly. But I feel bad for you and I'm sorry."

Alice lays a hand on his arm. "Don't feel

bad. First of all, she's already apologized to me herself, and second, you shouldn't have to apologize on behalf of anyone else. You mustn't worry. I didn't believe it anyway."

James visibly relaxes. "So, how have you been? We haven't seen you at the nursery for a few weeks. I've been worried."

"You have? That's so sweet. Actually there hasn't been anything I've needed."

James nods. "Of course. I was just worried, we'd got so used to seeing your face. We've missed you, and your friend was asking about you. I think he was expecting to have seen you already."

"Friend? What friend?"

"Your friend from England. Harry. He was just asking me on Friday whether I thought you'd be in soon."

Alice looks at James with a frown, total incomprehension on her face. "Harry? What are you talking about?"

"Harry's at the nursery. He took me up on the job offer. He's been working here the last few weeks."

"What? Harry's *here?*"

"I can't believe you didn't know. I assumed you knew." James shakes his head at the strangeness of it all. "You *are* friends, aren't you?"

"Sort of." Alice is still in shock. "He was

going out with my best friend. But he's here? In Highfield?"

"Yes. It seems as if he'd really like to see you. You should pop in and see him."

Alice doesn't say anything. Just sits quietly, watching her legs as she circles them in the warm water.

"Kay will probably kill me for talking to you," James mutters as he stands up. "Oh God. Sorry. No offense."

"Don't worry." Alice looks up at him and smiles. "None taken. Thanks, James."

"What for?"

Alice shrugs. "For the apology. For . . . nothing. I think I'll come in on Monday. I'll see you then."

"Great!" James starts walking back to Kay, who's giving him murderous looks from just inside the French doors. "See you Monday." And off he goes.

30

Joe is beginning to think that Josie might not be such a good idea after all.

He had thought she was tough, independent, self-sufficient. He had assumed she wanted nothing from him other than great sex, would follow the rules and not expect him to be with her full time, or make demands he wasn't prepared to fulfill.

Not to mention the fact that the greatest turn-on for Joe was the very fact that Josie was forbidden, the thrill that they were engaging in an illicit affair, and the potential danger that involved.

The day he broke up with Alice everything changed. Joe thinks that it is Josie's fault, that Josie has decided she is going to be his next wife, and while there is an element of truth in that, he hasn't considered that he has just grown bored, that without the element of danger there is no excitement left for him in sleeping with Josie.

And poor Josie has fallen for Joe. She had refused to admit to anyone that her move to New York might be for reasons other than professional, but she knew, the minute the job offer arrived, that she would be seeing Joe again.

All those months in London she had tried not to entertain the possibility that Joe would leave his wife for her. She was neither that naive nor that optimistic, but there was always a tiny hope that she tried to push well out of the way. And now, suddenly, her hope has materialized. And while she is well aware that technically Joe didn't leave his wife for her, she can't help but think that Joe might have wanted to be found out. After all, who does not junk potentially dangerous e-mails such as the ones they had been sending one another? And she can't help but think that Joe needs a woman, and she is the perfect girl to step into the shoes that Alice has so recently vacated.

Joe did, after all, beg her to stay that day she came round and discovered the marriage had broken up.

Joe is more vulnerable than Josie ever imagined, and his seeming incapacity to look after himself has brought out Josie's maternal instincts, instincts that quite frankly she didn't think existed.

For the last six weeks Josie has been dashing over to Joe's apartment and cooking him meals. She has been the one to drop his dry-cleaning off in the morning on the way to work. She left work early to let herself into his apartment to wait for the cable guy.

In short, Josie is doing everything that Alice once did. She thinks that if she makes herself indispensable, Joe will make her his second wife. She is convinced that the more she does for him, the better she looks after him, the more Joe will realize he cannot do without her.

She doesn't think that there might be anything strange in their not making love quite as often as they did before. That Joe is climbing into bed beside her, giving her a perfunctory kiss on the cheek before claiming exhaustion and rolling over on his side to go to sleep.

Josie doesn't realize that in trying to make herself indispensable, she has lost her sex appeal for Joe, and while he is comfortable being looked after, having someone beautiful on his arm (and why wouldn't he be, having had exactly the same in Alice for the past six years?), he is growing as turned off by Josie as he used to be by Alice.

Joe's eye has started wandering again. Here he is tonight, in the lobby of the Royalton, having a drink with Fred, a colleague from the office. All around him there are beautiful women, and it doesn't take long before they are joined by two of them, Andrea and Kathleen.

Andrea, the lovelier of the two, is brazen in her flirting. Joe looks at his watch. This was supposed to be a quick drink. He's supposed to be at Josie's apartment tonight. She's cooking him dinner and they're meant to be having a quiet night in. He looks back at Andrea, who is staring at him coquettishly, raising an eyebrow.

"Don't tell me you're going somewhere already?" Her voice is sultry, her look suggestive.

"Why?" Joe grins. "Do you have a better idea?"

"My apartment's around the corner. I was thinking perhaps you'd like to come up and have a drink. We could get to know one another better." With that she slips off a shoe and strokes Joe's calf with her bare foot. Joe closes his eyes for a second. He can't do this. He shouldn't do this. Josie's waiting. Oh, for fuck's sake. He's just split up with his wife. He deserves to have some fun.

"I just have to make a phone call," Joe says.

"The wife?" Andrea smiles, not really caring.

Joe smiles and shakes his head. "Nope. I'm separated. Just a friend I was going to meet for dinner."

"And you're canceling?"

"Should I?"

"You very definitely should."

"In that case please excuse me for a couple of minutes."

Joe leaves the table and walks outside the hotel, pressing Josie's speed dial.

"Hi, it's me."

"Hi! I'm just in the middle of cooking. Where are you?"

"Jose, I'm so sorry. I'm having a drink with Fred, and Richard and Don from Goldmans have just walked in, and you know they're joint books on this huge deal I'm doing, and we've started talking work, so I really think I should stay."

"Oh." Josie's disappointment weighs her down, prevents her from saying anything else, and she stands in her tiny galley kitchen, wooden spoon in hand, phone cradled in her shoulder, waiting for him to say he'll be over later, hoping that even though she's gone to all this trouble for a meal he won't be eating, at least he'll come over later and stay the night, keep the loneliness from the door.

"And I know you've made dinner and I'm so sorry, but I need to be involved in this and they're going out for dinner. I think it's probably best if I stay at my place tonight."

"Okay." Josie pulls herself together and tries to make her voice as bright as possible. "Do you want me to come over? I could come later."

"Don't worry. I think it may be a late one. But I'll see you tomorrow."

"Okay. Have a good time."

"I'm sure it will be boring as hell, but it needs to be done. Take care, darling." And Joe clicks the phone shut, leaving Josie standing in her kitchen, praying that she's not losing him already.

Joe goes back to Andrea's apartment. She makes no pretense of offering him a drink, but entwines herself around him the minute they step out of the elevator, and they stumble together to her bed.

And it is, as it always is for Joe with these brief encounters, fantastic. She is tireless, inventive, and best of all as far as Joe is concerned, filthy.

They go to sleep in each other's arms, he is woken up by her oh-so-clever mouth, they have more sex in the morning, and then he leaves.

"Call me if you ever feel like a fun night again," Andrea says, waving him good-bye from her bed before she turns over and goes back to sleep.

Joe doesn't bother telling her he doesn't have her number. He just leaves, unable to wipe the smile off his face all day. Why would he need Andrea's number when there are plenty more where she came from?

Hell, he's spent six years married. Finally he has freedom. The very last thing he needs is to settle down again. But meanwhile, how can he let Josie down gently?

Joe cares about Josie. Genuinely. And he's used to being looked after, and even though Josie is rapidly losing her sex appeal, the fact remains that he's comfortable with her.

And why would Josie have to know? He's

already spoken to her this morning, and although she was clearly upset at first, by the end of the conversation he had won her over, and he is taking her out tonight to a charity benefit.

Joe is a man who is used to both having his cake and eating it. It's far too soon to get rid of Josie, plus he's never been much good at getting rid of women — he usually behaves so badly he forces them to do the dirty deed themselves. He'll just carry on as he is right now, seeing Josie, and if other opportunities present themselves, well, good Lord, he's newly single and only human after all.

As for Alice, Joe phones her from time to time because he feels it's the right thing to do. He doesn't exactly miss her, he misses the *habit* of her, and although he's now fairly sure he hadn't been in love with Alice for years, he does still care about her and wants to check she's okay.

But oh how lovely it is not to feel pressured to go down to that dump in the middle of nowhere. The more Joe thinks about it, the more amazed he is that he ever spent any time there whatsoever. Bloody countryside. Bloody bugs. He can't believe he schlepped down to Highfield on the train to spend weekends doing all the things he hated.

What a relief it is to be in Manhattan every weekend, not to have to explain to anyone why he won't be arriving or to have to think of yet another bloody excuse.

He's not looking forward to the actual divorce — God knows he's worked hard enough for his money, he's not exactly happy about giving any of it up — but all in all he has to admit this is probably for the best. He and Alice have grown so far apart. Alice has changed so much, it's a wonder they survived as long as they did.

On Monday morning Alice puts Snoop in the car and drives over to Sunup nurseries. She pulls up in the forecourt and looks out of the windshield, trying to see if Harry's around, but she doesn't get out of the car.

She wasn't going to do this. She sat in her kitchen yesterday evening thinking about what James had told her. She thought how bizarre it was that Harry should be here, that he hadn't called her, but then she remembered the feel of the grass on her back, his lips on hers, and she knew that he wouldn't call her, that he would wait until she appeared in the nursery.

Now that she's here she can't get out of the car. She can remember the feel of his lips, the smell of his skin, but she can barely remember what he looks like. And what will she say to him? Fancy seeing you here? What a surprise?

Then there's Emily to consider. They've only just gotten back on track again, reverting to their regular laughter-filled phone calls. Alice nearly lost Emily once; she's not prepared to do it again. And even though Alice isn't thinking about Harry as anything other than a friend (at least she's trying), it's only been six weeks since her marriage broke up and she's hardly ready for someone else, let alone a disastrous rebound relationship with her best friend's ex.

How will she tell Emily she's seen Harry? How will she tell Emily Harry is here? Alice sighs and rests her head on the steering wheel as Snoop raises his head from the passenger seat and looks at her with concern.

"What am I doing here?" Alice whispers to Snoop as she shakes her head and turns the ignition key. "I must be nuts. This is ridiculous. Come on, Snoop, let's go home." And off they go.

★ ★ ★

Alice goes home, cleans up the kitchen, makes some phone calls, then takes a large mug of tea outside to soak up the warm midafternoon sun. She takes her phone down to the pond and sits on the bench looking at the water, smiling as she thinks how lucky she is, how she would never believe she could be this calm or at peace, given that her marriage has just broken up.

The silence is broken by the shrill ringing of her phone.

"Hey, you." It's Emily.

"Hey, you," Alice smiles. "What are you up to?"

"Writing a piece about a madwoman who runs workshops teaching women how to empower themselves."

"Doesn't sound mad, sounds like a good idea. Have you done the workshop?"

"No," Emily groans. "That's the awful part. I'm starting tomorrow."

"And? What's so awful?"

"Oh God, Ali. Let's just say part of the workshop involves mirrors and vaginas."

Alice splutters with shocked laughter. "You're *joking!*"

"No," Emily says miserably. "I wish I bloody was."

"But not in front of other people, surely?"

"Yes in front of other people. That's part of the empowerment apparently."

"Sounds more like the madwoman's fulfilling a sexual fantasy."

"I know. That's what I thought. Oh God. Isn't it horrific?"

"I hope you've had your legs waxed." Alice keeps laughing.

"My legs? I've had *everything* waxed."

"Ouch!"

"Yes, bloody ouch. It was a killer."

"But at least you'll have the prettiest vagina there." Alice splutters with laughter.

"Oh God. I should never have told you."

"Just tell me why exactly you're doing this?"

"Because it's a commission from *Elle*, and I've been dying to get in with *Elle* for years. This could be my big breakthrough, but I hope to God it's worth it. I think I could be about to have the most embarrassing day of my life."

Alice takes a deep breath. "Em, there's something I have to tell you."

"Uh-oh. Why does that always make me think I'm about to hear bad news?" And she gasps. "Oh no, don't tell me you're pregnant. You're not, are you?"

"No, I'm not pregnant. Nothing like that. Harry's here."

There's a brief silence as Emily digests what Alice has just said, not quite understanding. "Harry? *My* Harry?"

"Yes. That Harry."

"What do you mean he's there? He's staying with you?"

"No! Christ, Em, I wouldn't do that, I mean, that would never . . ."

"Okay, okay. Sorry. But what do you mean?"

"I know, it's completely bizarre, but I was at Gina's on Saturday and James was there and remember when James jokingly offered Harry a job on New Year's Eve? Well, it seems he accepted."

"Oh." There's a pause. "No. I didn't know that. So have you seen him yet?"

"No! Emily, I told you, there's nothing between us. I don't plan on seeing him. I just thought you ought to know because, well, you know how small this town is. I may well bump into him, and I didn't want you to jump to conclusions."

Emily doesn't say anything for a while.

"Em? Are you still there?"

"Sorry. I was just thinking. You know, you two are perfect for each other."

"What?" Alice is shocked. This was the

very last thing she expected Emily to say.

"Well, you are. I know I was devastated last Christmas and don't worry, you don't have to explain again. I know that these things happen, but you know I've had a lot of time to think since then, and you and Harry just make sense."

"Emily, that's ridiculous. First of all, I don't find Harry attractive, and second, I'm still married."

"Separated."

"Okay, but technically I'm still married. I've only been on my own for six weeks. There's no way I want to get involved with Harry. Or anyone. God! I wasn't even thinking that."

"But, Alice, it's true. The two of you are perfect together. And you do find Harry attractive. You told me when I was going out with him."

"Maybe I was just saying that to keep you happy."

"Bollocks. You should go and see him."

"Oh God. No. I can't. What would I say?"

Emily giggles. "Tell him Emily says hi."

"Oh, ha bloody ha."

"Just say hello. Tell him you heard he was working there and you thought you'd come and see him. Then invite him over for dinner and have wild passionate sex with him on the kitchen table."

"Emily!" Alice is shocked.

"Oh, get over yourself. First of all, he's fab in the sack, and second, I'm very happy with Colin, thank you very much, so I don't mind at all. You know what, I want you to be happy, especially after the way that fuckwit Joe treated you, and I know Harry would make you happy. The two of you could garden your way into the sunset together."

"If I didn't love you so much I'd tell you to fuck off."

"If I didn't love you so much there's no way I'd be pushing for you to get together with my ex-boyfriend. But seriously, I can't think of two people better suited for one another. Go and see him. Please. For me."

"I can't believe I'm hearing this."

"I can't believe I'm saying this."

"Are you serious?"

"More serious than I've ever been about anything in my life."

"Emily, I love you."

"I know. And I love you too, which is why I'm giving you my blessing. You deserve him. He wasn't right for me but he's lovely. Just make sure I'm the maid of honor at your wedding."

Alice snorts. "Oh, shut up."

"And what kind of way is that to talk to your best friend?"

Alice spends the rest of the evening mulling over what Emily has said. In some ways she can see her point. Harry and she do have so much in common, and yes, she certainly finds him attractive, but there's no way she's ready for a relationship, not with Harry, not with anyone.

She needs time to heal. She needs time to adjust to being single again. She needs to get used to not being a married woman, to being a divorcée. (The very thought of the word makes her shudder.)

Alice walks upstairs and takes *The Winding Road* to bed, finally managing to finish the book in the early hours of the morning. She lies for a while, staring up at the dark ceiling as she thinks about Rachel Danbury, how she must have felt, and how bizarre that Alice's own life so closely echoes that of the writer in whose house she now lives.

She's more surprised that Rachel continued to live in this same house, even while she was unhappy, because this house has woven a spell around Alice, has wrapped her in its warmth and love, and if

Alice didn't know better, she would have said the only memories the house had held were good ones.

Perhaps Alice was meant to come and live here. Perhaps Alice is the one who was supposed to right the wrongs Rachel Danbury wasn't able to, and as she lies in bed Alice thanks the stars she didn't become Rachel Danbury, lying awake night after night, knowing that Joe was downstairs sending e-mails, planning trysts with God knows how many lovers. Thank God she found out and had the strength to end it.

Alice reaches over to switch off the light and falls into a deep, dreamless sleep.

31

Snoop wakes Alice up with a start. Barking furiously, he jumps off the bed and tumbles down the stairs, leaping up and down by the side door.

Alice calls out to quiet him and eventually pulls a robe over her T-shirt and goes to see what all the fuss is about. As she walks toward the door she sees Harry, peering in through the glass.

"Morning," he smiles, as if he had seen Alice only yesterday, and he pushes past her with a brown paper bag and a cardboard tray containing two cups of steaming coffee, setting them down on the table. "I've brought breakfast."

"I can see." Alice, fast asleep less than a few minutes ago, is now wide awake. "And nice to see you too, Harry." Harry is already sitting at the table, pulling fresh bagels and muffins out of the bag. "Do sit down," Alice says with a hint of sarcasm as Harry winces.

"Okay." He stands up and bows his head in apology. "I didn't want this to be awkward so I'm trying to be natural, but clearly I've gone to the other extreme and am being completely overfamiliar."

"Just a touch," Alice smiles, but she approaches the table, drawn by the smell of freshly baked bread, and pulls out the chair opposite Harry. "But it's okay," she says, gesturing for him to sit down again, which he does. "It's a lovely surprise. I wish I could tell you that I didn't know you were here, but James told me on the weekend. Why haven't you been to see me?"

Harry looks embarrassed. "I feel very stupid. James told me he'd told you, and then I saw you pull up outside yesterday, and I realized how ridiculous it was that I was here and hadn't seen you. To be honest, I was embarrassed after what happened." He looks up and meets her eyes, and Alice looks away first.

"You didn't have to be embarrassed," she says eventually.

"Well . . . anyway, I didn't want to impose. And then I'd heard about you and

Joe, and I didn't know what to say or whether you'd want to see me, so I figured I'd better stay away."

"Until this morning?"

"Well, after I saw you yesterday I just realized how silly I was being."

"So here you are. May I?" Alice picks a banana nut muffin and takes a big bite.

"Of course. So here I am."

"Mmm. This is delicious." Alice finishes her mouthful then takes a sip of coffee. "But I still have to ask, what on earth are you doing here? In America, I mean, not *here*, this morning, obviously."

Harry shrugs. "James's offer seemed too good to turn down."

"But I didn't think he was serious when he made it. God knows most of us were shit-faced at that party."

Harry grins. "Speak for yourself."

"I'll speak for you too if you don't mind."

"I don't mind."

"Good. So are you enjoying it? Do you like it here? Shit! I still can't believe you've been here for weeks and you didn't get in touch."

"I know. I'm sorry. And the answer to your question is yes. I love it here. I'm having a great time."

Alice shakes her head. "But I can't believe I didn't know, I can't believe no one told me."

"James told you."

"I suppose so. I still think it's very peculiar." She peers at him. "Actually I think you're rather peculiar for being so secretive."

Harry shrugs. "I have been called worse things in my time."

"I bet. And some by Emily, I would think."

Harry reddens ever so slightly. "Has she forgiven you? Are you still friends?"

"Yes and yes. But it took a long time to get back to where we were. I think we're back on track now."

"Good. You two were too close to let, well, that . . . you know . . . that night come between you."

"That's what we thought."

"So did you tell her I was here?"

"Yes."

Harry's eyes widen in shock. "You did?"

"Yup."

"What did she say?"

"Ah." Alice considers the possibility of telling Harry the truth. She gazes at him over the rim of her cardboard coffee cup and wonders how, in fifteen minutes,

Harry can look as if he has always belonged here, can fill the kitchen, the house, with his personality. His jacket is thrown over the back of the chair, his long legs stretched out, ankles crossed, under the table, and he is happily chewing a sesame bagel.

Could Emily be right? Alice thinks. Could Harry and I be destined to be together? No, that's ridiculous. Alice might have believed in soul mates once upon a time, but no longer, and anyway, she's not even divorced. The very last thing she needs is to be getting involved with someone else. Even someone as familiar and comfortable as Harry.

Especially someone as familiar and comfortable as Harry.

"I take it she wasn't happy?" Harry prompts Alice.

"No, actually, she was fine. Glad that you might have found your niche."

"Do you think she'd mind me seeing you?"

"No. She said we ought to get together. She said we'd be . . . friends. We should be friends."

"She said that?"

"Pretty much."

Harry raises his eyebrows. "I'm impressed. Does she have anyone?"

"I think so."

"You think so?"

Alice winces. "I'm not sure how much I'm supposed to say."

"Well, I'm glad. She deserves someone special."

"Rather than you?"

Harry shrugs. "We just weren't right for each other, that's all." He leans over and takes a second blueberry muffin.

"Good Lord, are you going to eat your way through everything in the bag?" Alice laughs as she surveys the pile of food spilling out onto the bleached pine of the kitchen table.

"I tell you, that gardening really gives you an appetite. Am I eating too much?"

"Not at all. It's nice to see a man enjoying his food. Do you want some orange juice?"

"Love some."

Alice pads over to the fridge in her bare feet, rewrapping her robe and tying it even more tightly as she stands with her back to Harry. She is acutely aware of her just-got-out-of-bed appearance, and she runs a hand through her curls as she reaches for the juice, hoping she doesn't look as bad as she fears.

She pours the juice for Harry then sits down. "So what time do you start work?"

"Usually nine, but today's my day off. I thought maybe we could do something, that is, if you're not already doing anything."

"Oh. Well . . ." Alice tries to think what she had planned. She knows she has some errands to do and she's supposed to be having coffee with Sandy, but nothing that couldn't be postponed or rearranged. "I'm not doing anything important," she says. "What did you have in mind?"

"We could start with taking Snoop for a w-a-l-k." Harry spells the word out as Alice starts to laugh, Snoop's ears pricking up at the first letter, Snoop now leaping at Harry's legs. "I don't believe it," Harry says. "Snoop can spell?"

"Only a couple of words," Alice grins. "He may be a genius, but he's not that much of a genius."

"How about the b-e-a-c-h?"

Snoop twirls in circles, whining deliriously.

"Should I presume that's his other word?"

"You'd be presuming correctly."

Harry laughs. "So what about it? Do you want to go there?"

"Sure. We could drive to the beach at Westport. Just let me go and get dressed."

Alice runs into the bathroom and is surprised to find herself smiling. She pulls her clothes off and jumps into the shower, then after toweling herself dry she scrapes her hair back into a ponytail and pulls on a thin pink sweater and a pair of faded jeans.

She studies her face in the mirror, then rummages around in a drawer until she finds an old tube of lip gloss and coats her lips with a thin layer of pink. It looks pretty. And obvious. She grabs a tissue and smears it off. Why on earth, after all these months without makeup, is she suddenly putting on lip gloss?

Why indeed.

Minutes later a makeup-free Alice walks back downstairs, and the three of them — Alice, Harry, and Snoop — climb into her car and drive on to the Merritt Parkway, on their way to the beach at Westport.

The beach is crowded with mothers and children, chairs and towels taking up almost every available inch, everyone trying to make the most of a summer that's very nearly over.

Alice keeps Snoop on the leash as they

set off along the road that runs alongside the beach, turning to look at the sunlight on the waters off the sound, smiling as she surveys the scene.

"It's gorgeous, isn't it?" Harry says, striding leisurely alongside her, watching her as she smiles.

"You know, it's ridiculous how much I love it here." Alice turns to him. "I feel like I ought to be moping around my house feeling sorry for myself, especially now that I'm on my own, but every morning I wake up feeling as if the house and this place has cast a spell on me, and I'm not allowed to be miserable. I just can't help smiling."

Ah. The forbidden subject. Harry's ears prick up at Alice's mention of now being on her own. He's only heard secondhand gossip, and he didn't think Alice would be ready or willing to talk about things, but then again, he didn't expect to find Alice looking so happy.

He had rather expected her to be desperately unhappy. He had ridiculous visions of taking care of her, being the one to bring her back to life, her knight in shining armor. He has gotten so used to his daydream of rescuing her, he's slightly lost in this reality that is so far from his fantasy.

But oh how good it is to see her again.

After all these months of thinking about her. None of the women he has met during the past few months have held his interest in the way that Alice did — and does.

He went out with some of them. Slept with a few of them and continued to see even fewer, but they just didn't have the magic something that he knew Alice had.

And God knows he'd tried not to think about her. He knew his fantasies were both unrealistic and unlikely ever to come to fruition, but when James sent him the e-mail saying one of the gardeners had left Sunup and they had a position should he be interested, how could he possibly refuse?

Especially when the lease on his flat was up anyway, and there was little keeping him in London other than a few friends who were now married with babies and whom he rarely seemed to see anymore.

He'd expected to see Alice weeks ago. His fantasies had changed from the sexual to the platonic — he had hoped they would become friends, that Joe would somehow disappear from the picture, and that he would step in as, well, as whatever Alice would want or need.

But little did he think his fantasies would ever come true. And even less did he think he would be unhappy about it. Or perhaps unhappy is too strong a word. He had spent so many months imagining a scenario in which Alice and Joe would break up, he thought that should it ever happen, he would be delighted.

And when James had come in that day and told him that apparently Alice had caught Joe with another woman and kicked him out, Harry had been so concerned about Alice it was all he could do not to drop everything and run to her house.

Harry knew he couldn't do that. He knew he had to wait for a while, see what happened, hope that she would come into the nursery, and take it from there.

Yesterday, when he saw her in the car, his heart almost stopped with the familiarity of her face, and he knew he would have to see her, he couldn't put it off any longer. James said he had mentioned it to her, and winked and told him he thought Alice would be glad to see him.

And now here he is, walking next to the woman of his dreams, feeling more comfortable and relaxed with her than he has ever felt with any woman he has ever met, and she is no longer living with her husband, and for the first time in his life

Harry thinks there may be a God after all.

What can I tell you about Alice and Harry that you might not already know? I can't tell you they live happily ever after because, as we all know, real life doesn't happen like that, and anyway, that's another book in itself.

But I can tell you that they become more than friends. That Alice remembers exactly why she always liked Harry so much, and that the more time she spends with him the more she likes him, and that when, on New Year's Eve, Harry and Alice find themselves in the garden again at Sally's annual party, their kiss is much slower and sweeter than the previous year, and lovelier still now that neither of them has any guilt.

Emily is thrilled that Harry and Alice have become friends, and knows that it will become more, but stops haranguing Alice after she tells her that the more Emily talks about it, the less interested she becomes. Not true, but it does the trick, and Emily stops teasing Alice and waits for the phone call when Alice will tell her the good news.

Colin didn't work out for Emily. It all went horribly wrong when Emily became pregnant and, knowing she wasn't ready for a child, didn't feel mature enough, or financially stable enough, or *anything* enough, had an abortion. It left her physically and emotionally drained, and although Colin stayed around for a few days, he phoned less and less after that, and always seemed to have an excuse as to why he couldn't see her.

For a while Emily was devastated. It became Alice's turn to phone *her* every day, to check that she was coping, but Emily is nothing if not resilient, and soon she had thrown herself back into single life with a passion and was regaling Alice with stories of her latest dates.

And Joe? Joe hasn't quite managed to let Josie go. She is so clearly in love with him, and so good at looking after him, and even though she may still be known as a ball-breaker in the workplace, she is not nearly so strong or forceful in the home.

In fact, Josie has filled Alice's shoes in more ways than she could have imagined. She looks fantastic, she's eager to please Joe, and she's so frightened of losing him she doesn't question where he is or what he's doing.

Occasionally Joe feels guilty about the women he sleeps with, but not so guilty as to stop, and anyway, they have no bearing on his relationship with Josie. As long as she doesn't know, how can it possibly hurt her, for Joe would never want to hurt Josie, just as he never wanted to hurt Alice.

He was lucky with Alice. Lucky that she didn't allow herself to be worn down by him, worn down by the lies until there was nothing left of her at all.

Alice was lucky because she discovered her true self before it was too late. She rediscovered her dream and was able to live it.

Right now it doesn't look as if Josie's going to be that lucky. Josie's still trying to be everything that Joe wants her to be. Josie is, astonishingly, quite as malleable as Alice once was, and even more eager to please.

Look at her now. Poor Josie. Lying in bed staring at the clock, watching the hour grow later and later, every muscle in her body tense as she waits for Joe to come home, already two hours later than he said.

She is fighting not to call him. She wants so desperately to pick up the phone and call his mobile, but she still has a shred of dignity left, and she knows how furious he will be if she does, how he will say he needs a break for a few days, and she won't be able to go through that again.

As she lies there the knot in her stomach

grows ever so slightly bigger, her self-esteem ever so slightly smaller, but it will take many more years before Josie is able to understand the damage Joe has caused, more still before she moves on to allow Joe to start living with the next Josie.

Josie will eventually end up with Al, so there is a happy ending of sorts in store for her. He will make her happy, but she will always feel that there is something missing in her relationship with him. She will never feel that she is head over heels in love with him, but it will not be until she is in her late forties that she realizes that what she has with Al is enough, that the friendship and trust and ease she has with Al make her so much happier than the knife edge on which she was living during those years with Joe.

Nevertheless, a part of Josie will always miss the danger, the excitement, the roller-coaster ride she experienced with Joe.

Luckily, the same cannot be said for Alice. Alice rarely thinks of Joe these days. He gave her the house in Highfield as part of the divorce settlement, and that was it. She didn't want anything to do with the apartment in New York or the house in London.

And Joe was delighted he got off so

lightly. He'd heard all the stories about colleagues who had been forced to part with half of everything they owned. Even his divorce lawyer was amazed, as was Alice's, who begged her to take the house in London, told her repeatedly that she deserved more, but Alice wouldn't hear any of it.

Alice once had a dream of a house in the country, a house with wisteria growing over the front and climbing roses tumbling over the back. She had a dream of acres of land filled with children running and jumping and animals playing.

The wisteria is growing slowly but surely. The roses are climbing and tumbling happily and heartily, and Snoop and Dharma have been joined by a Labrador called Floozy, Calvin the cat, and five chickens named Maisie, Corny, Mealy, Grainy, and Rice.

As for the children, we'd have to ask Harry about that, but Alice is blooming just as steadily as her garden these days, the sparkle in her eye brighter than it has ever been, her hair as luscious and thick as it has ever been, and don't they always say that's one of the signs?

Take a closer look at her stomach. Is it

our imagination, or is it ever so slightly more curved than we are used to seeing it? It could of course be happiness that is causing her to eat more, but then again, she does seem to stroke her stomach rather more often than she ever has before.

But as I said earlier, that's a story for another day.